THE
ADVERSARIES

An American Family Portrait

BOOK FOUR

The Adversaries

Jack Cavanaugh

Chariot VICTOR
PUBLISHING
A DIVISION OF COOK COMMUNICATIONS

Editor:
Greg Clouse

Cover Illustration:
Chris Cocozza

Design:
Paul Higdon

Maps:
Andrea Boven

Victor Books is an imprint of Chariot Victor Publishing,
a division of Cook Communications, Colorado Springs, Colorado 80918
Cook Communications, Paris, Ontario
Kingsway Communications, Eastbourne, England

Library of Congress Cataloging-in-Publication Data

Cavanaugh, Jack.
 The adversaries/Jack Cavanaugh.
  p.   cm.—(American family portrait; bk. 4)
 ISBN 1-56476-535-0
 I. Title. II. Series: Cavanaugh, Jack. American
family portrait: bk. 4.
PS3553.A965A66 1996
813'.54—dc20   95-39588
                                                 CIP

Chariot**VICTOR**
PUBLISHING
A DIVISION OF COOK COMMUNICATIONS

To my parents, Bill and Marge Cavanaugh—
you taught me what family
is all about.

ACKNOWLEDGMENTS

To John Mueller, Barbara Ring, Kim Garrison, and Karen Stoffell—your critiques of my story line are always insightful. You correct me, sometimes chastise me, but never fail to encourage me. May God bless you for your partnership in this effort to communicate His spiritual truths through fiction.

To Linda Holland—thank you for your research on Mary Ann Bickerdyke. It inspired a key scene in this novel.

To Greg Clouse—my editor, my friend, my conscience when I get behind.

To the staff at Victor Books—with this book we pass the halfway point in the series; working with you just keeps getting better and better.

To all the Civil War buffs who read this novel—thanks to all of you who catch historical errors and don't bring them to my attention.

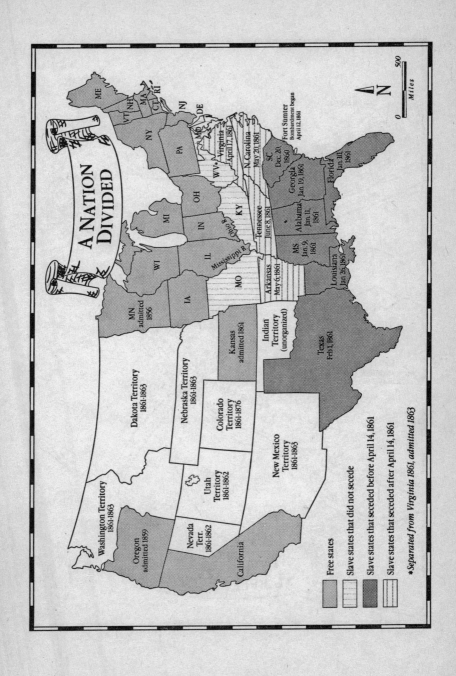

A NATION DIVIDED

Washington Territory
1861-1863

Oregon
admitted 1859

Nevada
Terr.
1861-1862

California

Utah
Territory
1861-1862

Dakota Territory
1861-1863

Nebraska Territory
1861-1863

Colorado
Territory
1861-1876

New Mexico
Territory
1861-1863

MN
admitted
1856

IA

Kansas
admitted 1861

Indian
Territory
(unorganized)

Texas
Feb.1, 1861

WI

IL

MO

Arkansas
May 6, 1861

Louisiana
Jan. 26, 1861

MI

IN

OH

KY

Tennessee
June 8, 1861

MS
Jan. 9,
1861

Alabama
Jan. 11,
1861

Georgia
Jan. 19, 1861

Florida
Jan. 10,
1861

Mississippi R.

Ohio R.

ME

VT NH

MA
CT RI

NY

PA

NJ

MD DE

WV*

Virginia
April 17, 1861

N. Carolina
May 20, 1861

SC
Dec. 20,
1860

Fort Sumter
Bombardment began
April 12, 1860

Free states

Slave states that did not secede

Slave states that seceded before April 14, 1861

Slave states that seceded after April 14, 1861

*Separated from Virginia 1861, admitted 1863

N

0   500
Miles

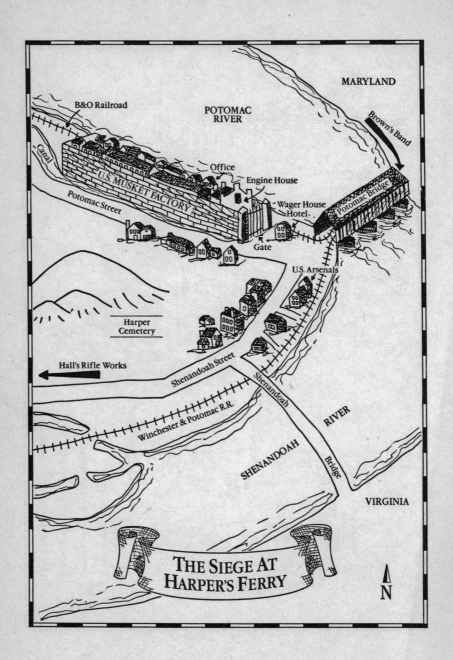

THE SIEGE AT
HARPER'S FERRY

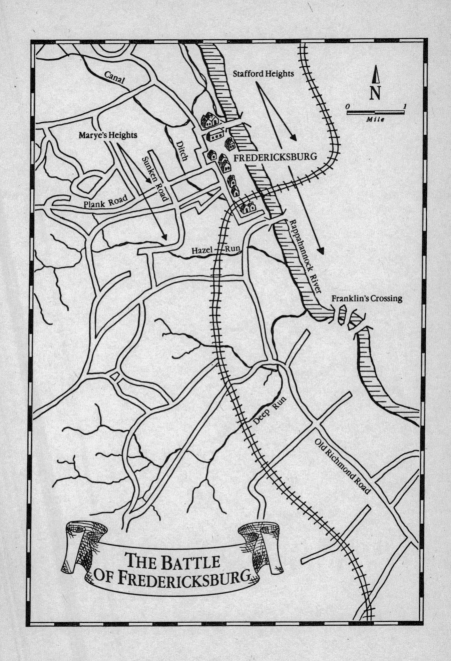

THE BATTLE OF FREDERICKSBURG

Chapter 1

A STREAM of Negro slaves backed out of the two-foot-square opening high above the ground on the side of the house. Moments before, a flush panel hid the opening to casual eyes. Now, one by one, the runaways emerged, feet searching blindly for the first rung of the splintery ladder. The wooden stairway shivered, taking on the fear of those descending it.

Marshall Morgan stood at the foot of the ladder with a musket-rifle in his hands. A young man of twenty-one, he oversaw the procession. With rare exception, upon reaching the ground, each slave would cast a suspicious glance in his direction. Their gaze usually worked its way up from the ground to his chest, his clean-shaven chin, then his brown eyes. When they reached the white streak in his full, brown hair, their own eyes bulged with fright. The unusual birthmark stretched from forehead to crown. The runaways stared at the streak like it was the mark of Cain. Over the years Marshall had grown accustomed to the reaction. His father said it was Marshall's wild streak coming out.

As runaway after runaway poured out of the opening, Marshall wiped a river of sweat from the side of his head with the back of one hand. With each new appearance at the top of the ladder, he grimaced.

"Cato, how many are there?"

A heavily perspiring, middle-aged Negro slave, his back a maze of crisscrossed scars, stood beside him. It was a scorching August day which made it that much hotter for the slaves hiding in the attic of Thomas Goodin's house.

"Twenty-eight in all, Mas'r Morgan."

"Twenty-eight?" Marshall shouted.

"Is dat not good?"

"Cato, I only have three skiffs."

"We's fit in 'um. We's see to that," the runaway insisted.

Despite the heat, the growing pool of slaves huddled close to one another. There was more than a dozen of them already, of all sizes and description. Most were barefoot. Some carried small bundles of clothes, others carried nothing more than the rags they were wearing. But as different as they were from one another, the runaways standing next to Tom Goodin's house were alike in one thing—without exception, they craned their necks in the direction of the Ohio River which, though a short distance away, was still hidden from their view by a ridge. When an occasional gust of moist air from the river blew over the ridge, the runaways lifted their faces and sniffed it like bloodhounds on the scent. For them the Ohio was a mystical river, not unlike the pearly gates of heaven. It was the frequent setting of late-night stories told around slave campfires by visionaries who defended its existence, but who had never seen it themselves. It was a watery boundary line between two worlds. On this side was Kentucky and slavery; on the other side was Ohio and freedom.

Marshall Morgan and his two brothers assisted runaways in crossing the boundary. A secret network of houses and other resting places were linked like an underground railroad that transported slaves to freedom. The Morgan brothers' portion of the line went from Tom Goodin's house in Kentucky to the Zion Baptist Church in Cincinnati, Ohio. And though Marshall had assisted hundreds of runaways across the Ohio

River, he never tired of their reaction when the river of legend came into sight. He thought of Cato's comment about crowding into the skiffs. *Yes, Cato, somehow you will find a way to fit twenty-eight people into three skiffs. Of that I have no doubt.* Wiping away another stream of sweat from his temple, Marshall nervously glanced over his shoulder. While the attention of the slaves was drawn to the river, his was drawn to the road at the front of the house. He was expecting unwanted company. He hoped to be across the river when they arrived.

A tuft of trees obstructed his view of the dirt road, so Marshall looked for rising dust. The air above the road was clear. *Good.* But he knew it wouldn't stay that way for long.

There was a break in the flow of traffic down the ladder as a slight, elderly woman paused on every rung, steadying herself on each step before continuing. Cato moved to the foot of the ladder to assist her. The woman's slowness prompted Marshall to cast another agitated glance toward the road.

"Three more steps, Mother Kinney," Cato said, reaching out to her. "Three more steps clos'r to freedom."

"Is we at the Ohio?" The old woman planted an uncertain foot on the ground.

"Nearly there, Mother Kinney, nearly there."

The woman was bent with age. Her arms and hands and face were draped with wrinkles wet with perspiration. "Are you the one ferry'n us 'cross de river to de promised land?" Ancient eyes stared at the white streak as she spoke. There was a fair gazing distance between the old runaway's eyes and his, she being so small and he of good height.

"Yes, ma'am. I'll get you across the river."

The old woman scoffed at his politeness. "I ain't no ma'am. Jus' Mother Kinney."

She held out her hand. Marshall reached for it. Two silver dollars plopped into his palm.

"It's all I got," she said. "Will it get me 'cross dat Ohio River?"

The two coins weighed heavy in Marshall's hand. They represented untold hours of extra work on some slaveholder's plantation, or possibly months of late-night basket weaving to produce a product that sold for pennies. It was the old woman's lifetime investment in her freedom. From experience, Marshall knew that runaway slaves with money had a better chance of making it than those without. Even then there were no guarantees. Sometimes runaways handed their money to imposters who claimed to work for the underground railroad. After taking the slaves' money, the unprincipled men would then turn them over to slave hunters for a price, making a double profit.

Cato stared hard at Marshall to see what he would do with the old woman's money.

Marshall returned the coins to her.

"I don't want your money, Mother Kinney," he said. "You'll need it to start your new life in Canada."

The old woman couldn't have looked more pleased if the angel Gabriel himself had just returned the coins.

"See, Mother Kinney?" Cato said. "I tol' you he was a good man."

"I knows he's a good man," Mother Kinney said rather testily, "but not 'cause you says he was. I knowed it 'cause God done tol' me I could trust him." She patted Marshall on the arm. "Lor' bless you, Mas'r Morgan," Mother Kinney said. "Lor' bless you real good. Now where's dat river I's heard so much about?"

Cato assisted Mother Kinney to the huddle of runaways next to the house as the last of them came down the ladder. Marshall looked to the road again. *Still no dust.* Maybe the alarm was false; maybe, just maybe, they'd make it across the river without being discovered; maybe he should ask Mother

Kinney if God spoke to her about their chances.

"Cato, come here!" Marshall pointed to the ridge that separated them from the river. "See the elm tree in the notch of that ridge?"

"I sees it."

"Just beyond that tree there's a path that leads down to the river. Tom Goodin is there with the skiffs. Get everyone loaded into them as quickly as you can. Have them hunker down and cover them with the tarps. Do you got that?"

"It's mighty hot fo' tarps, Mas'r Morgan."

"I know, but it can't be helped. Ordinarily we wait until dark. Today we have no choice. It's not enough just to get you across the river, Cato. If you're seen you can still be captured and brought back from the Ohio side."

"I knows dat," Cato said indignantly. "It's still gonna be mighty hot under dem tarps."

"But they're necessary cover. Hurry now."

"Ain't you comin' wid us?"

Marshall patted Cato on the shoulder and gave him a shove in the direction of the ridge. "I'm right behind you. Someone has to put the panel back in place and get rid of this ladder." Marshall looked to the road again. A cloud of dust billowed over it like an approaching storm. "Go, Cato! Hurry!" he cried.

Cato ran for the ridge, yelling for the slaves to follow him. Marshall dropped his musket-rifle and vaulted up the ladder. Halfway up he stopped. Below him a column of runaways bunched up at the notch in the ridge like grains of sand squeezing through the mid-section of an hourglass. On the other side of him the cloud of dust loomed closer. Marshall looked at the opening in the side of the house. *No. No time. I can't let them see me,* he thought. *Got to get away.*

He jumped from the ladder and landed next to his rifle with a thud. He could hear the horses coming up the road.

Two? Three? He couldn't tell. Grabbing his firearm, Marshall Morgan ran as fast as he could toward the ridge, frightening the last of the slaves as he dove past them over the embankment. From behind him came a grating voice:

"There! Stop right there! Stop or we'll shoot you like dogs!"

Marshall tumbled down the ridge, slamming into the base of a bush, his rifle clattering next to him on the ground. Cato and the first of the runaways had just reached the river's edge. Tom Goodin was holding the lines of three skiffs. At the sound of the shouting, the Negroes who had made it over the ridge froze and stared in panic in the direction of the voices. Those closest to Marshall looked at him sprawled against the bush. Their faces were portraits of shock and disbelief. Could they have come this far, only to be turned away at heaven's gate?

"Stop dead in your tracks! I swear I'll shoot!" the voice bellowed. "Ain't shot no slave all day and I'm achin' to bag me one!"

The voice was drawing closer to the ridge. The eyes of a dozen slaves pleaded silently to Marshall for help. He scrambled to his feet. Cato and Goodin were looking his direction too. Motionless, they waited for some kind of guidance or signal. What should they do? In horror they watched as Marshall snatched up his rifle and darted into the bushes. He disappeared upstream before the voice on the other side of the ridge materialized into a face.

Just like old times!

Forty-seven-year-old Jeremiah Morgan smiled and leaned back contentedly in the wooden lawn chair. He rested a glass of lemonade on his stomach, balancing it with two arthritic hands. Next to him in an identical chair and sharing the shade of the tree with him was his best friend, Seth Cooper. It was a lazy, hot Sunday afternoon. Earlier Seth had preached a rousing sermon at Jeremiah's Point Providence Heritage Church, lecturing the men of the congregation on their responsibility to be the spiritual heads of their households. Both sermon and preacher had been well-received, which didn't surprise Jeremiah. Ever since seminary days Seth had been the better preacher of the two, a fact that bothered Jeremiah not one bit. Any spirit of competition would have starved to death long ago had it depended solely on Jeremiah Morgan and Seth Cooper for its sustenance.

The friendship between the two men had roots that stretched deep into the lineage of both families. In the early nineteenth century, their fathers had been cofounders of the Heritage Churches of America, a denomination that emphasized salvation by grace through faith in Jesus Christ, the Bible as the final authority for all of life, and the importance of the family for the propagation of the faith. In fact, their fathers were so close, Seth was named after Jeremiah's father. Even so, the Morgan and Cooper family roots intertwined on a deeper level. More than two centuries before either man was born, the Morgans and the Coopers had shared a dramatic moment in the small English village of Edenford. It was there that Drew Morgan risked his life to save little Thomas Cooper who had fallen into a vat of blue dye. Both were burned badly and it was believed that, despite Drew's heroics, the Cooper boy would not survive. But by the grace of God, he did; which was fortunate for Seth Cooper. For had the boy died, Seth would not exist. The Cooper family traced their lineage back through the boy dyed blue.

Drew Morgan and the Coopers fled from England in 1630 to escape the murderous reach of Drew's former mentor, London Bishop William Laud, who persecuted Puritans for ignoring his edicts which, they felt, contradicted the Bible. Landing safely in the New World, both families settled in the

Massachusetts Bay Colony. Over the years, a deep and lasting friendship developed between Drew and Thomas, who remained heavily scarred from the vat incident for the remainder of his life.

After marrying the beautiful and talented Nell Matthews, Drew began a family tradition by choosing one of his children to be responsible for ensuring the continuance of the family faith into the next generation. During a private ceremony, Drew presented the family Bible to his son, Christopher. The boy's name was printed in the front of the Bible under his father's. Then, Drew charged his son to perpetuate the family faith and someday to hold a similar ceremony with one of his heirs.

When Thomas Cooper learned of the Morgan family tradition, he began an identical tradition with his family and their family Bible. Since then, the descendants of Drew Morgan and Thomas Cooper had kept the tradition alive for more than two centuries.

In the late eighteenth century two of their descendants introduced the tradition to other families. Matthew Morgan and Charles Cooper, both religious educators, were so moved by the number of men and women who expressed interest in starting the tradition with their families, that they began holding meetings to promote the practice. Soon, likeminded families formed covenant groups for fellowship and support. Some of the groups organized into churches. Not long afterward, the churches banded together in a denomination, calling themselves the Heritage Churches of America.

The organization's doctrinal statement emphasized the Bible and the family. It was the early leaders' belief that should these two things endure, there would always be a remnant of Christian believers in America. Their vision ignited an explosion of new churches in every state. The common element among them was the use of a family Bible following the pattern of the Morgans and Coopers.

It was Matthew Morgan's and Charles Cooper's grandsons who sat in the shade beside the Point Providence parsonage on a hot Sunday afternoon. Seth was the keeper of the Cooper's Bible; Jeremiah had the Bible that had once belonged to Drew Morgan.

Jeremiah and Seth met at a New York college. It wasn't long before they discovered their common heritage, and they were inseparable. They shared everything—class notes, denominational gossip, personal hopes and fears, even affairs of the heart.

Of the two, Seth was the better student. By his second year he was considered the denomination's most promising leader and preacher. He had a keen intellect, ready wit, and passionate fervor for spiritual things. Jeremiah, on the other hand, was an average student and a fair preacher. His mild temperament suited him to be more of a supporter than a leader. While Seth's emotions flared from meteoric highs to cavernous lows, Jeremiah was even-tempered and steady, day after day. This seemingly mismatched relationship confounded most campus observers, but to Seth and Jeremiah it was a perfect match of opposites. Each man gave to the friendship something the other was lacking, while mutual admiration provided the glue that held them together.

If the unlikely pairing of Seth Cooper and Jeremiah Morgan wasn't enough to amuse the college campus, the amorous exploits of the two men made up for it. When it came to matters of the heart, it was as if the two men swapped roles. For the duration of his college days, Seth Cooper disdained all local feminine temptations and remained ever faithful to his childhood sweetheart back home, Emma Longstreet, a shy, rather plain Virginian belle. Jeremiah Morgan, on the other hand, wooed and won the vivacious Elizabeth McKenna, daughter of a politically prominent New York banker. In doing so, he beat out a host of wealthy, prominent bachelors from every corner of New England.

Although marriage into the McKenna family for any man meant immediate wealth and assured success, Jeremiah cared for none of these things. He was attracted solely to Elizabeth. The attraction was mutual.

Since the day she came of age, the daughter of wealthy Caleb McKenna had been bombarded with the attention and propositions of an endless line of suitors. They all seemed to have two things in common—pompous ambitions and inflated egos. She disdained both. For her, Jeremiah Morgan was a rose among thorns.

They met at the Heritage Churches of America annual meeting. Though Elizabeth was introduced to Seth Cooper, it was Jeremiah Morgan standing quietly by his side whom she noticed. Throughout the remainder of the evening, his lack of pretension and sincere faith became more evident every time he spoke. Seth recognized immediately the attraction between them and fended off anyone who attempted to take Elizabeth away. That night the love between Jeremiah and Elizabeth took root. It blossomed into a storybook romance of a rich New York socialite and an unassuming, devoted minister.

Actually, the differences between the two lovers was not as great as many made it out to be. Though they lived in two different financial realms, Jeremiah and Elizabeth shared a common depth of spiritual faith. So it wasn't difficult for Elizabeth to imagine a life of meager subsistence with the man she loved. She was more than willing to exchange the pressure and pretense of New York society for a life of service with this quiet man who so captivated her.

Her father, however, did not share her fascination with Jeremiah Morgan. Caleb McKenna, a self-made man, had taken a small inherited fortune and built it into a massive fortune through reckless and sometimes ruthless speculation in the banking industry. He was a man who loved his wealth and the power that came with it. Although he had no political ambitions himself, he loved politics and was a formidable political force, both in the national arena and in the Heritage Church denomination. He liked to think of himself as a king-maker. For him, there was no greater feeling than to have a parade of political hopefuls — mayors, governors, congressmen, senators, and even presidents — beat a path to his door and, with hat in hand, court his influence, his money, and his vote. The thought of his only child marrying an unexceptional preacher was revolting. Elizabeth had been reared to be the wife of a senator or governor, possibly even the first lady of the nation. Marriage to Jeremiah Morgan was out of the question. However, affections of the heart produce uncommon courage, and Caleb McKenna found his daughter and her love to be surprisingly skillful adversaries.

When McKenna forbid Elizabeth to see Jeremiah again, she defied her father by arranging a series of secret rendezvous with the man she loved. And when McKenna bribed Jeremiah to stay away from his daughter by offering him his choice of positions within their denomination, or any church in New England for that matter, his offer fell on deaf ears. But the New York banker, accustomed to getting his way, was not easily deterred. When intimidation and money didn't work, he decided to send Elizabeth away. Once she was safely away, he would deal with Jeremiah in a more direct — and permanent — manner.

On the eve of Elizabeth's scheduled departure for France, for a thinly disguised "cultural tour," she and Jeremiah made a bold countermove. It was Elizabeth's idea. So, in a way, it was she who proposed to Jeremiah. Marriage was the only solution, she argued. Her father would never relent until they were married. That night — the same day of Jeremiah's graduation from college — the New York socialite and the poor preacher eloped. They surfaced a few weeks later at Morristown Heritage Church in New Jersey, where Jeremiah became the new pastor of a congregation of twenty-five.

For months afterward, Caleb McKenna blustered and bullied the newlyweds to get an annulment. When that tactic didn't work, he tried to intimidate the church through the denominational channels. But his salvo of rage and coercion had little effect. The marriage was legal, the newlyweds were inseparable, and the church had fallen in love with both of them. Each new intimidation from New York only served to force them to tighten their ranks in defense of their right to be happy.

For Jeremiah and Elizabeth the first year of marriage was one of unending bliss. They loved each other. They loved the unhurried, simple life of a small town. And their congregation was patient and supportive of Jeremiah's early, stumbling efforts at preaching. Then, as if things couldn't get better, within months after their marriage, God blessed the union of the newlyweds with the hope of new life and the promise of a continuation of the Morgan family line. Elizabeth was with child.

It was a difficult pregnancy from the start, but Elizabeth bore the various pains with uncommon grace.

"I'm bringing another Jeremiah into the world," she shrugged with a smile. "How can I complain about a little pain?"

However, as her term progressed, it became increasingly obvious that this would be a difficult birth. Her father, in a rare demonstration of compassion, dispatched a private midwife to care for her and the baby. Jeremiah and Elizabeth gratefully received the offer of help as a gesture of reconciliation. It gave Elizabeth an added measure of courage to endure the pain. She thought of the little one inside her as a peace-child. She envisioned the newborn child placing one chubby hand in her hand and the other in her father's, and bringing them together again.

As if in a hurry to complete its mission, the baby insisted on coming before its time. On the morning of the birth, Elizabeth kissed Jeremiah one last time before the midwife ushered him out of the room. "The next time you see me," she said between birth pains, "I'll be holding our son."

"Or daughter," he replied, mopping her forehead with a towel.

"Or twins," she replied.

"Twins? Really?" The idea hadn't occurred to him.

Elizabeth smiled at the comical look of surprise on his face, then grimaced at the onset of another pain. "One at a time," she said. "But this one's a boy," her eyes squeezed back the pain, "and a strong one at that."

"I love you, Elizabeth."

A weak smile. "You're going to make a good father," she replied.

Eighteen hours later, a sullen midwife emerged from the bedroom. Her face was drawn and troubled. It had not gone well. Not well at all. Elizabeth had clung to life for both her and the baby until her strength gave out. But it wasn't enough. She was dead. And so was their son.

For a night and a day, a broken Jeremiah Morgan wept over the lifeless form of his beautiful, beloved Elizabeth. Church members congregated outside his door, but he refused to see any of them, nor did he allow any light in the house. At one point he screamed for the midwife to bring him the body of his son. Clutching the cloth bundle to her bosom, she pleaded with him not to unwrap it.

"That's not the way you want to remember your son," she cried.

As Jeremiah began to pull away the layers, the midwife buried her tearful face in her hands, imploring him not to unwrap the boy. Jeremiah relented. He handed the delicate bundle back to the midwife and returned to Elizabeth's bedside.

In the early morning hours, a ray of sunlight broke through the closed shutters and fell on his face. Angrily, he grabbed a piece of bedding to stuff into the crack and shut out the offending intrusion into his darkness. Then, in the light, he saw Elizabeth, clothed in radiance and cradling an infant in her arms. Her communication was inaudible, but clear. A sweet smile. A knowing look. The pain was gone. They were happy. Then the sun's rays broke through the vision and Elizabeth was gone. Jeremiah opened the door and allowed himself to be comforted.

Caleb McKenna blamed Jeremiah for his daughter's death and the death of his grandson. The man's rage built up like a thundercloud. His vindictiveness knew no bounds as he used his influence and wealth to destroy Jeremiah.

Through intermediaries, Caleb McKenna purchased the testimony of disreputable women. The resulting scandal forced Jeremiah to resign his church position. Not satisfied with a single victory, McKenna chaired an ethics committee within the denomination that censured the preacher.

When long-time friend Seth Cooper rose to Jeremiah's defense, he too incurred the wrath of the powerful New York banker. Using the argument of guilt by association, McKenna succeeded in tarnishing Cooper's growing reputation among the denominational leadership. And though he tried for direct sanctions against Cooper, he soon discovered that his influence stopped at the Virginia state line. Sectional emotions were rising dramatically and even disreputable Virginians were unwilling to go along with the Yankee banker's blood feud. So McKenna turned his attention once more to Jeremiah.

To avoid further painful confrontations with his father-in-law, Jeremiah Morgan fled from the East. Seth Cooper urged him to come south. But Jeremiah knew that despite Cooper's widespread influence, Southern churches would never accept a Yankee minister. Nor could he accept them. He knew he could never reconcile his theological beliefs with a ministry to a congregation of slaveholders. So he wandered west, settling in Point Providence, Ohio.

Concluding his ministry days were over, he took a position as clerk in Horace Grimes' general goods store. Over the course of two years he established a favorable relationship with the townspeople, his employer, and—to a greater degree—his employer's youngest daughter, Susanna.

In the same way Elizabeth McKenna embodied all the sparkle and allure of big-city New York society, Susanna Grimes was the epitome of Point Providence—small, plain, but with an easy, underlying warmth. There was a comfortableness about both the town and the girl; a welcome feeling after the recent, highly-charged years of his life.

He and Susanna were married after a year of courting. Shortly after they celebrated their first anniversary, their first child was born—a son. They named him John Drew Morgan, his middle name in honor of the first Morgan of their line to come to America.

It was Jeremiah's father-in-law who first approached him about returning to the ministry and starting a Heritage church in Point Providence. Although Jeremiah longed to be a pastor again, he rejected the idea. A few Sundays later he and Susanna were invited to the Grimes' for dinner following church services. When they arrived, to their surprise, eight families awaited them. They were in unanimous agreement that they wanted to start a Heritage church and they wanted Jeremiah to be their pastor. This time when he declined the invitation, they were not as easily dissuaded as his father-in-law had been.

Feeling he had no other recourse, he informed them of how

he had been asked to resign an earlier church and been censured by the denomination. (Prior to this time the Grimes' were the only family to know his controversial ministerial past.) They asked him if the charges were true. He replied they were not. His word was good enough for them. Without dissent, they voted to start a new church and call Jeremiah Morgan as their pastor. And that was how Jeremiah Morgan returned to his original call from God and began ministering to the townspeople of Point Providence along the great Ohio River.

The church and the Morgan family grew together. As more and more families came into the congregational fold, the pastor and his wife did their part to add to the church by having three more children—Marshall, Sarah, and William, who was born with a deformed right foot.

Years passed and the growing national spirit of sectionalism succeeded in doing to Jeremiah Morgan and Seth Cooper what the powerful Caleb McKenna was unable to do—create a rupture in their friendship. It was in 1854 at the Heritage Churches of America annual convention in Philadelphia that the delegates split over the slavery issue. The Southern delegates, angered over the Northern delegates' increasingly hostile and denigrating rhetoric regarding Southern slave owners, walked out. They traveled straight to Charleston, South Carolina where they wrote a new constitution and formed a new denomination. The debate on the floor preceding the walkout was loud and rancorous. New York power-broker McKenna was one of the loudest advocates for the abolition of slavery. And as painful as it was to him, Jeremiah found himself siding with Caleb McKenna against his best friend, Seth Cooper. Seth, who owned two household slaves, walked out with the other Southern delegates.

Jeremiah knew his friend was morally opposed to slavery, but one could not easily dismiss the entire Southern economy. He'd often heard Seth state his position with a quote from Thomas Jefferson: "Slavery is like holding a wolf by the ears—you don't like it, but you dare not let go."

And so the Heritage Church convention split with Jeremiah Morgan on one side and his best friend Seth Cooper on the other. It was a great personal loss for both families.

Prior to the split, the two families exchanged visits every summer. It was a highlight of the year for both families. J.D. (John Drew's nickname) and Daniel (Seth and Emma Cooper's only child) became the best of friends. In fact, all the Morgan children looked forward to the summer days spent with Daniel, though the Cooper boy was outnumbered four to one. Somehow, he had developed a unique bond with each of the Morgan children; especially Sarah, as she matured in her teenage years. Their not-so-secretive glances at each other prompted quiet discussion among the adults of a possible marriage between the Morgans and Coopers. It was a happy speculation. At least until the Southern delegates walked out in Philadelphia. On that day, everything changed for the Morgans and the Coopers. It was as if by the stroke of a denominational gavel, they became two hostile nations. Now that the South was forming its own convention, there was a greater possibility that a Jew would marry a Gentile than there was that a Southern Cooper would marry a Northern Morgan.

It was heartsickness for his old friend that eventually prompted Jeremiah to invite Seth to preach at the Point Providence Church. Jeremiah hoped that the spiritual basis of the invitation might bridge their political differences. To his surprise and delight, Seth Cooper accepted.

The news that a Southern slave-holding preacher was going to preach at Point Providence caused no small stir among the congregation and townspeople. More than a few longstanding church members spoke out against the prospect of having a

Southern preacher in a Northern pulpit. They argued that since slavery was a sin, it would be nothing less than scandalous to allow a slaveholder, and the pastor of slaveholders, to preach in their church. Ordinarily, Jeremiah would have agreed with them. But this was Seth Cooper, his trusted and best friend.

Jeremiah publicly vouched for his friend's spiritual nature and call to the preaching ministry. He pleaded with the congregation on the point of personal privilege to give the man a hearing. He promised Seth would not talk of slavery or politics, but about the importance of the family; that the Southern preacher would not be promoting his own ideas, but would be extracting truths from the Bible. Regarding the charges that any slaveholder was a sinner, Jeremiah could not argue; but who among them was without sin?

A tentative agreement was worked out between pastor and people. Out of respect for their pastor, the majority of members agreed to give Dr. Cooper a hearing. Others refused to attend, but they further agreed to limit their disagreement to quiet absence from the meetings. There would be no public demonstrations. And so the stage was set for a Southern minister to preach in a Northern church.

For weeks prior to the meetings, Pastor Jeremiah Morgan prayed that the fragile peace would hold. When the Coopers arrived, it was like a family reunion. Since they'd seen him last, Seth had grown a full beard with no mustache. He looked a little paunchy and a little older. Emma was prim and stylish, every bit the Southern lady. And Daniel was a strapping young man with a huge, clean-shaven, boxlike jaw; coalblack hair fell over his ears; his eyes were dark and intelligent. It was just like old times. The Morgans and the Coopers were together again. There was no talk of politics, only churches and families and the good times of the past.

Enjoying the shade of the tree, with his drink balanced on

his stomach, Jeremiah glanced over at his friend in the chair beside him. Seth's head lay back, his eyes were closed. He was gently snoring. Jeremiah sighed contentedly. It was going to be a good week; a chance for the two of them to renew their friendship, a chance once-for-all to prove that the bond between Christian brothers was stronger than sectional politics.

Backing them up against the Ohio River, Frank Toombs held a steady rifle on the line of runaway slaves. Tom Goodin, still holding the lines of the three skiffs in his hand, stood with them. Toombs, a short, rotund slave hunter, removed his left hand from his rifle briefly to wipe the sweat from his patchy, bearded cheeks and reposition the two revolvers in his waistband. He was in good spirits despite the fact that there were twenty-eight of them—twenty-nine if you counted Goodin—and only one of him.

The slave hunter chuckled to himself as he surveyed the runaways standing meekly beside the river. *Sheep. That's what they are. Sheep waiting to be herded back to their pens. If they weren't so stupid,* he thought, *they'd realize they could overpower me simply by rushing me.* Even if he was able to get off every shot, he could stop only thirteen of them—with six shots from each pistol and one from the rifle. That would mean fifteen of them would go free. More than half. *Besides, what are the chances of getting off thirteen shots?* But, lucky for him, runaways didn't think things like that. That's what made his job so easy. They were sheep. Superior intelligence, that's what made the difference between him and them, he sniffed. They were no match for his superior intelligence.

"Hey, Frank! Whatcha got there?"

Toombs jumped at the sound of the voice behind him. A quick glance over his shoulder brought a grin. "Morgan! Come here! Look what I got! I bagged me some runaways."

"Well, so you have!" Marshall Morgan sauntered down the ridge to the river's edge, his musket-rifle slung casually over his shoulder. "You captured all of them by yourself?"

"Watkins and me done it," the slave hunter proclaimed proudly. "He's off to Maysville for chains and a few more hands."

"A good day's work," Marshall said, surveying the runaways. A mixture of expressions greeted him ranging from disgust to outright hatred.

"See what else I got?" Toombs jabbed the rifle barrel in the direction of the only white man standing among the runaways.

"Tom Goodin! Is that you?" Marshall said with a tone of disbelief.

Goodin didn't respond.

"Who woulda thought that quiet ol' Tom Goodin was runnin' slaves," Toombs said, "him bein' a deacon in the church and all?"

"I never would have guessed it," Marshall replied.

"Neither did anyone else in Maysville when I told 'em so! They wouldn't believe me when I told 'em it was the honest truth! That's why Watkins and me had to come alone."

"How did you find out about Goodin?" Marshall asked.

Toombs grinned a jackal's grin. "A runaway," he said.

"You torture him or something?"

"In-tim-ee-da-tion," Toombs boasted. "Just scared it right outta him. Watkins shoved the end of a rifle barrel in his mouth, threatened to blow his fool head off!" He laughed devilishly. "Amazin', ain't it? For all their singin' of heaven, most of 'em don't want to go to the pearly gates none too soon."

"Need any help with these slaves?" Marshall asked, taking his rifle from his shoulder.

"Naw, they's not going anywhere," Toombs said.

"You just don't want to share the reward money," Marshall complained.

A twinkle came to Toombs' eye. "Look at it from my point of view, Morgan. I can split the money two ways or three ways. Which would you do if you was me?" he chortled. "Besides, these worthless folk ain't anythin' I can't handle."

There was a moment of silence. "Who would have thought Tom Goodin was a slave runner?" Marshall said again.

"Yeah, who woulda thought?"

"And who would have thought that I work with him?" Marshall Morgan pointed his rifle at the slave hunter's head.

A nervous grin creased the slave hunter's face, then quickly disappeared. "I find no humor in this, Morgan."

"I intend no humor, Frank."

Toombs fidgeted in place, his rifle still pointed at the runaways. "What . . . what are you gonna do?"

With teeth gritted, Marshall answered, "I was thinking about shoving the barrel of my gun into your mouth to in-tim-ee-date you into lowering your gun." Marshall's face flushed as he fought to control the wild beast inside him that wanted to tear into the slave hunter.

Toombs chuckled nervously. "You wouldn't kill me . . . I know you. Seen you in Maysville hundreds of times. Son of a preacher. You wouldn't shoot a white man."

Marshall touched Toombs' bottom lip with the barrel of his rifle. "You don't know me as well as you think you do," Marshall seethed. "You're wrong about me and slaves. You see, I'm the conductor of this underground railroad. And I take personal offense to anyone who disrupts my schedule. Now, do you want to find out if you're also wrong about my ability kill a slave hunter?" Trembling with rage, the rifle barrel jerked in his hands, pinching Toombs' lip between the weapon and his teeth. A trickle of blood appeared.

Toombs' leaned backward slightly. His tongue tasted the

blood on his lip. "W ... wh ... what do you want me to do?" he stammered.

"I already told you. Lower your rifle. Let it fall to the ground."

A heavily perspiring Frank Toombs dropped his rifle.

"Now the pistols, one at a time."

There were two soft thuds as the pistols hit the ground.

"Them slaves ain't worth it, Morgan!" Toombs said looking to the ridge in hopes of spotting reinforcements. There were none.

Marshall read his thoughts. "No way Watkins could be back this soon," he said as he kicked the slave hunter's weapons further out of reach. "He's probably just reaching Maysville about now. It'll take him the better part of an hour to round up help and get back here. By then we'll be long gone."

A look of pleading appeared on Toombs' face. "All right, all right!" he cried. "I'll cut you in on the reward money. That's what you want, isn't it? Twenty-eight runaways, more than enough money to go around."

"I don't want the money."

"Sure you do!" Toombs cried. "Them runaways ain't nothin' to you! Even if you let 'em go, word will get out and they'll be picked up by some other slave hunter before they reach Cincinnati. Then he'll get the money. The way I see it, someone's gonna get a heap of money for them slaves. Better us than someone else, right?"

A sober look crossed Marshall's face. "When word gets out ... " he pondered Toombs' statement. His thumb played with the rifle cock. "There's only one way word can get out, Frank."

Cato yelled from the river's edge. "Tha's right, Mas'r Morgan! Don't let him go. Shoot him! Shoot him!"

Frank Toombs turned white with fright. "You're not gonna

take directions from a Negro, are you, Morgan? Just let me go . . . I promise I won't tell nobody nothin' . . . I promise . . . I'm even willin' to forget we was even here together . . . just don't . . . "

"Into the skiff," Marshall ordered.

"What?"

"Into the skiff! We're taking you with us."

"You can't do that!" Toombs shouted.

"There's no room!" Cato shouted. "We's too crowded already. Shoot him!"

"Either you get in willingly," Marshall said to Toombs, "or I'll ask Mr. Cato and a few of his friends to assist you."

Cato was breathing heavily. The memory of a dozen scourgings churned his hatred for the slave hunter.

"Morgan, no . . . wait . . . " Toombs pleaded, not taking his eyes off Cato, "you're forgetting Watkins! By now half of Maysville knows about these slaves."

"All they know is what Watkins told them," Marshall replied. "And just a few moments ago you said that no one in Maysville believed you earlier when you told them Tom Goodin was running slaves. I imagine the good townspeople of Maysville are going to be mighty irate when they get here and discover it was all a prank. They'll come looking for slaves, but all they'll find is quiet Tom Goodin going about his daily chores. Of course, Watkins will persist in his story. But who do you think the townspeople will believe? Slave hunter Watkins or deacon Goodin?"

His voice turned harsh. "Now get into the skiff."

At gunpoint, Frank Toombs lay on the bottom of the first of the three skiffs. He moaned and complained as runaway after runaway piled in on top of him. Then, large tarps were thrown over the skiffs to conceal the human cargo. The heat under the tarps was stifling, but the only one heard to complain was Toombs and his voice was muffled by all the bodies stacked on top of him.

After the slaves were loaded, Marshall's anger gradually subsided and the trembling in his hands stopped. Turning to Tom Goodin: "Will you be all right?"

Goodin hadn't quite regained his composure. "It will take a while for my nerves to settle down, but I'll be fine." He chuckled nervously. "Marshall . . . thanks. I thought it was over for us all."

Marshall patted him on the shoulder. "So did I." He turned to board the skiff. Goodin grabbed his arm.

"Standing by the water's edge," Goodin's voice quivered as he spoke, "I thought that even if somehow we escaped, I'd have to become a runaway myself . . . leave my home . . . you know, once word got out I was runnin' slaves. But now, it looks like I'll be able to stay. Can't thank you enough."

Marshall extended his hand. Goodin gripped it tightly with both of his hands. "I didn't have time to replace the panel in the attic," Marshall said. "You'd best nail it in place before Watkins returns."

Goodin nodded. Marshall stepped into a skiff.

"Marshall?" Goodin's eyes were downcast. "Um . . . I hope you'll forgive me for what I thought of you when you ran away. You know, when Toombs and Watkins first appeared. It's just that I thought you were running out on us."

Marshall shrugged. "I would have thought the same thing had it been you."

"Anyway, thanks again. God be with you, son."

Gripping a long pole, Marshall Morgan pushed off, and the first boatload of runaway slaves lumbered into the Ohio River. Cato and another slave, piloting the second and third skiffs, launched their boats. As Marshall poled his skiff into deeper water, the river sloshed over the sides of the overloaded craft prompting startled cries from the runaways under the tarp.

"Is we sinkin'?" a male voice cried.

"Lay still!" Marshall shouted. "We're low in the water, but if you stay still we'll make it across." *I hope,* he added silently to himself.

From beneath the tarp Marshall could hear the voice of Mother Kinney. "Carry us safely 'cross dis river, Lor'. We's Moses in the basket. Float us into de gentle arms of Pharaoh's daughter."

Chapter 2

AS it turned out, the arms of safety Mother Kinney prayed for belonged not to a Pharaoh's daughter, but to a hulking Negro layman of Cincinnati's Zion Baptist Church. And the skiff carrying the runaways proved less seaworthy than the basket Moses' mother made. Midway across the river the lead skiff began taking on water.

"Here dey come!" John Hatfield pointed upriver to the three skiffs. He was a massive black man with a large chest, hairy arms, and a bald head.

Standing next to him, Willy Morgan pushed up on his crutch to get a better look. "There! I see them," he cried. Willy stole a glance at his underground railroad partner. He had never known a man larger than John Hatfield. Nor had he known a more sensitive man. Having performed over a dozen operations together, Willy noticed that the giant Negro wiped tears from his eyes every time he saw the skiffs coming toward shore.

"Looka dat firs' boat!" Hatfield shouted. "Dey's frightfully low in da water! How many dey got in dar anyhow? They's not gonna make it!" He lumbered over the edge of their lookout position, barreling his way through the underbrush to the river bank. From the water's edge, he looked back.

"You need help?" he asked.

Willy swallowed a retort. He hated being treated like an

invalid. Just because he had a clubfoot and couldn't move as quickly as everyone else didn't mean he was helpless.

"I can make it down fine by myself," he said.

"Suit yourself."

Hatfield proceeded up the river without waiting for him. Willy planted his crutch on the hard, sun-baked ridge. Just as he was transferring his weight to it, it slipped a few inches before catching hold on a rock. The sudden jerk rammed the crutch into Willy's armpit. He winced but made not a sound. It was a practiced response. Cries of pain brought unwanted attention to his deformity. It wasn't that Willy didn't want attention. He craved it. He just didn't want the head-shaking-pity kind of attention he usually got when people screwed up their faces and stared at his twisted foot.

At eighteen years of age, Willy was the youngest of the four Morgan children. He was also the shortest, which only served to remind him constantly that he was the runt of the litter. It was one of a multitude of daily reminders. Every time he looked in a mirror, or stood next to his brothers, or tried to keep up with them, he was reminded he was different; every time he picked up his crutch and hobbled across a room, he was reminded that when God was passing out good looks and intelligence to the Morgans, the supply ran out before He got to Willy. Whereas J.D. was brilliant and handsome, and Marshall was strong and bold as brass, and Sarah was attractive and articulate, Willy was the short runt with the clubfoot who walked with a crutch.

He didn't blame his brothers and sister for his shortcomings. Nor was he angry with them for being comely and fit. In fact, he idolized them. After all, it wasn't their fault he was the way he was. *Why blame them for something God did to me?*

With each step down the slope, Willy secured the crutch, transferred his weight, then took a hop. He was quite accomplished at it. Still, it was slower than people with two good feet and he found himself falling behind Hatfield. That was common for Willy. Always slow. Always falling behind.

Suddenly, the hardened dirt gave way. The crutch slipped. Willy tried to stop his momentum by reaching for the branches of a bush. He came up with only a handful of leaves. Acting like a pivot, his good foot swung him around. Groping wildly, Willy fell backwards down the slope, tumbling, heels flying upward, turning over and over, caroming off rocks and bushes until his momentum was spent. He lay head and shoulders in shallow water, his shirt soaking up the river. Mud coated his arms and face and tasted gritty in his mouth. His crutch sprawled uselessly in a bush halfway up the slope.

"Willy! You all right?" Hatfield called to him.

"I'm fine," Willy yelled angrily. He spit grit and mud from his mouth, then struggled to a sitting position. Hatfield was running toward him. Willy waved him off. "I said I was fine. Go get the skiffs."

The giant Negro ignored him, working his way up the slope to retrieve Willy's crutch. By the time Hatfield made it back down to the river's edge, Willy was standing, balanced on one foot. Hatfield placed the crutch under Willy's arm like he was propping up a sagging fence. Once more, Willy endured the humiliation in silence.

"Willy! John! We need help!" The voice was Marshall's. The lead skiff was still a hundred yards upriver and an equal distance from shore. It was so low in the water, the boat's sides were barely visible. Every minor tilt brought a flood of fresh water over the sides. Marshall—flushed from exertion, soaking wet, his arms heavy—paddled with all his might. The skiff responded sluggishly to his efforts to bring it ashore.

"Go! Go!" Willy urged Hatfield. "I'm right behind you."

Hatfield ran upriver until he was parallel with the sinking skiff. "What you wants me to do?" he yelled to Marshall.

Marshall's answer was to throw a line toward shore. It fell

woefully short. The giant black man splashed into the river after it, keeping his footing. Marshall coiled the line and threw it again. With the water up to his shoulders, Hatfield managed to grab hold of the rope. He wrapped it around his hand, dug his feet into the bottom of the river, and pulled with all his might. Marshall resumed rowing. He could hear Mother Kinney praying for them beneath the tarp.

The other two skiffs had passed Marshall and, upon his direction, were making their way toward shore.

Reluctantly the lead skiff conceded to their efforts to bring it ashore. Marshall exchanged his paddle for a pole while Hatfield played tug-of-war with the Ohio River, his strong legs and feet gouging the river bottom with each step as he emerged onto dry ground. Willy grabbed the rope behind him with one hand and pulled. With a thump, he fell to his seat. Realizing he could do more from this position, he tossed his crutch aside and now pulled the rope with two hands, his good foot scratching the ground for leverage. Hand over hand, they pulled the skiff toward shore.

Then, just as they were making good progress, the line froze. The skiff would go no farther. Marshall poked at the river's bottom with his pole.

"We've hit a sandbar!" he yelled.

"How deep is it this side of the bar?" Hatfield yelled.

Marshall leaned forward on the bow, probing the water. The twelve-foot pole sank freely for as far as Marshall could reach.

"I can't touch bottom," he cried.

"Can you push off the bar?" Hatfield yelled. "We can pull you in further downstream."

Marshall planted the pole and pushed. The skiff didn't budge. He pushed again, grunting from exertion. They were stuck fast. The skiff groaned as the river's current pushed against its side. The hot afternoon sun sparkled on the water.

Marshall remembered the many times he and his brothers played in the river on hot days like this, jumping from tree limbs or piers, splashing, laughing. But it seemed that today the sun and the river were refusing to play with him, as though they'd forgotten those former carefree summer days. While the sun hammered him from above, the river clawed at the skiff, trying to tear it apart.

"We're going to have to swim for it," Marshall cried. "Keep the line tight!"

He threw off the tarp. More than a dozen faces shielded themselves from the sudden light.

"Everybody move slowly," Marshall said. "We're stuck on a sandbar and have to swim ashore."

A chorus of cries erupted. "I's can't swim, Mas'r Morgan! O Lor', help us! Don' let us drown, help us!" The tumult rocked the skiff. Water flowed over the sides. The runaways began to panic.

"Quiet! Listen to me!" Marshall yelled. "Listen to me! There's a rope from here to shore. All you have to do is hold on to the rope!"

"But whats if we drowns, Mas'r Morgan? Whats if we drowns?"

Mother Kinney answered them. "The good Lor' didn't bring us this far to forsake us now!" she cried. "We's just gots to trus' Him, thas all!" To Marshall: "I's never swimmed a lick in my life, but if you'll jus' get me to dat rope, I'll be makin' my way to the promised land."

The boatload of runaways watched as Marshall assisted the elderly woman to the front of the skiff and lowered her over the side. Wrinkled black hands gripped the taut line. Mother Kinney closed her eyes and didn't move.

"O Lor'," she prayed, "help your child Mother Kinney right now or takes her to glory. Thy will be done. Amen."

The oldest of the runaways worked her way toward shore,

hand over hand with surprising ease.

"Look at dat!" she cried. "It's a miracle! I's as light as a feather! God done sent His angels to make me light as a feather!"

Marshall couldn't help but smile at the old woman's faith and her discovery of water's buoyancy.

Encouraged by Mother Kinney's faith, one by one the other runaways lowered themselves into the water and worked their way in similar fashion toward shore. By now the occupants of the other two skiffs had landed. Hatfield turned the line over to them with orders to keep it taut while he waded out into the river up to his chest to assist any who needed help.

Frank Toombs, who had been on the bottom of the pile in the lead skiff, came up coughing and sputtering as the last of the Negroes climbed off of him. Being on the bottom of the sinking skiff, his had been a desperate struggle to keep his head above water.

"I almost drowned under all them slaves!" he screamed. "Morgan, I'm gonna get you for this! I swear if it's the last thing I ever do, I'm gonna . . . "

The skiff lurched, cutting him off mid-sentence. It was breaking up. Four runaways, their eyes filled with terror, clung to the bow waiting for their turn at the rope.

Sweaty, plump white hands grabbed Marshall's shirt. "I can't swim, Morgan! I can't swim! This thing's fallin' apart, and I can't swim!"

Another jolt. Marshall could see the seams on the stern separating. The skiff began to list. Toombs' fingernails clawed Marshall's chest in panic.

"She's comin' apart!" Hatfield yelled.

"I know!" Marshall cried as he fought to extricate himself from the slave hunter's grip. "Toombs can't swim."

Surprised to see Toombs standing in the skiff, Hatfield

muttered, "That's the whitest Negro I've ever seen!"

Marshall succeeded in prying Toombs' hands off of him. "Follow the others and you'll be safe!" he cried. "Just hold on to the rope!"

"I can't do it!" Toombs whimpered. "Don't let me drown, Morgan. I'm beggin' you, don't let me drown!"

"It's either the rope or drown! Take your pick!" Marshall yelled.

The skiff groaned and jerked again. Toombs didn't move.

Exasperated, Marshall grabbed Toombs by the wrists and placed his hands on the edge of the creaking skiff.

"Hold on to the side of the boat and work your way forward!"

"What are you going to do?" Toombs wailed. "You can swim, can't you? You're gonna leave me here to drown, aren't you?" The slave hunter's voice was punctuated with sobs, his hands shook violently. He could barely maintain his grip on the boat.

"I'm going to steady the skiff while you climb out to the rope," Marshall yelled at him. "Hurry! We don't have much time! Work your way to the bow and grab the rope."

Marshall didn't wait for Toombs to respond. He jumped over the side of the skiff onto the sandbar. He splashed feet first into the water. But instead of hitting a solid sandbar, his feet plunged deep into loose sand. It encircled his ankles and calves up to his knees with a deadly grip that tried to pull him under. His arms flailing, Marshall grabbed the only thing within reach, the side of the skiff. His grip caused the boat to list radically, knocking Toombs off his feet.

The slave hunter let loose a nerve-rattling scream as he fell upon the opposite side of the skiff, clutching it with all his might.

"Quicksand!" Marshall cried. "Hatfield! I'm in quicksand."

It was as though the devil had reached up from the bowels

of the earth and was trying to pull him into hades. The water rose to his chest, then his chin. Marshall's only hold this side of a watery grave was the wooden skiff, and it was breaking apart.

"I can't swim, Marshall!" Hatfield called to him. "What am I gonna do? I can't swim!" The huge deacon turned toward the shore and pleaded. "Can anyone swim? Anyone? Marshall's drowning!"

In the skiff Frank Toombs' wails grew louder and louder. The runaways huddled on the shore watching helplessly. No one came forward. With the water up to his nose, Marshall had to tilt his head back to breathe. Willy was working his way into the current. He was in the water up to his knees, using his crutch to keep his balance. Willy never ventured further than that into the river, not without something to keep him afloat.

Marshall shook his head and tried to shout, "Willy, no!" But all he succeeded in doing was swallowing a mouthful of water, causing him to cough and sputter.

Willy waded further out until the water was up to his waist. His mouth was a thin line. Worried eyes overflowed with tears. He wanted to go farther. He wanted to push out into the river, to save his brother. But he didn't. Something held him back.

The skiff groaned as the stern cracked open and the river forced its way into the back of the boat. Toombs was whimpering. His hands reached for the bow of the boat as the water inched its way up his legs. Marshall could feel the skiff giving way. He was sinking lower and lower. He tilted his head back to keep his mouth and nose above the surface.

"Hatfield, get Toombs out, then throw me the line!" he yelled.

The large Negro called to the slave hunter. "Mas'r Toombs. Grab holda da rope! I'll pulls you in!"

"I can't!" Toombs yelled.

"Yes you can!" Hatfield replied. "Grabs holda da rope!"

"No, I can't. I can't!"

Marshall was fighting for air now. The sloshing of the water was getting into his nose and mouth.

"He's not gonna do it, Marshall! I's gonna cut da line free!"

"No!" Marshall cried. "Toombs! Climb over the bow! Grab the rope. Now!"

The only response was a series of uncontrollable sobs. Marshall was getting more water than air now. He was losing his grip on the side of the skiff and beginning to black out. The surface of the water closed over his head. Sounds were muted. Cries. Shouts. Indistinct sounds, yet some recognizable. *J.D. . . . Marshall . . . skiff . . . one inside. . . .* The words were a strange juxtaposition of the realms of water and air. *So this is what it is like to die.* A curious sensation. He was no longer breathing air. Yet his body was at peace. And everything was clear. The river bottom. Rocks. Plants. Then, beginning with the outer edges of his vision, a darkness started to creep over him.

Hands encircled his chest. *Mother Kinney's angels coming to take him to heaven?* They were placing some kind of cord around him, under his arms. Strange. He'd always thought that people floated up to heaven. Come to find out, God pulls them up on a rope.

The cord yanked him out of the sand. Moments later he broke the surface of the water and was pulled to shore. But instead of finding himself in the arms of an angel, he found himself face-to-face with the brown mustache and kindly brown eyes of his older brother, J.D.

For several minutes Marshall rediscovered the joys of breathing while J.D. rushed over to help Daniel Cooper with the floundering Frank Toombs. As the last survivor of the lead skiff was pulled ashore, the remains of the skiff broke away from the sandbar and floated down the river. While Daniel panted from the exertion, J.D. returned to Marshall. Willy was sitting next to his brother, quiet and sullen.

"Thought you weren't going to help us today," Marshall said to J.D.

J.D. plopped down beside him. "I leave you two alone for one minute and you get into trouble. Can't you do anything right without me?" A grin accompanied the chiding. Leaning closer, he whispered, "What went wrong? You should be halfway to Cincinnati by now."

Marshall nodded his head toward the slave hunter who lay on the shoreline, gasping for air. Toombs looked like a beached white whale. "He held us up," Marshall said with a twisted grin. "It took us a while to get free. Then the skiff sprung a leak and slowed us down. It's not been a good day."

J.D. sighed heavily. "It's going to get a lot worse if Daniel tells his father about this."

Marshall grimaced at the thought. "Do you think he will?" J.D. shrugged.

"Do you think Daniel knows we're running slaves?" Willy asked.

Marshall and J.D. looked at their brother in disbelief.

"Well, maybe he thinks we're slave hunters and we captured them!" Willy offered.

"Willy," J.D. said, "you're headed the wrong direction with the slaves to be slave hunters. If we captured them, we'd be taking them south."

"Oh yeah."

Marshall to J.D.: "Not that I'm complaining, but what were you doing down by the river?"

"The girls wanted to take a walk along the river. Had I known you were running behind schedule, I would have diverted their attention somehow."

"Lucky for me, as it turns out," Marshall said.

"Don't feel so fortunate yet. I may have saved you so Father can kill you. You know how hard he's worked to avoid any discussion of slavery or states rights while the Coopers are here. This week means a lot to him."

"Yeah, I know."

Toombs had propped himself up on his arms and was talking to Daniel. Hatfield was speaking in hushed tones to the runaways, assuring them that they were safe.

J.D. stood and brushed some of the mud from his pants. "I'll see if I can keep Daniel from saying anything. Sarah will help me. Will you be all right? You swallowed half the river. Maybe I should help you take the slaves the rest of the way."

Marshall struggled to his feet. His voice was steadier than his legs. "I'll be fine. Besides, I've got Willy here to help me."

It was a gratuitous comment to make his younger brother feel better, and it did.

"That's right, he's got me to help him," Willy said.

Marshall to J.D.: "You just take care of Daniel, or I'm a dead man when I get home."

"I'll do my best." J.D. turned his attention toward Daniel and Toombs.

Marshall called after him. "J.D.?"

"Yeah?"

"Thanks."

"What are brothers for?"

The oldest Morgan brother collected Daniel and the two of them walked upriver toward the Morgan home. Beyond them, on a bluff, Marshall could see Jenny and Sarah waiting for them.

"Let's go, Willy!" Marshall slapped his younger brother playfully on the arm.

"Marshall?"

"Yeah, Willy?"

"I'm real sorry."

"About what?"

"I couldn't rescue you. You needed me and I couldn't rescue you. I feel real bad about it. If J.D. hadn't come, you'd be dead. It would be my fault."

"Nonsense! It wouldn't be your fault, Willy. Besides, everything's fine now."

Willy nodded. But the grim line across his mouth indicated that Willy felt like a failure, once again.

"Emma!" Seth Cooper burst through the door. His face was crimson, his eyes fiery. "Pack our things! We're leaving."

His thundering appearance startled the two middle-aged women sitting at opposite ends of the sofa; their half-empty teacups rattled and spilled as the visiting preacher stormed by them on his way upstairs to the guest bedroom. The front door slammed open a second time. Jeremiah followed in Seth Cooper's wake.

"Seth! Let's talk about this . . . don't let this one incident spoil the entire week. . . . "

A startled Susanna attempted to intercept her husband. "Jeremiah, what on earth is going on?"

Jeremiah followed his friend as far as the foot of the stairs, stopped, and watched as Seth slammed the bedroom door behind him. Jeremiah pounded his fist on the railing.

Emma Cooper excused herself and followed her husband upstairs.

"Jeremiah, are you going to tell me what's going on?"

Before he could answer, the front door flew open. Daniel Cooper, his wide jaw firmly set, his clothes soaking wet, stomped into the room and headed for the stairs. Sarah tried to grab him by the arm. She had no effect in slowing him down.

"At least try to reason with him!" Sarah pleaded.

She got no response. Daniel's unblinking eyes were set

straight forward; he refused to look at her. Jeremiah stepped out of the boy's way as Daniel followed his parents up the stairs.

Sarah stopped next to her father. With tear-stained cheeks, she watched Daniel disappear. She looked at her father. Her lower lip trembled; her hazel-brown eyes were reservoirs about to spill over. With an exasperated groan she stomped her foot and fled outside, nearly knocking over J.D. and Jenny who were just coming through the front door.

"J.D., just look at you!" Susanna cried. "What have you and Daniel been doing? Will someone please tell me what's going on?"

The bedroom door flew open. Seth Cooper's voice boomed from the top of the stairs. His tone was one of forced civility. "Morgan! Will you please arrange for our carriage?"

"Seth, let's talk. Don't let it end this way," Jeremiah pleaded.

His plea had no effect on the stony presence at the top of the stairs. A piercing glare was Cooper's only response. Moments later, Daniel came storming down the stairs.

"Is someone going to tell me where the bridles and reins are, or do I have to find them myself?"

He didn't wait for an answer, nor did he look at anyone directly as he walked out the door. Jeremiah motioned to J.D. to assist Daniel.

"Jeremiah Morgan," Susanna cried, "I insist you tell me what is going on right now!" Her arms were folded and her hands cupped her elbows, rubbing them nervously. Jeremiah recognized the mannerism. Whenever Susanna rubbed her elbows like this, she was frightened and upset. He moved toward her. In as calm a tone as he could produce, he said, "Seth is angry because . . . "

KA-THUMP! KA-THUMP! KA-THUMP! The sound on the stairway interrupted him. Seth was pulling a heavy trunk down the stairs by himself, one step at a time. The unmanned end of the trunk hit each step with a resounding thump.

"I can't believe this!" Jeremiah bellowed. "Well, if you're in that much of a hurry to get out of my house, then here, let me help you!"

"I don't need your help!" Cooper yelled.

"You're going to get it anyway. I wouldn't want you to accuse me of being an ungracious host too!"

"Ungracious host? That's the understatement of the year! What kind of host is it that runs slaves right under our noses on a Sunday afternoon?"

"Nothing that was done today was done to offend you," Jeremiah shouted.

"Well, it did offend me!" Cooper replied. "And I think you could have at least had the courtesy to suspend your abolitionist activities for the duration of our stay. We left Elijah and Abel at home because we knew that you wouldn't feel comfortable with our house servants. But apparently, polite consideration only goes one way in this friendship."

"What kind of friendship is it that takes offense so easily?"

With a steely glare, Cooper said, "I do not take offense easily. It is one thing for you and your boys to run slaves, it is quite another thing to involve my son in their abolitionist activities."

"Daniel was saving lives."

"Are you going to help me with this trunk or aren't you?"

Cooper picked up his end of the trunk and began to drag it toward the door. Jeremiah rolled his eyes, then chased after the other end of the trunk. As the two men clambered out the door, Emma came downstairs, her hat on, carrying a small bag. Her eyes were red and swollen.

Susanna went to her. "Emma, dear, please don't go."

Emma refused even to look at her. Her eyes revealed more hurt than anger. Without saying a word, she followed after her husband.

Susanna let out an exasperated scream. "Jenny, can you tell me what is happening?"

The black-haired Jenny Parsons sighed, then said, "The four of us—Daniel, Sarah, J.D., and me—were walking along the river. We saw three boats. Daniel recognized Marshall in the first boat . . . "

"Susanna!"

Jeremiah called to his wife from the front of the house. Susanna shook her head sadly and went outside. Jenny followed after her.

The Cooper's carriage rumbled down the country road, its wheels kicking up a swirl of dust. Jeremiah stood off by himself watching it go. His shoulders were slumped. Behind him, arm in arm, stood J.D. and Jenny. Susanna was in the doorway. Sarah was nowhere to be seen.

"Is somebody going to tell me what happened?" Susanna asked.

"You'd better get out of those wet clothes," Jenny said to J.D. as she pulled at his shirt that stuck to his belly like a layer of skin. "I'll stop by tomorrow."

"Let me walk you home," J.D. said.

"Go dry yourself. I can walk home by myself."

Moments later Susanna and Jeremiah were alone in front of the house. He hadn't moved, even though the carriage was no longer in sight.

"Well?" Susanna said.

With a heavy sigh, Jeremiah accompanied his wife inside. In their bedroom, he sat dejectedly on the edge of the bed and told her of the day's unfortunate sequence of events.

"Seth and I were sitting under the shade tree, drinking our lemonade. We saw Daniel and Sarah with J.D. and Jenny strolling along that grassy bluff overlooking the river. We started talking about Daniel and Sarah, how we used to think they would someday get married."

"There is still something between them," Susanna said.

"Do you think so? What makes you say that?"

"The way they look at each other. Emma noticed it too."

"Well, there's no chance of them ever getting together now." Jeremiah sighed again. "Anyway, we got to talking about other things7 Then, all of a sudden Seth noticed that the boys had disappeared. Sarah and Jenny were staring down at the river, like something had happened. When they didn't move and the boys didn't return, we grew concerned. So we got up to investigate. Then the girls disappeared too. Well, by the time we reached the bluff, here come both couples and J.D. and Daniel are soaking wet. The first thing we hear is Daniel saying, "I don't like it, but for your sake I won't say anything" And Seth says, "Won't say anything about what?""

Jeremiah chuckled.

"You should have seen the look on their faces. I haven't seen that look since the time I caught J.D. and Marshall smoking that cigar when they were boys. All four of them looked guilty as sin."

"What did they say?" Susanna asked.

"They didn't have to say anything. Behind them, downriver we could see Marshall and Willy herding a group of runaways up a path to the road."

"Oh, no!"

"Oh, yes."

"And Daniel was helping them?"

"Not exactly. Apparently there was trouble when one of the skiffs sank. J.D. and Daniel saw it and went down to help. So now Seth is convinced our boys deliberately lured Daniel into helping runaway slaves."

"They didn't, did they?"

"Of course not. J.D. wouldn't do that. But I fail to understand why they were moving slaves on Sunday and in the middle of the day. It's foolish! And you'd better believe when Marshall gets home, I'm going to get some satisfactory answers."

"Wha's dat fo'?" Cato asked.

A rough, pine coffin rested on a cart which was hitched to a mule.

"We can't just parades you up and down the roads in broad daylight," John Hatfield said. "So we's gonna have a funeral."

"Whose funeral?" Cato cried.

"It's nobody's funeral," Hatfield replied. "It's a pretend funeral. That ways, nobody thinks twice about why we's all on the road at the same time."

Cato was still skeptical. And from the looks on the faces of many of the runaways, he wasn't alone; only the most vocal.

"O, I jus' loves funerals," Mother Kinney cried. "Some of da bes' preachin' is done at funerals."

"We're going to need a corpse," Marshall said.

"Mas'r Morgan, we done this afore and we ain't never needed a real corpse," Hatfield said. "Mos' people don' want to look inside a coffin."

"I just think it best we have a corpse today, just in case. But we're going to need a volunteer. Are there any volunteers, Toombs?"

With the absence of firearms, all of them being lost in the river mishap, several of the larger black male slaves had been entrusted with the care of Frank Toombs. Only once did the slave hunter try to in-tim-ee-date them. Cato put down the effort with a little intimidation of his own which nearly escalated into violence before Marshall involved himself. Toombs realized that if Marshall's restraining authority were ever removed, he would be seriously harmed by the runaways. So, until now, Toombs had followed along rather meekly. But at the suggestion he be shut up in a box, he came to life.

"I'm not getting in there," he cried. "It's bad enough I nearly drowned in their sweat in the bottom of that boat. You're not going to put me in that coffin."

"Ah come on, Frank. Just try it on for size. Cato, why don't you and your friends help Mr. Toombs?"

Toombs was outmuscled. The coffin cover was removed and he was placed inside. It was a tight fit, but he made it. All the while Toombs was pleading to Marshall to let him out. Marshall leaned over the coffin and looked down at the slave hunter.

"It's only a short way to the cemetery, Frank. Enjoy the ride."

"You put that lid on, Morgan, and I'll scream. Anybody who passes by will know something's up if they hear a screaming corpse!"

"That wouldn't be wise, Frank. The way I figure it, you're our corpse for the day. Now you can do it voluntarily, or we can make it official."

The threat would have carried little weight had it come from Marshall alone. But the way Cato's eyes lit up at the idea silenced Toombs' complaints. As the lid was being lowered, he said, "I'll get you for this, Morgan. I swear it."

Marshall spoke to the sides of the pine box, "This whole experience will give you a deeper appreciation of life, Toombs."

"Do you think puttin' him in dar's wise?" Hatfield asked.

"We can't run the risk of him doing anything that will draw attention to us. This will keep him quiet."

With a wailing Mother Kinney leading the way, the funeral procession wound its way up the road toward Cincinnati accompanied by loud weeping and groans and shouts and tears. The runaways were a convincing funeral procession. More than once Marshall had to remind himself that it was a performance, as he felt the uneasy tightening in the pit of his stomach that he'd always associated with funerals and things related to death.

They passed several travelers, some who stopped in reverence for the procession to pass, while others simply steered to the far side of the road so they wouldn't get too close to the Negroes, or to death. Marshall didn't know which unsettled them more.

The procession reached the cemetery on the outskirts of the city as the sun was setting. The runaways were chilled and hungry and exhausted. Spots of blood in the dirt marked their path as blisters on their feet split open. Yet, despite their suffering and exhaustion, there was an underlying current of joy. This was their first day on free soil, and nothing could dampen their spirits. It was as though they were going to the cemetery to put slavery into the ground forever.

Upon reaching the backside of the cemetery, Hatfield ushered them into a ravine. They would wait there until dark. Giggles and laughs echoed against the dirt walls, prompting Marshall to scold the runaways for making too much noise.

"You can't stop 'em," Hatfield said. "They're so full of tickle they can't help themselves."

After a while, the noise subsided. Someone complimented Mother Kinney on her ability to wail during the funeral procession.

"Been to lots a fun'rals. Nothin' like a good fun'ral," Mother Kinney said. "There's nothin' like fun'ral preachin' to lift a person ta glory. Once, I gots to hear John Jasper hisself at a fun'ral!"

Blank looks on the faces of the other runaways indicated they'd never heard of the man. Neither had Marshall.

"O Lor'! Nobody preaches a fun'ral like John Jasper!" she cried. "He was a tobacco stemmer on a Virginia plantation afore da Lor' got ahold o' him. Oh, he was a wild one—

smoked and drank and cussed. Den one day God's arrow of conviction struck him right in his proud heart, and after that he started preachin' da Gospel."

Mother Kinney paused as visions of the man appeared in her mind. The others sat quietly, waiting to hear more. A spreading smile across the old woman's face indicated the telling of a fond memory was forthcoming.

"Firs' time he ever spoked in public was at a slave's fun'ral," she began. "A white preacher preached da sermon, den asked Jasper to dismiss everyone wid a prayer. Well, I's tell you, brother Jasper's prayer lifted everyone right up ta glory. Afterwards, even da white folks was sayin', 'From now on at fun'rals, we wants to hear John Jasper!' "

A couple of *Amens* and *Praise the Lords* echoed through the ravine.

"Da only time I heards him directly," Mother Kinney continued, "was at da fun'ral of William Ellyson and Mary Barnes." She clasped her hands to her chest and closed her eyes. "Till my dying day, I's never forget da picture he done painted of heaven." With a wide grin she added, " 'Course den I won't needs ta remember it no longer, cause I's be there!"

Maybe it was the lateness of the hour or the nearly fatal events of the day, but Marshall found himself drawn into Mother Kinney's story in an unusual way. He noticed that even the recently resurrected Frank Toombs was listening intently.

"He begun wid William Ellyson." Mother Kinney deepened her voice to approximate the tone of John Jasper, speaking the words as she remembered them: " 'Lemme say a word about dis William Ellyson. I say it da first and get it off my mind.' Jasper was always like dat, speakin' da truth no matter what. He says: 'William Ellyson was a no-good man—he didn't say he was; he didn't try to be good, and they tell me he die as he live, without God and without hope in da world. It's a bad tale to tell on 'em, but he fix da story hisself.' "

Marshall watched Frank Toombs fidget.

Mother Kinney continued: " 'But my brethren,' says Jasper, 'Mary Barnes was different. She was washed in da blood of da Lamb and walked in white; her religion was of God. You could trus' Mary anywhere; never caught her in them playhouses nor friskin' in them dances; she weren't no streetwalker traipsin' round at night. She loved da house of da Lord; her feet clung to da straight and narrow path; I know'd her,' he said. 'Our sister, Mary, good-bye. Your race is run, but your crown is sure.' "

Mother Kinney closed her eyes. Her breathing increased as she continued.

"Den brother Jasper talked about what it would be like to go to heaven. 'First of all,' he said, 'I'd go down and see da river of life. I loves to go down to da old muddy James,' he says, 'but it ain't nothin' like da river which flows by da throne. I longs for its crystal waves, to be drinkin' its water and restin' under those trees. Oh, what it must be like to be there!

" 'After that, I'd go see some of dem fine mansions. I'd stroll up dem avenues where da children o' God dwell. Father Abraham, I'm sure he got a great palace, and Moses, what escorted da Children of Israel out of bondage, he must be powerful upset bein's such a man as he is; and David, da king that made pretty songs, I'd like to see his home.' "

" 'Den,' says Jasper, 'I'd cut roun' to da back streets and look for da little home where my Savior's set my mother up to housekeepin'. I 'spect I'll know da house by da roses in da yard and da vine on da porch. Oh, what it must be to be there!

" 'And den I'd take a trip to da throne and see da King in His royal garments. And visit da ransomed of da Lord. Here's brother Abel, da first man what got here; and brother Enoch what took a stroll and straggled into glory; and there's Elijah, what had a carriage sent for 'im; and . . . well, here she is; I know'd she'd get here. Why, Mary Barnes, you got home, did you? Oh, what must it be to be there!' "

The ravine beside the cemetery was stone quiet when Mother Kinney finished her account of Jasper's funeral sermon. It was their first night on free soil and the level of excitement among them was already high, but Mother Kinney had taken them to even greater heights.

It was dark now. John Hatfield was joined by four other laymen from his church and the runaways were spirited out of the ravine. From there they would go to another stop on the underground railroad where they would be fed and given clothing, provided by the Antislavery Sewing Society. Then, once again using darkness to hide their movement, they would continue their journey to Canada.

"What should I do with Toombs?" Hatfield asked.

"Take him to Canada. He might like it there," Marshall replied.

Toombs objected. "Morgan! Don't leave me with them. They'll kill me! Whatever you want, I'll get it for you, but please . . . please, don't leave me with them."

There was real fear in his voice, and seeing the hunger for revenge in Cato's eyes, Marshall knew there was valid grounds for his fear.

"Tell you what I'll do for you," Marshall said. "I'll put you in someone's charge. Someone who can protect you." Looking around, he called, "Mother Kinney, come here."

The old woman broke away from the others and stood next to Marshall.

"Mother Kinney, you're a good Christian woman and I know people listen to you."

"'Tain't me. I am what I am by da grace o' God," Mother Kinney said.

"Well, you see, Mr. Toombs here is afraid to go with you to Canada. I want to guarantee his safety, but I'm not going any farther with you. So I need someone to look after him. Will you see that he gets to Canada unharmed for me?"

Mother Kinney's lower lip protruded as she looked Toombs up and down while weighing the request. "Dis man is from da devil, of that I's sure," she said. "But you done been so good to us, Mas'r Morgan. I's do it fo' you."

Looking up at Toombs, Marshall said, "Mother Kinney will protect you, Frank. And Lord help the person who tries to cross her."

"You can't be serious, Morgan!" Toombs cried.

"Good luck in Canada, Frank."

Mother Kinney walked ahead. When Toombs didn't follow her, she stopped in the middle of the road and placed her hands on frail hips. "Don' dawdle, Mas'r Toombs. We's got a long ways to go."

Toombs folded his arms and refused to take a step. Whereupon, Mother Kinney motioned to several large Negroes. They moved toward him. Frank Toombs quickly waved them off. "I'm coming! I'm coming!" he cried.

"Frank!" Marshall called out after him, "If you know what's good for you, you'll be nice to Mother Kinney."

"I'm comin' back to get you, Morgan!" Toombs yelled over his shoulder. "I swear I will. I'll get you!"

A laughing John Hatfield shook hands with Marshall and Willy. "It got a mite scary there at da river," he said.

Marshall shrugged it off. "It wasn't one of our smoothest runs. And it's not over yet. If my father and our house guest find out we've been running slaves today, the worst is yet to come."

"I'll pray for you," Hatfield said.

"We'll need it."

While John Hatfield hurried to catch up with the weary but

jubilant runaways, Marshall and Willy Morgan walked side-by-side back to Point Providence and their uncertain homecoming.

Jeremiah Morgan sat in the dark under the shade tree. The chair beside him, which had recently been occupied by his best — now former — friend, was empty. The evening service at his church had been humiliating for him. Not only did he have to explain the absence of the visiting preacher and call off the remainder of meetings for the week, but he also had to preach a sermon without having time to prepare. The eloquence of Seth Cooper from the same pulpit a few hours earlier made Jeremiah's sermon sound worse than it actually was. And he knew the balance of the week would fare no better. The day's events were sure to fuel the gossip fires among those who opposed the coming of a Southern preacher in the first place.

Jeremiah sighed a long, protracted sigh. He would survive the gossip. In fact, given the same set of circumstances, he would do it all over again for the chance to reconcile with Seth. What he couldn't live with was the way things turned out with Seth. The empty chair next to him was a monument to his failure. For all of his professional life, he had preached that God's love was the mightiest force in the world; that it was God's love that held marriages together; that God's love was the glue of the Christian family; that nothing and no one could separate those who were bound together by God's love. He not only preached this, he believed it.

But now he wasn't so sure. He had just witnessed the destruction of a friendship that he once believed could survive anything. Maybe there were some things that even God couldn't hold together.

The sound of crunching gravel drew his attention to the private road leading to the house. The summer moon bathed the open field that lay between him and the road with white light, casting dark shadows along the fence and trees lining the far side. The silhouetted figures of Marshall and a limping Willy appeared and disappeared among the shadows. Not until they were within a few feet of the house did they see him. They stopped. For several tense moments no one spoke.

"Willy, go inside. I want to talk to Marshall."

A frown covered Willy's face. He looked to Marshall. His older brother shrugged in response. With an exasperated sigh, Willy limped into the house. The door slammed closed behind him.

"It's been an eventful day for you," Jeremiah began.

Marshall's eyes squinted as he tried to determine how much his father knew. He ran his hand through his hair like a comb. The white streak stood out prominently in the moonlight.

"It hasn't been an average day," Marshall replied.

"Thank God for that," Jeremiah said.

Marshall hitched his pants and offered nothing more, willing to let his father determine the course of the conversation.

"Where have you been all day?" Jeremiah asked.

"I don't feel like playing question-and-answer games," Marshall said. "It's obvious you're agitated about something. What have I done wrong now?"

Jeremiah Morgan rose and stood face-to-face with his son. Marshall was slightly taller, causing Jeremiah to have to look up at his son when he spoke.

"All right. Why were you running slaves today? On the Sabbath! And when the Coopers were under our roof! What did you do, get up this morning and say to yourself, 'Now what can I do that will cause the most trouble?' Because you couldn't have picked anything that would have ruined things worse than you did today!"

"We had no choice," Marshall defended himself. "Tom Goodin learned that his house had been identified as a runaways' station. We had less than an hour to move the slaves across the river. I don't understand what all the fuss is about. You know we've been doing this."

"But not on the Sabbath!" Jeremiah shouted. "And not when the Coopers were here!"

"Jesus helped people on the Sabbath!" Marshall shouted back. "What would you have me do? Tell twenty-eight runaways that they have to return to slavery because this isn't a good day to help them? As for the Coopers, I happen to think that the lives of those slaves are more important than being courteous to guests. Besides, what kind of friendship is it if they are so easily offended?"

Jeremiah's hands clenched. He winced in pain, but didn't unclench them. He wasn't a fighting man, but Marshall's verbal blow hurt. He fought to keep himself from hitting his son.

Realizing he had pushed his father to the edge of violence, Marshall backed off. His tone was softer as he said, "I can't believe Daniel told on us."

"He didn't. We saw you ourselves."

"I'm sorry," Marshall said. "If you wish, I'll apologize to Dr. Cooper."

"The Coopers have returned to Virginia."

The news saddened Marshall. He understood better his father's anguish. "What more can I say?" Marshall asked. "I'm sorry. But it couldn't be helped."

"Marshall, this week was important to me!" Jeremiah shouted.

"Helping people escape the bonds of slavery is important to me! And if you ask me, their suffering is far greater than anything we or the Coopers have suffered today!"

It was a powerful blow. A near knockout.

"Now, if you don't mind," Marshall said, already walking toward the front door, "I'd like to get out of these dirty clothes and get to bed."

Jeremiah didn't stop him.

Chapter 3

THE woodpile behind the Morgan house grew considerably the day following the Sabbath slave run. As the sweat rolled unhindered down Marshall's face, he placed another log on the stump. Gripping the handle until his knuckles hurt, he heaved the ax with all his might. The blade swung in a swift and even arc. There was a grunt and a thud. Two pieces of kindling fell to the ground. Without pausing, Marshall loaded the stump with another log.

Since the days Marshall was old enough to think for himself, the Morgan's firewood supply had always been the beneficiary of his disagreements with his father. Their supply never ran low.

The topics of their arguments changed as Marshall grew older. Early differences of opinion between parent and child over time spent working compared to time spent playing gave way to heated political discussions between adults. The thing that irritated Marshall most was that his father didn't give him credit for having a brain. Just because he was active didn't mean he never took time to think. He had always been the most active of the Morgan children—never able to sit still for long, always fidgety at church, at the dinner table, in the company of guests. Marshall thought it unfair of his father to interpret his excessive energy as a deficiency in brains and maturity. "You are forever acting first and thinking later, if at all," was one of his father's fondest sayings.

For the longest time, Marshall accepted that assessment of himself. Then, as he grew older, he discovered that not only did he have a fully functioning brain, but a quick one as well. Things that were immediately obvious to him were gradually realized by others. By the age of twelve he saw the illogic, immaturity, and oftentimes downright stupidity of most adults. But when he pointed out their errors in logic or fact, his father rewarded him with public chastisement, calling him impertinent. Even now, as an adult, Marshall's opinions were dismissed as ill-considered and wild. *Why couldn't his father give him the same measure of respect that was given to J.D.?*

Another swing. Swoosh. Grunt. Thud. Two more pieces were added to the woodpile.

The difference between him and his father, Marshall reasoned, was that his father was a talker and he was a doer. Take the slavery issue. They both detested it as morally untenable. But when it came to doing something about it, his father did nothing more than preach an occasional sermon against it. To Marshall, preaching against slavery was like shooting a rifle in the air. The noise might get people's attention, but all-in-all it was a waste of a good bullet.

Marshall didn't put much stock in words. *What good did they do?* If words were drops of water, Washington politicians would have drowned themselves long ago. *And what had they accomplished in their efforts to dismantle slavery?* Nothing. City after city held debates on the issue. One man would speak for it, another against it. Then they'd shout at each other for a while. Sometimes they'd even shout at the audience. Many of them would do nothing more than shout at opponents who weren't there to defend themselves. *And what did all this shouting accomplish?* Nothing. Invariably, the two debaters would step down from the platform, shake hands, call each other worthy opponents, then go on to the next city to do it all over again. In Marshall's opinion, if they really wanted to settle their debate, they'd exchange their written speeches for dueling pistols. That would settle the matter once and for all. And there would be no mistaking who won the debate and who lost.

Grunt. Swoosh. Thud. Never had the Morgan's woodpile been this high.

Marshall's mind wandered to some newspaper clippings tucked between the pages of his Bible in his upstairs bedroom. All the clippings were of one man, John Brown. *Oh, to be his son*, Marshall thought as he balanced another log on the stump. In Marshall's opinion, John Brown was abolitionism incarnate. Though a white man, Brown once settled his family in a black community in New York. He was obsessed with winning justice for the Negroes. More importantly, he wasn't afraid to use force to do it. One of the clippings told of how armed Southern sympathizers from western Missouri crossed the border into Kansas to ensure the election of a proslavery legislature in the new state. John Brown responded by going to Kansas with his sons to join the antislavery forces.

The series of news accounts detailed the summer's activities of 1856. One headline described the state as "Bleeding Kansas." On May 21st, the town of Lawrence, heavily fortified by Free Staters like John Brown, was attacked and sacked by proslavery "Border Ruffians." They burned the Free State Hotel, pillaged homes, and destroyed the offices and presses of *The Herald of Freedom* and *The Kansas Free State*. In retaliation for the attack, on the night of May 24th, John Brown, his sons, and companions carried out a raid of their own. Five proslavery colonists living near Dutch Henry's Crossing at Pottawatomie Creek were executed. According to the news story (this part Marshall had underlined), Brown was quoted as saying his was a divine mission of vengeance.

While Kansas was bleeding, so was the Senate chamber in

Washington. A related article Marshall kept in his Bible was dated May 23, 1856. It described the brutal attack on Massachusetts Senator Charles Sumner on the Senate floor. A few days earlier, Sumner had delivered a speech during the Congressional debates on Kansas. His was a bitter, sarcastic denunciation of what he called the rape of Kansas. In it, he denounced by name several prominent proslavery senators, particularly Andrew Butler of South Carolina. On the 23rd, while Sumner was sitting at his desk in the chamber, Butler's nephew, Representative Preston Brooks, approached him. According to the newspaper account, Brooks shouted: "Mr. Sumner, I have read your speech against South Carolina, and have read it carefully, deliberately, and dispassionately, in which you have libeled my state and slandered my white-haired old relative, Senator Butler, who is absent, and I have come to punish you for it!" Brooks then brandished a cane and pummeled Sumner with it until the senator was unconscious.

Every time Marshall read the newspaper account of the Sumner-Brooks affair, he fumed. Particularly as he thought of the outcome of the assault. The attack incapacitated Senator Sumner physically and emotionally. Since the attack three years earlier, Sumner had been able to attend only a single day of Congressional sessions. As for Brooks, all attempts to expel or censure him for his actions failed, blocked by Southern senators and congressmen. And though Brooks resigned his seat, he was unanimously re-elected by his South Carolina district. It was clear the South approved of Preston Brooks' violent attack on the Northern leader. It was this sort of nefarious activity that convinced Marshall that physical force was the only effective argument the South would understand. That's what attracted him to John Brown. Few men comprehended this fact more clearly than he.

Marshall craved any news of Brown's activities. The most

recent printed piece he'd seen placed the radical abolitionist in Chatham, Ontario. It was a pamphlet which gave an account of a convention of blacks and whites in which Brown announced his intention to establish an armed stronghold in which escaping slaves could find refuge. He picked the Maryland and Virginia mountains as the site of his sanctuary. The mountainous terrain would allow a few armed men to defend against any attack by superior forces. The Chatham convention adopted John Brown's proposal and wrote a provisional constitution of which John Brown was elected commander-in-chief. The project was backed financially by Gerrit Smith and several prominent Boston abolitionists. The idea of such a sanctuary captivated Marshall. He eagerly wanted to know how the project was developing.

Additional news of Brown's proposed sanctuary came by way of rumor from Henry Wier, Point Providence's telegraph operator. According to Wier, news over the wires purported that John Brown had established a headquarters at a farmhouse in Maryland. As Wier heard it, Brown was training men in preparation of launching an offensive that would lead to the establishment of the sanctuary.

Grunt. Swoosh. Thud. The woodpile increased by two more pieces.

A half-hour of chopping wood normally took the fight out of him. Not today. In fact, the opposite seemed to be true. Today, the more Marshall chopped, the angrier he grew. He couldn't help but feel he was wasting time staying in Point Providence. *What was here for him?* Family. But they would always be here. *Girls?* He had no romantic involvements like J.D., nor did he want any. What he wanted was to do something that would make a difference. *So much was happening all around him, and what was he doing?* Chopping wood. He could see his epitaph now: "Marshall Morgan: Chopped more wood than any other man in the history of America." He sighed. If only he were in Maryland instead of Point Providence.

The idea stopped Marshall mid-swing. *Why not? Why not Maryland? What was stopping him?* Certainly John Brown could use one more dedicated fighter to create his city of refuge. Think of it. Marshall Morgan could be part of an historic effort that schoolchildren would read about someday. The ax hung at rest by his side. Marshall grinned as his wishful thinking took on the flesh and bones of reality. *Why hadn't he thought of this before? He could do this!* The more he thought about it, the more he felt as if his destiny was calling to him. Suddenly, he realized his anger was gone. In its place was a sense of purpose and determination.

With a triumphant swing, Marshall Morgan lodged the ax into the top of an empty stump.

J.D. Morgan felt he knew something of the family situation of Joseph, the Old Testament boy who was sold by his jealous brothers into slavery. Like the eleventh son of Jacob, J.D. was his father's obvious favorite. And though Jeremiah Morgan hadn't given his eldest son a coat of many colors, he demonstrated undisguised favoritism in a hundred different ways. J.D. sat next to his father at meals and was always served second. Most of the mealtime conversation centered on him—his progress in school, his opinion of church business, town meetings, and national politics. When it came to family matters, Jeremiah would take his eldest son aside and discuss the situation at hand even before consulting with his wife. In church, a front-row seat was reserved for J.D. while the other Morgan children sat several rows back with their mother. Preference was always given to J.D.'s opinions, his needs, his development. This was his lot in life as the firstborn male of the Morgan household. His birthright placed him on elevated status over his brothers and sister.

He was the chosen one, the one who would inherit the Morgan family Bible and with it the responsibility of carrying on the family faith into the next generation. In this too, J.D. found another Bible character with whom he could identify—Jesus of Nazareth. Both had been selected by their fathers before birth for a specific spiritual mission. Accordingly, their upbringing, relationships, and associations were all carefully guided in preparation for their task. Of course, that's where the similarity with the Son of God ended. J.D. had no allusions that he was another Jesus Christ. After all, the Ohio native was not expected to be the savior of the world, only of his family.

A sense of mission was instilled in him at a young age. One of his earliest memories was sitting on his father's lap when he was four years old. Encircled by his father's strong arms, the Morgan family Bible was held open before him. The names of his Morgan ancestors—the ones printed inside the front cover—were read aloud to him. Each name was spoken with holy reverence. It was a roll call of heroes, each one proudly advancing the Morgan family faith.

His father pointed to the name at the top of the list. "Drew Morgan," he read aloud. "He fought the powerful and wicked Bishop Laud of England and was the first Morgan to come to America. This is his Bible. The one he brought over with him by sailing ship."

Little J.D.'s eyes grew wide with wonder at the mention of the sailing ship.

"You were named after him. J.D., John Drew." Pointing to the next name, he continued, "Christopher Morgan. He was a great missionary to the Narragansett Indians. He taught them lessons using this very Bible. Then there was Philip Morgan. Philip went searching for the Bible when everyone in Boston thought it was lost. But it wasn't really lost. It was with Christopher Morgan who was still on the Indian reservation, only he was very, very old. At first Philip didn't recognize him because he was so old and because the Indians called him Nanouwetea, which means leader. Then there's Jared Morgan, Philip's younger brother. He was a pirate."

"Wow! A pirate!" four-year-old J.D. cried.

"He was a good pirate, though, not a bad one. Even during sword fights, he refused to kill his enemies. Jared was given the Bible when Philip returned to the Indian reservation to marry Weetamoo, a beautiful Indian maiden, and carry on the work of Christopher Morgan. That was the first time the Bible was given from brother to brother, rather than from father to son." Pointing to the next name, he said, "Jacob Morgan. Look here. After his name it says, 'Esau's brother.' That's because Esau died in his brother's place during the great Revolutionary War. Jacob was so grateful, he wanted to make sure that everyone remembered. Then there's Seth Morgan. That's your grandfather. He was the one who founded the Heritage Churches of America. Then, last on the list is my name, Jeremiah Morgan. My father wrote my name in this Bible and gave it to me. And see this empty space below my name? Someday your name will be written there." He pretended to write the name with the tip of his finger. "I will write *John Drew Morgan*, and put the date and a Scripture reference, just like all the other names."

Of course, at age four, J.D. wanted his name written in the Bible that very moment. His father told him he would have to wait until he completed school and got married, because it was important that J.D. have children so that he could have a son whose name could be written in the Bible under his.

Naturally, with the future of the Morgan line depending on his choice of a wife, the matter of courting was no small concern, one that was best not left to the unpredictable tides of romance. Even before J.D. took an interest in girls, Jeremiah was looking for him; and when J.D. began feeling an attraction to girls, his father had a list ready of approved prospects.

The courting process did not go smoothly. None of the girls who were attractive to J.D. were on the list, nor could he convince his father to add them; and the girls who were on the list were not attractive to him, nor could his father convince him that they were the ones worthy to bear his children. For nearly a year J.D.'s response to the impasse was not to court anyone at all. Jeremiah patiently bided his time. Why waste words when youthful drives would win his case for him? Sure enough, J.D. eventually spoke of courting again. The dam was breached and a flood of words poured forth from his father, a lengthy lecture that had been stored up for this inevitable moment. Jeremiah reminded his son about the transitory nature of beauty, the importance of family responsibility, and the fate of future generations. J.D. capitulated to the onslaught. He agreed at least to consider some of the names on his father's list.

J.D. ranked the names from the least offensive to the most offensive. Then he systematically began the courting ritual starting with the least offensive name. He felt like the prince in Frenchman Charles Perrault's story of Cinderella who was given the task of calling upon all the ugly step-sisters in the kingdom in his search of a princess. The analogy failed in that J.D. didn't think of himself as a prince, nor did he consider himself a great prospect as a husband. His family was of humble means, though well respected in the town. His prospects for income, likewise, were humble, since he intended to follow in his father's ministerial footsteps.

Nevertheless the families of the girls he called upon treated him like royalty. One would have thought he was the crown prince of England the way they fawned over him. The girls' fathers slapped his back a lot and muttered crude asides to him regarding married life. The mothers shoved food in front of him and insisted he eat it while they watched. They were offended if he declined the least morsel. Most often his arms were loaded with food as he said his good-byes. As for the ladies he was calling on—they stirred the wind batting their eyelashes at him, giggled incessantly, and acted in ways he'd never seen them act before in public. The whole process was unsettling; it seemed so forced and unnatural. What made things worse, the same scene was played out at every house. He had the same conversations, heard the same crude jokes, saw the same batting eyelashes, and gorged himself with an orgy of food. Working his way down the list of names was like a recurring nightmare. Each night he hoped it would be different. It never was.

The last name on the list was Jenny Parsons. Her name was last because J.D. hated her. Fortunately for him, the feeling was mutual. He had hoped that he wouldn't make it this far down the list. J.D. wasn't sure why Jenny hated him, nor did he care. All he knew was that their mutual hostility first surfaced when they were children.

The incident that started their private war occurred on a Sunday. Both of them were eight years old. During the church service J.D., prompted by his father, stood before the congregation and flawlessly recited the names of all sixty-six books of the Bible from Genesis to Revelation. Afterward, J.D. took his seat, smugly satisfied with his accomplishment. His father glowed with parental pride and the congregation applauded appreciatively—everyone except Jenny Parsons, whose arms were folded tightly across her chest.

Following the service while the adults shook Pastor Morgan's hand and chatted amiably in small clusters, the children congregated behind the building. There was the usual horseplay—the boys poking, pinching, and teasing the girls; the girls squealing in protest and slapping hands that came near them, yet coming back for more. The boys shoved and tripped each other, thinking that in some way it impressed the girls. J.D.'s artful recitation of the Bible books had been long forgotten, until Jenny brought it up. After gaining everyone's attention she dramatically compared his performance to that of a trained monkey in a traveling circus. To everyone's amusement, she proceeded to mimic his performance adding the antics of a chimp.

"You're just jealous," J.D. shouted, "because you can't do it."

"You think you're so smart," Jenny said, "but you're not. You're just a show-off."

"I knew she couldn't do it!" J.D. crowed to the boys. "However, her imitation of a monkey looked real natural." The boys roared with laughter.

"Very funny," Jenny replied dryly. "But it doesn't take any brains to do what you did today, which explains why you did it—you have no brains." Now it was the girls' turn to laugh.

Young Jenny Parsons was gangly, taller than the average girl with shoulder-length black hair that was parted down the middle and curled into ringlets that bounced whenever she tossed her head. Her eyes were dark and intelligent; her nose thin and pronounced. Like J.D., she had been born and raised in Point Providence. Her parents had attended the Heritage Church since before she was born. The two young combatants behind the church building had known each other all their lives.

"At least I'm smarter than you," J.D. shouted back at her. "So if I'm dumb, you're dumber! In fact, you're so dumb, you probably can't even recite the names of the first five books of the Bible!"

"Shows how much you know. I can recite all the books of the Bible," Jenny sniffed. "But you won't see me showing off like you."

J.D. scoffed. "Liar! If you can say the books of the Bible, I dare you to do it, right now!"

Jenny studied him for a moment, then said, "No. I don't have to prove anything to you or anybody else. And I don't have to perform for people's applause to feel important, like some people."

"Ha! Just as I thought!" J.D. paraded before the boys like a stumping political candidate who had just won a debate. "She can't do it. So now she's backing out!"

That angered her. "Oh, I can do it," Jenny said coolly. "In fact, I can do it the hard way. Backwards. From Revelation to Genesis. Can you?"

J.D. froze momentarily, stunned by the audacity of her boast. "You're a liar," he said. "You can't say all the books of the Bible backwards!"

"Can too."

Her calm response unnerved him, but there was no backing down now. "Prove it then! Say the books of the Bible backwards."

"How can I? You're so ignorant, you wouldn't know if I was right or not!"

J.D. called to a short, bespectacled boy standing nearby. "Douglas! You have a Bible, don't you? Get it." Douglas retrieved his Bible from atop a clump of discarded coats next to the church. J.D. to Jenny: "We'll let Douglas be the judge. He can follow along in the table of contents. So what's your excuse now?"

"No excuse," Jenny said. "I can do it. I just don't want to."
The boys groaned loudly in unison.

"What's the matter now?" J.D. pressed her, confident now that she was lying. "If you can do it, why not prove it?"

"Why should I?"

"To prove to us how smart you are."

"I already know I'm smart. At least, smarter than you."

"Put your Bible away, Douglas," J.D. said with a note of

triumph, "she can't do it."

"I'll do it under one condition," Jenny said.

"What condition?"

"If I do it . . . " she hesitated for emphasis, " . . . you have to kiss a bullfrog." Hoots and shrieks reverberated all around. "On its mouth!" she added. The shouts of delight from both sides grew even louder.

J.D. looked around him. He was in an arena of his peers standing face-to-face with Jenny Parsons—in his mind, evil incarnate. The cold hand of dread clutched his insides. It was clear now. She'd set him up for this. *But what could he do?* He couldn't back down now, not in front of everyone. His only option was to agree to her terms and hope she couldn't do it, or if she could, that she'd make a mistake.

"Agreed!" he said. Then before the shouts grew too loud, he added: "But what happens if you can't do it?"

"Then you'll be proved right. And everyone will know that you're smarter than me."

"Not good enough!" he cried. Those watching fell to silence to hear what J.D. had in mind. "If you can't do it," he said slowly and deliberately for effect, "if you make even one mistake . . . then you have to kiss . . . a cow!" A crescendo of howls. "On the mouth!"

He thought he had her, for the smug smile disappeared as the image of bovine lips appeared in her mind. But just as quickly as the smile disappeared, it reappeared. She agreed to his terms. Too readily in J.D.'s opinion. And once again the icy fingers of dread squeezed his insides. For the rest of the children of Point Providence, it would be a memorable day one way or another. For on this day one of their number would kiss a member of the animal kingdom. No matter who won the contest, there was going to be an exciting conclusion.

J.D. cast a wishful glance toward the front of the church,

hoping to see his father motioning to him to hurry home for Sunday dinner. He was not so lucky. Oblivious to their son's predicament, Pastor and Mrs. Morgan were immersed in a conversation with Jenny's parents and one other couple. J.D. had no choice but to go through with this. *Why was she doing this to him?* he wondered. This Jenny Parsons was a crafty one. She had baited her hook and cast the line, and like a dumb fish he swallowed it whole. Now she was reeling him in.

Beginning with Revelation Jenny proceeded to name the books of the Bible. She marched backward through the New Testament with ease, and J.D. felt his impending doom. When she successfully navigated the rocky shoals of the minor prophets and sailed smoothly through the major prophets and into the books of wisdom, he knew it was all over.

"Deuteronomy . . . Numbers . . . Leviticus . . . Exodus . . . Genesis!" Jenny said.

There was a moment of silence. Then Douglas, the appointed judge, cried, "Perfect!"

The girls squealed with delight. Even the boys turned on their friend in their eagerness to see someone kiss a bullfrog. Triumphantly, Jenny led them all down to the river where a throaty brown bullfrog was fished out. She insisted on holding the amphibian herself. With the wicked grin of a conqueror, she held out the frog for J.D. to kiss. J.D. inched his way toward the frog that had been chosen to receive his affection. Bugged eyes stared at him indifferently, and why not? The other frogs wouldn't be teasing him for the rest of his life just because he kissed a human.

J.D. heard an assortment of groans and guffaws as he moved closer. Inches away now, he closed his eyes. *One swift peck and it will be over*, he thought. But Jenny Parsons had something different in mind.

The moment J.D.'s eyes closed and his lips were about to

pucker, she shoved the frog into his face. The front half of the amphibian disappeared into J.D.'s mouth. And, instead of a wet peck, J.D. felt the slime of the frog scrape off on his front teeth and coat his mouth and tongue. The feet of the frightened frog slapped wildly against J.D.'s lips and chin in a desperate attempt to free itself from the black cavern with teeth.

Instinctively, J.D. pulled back and slapped at Jenny's hands. The frog went flying back into the river with a sploosh. Spitting profusely, J.D. wiped his lips and tongue with his arms and then with his shirttail while the assembled boys and girls of the church roared with laughter.

"You should have seen the look on your face!" Jenny cried as she wiped tears of laughter from her cheeks. "You looked so ridiculous with a frog's backside sticking out of your mouth!" She laughed so hard, she staggered and nearly fell over.

It took most of the day before the mossy, dirty, gritty, slimy taste of the frog left his mouth. But it took a lot longer than that before he was able to laugh with his friends when they recalled the incident, which was frequently. But he never forgot that it was Jenny Parsons who orchestrated the humiliating event, and he vowed never to forgive her. It was a vow he broke the day he fell in love with her.

J.D. didn't want to love Jenny Parsons. It just happened. But it never would have happened had her name not been on his father's list. One day while he and his father were repairing the wooden fence that ran parallel to the road leading to the house, J.D. announced that he had completed the list with no success.

"Completed the list?" Jeremiah echoed.

"Yes, sir."

"You called on every girl on the list?"

"Yes . . . well, nearly every girl. Every girl except the last one."

When Jeremiah heard who was the last name on the list, he said, "The Parsons family are good people." He held a plank steady while J.D. hammered it. "And Jenny is a fine girl, intelligent, attractive. You should call on her."

The hammer hit the board with extra force. "I'm not calling on Jenny Parsons," he said.

"Why not? Nothing has come of your visits to the other ladies . . . has it?"

J.D. grinned at his father's attempt to pry into his romantic life. It didn't bother him that his father was prying; there was nothing to uncover. "Believe me, it just wouldn't work between Jenny Parsons and me," J.D. insisted. "We despise each other! We have ever since we were children." Another whack with the hammer. The sound from the blow echoed down the road.

"Are you still upset with her because she made you kiss that frog?"

J.D. lowered the hammer. "You know about that?"

Jeremiah chuckled. "I knew about it the day it happened. It's hard to keep that kind of thing a secret in a small town."

"Hold the board straight," J.D. drew his father's attention back to the fence. The board had slipped out of place as Jeremiah remembered the frog-kissing incident. He repositioned it. "That particular incident was only the beginning!" J.D. said as he hammered. "She's badgered me ever since that day, and I've done the same to her. We just don't get along."

"What do you mean? You've grown up together in the same church. You're friends!"

"We're not friends!" J.D. shouted.

With the fence board in place, Jeremiah stepped back and examined their work. "Why does Jenny dislike you?"

"I don't know. Jealousy, I guess."

"Maybe you should ask her. If you knew why she disliked you, you could resolve it and become friends."

"Not likely."

"Well, at least give it a try. Saturday evening would be a good time. At dinnertime. Her parents are expecting you."

"You arranged for me to go over to Jenny Parsons' house without asking me first?"

Jeremiah nodded. "We think you and Jenny would make a good couple."

"We?"

"Her parents, your mother, and me."

"I don't like the idea of a committee orchestrating my romantic life. Does Jenny know about this?"

A queer look crossed Jeremiah's face. "I don't know directly," he said. "But I don't think so."

"Sounds like a wonderful evening," J.D. said.

"You know, son, our ancestor Drew Morgan loved a girl named Jenny. A mighty fine woman, or so the story goes."

"Different times, different people," J.D. replied.

"She saved his life," Jeremiah continued.

"I thought his wife's name was Nell."

"It was. Jenny was Nell's younger sister."

"Too bad Jenny Parsons doesn't have a sister," J.D. replied.

"The point is, there was almost a Jenny Morgan once. The name has a good ring to it, don't you think?"

With hammer still in hand, J.D. put his hands on his hips. "That's a mighty thin argument."

Jeremiah smiled. "Best I could come up with on short notice."

"You're not going to let up on this until I go over to her house, are you?"

"What have you got to lose? It's only one dinner."

"Then will you forget about Jenny Parsons?"

A smirk formed on Jeremiah's lips. "I will if you will," he said.

A look of resignation formed on his face as J.D. dropped

the hammer in the toolbox. "Did the committee discuss what we would eat for dinner?" he asked sarcastically.

A twinkle appeared in the elder Morgan's eyes. "I understand they plan to serve frog's legs."

From the stoic expression on Jenny Parsons' face all through dinner, J.D. guessed that she had been informed of his coming just moments before he actually arrived. She said not a word during dinner, nor did she once look at J.D., despite her parents' efforts to strike up a conversation. When her mother suggested J.D. might like a second helping of green beans, Jenny passed the bowl to him with downcast eyes. When they requested she tell J.D. about her favorite riding horse, she said, "He wouldn't be interested in hearing about that." J.D. didn't disagree with her.

For J.D. the evening had all the attraction of the frog-kissing event. All he wanted to do was to hurry up and get it over with. When the meal was concluded, before he had a chance to excuse himself, Jenny's father invited him to join them on the front porch. Thanking Mrs. Parsons for the meal and saying he couldn't stay long, he followed his hosts to the porch. He wasn't free yet, but at least he was out the front door.

The elder Parsons sat in two wooden chairs which left only the wooden bench swing for Jenny and J.D. One would have thought the two of them were sitting down on hot coals the way they reluctantly lowered themselves onto the swing. For what seemed like two eternities, the four of them sat on the porch in silence. The sun lowered itself gloriously beneath the western horizon, a full moon was on the rise, and mosquitoes buzzed happily around them. J.D. and Jenny sat stiff and straight on the swing, inches from each other, careful not to move since the slightest fidget rocked the other.

Mr. Parsons broke the silence by offering to help his wife

clear the table. Jenny insisted on helping too. Swiftly and in unison her parents declined her offer, insisting she stay and entertain her guest. Then they, not too subtly, took their chairs with them inside, leaving J.D. and Jenny alone on the bench swing in the early evening twilight.

At the sound of the front door closing, Jenny was off the swing. She stood at the edge of the porch, her arms folded and her back to her guest. "You can go now," she said. "I'll make the appropriate excuses to my parents."

His first impulse was to take quick advantage of the opportunity to leave, but something stopped him. He wasn't sure what it was, but something inside him urged him to stay right where he was. It was spite. As eager as he was to end the evening, he didn't want her to think he was leaving at her command. Then again, there was something different about Jenny Parsons as she stood on the edge of the porch. Her hair was different. He hadn't noticed it until now. Gone were the ringlets. Parted down the middle, it was straight and gathered around the ears in the popular style. The back of her neck was pale and thin, her white dress hung gracefully on her shoulders, narrowing to a thin waist, then flaring out fashionably. *When had this amazing transformation occurred?* The Jenny Parsons standing at the edge of the porch tonight was no longer the stick-figured, obnoxious urchin who shoved the bullfrog into his face. Indeed, if it were any other female standing at the edge of the porch, J.D. would have found her attractive. The swing creaked as J.D. settled back into it.

Jenny turned and faced him. "Did you hear me? You can go now."

The change in her hairstyle that J.D. had failed to notice earlier in the evening was striking. From the top of her forehead, her long hair parted like a curtain, pulled back and gathered around her ears. The opened curtain of shiny black hair revealed the delicate eyes, nose, and lips of a lovely young woman.

"Why are you staring at me?" Jenny asked, suddenly self-conscious. Her mild embarrassment pleased J.D.

"I don't think I should go yet," he replied. "It would be impolite."

"Nonsense! You want this evening to end as quickly as I do. So good-night." She started for the front door.

"You can go inside if you want. I'll just stay out here and swing for a while."

Jenny froze at the door and let out an exasperated sigh. "Dunce! I can't go in until you leave. My parents would send me right back out here to keep you company."

"I know," J.D. said with a mischievous smile.

A look of familiar fury appeared from behind the parted veil of hair. "Get off my porch!" she ordered.

"Is that any way to speak to a guest? Is this how you treat all the fellows who come courting?"

Jenny's face flushed red from the hollow of her neck up to the part in her hair. "I do not consider you a guest, and I certainly do not consider you a suitor!"

"Then what am I doing here?" J.D. rocked the swing, his arm draped casually across its back.

"My guess is that you lost another dare or bet! Why else would you be here?"

"Because I wanted to come?" J.D. offered.

"I doubt if that's true."

"It isn't. I didn't want to come."

"Fine!" Jenny concluded. "So go!"

J.D. laughed. "I said I didn't want to come. I *didn't* say I didn't want to stay. Now that I'm here, I'm enjoying myself."

"I see," she said through gritted teeth. "You're staying just to annoy me."

"Perhaps."

Her jaw worked back and forth with indecision. She said, "If that's the way you want it." She strode across the porch to the swing and plopped down beside him. The swing took a sudden lunge backward. With arms folded and jaw set, she added, "I'll just sit here until you go, but I refuse to give you the satisfaction of seeing me annoyed."

"Too late for that." J.D. grinned.

Jenny's response was a stone face with eyes fixed forward. The clank of dishes and muffled voices of her parents could be heard from inside the house. A dog from the nearby property barked until a loud male voice ordered it to shut up. J.D. let out a sigh, thinking it might get her attention, or possibly a derogatory comment. It didn't. So he turned slightly in the swing and stared at her, hoping to prompt a response. He got none. Jenny Parsons was a statue. So he tried a more direct approach.

"Why do you hate me?" he asked.

Silence.

"You do, don't you—hate me, I mean?"

Still no response. Not even the flicker of an eyelash.

"After all, we've done a lot of mean things to each other over the years. In some ways it's been fun, really. I mean, it's been a challenge, always having to keep up my guard around you. Thinking of ways to embarrass you. It sort of keeps things from getting boring. And, don't get me wrong, I don't want things to change between us. Your hatred of me is something I've always been able to count on."

Had J.D. been talking to a tree stump he would have gotten more response than he was getting from Jenny Parsons.

"It's just that . . . " he paused to think how he wanted to say this, "I know you hate me, but I don't know *why* you hate me."

She gave no indication of hearing him, much less a willingness to answer.

"So, I'm asking you. Why do you hate me? I'd really like to know."

Unresponsive eyes stared forward into the distance.

J.D. sat back into the swing and stared forward too. "If you want me to leave," he said, folding his arms to match hers, "just answer my question, and I'll go. Otherwise, we can sit out here all night for all I care."

For nearly thirty minutes not a sound was made between them. The porch was dark now, except for what little light spilled onto the floor planks through the windows from inside. Any moment now J.D. expected one or both of her parents to come out and check on them. If they did, it would be just the excuse Jenny would need to bring the evening to a close without answering his question, thereby giving her a minor victory. That's probably what she was hoping for. *But what if he gave in first? What if, in a gracious way, he let her off the hook? Wouldn't that take away her victory? Wasn't there something about that in the Book of Romans? Didn't it say that by doing something kind to your enemy it was like heaping coals of fire on his head?*

J.D. got up from the swing. "You've been a gracious hostess," he said. "I mean that sincerely." She gave no response, verbally or otherwise. "And it was wrong of me to return your graciousness with spite. Please forgive me, and extend my thanks to your parents for a lovely meal. I only wanted us to be friends. But I respect your right to continue hating me. Good-night, Jenny."

His shoes sounded against the wooden planks with each step as he started walking away.

Jenny's words hit him in the back. "It won't work," she said.

"Pardon me?" He turned to face her. She was looking straight at him.

"Romans 12:20," she said. "It won't work."

"I'm afraid I don't understand what you're . . ."

Jenny Parsons rolled her eyes. She quoted the Scripture passage from memory: "Therefore if thine enemy hunger, feed him; if he thirst, give him drink: for in so doing thou shalt heap coals of fire on his head." Then she added, "That's what I hate about you! You treat us like we're dumb animals, and we're not!"

"Us?"

"Girls, females. Men don't give us credit for having minds. We're nothing more than breeding stock for you and I hate it!"

"When did I ever treat you like breeding stock?" J.D. protested.

Jenny's lips quivered as she fought to keep her emotions back. "You do it every day!"

"You're imagining things!"

"Imagining things, am I? Do you remember the day I shoved the bullfrog into your face?"

"Vaguely." He knew it was a stupid response, but J.D. didn't want to give her an opportunity to gloat. If the truth were told, with a little effort he could still recall quite vividly the brackish taste of bullfrog.

"That morning you stood in front of the church congregation and recited the books of the Bible."

"I remember. So what?"

"So what? That's my point exactly! Why were you chosen to do that? Why wasn't a girl chosen to recite the books of the Bible?"

He knew better than to claim that a girl couldn't do it. She proved she could recite the books of the Bible frontwards and backwards. "I never thought about it," he said.

"Well, you're half right," she replied. "You never thought."

"Now wait a minute! It wasn't my idea to do that. I was

asked to do it!"

"By your father."

J.D. shrugged. "He's the pastor of the church. He was just trying to encourage other families to emphasize the Bible in their homes. It's part of our heritage."

"But you enjoyed it, didn't you? You always enjoy getting up in front of other people and showing off. And your father gives you plenty of opportunities to do it."

"So now you're condemning me because my father's proud of me?"

"Maybe I am," she sniffed. "All I know is that you enjoy it, and it's not fair."

"I don't enjoy it!" J.D. protested.

"Now you're not being truthful." Jenny stood and reached for the front door. "Good-night, J.D."

"Wait!" He took a few steps toward her. "You're right. I do enjoy it. But who wouldn't? I feel good inside when my father is proud of me."

"I'm glad you feel good," she said sarcastically. Her hand grasped the door latch.

"Wait. Please, Jenny, wait."

She paused, her eyes downcast.

"All my life I've been trained to be a leader according to our denomination's teachings. It's expected of me. Until tonight I didn't realize that sometimes by stepping forward, others are pushed aside. I . . . you helped me see that. Thank you."

She turned toward him. Her eyes harbored skepticism. "Are those burning coals, or do you really mean what you're saying?"

"No burning coals," he replied.

"Then there may be hope for you yet, J.D. Morgan."

Their eyes met and for the first time that J.D. could remember, Jenny Parsons looked at him with something other than loathing. It stirred him inside.

"Good-night, Jenny," he said softly.

"Good-night, J.D."

As he descended the porch steps that night, he heard the Parsons' front door open and Jenny's mother's voice: "Did you have a nice time with J.D., dear?" she asked.

The door closed before he could hear Jenny's response.

In the weeks following, J.D. and Jenny spent many nights alone on the swing on the Parsons' porch. It became their private place, as private as any place can be for an unmarried couple. It was on that swing that they talked, laughed, got to know one another, and fell in love.

Chapter 4

*P*ALL, *that's the word I'm looking for.* Sarah Morgan slouched in the wooden chair beside her small writing table which she had strategically placed beside an open window in her upstairs bedroom. She found that fresh air and the elevated view inspired her best writing. At times she likened her vantage point to that of Zeus sitting on the clouds overlooking the civilization of the classical Greeks. Only, instead of marble columns and grapevines, she saw a field thick with grass bordered by a solitary row of elm trees. To the south she could see the sparkling Ohio River and Kentucky soil on the far shoreline. A dusty road with shallow ruts paralleled her side of the river. It was from this high perch that she watched in tears as Daniel Cooper and his parents made their hasty departure the day before.

Sarah mused over her word find. *An appropriate word, pall. A funeral word. It is as though a black cloth has been cast over our household this morning, as though someone has died. And why shouldn't this morning's feelings be related with that of a funeral? What is death but separation from a loved one? And isn't that exactly what has happened to Daniel and me? God alone knows whether I shall ever see him again. Isn't that similar to death? Some might argue that death is more permanent. But does not our Christian hope of life eternal make death a temporary separation? And yet, still we grieve, wounded of heart*

*at the parting. How much more so for me at this moment! Have
I forever lost my beloved Daniel? Will I ever see him again? Is
he dead to me?*

Sarah fought back her tears with a bustle of activity.
Straightening herself in her chair, she opened a box and from
it retrieved a piece of blank paper, an inkwell, and a quill pen.
Placing the paper on the desk, she sniffed back her feelings,
opened the inkwell, and loaded her pen with ink. Back
straight and head slightly cocked, she assumed her writing
position and began.

> *My dearest Daniel,*
>
> *A pall of black emotion cloaks our household as I write
> this letter. Your untimely departure yesterday could not
> have had a more woeful effect upon us. Mother works
> silently in the kitchen while Father broods in his chair
> under the tree. The sound of an ax splitting wood tells me
> Marshall's anger will once again result in an enlarged
> woodpile. I know not where Willy has gone, but J.D. has
> sought comfort in Jenny's arms. I envy his nearness to the
> one he loves.*
>
> *As for me, my beloved, my grief is by far the greatest, for
> you have been cruelly taken from me, and that done before
> I had a chance to say good-bye. I will forever regret that
> lost opportunity. My darling, can you ever forgive me? My
> heart was riven in my bosom as I watched from my bed-
> room window your lamentable exodus. My speech was re-
> duced to tremulous sobs. Forgive me, my dearest, but the
> thought of being separated from you devastates me.*
>
> *Do I speak too boldly? I cannot help myself. With our
> families and nation racing toward crisis, timidity is an ex-
> travagance I can ill afford. I must convey my feelings for you
> if such a thing is possible using mere words penned on imper
> manent parchment, lest you think my love is as fragile.*

Do you recall our marriage ceremony in the field behind the church when we were but children? How you talked J.D. into being our minister and how you picked dandelions for my bouquet? Remember how you had to threaten Marshall to get him to play along, whereas little Willy begged to be part of the ceremony? And do you recall when our ceremony was over, Willy wanted to marry me next? Dear, dear Daniel, who would have thought that our innocent playtime of those carefree days would someday bear fruit and mature into genuine love? Only now that it has, cursed politics and cruel miles separate us. For how long, my love? For how long?

I can only hope that God will smile down upon us, that the Almighty Himself will intervene and somehow find a way to bring us together again. This is my prayer, my love, and to this prayer I will cling. Whether our nation will continue or fail, I know not. But this I know — my love for you will never fail.

With all my heart, my darling Daniel,
Sarah

She rested her pen. The straight-backed writer slouched into the posture of an anguished young woman in love. Wet, hazel eyes rolled heavenward in a silent plea to God, begging Him to answer her letter's petition. At nineteen years of age, Sarah had a dual focus in life, both of which merged in this letter. First, she wanted to be Daniel Cooper's wife. If the truth were told, it was she who orchestrated the childhood marriage ceremony in the field behind the church; Daniel happily complied, but she instigated it. For her the ceremony was not pretend. On that day she pledged herself to Daniel and never once wavered from her pledge, despite the distance and differences between their families. Her second focus in life was writing. With a flair for drama and a love of words, she dreamed of someday publishing a serial novel in a major New York magazine, just like Harriet Beecher Stowe had done with the publication of *Uncle Tom's Cabin*. Through a fictional portrayal of the injustices of life, Sarah hoped to change the world for the better. As the confluence of the Allegheny and Monongahela rivers formed the river that flowed past her window, so her twin passions—Daniel and writing—merged to produce the letter that lay on the desk in front of her.

After addressing an envelope, she cleared her desk and replaced the single-page letter with a manuscript of nearly two-hundred pages. Sarah wrote best in the morning. Her parents, who encouraged their daughter's literary aspirations, allowed her an hour each morning to write, after which her daily chores began. On some days, no new pages were produced as she sat in silence and imagined what life was like for each of her characters; on other days, she could complete three or four pages in the hour, her mind producing the story at a pace too rapid for her hand to record. On this particular morning, she felt she was ready to write, but not just yet. First she wanted to think through some complications that had arisen in her story line.

Taking a hairbrush from the top drawer of her vanity, she stroked her hair as she thought. Light brown hair was parted down the middle of her head and pulled back in plain fashion. She rarely spent much time primping, preferring to downplay her femininity when Daniel wasn't around, since she was not out to attract suitors. Whom she would marry was not a question in her mind, the only question was when she would marry him. *So why spend time making oneself attractive to men only to have to discourage their overtures?* Despite her efforts, several young men of Point Providence found her attractive. She was tall for a woman, not thin—she had her father's frame—but not manly or plump either. Her eyes were nearly round, not elliptical like most people's. The round shape gave her a bright, innocent look. A ready smile and healthy teeth added to her naive, girlish demeanor, but her mind was mature and wise beyond her years. And should anyone mistake her appearance for simplicity of mind, a brief verbal exchange readily dispelled the error.

As she finished grooming her hair, she reviewed her novel's purpose. Whereas Harriet Beecher Stowe portrayed the evils of slavery in her book, Sarah Morgan—or if the book was published after she married Daniel, it would be Sarah Morgan Cooper; she smiled at the thought of having three names—wrote to expose the destructive natures of ignorance and sloth. Believing that God rewarded knowledge and hard work, she hoped to spur the nation's conscience to earn God's favor through faithfulness and industry.

She believed it was these two traits that had made a success of the Massachusetts Bay Colony—the colony of her ancestors—when other colonies failed. In preparation to write novels, she had started with shorter stories, their themes based on Bible proverbs. Some of her favorites were:

The soul of the sluggard desireth, and hath nothing: but the soul of the diligent shall be made fat. (Proverbs 13:4)

A just weight and balance are the Lord's: all the weights of the bag are His work. (Proverbs 16:11)

Even a child is known by his doings, whether his work be pure, and whether it be right. (Proverbs 20:11)

Based on these verses she had written three short stories in which a young boy or girl protagonist, by story's end, had learned the truth of the proverb. She read them to the children at church, and soon the adults not only began listening too but also asked for more. Although Sarah never told her

father this, more than one member of the congregation con-
fided in her that they got more out of her children's stories
than they did out of her father's sermons.

Encouraged by the receptivity to her stories, Sarah began a
larger work. It was a story of the continuing adventures of a
sixteen-year-old New York orphan named Truly Noble—Tru
for short. In the story Tru was raised amid filth and corruption on the big-city streets. One day, wandering into a
church, he heard the preacher read from the Bible this verse:
*The wicked worketh a deceitful work: but to him that soweth
righteousness shall be a sure reward* (Proverbs 11:18). Tru realized the value of the words he'd heard and, in search of his
sure reward, began sowing righteousness everywhere he went.
True to God's word, he discovered that honesty, hard work,
and love overcame power and greed and corruption.

Sarah's literary dilemma was that she had just written a
scene in which a powerful newspaper editor had ordered Tru's
capture. Because the virtuous orphan had faithfully planted
seeds of righteousness, New Yorkers were mending their
ways, thus reducing crime and the unsavory news stories it
generated. The loss in circulation threatened the newspaper
mogul's empire and he plotted to kidnap and dispose of the
source of his problem—Truly Noble. Sarah imagined two
thugs holding Tru's arms behind his back. The foul-mouthed,
cigar-smoking newspaper tycoon sat behind his desk gloating
that not only had he captured Tru, but also was holding
Charity Increase, the girl with whom Tru had fallen in love.
The thugs were jeering. The tycoon was laughing in triumph.
Charity's life was in danger. And Sarah Morgan didn't know
how to resolve Truly Noble's crisis.

She'd thought of having Tru kick the thugs in the shins to
make his escape, but she preferred to avoid violence to solve
Tru's problems. *What if he broke down in tears for his beloved?*
Maybe the tears of the innocent could melt the stone heart of

the tyrant. Or maybe Tru could quote Scripture, or better yet, pray out loud. The prayer of the righteous Tru could convince the thugs to side with him. This way, while one thug guarded the tycoon, the other could lead Tru to the warehouse where he could rescue Charity!

That will work, Sarah thought, returning to her desk. She turned the manuscript over face-down on the desk, grabbed the final sheet of the manuscript which was half used, and began writing. As she began, she made a mental note to get Willy to sketch a picture for her of Truly Noble struggling to break free from two thugs with a wicked newspaper tycoon in the background. Maybe an inset picture could show Charity tied up and gagged at the warehouse. "This is good," Sarah said to herself as she wrote. "This is very good."

Willy propped himself against the dirt embankment which formed one side of the narrow runoff that drained water from the Morgan property into the river. An artist's pad of paper rested on his lap. His bent legs formed a bridge over the bottom of the dry gully. On the embankment next to him lay his crutch. From this low position, he could see his house through a small break in the ridge opposite him. The row of oak trees on the east side of the property towered skyward in the distance. The silhouetted figure of his father sitting beneath the shade tree rested at the bottom of the V-shaped dirt gap.

Willy liked to draw from a bizarre perspective. This low position reminded him of a child's world view. Everything was seen from below, looking up. From this spot the underside of the gables of the house and the branch structure beneath the shade tree's leafy canopy were prominent. His father, even though seated in a lawn chair, loomed larger than life. With sweeping charcoal strokes the images before Willy began to appear on the sketch pad.

He had discovered and refined his artistic talent at an early age during the endless hours he sat alone while the rest of his family moved about freely from room to room, in and out of the house, doing chores, engaging in horseplay, and going about the daily routine of life. Willy's daily routine and chores were different, simpler, slower, restricted. Less was expected of him because of his disability. So he sat. And sat. To fend off boredom, he began drawing.

Even his earliest drawings demonstrated an artistic sense of balance and color. His people were proportional to their surroundings. His scenes captured the action and mood of the moment. At age fifteen, his pen and ink sketch of the town's Fourth of July celebration graced the front page of the local paper. The picture earned him town-wide acclaim and the publisher gave him several other assignments which Willy gladly accepted at first. Then he missed a deadline, the unpardonable sin for newspaper employees. And then another. He quickly earned a reputation for being talented, but unreliable. "A real shame," the newspaper publisher said. "The boy's got talent. Good enough to work himself up to a position with one of them big New York City dailies. But no editor in his right mind will hire him if he can't get the pictures in on time."

It had been more than a year since one of his pictures appeared in the newspaper. Believing in him more than he believed in himself, Sarah badgered him until he finally agreed to illustrate her novel featuring Truly Noble. But after two pictures he quit and hadn't completed another since.

In the gully, Willy's charcoal sketch was quickly done. It was a dark portrait of his world, grotesquely misproportioned. In the center loomed a black, menacing figure in a chair around which all the other picture elements swirled.

Beneath the shade tree, Jeremiah Morgan sat limp in the wooden lawn chair, his head resting backward. His eyes were closed but he wasn't asleep. The chair's arms supported fully his aching limbs. His only movement was the rising and falling of his chest and somehow that was all that seemed to matter. He was alive. Drained of energy, devoid of emotion, mind clouded and confused, but alive.

Yesterday he had hope. Yesterday Seth was here, seated next to him; their deteriorating relationship was being repaired. The future looked bright. Then, with a single blow, everything was destroyed. Their relationship, which he once compared to a fence in disrepair, was blasted into a million splinters with Seth's departure. Today, the chair next to him was hauntingly empty. Today there was no hope, only the oppressive weight of despair.

If the previous day was bad, his night had been worse. He lay in bed until the early morning hours before his anger and frustration had burned themselves out enough for him to drift to sleep. Then he wished he hadn't slept. The nightmare came again.

It was the kind of dark nightmare that was so draining it left him exhausted upon waking. As most dreams and nightmares, this one was a jumble of events and elements, including his family, the escalating sectional crisis, and the Bible. He called it his Job dream.

In his dream, Jeremiah was standing alone in a fallow field. The earth was soft and plowed, bits of stubble straw poked upward from the dirt at odd angles. The sky above was dark, tinted orange and brown with blowing dust. A stiff wind ripped at his clothing as he stood there, howling as it passed, making it difficult for him to hear anything but the wind's mournful cry.

Suddenly, a messenger appeared. A stranger. He fought the wind to reach Jeremiah, his clothes torn and dirty, his face and lips parched by the dry wind. He had to shout to be heard: "A proslavery raiding party from Kentucky swept down upon the town. They burned your church and put the congregation to the sword. I am the only one who has escaped to tell you!"

While the first messenger was still speaking, another messenger appeared and yelled, "Fire fell from the sky and burned your house and fields and livestock. Your wife was inside the house as it went up in flames. She is dead. I am the only one who has escaped to tell you!"

While he was still speaking, another messenger appeared. "Your sons and daughter were feasting at J.D.'s house when suddenly a mighty wind swept in from the south and struck the four corners of the house. It collapsed on them and they are dead, and I am the only one who has escaped to tell you!"

At this point in his dream Jeremiah Morgan would fall to his knees. In great anguish, he would tear his clothes, throw dust in the air, and wail bitterly, his face and fists lifted heavenward. His moaning and wailing would then cross the line from nightmare to reality and Susanna, awakened by the sounds, would assist his escape from darkness.

But the dream's dissipation was only partial. Its effects always stretched into the next day, more this time than ever before. Jeremiah was fully aware of the uncertainties of life. He knew life was fragile. Disaster common. He knew that seldom would a day pass without someone dying from natural or human causes. But the potency of his dream was its ability to take his rational awareness and turn it into a bone-chilling nightmare. In the dream, theory became reality; pompous intellectual conjecture was swallowed up by panic and dread.

His great fear was that the dream was more than a personal haunting. *What if it was a premonition?* Unlike some dreams, the distance between this one and reality was short indeed. Should the bloody events of Kansas spill over to the rest of the nation, should North and South go to war, he could very well see his dream played out. War made everything in life uncertain. He could lose everything. His church. His property. His wife. His family. Everything.

As he fought to suppress the nightmare's lingering dread, he reasoned that Seth Cooper's anger and sudden flight back to Southern territory had brought the dream one step closer to reality. *If two brothers in the Lord — two brothers who were as close to one another as he and Seth had been — could not escape the ruinous consequences of the rising national anger, was there any hope left for the nation?* Maybe he'd been naive to believe that Christian love could overcome the animosity of the secessionists. But to admit to himself that he was wrong, to admit that there was an anger greater than God's love, struck at the very heart of everything he believed. It was a chilling blow.

Yesterday's rupture left him feeling like a failure. His infinitesimal attempt to breech the gap separating North and South ended in disaster. Bring two men together, that was the goal. Two men who *liked* each other. *How hard can that be?* Yet he couldn't do it. He felt unworthy to have his name listed among the other Morgans in the family Bible.

The men on that list helped bring Christianity to the New World. They evangelized the Indians, built financial empires, secured independence for the nation, began new denominations. The Morgans listed in the front of the Bible had always been in the center of American history. *Where was he?* On the western fringe, having run away from influential places. *And what was he doing?* Nothing important. He was pastor of a small church in a small town. Anybody could do that. When stories were told of the Morgans whose names appeared in the front of the family Bible, his would be glossed over. A small-town pastor who did nothing extraordinary.

Such thoughts made Jeremiah want to hasten the ceremony that would pass the family Bible and its responsibility to J.D.

Then it would be back in the hands of someone who could make a difference. J.D. was young, bright, articulate, a natural leader. Perhaps it was J.D.'s destiny to do something that would help resolve this great crisis America was facing. If so, Jeremiah could then rest in the knowledge that his part in Morgan history was to train his son for the task. He could live with that being his place.

Jeremiah already had the Scripture passage chosen that would accompany J.D.'s name in the Bible. He'd chosen it just a few hours after learning that his and Susanna's first child was a boy. It was 2 Timothy 2:1-2: *Thou therefore, my son, be strong in the grace that is in Christ Jesus. And the things that thou hast heard of me among many witnesses, the same commit thou to faithful men, who shall be able to teach others also.*

The only obstacle preventing Jeremiah from arranging a date for the ceremony was the fact that J.D. wasn't married yet. He and Jenny had an understanding, but nothing was official. And it was important for them to be married before the Bible was transferred. Past near-tragedies taught them this.

Drew Morgan originally presented the Bible to his son Christopher who never married. This endangered the succession. The Bible was ultimately passed to a descendent of Christopher's younger brother, having skipped a couple of generations. That incident, and more recent ones among other families in which an unmarried recipient actually caused the extinction of the family line, prompted a great deal of debate among Heritage Church members. As part of the denomination's guidelines, it was strongly advised that the Bible be passed to a married progeny, preferably one who already had a male child. Although this was not a foolproof guarantee of continuous succession, it increased the chances of success.

The problem for Jeremiah was that J.D. was neither married, nor did he have an heir. On more than one occasion, as pastor of a Heritage church, Jeremiah had comforted couples to be patient and not pass on the Bible prematurely. *How could he now ignore his own advice?*

Jeremiah stretched, rose from the lawn chair, and turned his thoughts toward church work. Visits needed to be made. And he'd regret it if he didn't get something started regarding Sunday's sermon. The pressure of procrastination in this matter mounted as the week wore on and he'd learned at least to have a working idea by Tuesday. As he made his way to the house he reminded himself to inquire about J.D.'s plans regarding Jenny. *Why hadn't they set a wedding date yet?* He brushed aside the fleeting idea that such a thing was none of his business. He was J.D.'s father. Everything associated with J.D. was his business.

His thoughts of J.D. and the future had lifted his spirits some, but as he reached for the front door latch, Jeremiah Morgan could not escape the depressing aftereffects of his nightmare, nipping at his heels like a pesky, black dog.

Chapter 5

MARSHALL slipped out of Point Providence in the dark on a chilly mid-October morning. He would later remember it as the first time he marched off to war. But there were no drums or flutes to herald his departure. No hurrahs. No handkerchief-waving females. His exodus was accompanied by a band of crickets. And the only cadence of marching boots was one man's footfalls on a dirt road.

Willy had wanted to come along. Marshall refused. Not until he better knew the situation. It could be dangerous. Willy's temper flared, as it always did whenever he felt someone was treating him as less than a man. It took the combined efforts of Marshall and J.D. to convince Willy to remain behind, for the sake of the underground railroad station, they argued. J.D. couldn't operate it alone. Willy agreed to stay only after Marshall promised to send for him at the earliest possible moment.

Marshall's plan to join John Brown's brigade in Maryland was a secret shared by the three brothers until after he left. This was at Marshall's bidding. J.D. didn't agree with the clandestine tactic, but he understood his brother's reasoning. Their father would never consent to the plan. In the Morgan household the mere mention of John Brown's name was like jabbing a hibernating bear with sharp stick. Once done, there could be no peaceful resolution; a scrap was inevitable. J.D.

knew that the argument, if begun, would be a mere echo of the one that ensued over the bleeding Kansas incident. Marshall had insisted that John Brown was justified in what he did. The South could not be reasoned with, he'd argued, and once people lose their ability to reason, force is the only alternative. Father had countered that the events in Kansas were a senseless slaughter, plain and simple. "Use the brain God gave you!" he'd shouted at Marshall. "How can a lawless course achieve a moral end?" And so it went; and so it would go again given another opportunity. In the end, neither side would convince the other and Marshall would still leave. "My point exactly," Marshall had argued. "So why put the family through the turmoil?" J.D. saw his point. He and Willy agreed to keep quiet.

At J.D.'s insistence Marshall left behind a letter. Marshall had placed the letter on the kitchen table on his way out the door. He knew the words would hurt his mother and anger his father. But someday they would understand. He would make them understand. This was something he had to do.

The first light of day was breaking over the horizon as Cincinnati's Union Terminal came into view. Marshall pulled out his pocket watch. Nearly seven o'clock. Father was probably reading his letter right now. The mental image of the family at the breakfast table, his father holding the letter, activated a pang of guilt. The manly thing would have been for him to confront his father face-to-face. Marshall sighed. *Nothing could be done about it now. What's done is done. Then again,* he thought, *this way is best. Once the world learns that a free slave state has been established in the Appalachians, Father will have no recourse but to admit that I was right.*

The shrill whistle of an unseen locomotive sounded in the distance. Marshall plopped his bag on the station's wooden platform. He leaned his rifle against it. Folding his arms he stood tall. *No turning back now. History awaits me in Maryland.*

◆ ◆ ◆

The coach car jolted, throwing Marshall's head back. The steam locomotive hesitated. Belching thick black smoke, it surged forward as it pulled the train up a long grade. It had been a dusty, weary journey—sitting at the train station waiting to get underway; sitting on board the train; sitting at one stop for water and coal, at another for passengers. And so it went. Their next stop was Marietta, Ohio. There, he would catch the Northwestern Virginia Railroad to Grafton, Virginia, spend the night, and then on to Harper's Ferry aboard the Baltimore and Ohio Railroad. Traveling from there on foot, he would cross the Potomac into Maryland in search of John Brown's rented farm. The way Marshall heard it, the farm served as a training camp for the expedition that would ultimately found a sanctuary for Negro slaves in the Appalachian Mountains.

The car he was riding in was nearly empty. The only other travelers were two other men seated apart further up in the car—one wearing a suit and tie and the other in worn overalls—and a modestly dressed woman of middle age who sat closer to him across the aisle. She clutched a valise to her chest and cast suspicious looks alternately at each of the men sharing the compartment. Marshall lay his head against the window and closed his eyes. In a way the trip was disappointing. He'd expected to feel a sense of exhilaration. After all, for the first time he was completely on his own; he was journeying toward his destiny, and heading into almost certain danger. *He should feel excited, shouldn't he? Wasn't this the stuff adventures were made of, the kind of adventure stories Sarah dreamed up?* Yet he felt no sense of romance, no thrill of risk. He was disappointed in his feelings for not doing their job.

Dark questions lurked in the back of his mind, adding to his disappointment. *What if John Brown refused to let him join up with them? It wasn't as though he'd been invited to join.*

Would they require some test of loyalty from him? Some proof that he was truly sympathetic to their cause? And if so, what?

The locomotive's high-pitched whistle startled him. His eyes popped open. The woman was staring at him. Their glances met. Her face remained expressionless as she turned her head away and looked out the window. The stale smell of a cigar drifted back from the man in the suit. Its smoke mixed with the acrid odor of the smoke from the engine. Marshall repositioned himself on the hard wooden bench, attempting to get comfortable. His eyes fell on the randomly scratched initials and other cryptic symbols that defaced the seat in front of him. W.E.B.; Joseph + Abigail; Harold "Thunder" Anderson. These were the names etched in the wood. These were the names of the adventurers who had preceded him on destiny's train.

A mist was falling when he deboarded at Grafton. Following the conductor's directions, he made his way to a nearby tavern about half a mile from the tracks.

"You arrive on the 6:20?"

A sandy-haired man with a long face and overlapping front teeth greeted him at the door. Marshall's face and hands felt clammy from the mist.

"Just arrived," he answered with a nod. "The conductor said I could get a room here for the night."

"You got money?" A seasoned eye studied him.

"I don't have a lot."

"Didn't say you needed a lot," the long face retorted. Then the face turned toward two neatly dressed men sitting comfortably at a table in the corner. "Though if you was to offer me a thousand dollars, I'd be polite enough not to refuse your generosity. Right, Cyrus?"

The two men in the corner laughed obligingly at the long face's humor. One lifted his glass of ale in a silent toast. Marshall assumed that one was Cyrus.

"Come in. Come in," the long face said. "Name's Marcus Pollard. This here's my tavern." Toward the back of the room, he bellowed: "Ira! We got a hungry guest out here! Ellen, make up the bed. He's stayin'."

"My name's Marshall Morgan." Marshall shifted his bag to free his right hand. He extended it to the tavern owner.

Pollard pointed to an empty table. "Sit there," he said. Then, hurrying off without offering to assist Marshall with his bag, the long-faced tavernkeeper marched through a door at the back of the tavern. "Tonight, Ira! The man wants dinner, not breakfast!"

Marshall laid his rifle against the door jamb and dropped his bag to one side. While the two men at the corner table watched him, he took the seat indicated by Pollard.

"Come far?" The man who had hoisted his ale asked the question.

"Cincinnati. Well, actually Point Providence by way of Cincinnati."

"Fair piece of traveling."

Pollard appeared with a plate of food and a mug. A young boy of fifteen or sixteen with unruly blond hair followed in his wake carrying utensils and a napkin in one hand and a pitcher of ale in the other.

"I'd prefer to drink water," Marshall said.

"Ale comes with the price of the meal," Pollard said.

"Thanks. But I'd still prefer water, and plenty of it if you don't mind. It's been a long, dry trip."

Ira stood motionless behind his father.

"Well, what are you standing around for?" Pollard shouted. "You heard the man. Ain't you got no brain? He said he wants water. Go fetch it for him!"

The boy frowned, then turned and retraced his steps. Marshall wasn't sure if the frown was directed at him for causing the boy an extra trip, or if it was because of the way his father ordered him around.

"If you're thirsty," the voice came from the corner of the room, "there's nothing like a good ale."

"Maybe that's why he wants water," the second man replied. "He'll find nothing like a good ale at Marcus' tavern!"

The two men laughed at their host's expense. Pollard took the jesting in stride. "You'll sing a different tune when your mugs run dry!" he replied. To Marshall: "Don't mind them. Cyrus Hines—the one with the oversized belly—is the editor of the local newspaper, *The Daily Tattler*."

"*The Daily Bugle*," Cyrus corrected him.

"The other one, John Goss, owns the mercantile shop. They prefer spending their nights here because they married the two ugliest sisters this side of Philadelphia."

The two men at the corner table took no offense. In fact, they nodded their heads in agreement.

Pollard glanced angrily toward the back door. "Ira!" he shouted. No response. Shaking his head, he went after the boy, muttering, "Give him a simple job to do . . . the boy's a simpleton just like his . . ." Pollard disappeared out the door.

"Where are you headed, son?" Cyrus asked. The two Grafton businessmen leaned comfortably back in their seats. Their mugs of ale looked like natural appendages to their hands. They looked at him as though he was to be their source of entertainment for the night.

"Maryland," he replied. "I'm going to Maryland."

"A matter of business?" Cyrus asked.

"You might say that." Marshall forked a pieceof meat into his mouth and chewed it studiously, avoiding eye contact with the men in the corner. He was reluctant to speak too freely about his destination considering the political nature of his trip. He'd learned that public opinions were dry timber awaiting the spark of a careless word.

"By way of Harper's Ferry?"

Marshall chewed noncommittally. "Why do you ask?"

"Telegraph lines are down," the newspaperman said. "Everything east of Martinsburg is cut off. May be nothing, just a downed line or faulty equipment. But I'm a newspaper man. I get paid to be suspicious."

"Jumpy, if you ask me," John said.

"Can you blame me? Look what the proslavers did to Lovejoy! Shot him and dumped his press in the Mississippi River!" Cyrus exclaimed.

"That was in Alton, Illinois!" John replied.

Marshall recognized the reference. Elijah Lovejoy owned an antislavery paper. He was shot defending the paper against a proslavery mob.

"Who's to say the same thing couldn't happen here?" Cyrus said. "The first thing vigilantes do is cut down the telegraph wires. I think I have a perfect right to feel uneasy."

John lowered his mug mid-drink and grinned. "It's probably nothing more than the mutton we had for dinner here last night." He rubbed his belly. "Come to think of it, I've been feeling a mite queasy myself."

"Don't think I didn't hear that!" Pollard cried, emerging from the back room carrying a pewter pitcher and a new mug. He filled the mug with water and left the pitcher on the table. "There's nothing wrong with my meat!"

"If you like the taste of horses." John winked at Cyrus.

Marshall examined a cube of meat on the end of his fork.

"Don't pay any attention to them," Pollard said. His tone was one of unconcern. Marshall got the impression this kind of bantering was standard fare for this tavern.

His host pulled out a chair opposite him, turned it around and sat down, his arms resting on the back. He looked hard at Marshall, then over at the bag and rifle beside the front door. "If you ask me," he said over his shoulder to the two regulars, "it looks to me like the boy's goin' huntin'. The question is, 'Huntin' for what?' And why Maryland?"

"Doesn't make sense, does it?" Cyrus rubbed his chin thoughtfully, also staring at Marshall. "If he *is* going hunting, why travel east? Hunting's better in Ohio."

Fighting back a growing sense of uneasiness, Marshall concentrated on eating his food. *Let them guess*, he told himself. *Doesn't hurt anything.*

"You know . . ." Cyrus sat up suddenly, struck upright by a revelation. "Pollard has a point, but he's wrong in one regard. The boy's not an animal hunter. He doesn't look the type. No buckskin, or furs, or hides on him of any kind. He could be hunting something other than animals. A slave hunter? Better yet, a slave runner!"

Marshall pushed his food around the plate with his fork. He cleared his throat. "Mr. Pollard, does this meal come with dessert?" It was a transparent attempt to change the topic of conversation, but it was all he could think of at the moment.

"He could be an adventurer," John offered. All three men were staring at Marshall. The tavernkeeper didn't even acknowledge Marshall's question.

"Possibly an adventurer," Cyrus said, "but what in Maryland would attract an adventurer with a rifle?"

"Politicians?" John offered.

The three men laughed. Marshall laughed with them.

"What in Maryland," Cyrus continued, "would be so attractive to a young adventurer that it would lure him across several states?" Suddenly, his eyes grew wide. Then they narrowed into a knowing look, a cocky look, the kind of look a man gets when he's the first person to find the solution to a puzzle. "What choices are there for an adventurer?" he asked rhetorically. "Join the army? He could have done that in Cincinnati. Be a slave runner? A possibility, but again he'd most likely do that near his home, where he's familiar with the territory. My guess is that he's going to join up with other adventurers of like mind and purpose. But what other adventurers are there in Maryland?" Cyrus paused only for dramatic effect, for when his table partner raised a finger to answer, Cyrus blurted it out first, "John Brown!"

"That's what I was going to say," John Goss protested.

The newspaper man struck a triumphant pose, confident he'd solved the puzzle of Marshall's undisclosed destination. The other two participants studied Marshall for some sign of confirmation or denial. A wide-eyed Ira stood in the kitchen doorway.

Marshall did his best to maintain a neutral expression, to give nothing away. But the squinting scrutiny of the men staring at him made it difficult. They looked like schoolboys who had just heard a rumor that school would be let out early—hoping that the rumor was true, yet cautious because it was just a rumor.

"That's it, isn't it, son?" Cyrus pressed him. "You aim to join up with John Brown, don't you?"

Coolly, Marshall reached for the water pitcher. He poured and drank slowly while everyone awaited his answer. He was stalling, of course, trying to think of what to say. After several leisurely sips, Marshall set down his mug. "Suppose I were to tell you that you were right. What then?"

A victorious glint appeared in the newspaperman's eyes. "Well, for one thing, I'd want to interview you for my paper."

"Interview me? Why?"

"Quite simple. Your story would interest my readers. You see, everyone is talking about slavery—endlessly talking about it. And everyone has an idea what should be done about it. But if I am correct in assessing your intentions—and I believe that I am—then you are one of the few people in this nation willing to go beyond rhetoric and put your life in danger just

to stop this great evil. That kind of commitment takes courage. And it would make a good news story."

"And it would sell a lot of newspapers," John added, ribbing his friend.

"Exactly!" the newsman cried. "That's my business! I'll not
apologize for it. So tell me, Marshall—it is Marshall, isn't it?
Do I have a story?"

Marshall stared at his plate, doing his best to control a
burgeoning sense of excitement within him. A couple of
things the newspaperman said had kindled the sensation.
First, he called slavery a great evil. That statement placed the
newspaperman in the abolitionist camp, which meant he was
sympathetic to Marshall's point of view. But of greater interest to Marshall was the newspaperman's claim to value action
over rhetoric. *He called it courageous, didn't he?* This affirmation was a hundred times more refreshing to Marshall than
the pitcher of cold water to his parched throat. All his life he
had dwelt in the desert of inactivity and rhetoric, the land
where his father was king. Now, one day's journey away,
instead of being condemned for his thirst for action, he was
being commended for it!

"Well? Do I have a story?" The newspaperman repeated.

With the self-assured tone of a military leader, Marshall
said, "You have a story."

"Then you are going to Maryland to join up with John
Brown?" Cyrus confirmed.

"Yes."

Victorious whoops sounded all around. In the doorway, Ira
stared in admiration at Marshall as though he were George
Washington himself.

"Dear, are you still awake?" Susanna's voice was clouded
with sleep.

Jeremiah's eyes were open, yet he could see nothing. The

room was in total darkness. He lay on his back, his hands folded across his midsection. He felt a movement beside him. A hand touched his side, then groped its way up his arm to his shoulder.

"Are you ill?"

"I'm not ill. Go back to sleep."

The bed shook slightly as Susanna propped herself up on an elbow. His answer had failed to pacify her. They'd been married too long for such a simple reply to alleviate her concern. It was not like him to have trouble sleeping at night.

A dark form passed in front of his eyes. An instant later he felt a warm hand press against his cheek, then his forehead. "You're not hot," she said.

"I told you I wasn't ill," he said testily. "Go back to sleep."

The bed rolled as an arm stretched across him. He felt Susanna's head rest on his chest; the weight of her body pinned his arm to his side. He smelled the scent of freshly washed hair as a few stray hairs tickled his chin. Husband and wife lay this way in the silent darkness for several minutes.

Susanna was the first to speak. "You're worried about Marshall," she said.

"Marshall is old enough to be out on his own. He's capable of taking care of himself."

"Still, you're worried about him."

"I'm not worried about him."

"Then why are you lying awake in the middle of the night?"

Jeremiah didn't answer. He didn't want to discuss it, at least not now. He wanted to wallow in dark misery. This was something best done alone.

Susanna let out a sigh. Her breath was warm and moist against his chest. "I worry about him," she said. "I know he feels he's doing what he has to do. I'd hoped that this below-the-surface ferry activity would channel those energies."

"Underground railroad."

"That's what I meant. Underground railroad. But this John Brown fellow frightens me, with the killing and all. There are plenty of people who are more than willing to give to him as he's given, and I don't want Marshall standing nearby when they give it."

Susanna's cheek against his chest grew warmer, then moist.

With his free hand, Jeremiah stroked his wife's hair. "Marshall is quick and resourceful," he said. "Of our three boys, he is best at taking care of himself in a scrap. He's been in enough of them."

"It's not the same," Susanna sobbed. "This is like a war with bullets and knives and cannons and who knows what else. One stray bullet, that's all it would take."

Jeremiah maneuvered his pinned hand free. Wrapping both arms around his wife, he spoke soothingly. "Marshall's a survivor. His natural leadership abilities and instincts will surface when they're needed most. Besides, God will watch over him."

Susanna raised herself slightly as though to look at her husband. However the absence of light allowed them to see only vague forms. "Why don't you ever say these things to Marshall?" she asked.

"What things?"

"Just a minute ago you said he was quick and resourceful. Now you say he's a survivor with the instincts and abilities of a leader. You tell *me* these things, but you never tell Marshall."

Jeremiah's eyes shifted back and forth uneasily. He was grateful the cover of darkness hid them from his wife. "With Marshall it's different. I don't know, he makes it difficult for me to compliment him. I've always found it painful to talk with him."

"Or to wish him well."

It was nearly impossible to keep anything secret from the woman who had shared his bed for twenty-three years. Tears dotted the corners of his eyes. "I regret that Marshall felt it necessary to sneak away without saying good-bye."

"That's what's been keeping you awake," Susanna said. She lay her head on his chest once more, nestling against him tenderly.

"I'd always thought the day each of our children left us would involve a celebration—moving into a house of their own, going off to start a business, or riding away with their newly-wedded spouse. I never imagined any of our children would run away." He tensed. "It hurts. I've comforted other parents whose children ran away from home. Never did I think it would happen to us. . . . I'd always imagined that on the day they left us, I'd have a chance to tell each of them how proud I am of them. Marshall didn't give me that chance."

In the stillness of the night Jeremiah and Susanna clung to each other.

Susanna whispered, "God willing, you can tell him when you see him again."

"God willing," Jeremiah replied, his voice trembling.

The next morning Marshall Morgan boarded the B & O Railroad, destination Harper's Ferry, Virginia, with all the exhilaration that had been missing the morning before when he walked out of Point Providence. Dropping his bag and rifle on the seat opposite him, he settled himself contentedly next to a window. Outside, the brakeman and engineer walked the length of the train, pausing every few steps to bend over and examine the undercarriage. The brakeman would occasionally lean in with his oil can and tend to one of the hundreds of moving parts. Marshall followed the crewmen's progress all the way up to the locomotive. Without giving it a thought, they passed through a small stream of steam escaping from the engine. It hit them in the pants legs.

Since the first time Marshall saw a train as a little boy, walking through the locomotive steam was something he'd always wanted to do. For Marshall it was the white discharge that gave the train its fairy-tale quality. He'd often wondered what it felt like, not only to pass through the steam, but to stand in the middle of it with it billowing up all around him. He'd always imagined that the sensation would be like standing on a cloud. It wasn't until later he learned that the massive discharge of steam was called "blowing down," and standing in it would be far from heavenly. The heat of the steam would more resemble heaven's counterpart. Still, boyhood dreams die hard.

"Tickets!"

With the train getting underway, a stout, scowling train conductor with a knobby chin made his way down the center aisle, snatching tickets from the outstretched hands of the sparse population of travelers. His scowl deepened if he had to slow his progress to wait for a ticket to appear. Marshall scrambled to produce his ticket and held it up well before the conductor reached his row. Still, the scowling ticket-taker halted upon reaching Marshall. The conductor made no sound. He stared at Marshall—particularly the white streak in his hair—then at the rifle on the opposite seat, then back at Marshall. His hard, dark eyes narrowed as if the focused gaze would burn its way into Marshall's head. Still not saying a word, the conductor slowly took Marshall's ticket and examined it at length. Then he continued down the aisle. No words were exchanged but the conductor's message was clear. He wanted no trouble from the rifle-toting passenger.

Marshall leaned back and smiled. It would take more than a

surly conductor to sour this day. This was his day of destiny, the day he would at long last join up with John Brown. Remembering something from the previous night, he looked out the window just as they were passing Grafton's main street. The small town's primary thoroughfare was a wide, rutted, dirt road lined on both sides with boardwalks. Business fronts stood ready for the day's activity. On the right there was a mercantile shop, Grafton Bank, and Priscilla's Millinery Shoppe. Two thirds of the way down the street on the left side he spotted a sign that prompted an unabashed grin — *The Daily Bugle.*

Marshall folded his arms then propped his feet up on the opposite bench, crossing them at the ankles. He thought of Cyrus Hines. Thanks to him, in a day or two everyone in Grafton, Virginia would know the name Marshall Morgan. The interview with the newspaperman had stretched late into the night. Question after question was fired at him. Every word in response was copiously recorded as John Goss and tavern owner Marcus Pollard listened with fascination. So did the tavernkeeper's son, Ira Pollard. At least for a while. When Pollard caught his son standing idly in the kitchen doorway, he threatened the boy with a thrashing for neglecting his chores. The boy quickly disappeared. Moments later Marshall caught the movement of a shadow lurking near the kitchen door. Ira remained out of his father's line of sight, but not out of earshot.

When the newspaperman's supply of questions was exhausted, Cyrus Hines rose to shake Marshall's hand. Tapping his notepad, he predicted that the printed story would be a good one. "One that will be an inspiration to a lot of people," he said. John and Marcus thrust their hands forward, wanting to touch Marshall. Each man commended him for his bravery.

The tavernkeeper then escorted a weary Marshall to his

room, all the while shouting orders to his wife and son who scurried here and there getting fresh linen, extra pillows and comforters, and a better lamp. Never before had anyone treated Marshall in this manner. He found himself liking it.

For a long time he lay in bed fully clothed with the lamp burning. He reviewed the events of the evening—the manner in which the men regarded him, the questions Cyrus Hines had asked him, his answers, and the pleased look on the newspaperman's face as he recorded Marshall's comments. In all truthfulness, Marshall found it hard to understand their fascination with him. But that didn't stop him from basking in the glow of the moment.

He remembered one question in particular that prompted astonished looks on the faces of his small audience. The newspaperman said: "You say you are willing to fight for the Negro's freedom—an admirable conviction to be sure. But let me ask you this: Are you willing to die for the Negro's freedom?"

Marshall had to pause before answering. In truth, he had never thought about dying. Dying was something that happened to other people, other people who were much older. He supposed it could happen to him; death was always a possibility when men pointed guns at each other. But whenever he'd imagined a gun pointed at him, he'd always imagined an escape—a tree to dive behind, a timely distraction, a quicker response than his opponent. In his mind there was always an alternative to death.

Cyrus Hines awaited an answer. From somewhere in the back of Marshall's mind a response came to him. It sounded good, so he verbalized it. By the pleased expressions on the faces of his three-man audience, it must have sounded good to them too. Marshall said, "Anytime you take up arms to defend someone's right to freedom, there is a possibility of dying. But if freedom is not worth dying for, what is?" It was from this quote that Cyrus said he got his headline for the story: "Freedom Worth Dying For."

Marshall slept little that night and what little sleep he got was interrupted. The steady shaking of a hand on his shoulder pulled him out of slumber's deep pit. All was quiet except for the rhythmic squeak of the bedsprings as Marshall's shoulder bounced up and down.

The dimly lighted form of Ira Pollard hovered over him. The boy was bare-chested. A thin rope gathered baggy pants around his midsection, but because the boy had no hips a spare hand was needed to hold the pants in place. His other hand continued rocking Marshall's shoulder, unaware that Marshall was awake because Ira was looking back toward the door. Disheveled blond hair framed a face that was anticipating terror, as though at any moment a fire-breathing dragon would appear at the door.

"Ira, what are you doing in here?" Marshall's voice was rough from sleep.

The boy jumped back, his Adam's apple bobbing futilely.

"What's happening?" Marshall cried.

"Shhhh!" Ira's spare hand shot up to his mouth. He nearly lost his pants in the process. The boy shot a nervous glance at the doorway. Seeing no dragon, he approached the bed again. "Take me with you tomorrow," he whispered.

"You want to go with me?"

Ira's head bobbed enthusiastically, blond hair tossing about.

"Why?"

Another glance at the door. "There's nothing for me here," the boy replied. "I want to fight with John Brown, just like you."

"How old are you?"

"Sixteen."

The boy looked more like fourteen, fifteen at best. "Have

you talked to your father about this?"

"He'll be glad to get rid of me." Apparently the boy saw some doubt on Marshall's face, for he added quickly, "Really! He hates me. He'll be glad I'm gone."

Marshall looked down and shook his head. "I don't know ... "

"Please, Mr. Morgan! I'll do anything you say. I'll carry your bag and rifle for you!"

Marshall continued shaking his head.

Ira's face made an instant transformation from that of a pouting little boy to one of fierce determination. "Then I'll run away. I can find Mr. Brown's farm by myself. I don't need you." Still gripping his pants, he turned toward the door.

Marshall called after him. "Tell you what," he said. "You can come with me if your father approves." Ira's face burst with a smile. "But you'll have to pay your own way!" Marshall added. "I have only enough money for me to get to Maryland, no more."

"Deal!" Ira silently clapped his hands. Without the added restraint, his pants began to slip. He caught them just in time.

Ira's childish response made Marshall feel uneasy. He determined to talk to the boy's father in the morning before allowing Ira to accompany him. As Marshall pulled up his comforter in an attempt to get back to sleep, the image of a hand-clapping Ira came to mind. "At least he has quick reflexes," Marshall muttered.

Come morning Ira was conspicuously absent. Marshall was fed a hero's breakfast of pancakes, eggs, and steak, then escorted by his host to the train platform. Marshall gave no more thought to the boy. He figured the permission-seeking conversation between the boy and his father had not gone well and that Ira was probably somewhere sulking. Marshall was satisfied with the outcome. Having had more time to reflect on the possibility of Ira's companionship, he preferred being alone. He would have felt responsible for the boy.

The train's screeching whistle sounded. With a jolt the car began to pick up speed. The town of Grafton, which had given Marshall such a grand reception, slid out of view.

"There he is!"

A familiar young voice came from behind him. Marshall closed his eyes and groaned silently. It was the same voice he'd heard in the dark the night before. Marshall turned and looked down the aisle to confirm his fear. With a grin too large for his face, Ira Pollard bounded up the aisle. Following behind him were two other boys, both smaller. All three carried a bundle of clothing and firearms of sorts. One looked like an ancient Revolutionary War musket.

Ignoring Marshall's propped-up feet, Ira plunked down on the seat opposite him. Marshall lowered his feet and Ira nodded obligingly and scooted toward the window. One of the other boys fell in next to him. The third boy, the youngest-looking one, stared at the empty space next to Marshall then chose to sit across the aisle from them.

"Ira, what are you doing here?"

The boy's grin disappeared. He was stunned by the question. "You said I could come with you!" he whined.

"Did you talk to your father like I asked you to?"

Ira looked down and fidgeted. "He doesn't care what I do. Glad to get rid of me. Same with them." Ira indicated the other two boys. They confirmed Ira's assessment of their parents with vigorous nods.

Marshall looked out the window, away from the boys. Trees and grass slipped by them; slowly in the distance, in a blur the closer they were to the train. *What am I going to do with them?* he wondered. Then a truly condemning thought came to him: *How can I berate them for leaving home without their father's permission when that's exactly what I have done?*

But it's different for me. I'm older.

Marshall's self-justification was not convincing.

"I only have enough money for myself," Marshall said.

Ira grinned. He pulled back his coat and patted a bulge in his shirt. Coins clinked. "I got enough for all three of us." Two more grins joined Ira's grin, making it a total of three boyish grins to Marshall's none.

"This is serious business," Marshall said. "You could get killed."

"Oh, we know that!" Ira cried. "But we won't, will we, boys? Because we got guns!"

Each boy held up his firepiece as proof. Marshall checked nervously for the sour-faced conductor. He was nowhere in sight.

"All right, all right. Put the guns away," Marshall cried. They quickly obeyed him. "I'll take you with me to John Brown's farm," he said. "After that, you're on your own. And remember, it's not up to me whether you get to stay or not. It's up to Mr. Brown."

Three grins atop three bobbing heads answered him.

Marshall sighed. "If I'm going to lead a children's crusade, I might as well know your names."

Ira designated himself to do the introductions. "This here's Alfred Hunter. He's the same age as me and is really good at sneaking up on people. And he can burp at the drop of a hat. Show him, Alfred!"

Before Marshall could refuse the demonstration, the brown-headed boy seated next to Ira opened his mouth and squeezed out a belch that commanded everyone's attention in the car.

"That was a good one, Alfred!" the younger boy squealed. His delight withered under the disapproving stares of the adult passengers onboard.

"That there is Thomas Johnston," Ira said, motioning toward the boy on the other side of the aisle. "He's sorta scrawny, but he runs real fast. No one faster in these parts." Thomas took the compliment in stride. Pulling up his legs, he wrapped his arms around them and rested his chin on his knees.

Marshall sized up his followers. "We're just overflowing with talent, aren't we?" he said. "All right, settle in and get some rest. You'll need all your energy once we reach Harper's Ferry. From there we walk to Maryland."

Marshall leaned back in his seat and pulled his hat over his eyes; partly as an example to the boys, mostly so he didn't have to look at their silly grins all the way to Harper's Ferry.

The B & O lumbered its way into western Maryland, past Lonaconing to Cumberland where it skirted the north side of the Potomac River. Then it crossed back into Virginia and followed the river's eastern course downstream on the south side until it reached Bath where it parted ways for a time with the Potomac and headed south to Martinsburg.

Marshall lifted his hat as the Potomac came into sight again. He knew they were nearing Harper's Ferry, which was situated at the point of the confluence of the Potomac and Shenandoah rivers. Paralleling the river's course the train rode a sliver of land with the river on one side and a canal on the other. Rocky heights filled the windows on both sides of the train.

"Why are we going so slow?" Ira asked.

Until Ira asked the question, Marshall hadn't given the train's deceleration any thought. But the boy lived in a train-stop town and was more familiar with the comings and goings of the iron monsters. The other passengers were also taking note of the train's slow rate. They pressed their heads against the windows trying to see what was causing the slow-down. Marshall joined their effort. To him it looked like the train was squeezing into the town. The tracks ran a narrow

line between the river on one side and a row of factory buildings on the other, identified by signs as the U.S. Musket
Factory. But it wasn't the narrow passage that was causing
the delay, it was people. They were everywhere—bunched
against the factory buildings, beside the tracks, some even on
the tracks. What was even more noticeable was the number of
armed, uniformed soldiers among them. Marshall also noted
several bands of armed men without uniforms, possibly
militia.

The inside of the train was abuzz with questions for which
no one seemed to have answers. They stared in drop-jawed
wonder, their faces pressed against the town-side windows.
The town was a panorama of confusion. Residents of
Harper's Ferry ran everywhere, shouting and cursing and
brandishing firearms. A company of federal cavalry soldiers
burst past the train heading in the opposite direction. Women
pulled children through doorways, then slammed the doors
lest the chaos of the streets somehow trail in behind them.
The air was heavy with dust. Harper's Ferry looked like a
town under siege.

In the distance Marshall noticed something strange on the
southern side of the covered bridge that united Virginia and
Maryland. A downed telegraph line was being repaired. *The
first thing vigilantes do is cut down the telegraph wires*, Cyrus
Hines had said. While workers raised a ladder, the wire, like
an injured limb, drooped uselessly against the pole. Yet still it
relayed a message. Not with a series of electric clicks, but
with its silence. The message was this: CAUTION, DANGER
AHEAD.

Marshall hurriedly collected his belongings. He looked behind him to make sure the boys were following. Ira remained
in his seat, his tongue sticking out of the side of his mouth in
concentrated study as he clumsily tried to load his weapon.

Chapter 6

H IS name was on everyone's lips.

The stationmaster: "John Brown rode into town Sunday evening in the rain with a wagonload of guns. Thirteen white men and five black men accompanied him. Death seems to follow that man. He wasn't here a day before someone was killed."

The telegraph operator: "It was John Brown's men who cut the wires. Would have smashed my key too, but I hid it from them. When they attacked the federal arsenal, we had to send for help the old-fashioned way—by horseback."

A black porter: "Like a dog in the street, that's how John Brown's men shot him down." Through watery eyes, the trembling porter described the death of his friend on the night Brown's men stormed the town. "Why did they shoot him? He was just the baggage man! He didn't never harm nobody. And he was a freeman too! That don't make sense, do it? Why would John Brown's men shoot a free black man?"

A broad-shouldered, grisly farmer: "I reckon ol' John Brown didn't figure we'd protect ourselves. Surprise was on *him*, though. Fact is, we don't cotton to men invadin' our town, even if they did good in bloody Kansas. Never seen people around here so angry when they heard what he was doin' at the armory. Took to the streets like vigilantes, we did. Cornered him like a rat in the fire engine house. 'Course they fired at us. But we fired back and killed one of 'em. Cut these here ears off the dead man myself!" The unshaven farmer proudly displayed two severed black ears. "Like I said, John Brown didn't know who he was tanglin' with when he rode into Harper's Ferry."

The prim stationmaster's wife: "I used to admire John Brown, at least until day before yesterday. Thought he was a righteous man! That was before he started shooting people and taking hostages! A man who holds innocent people hostage is no better than a scoundrel! Did you know that one of his hostages is Colonel Lewis Washington, the great grandnephew of George Washington himself? The way I heard it, not only did he take the colonel hostage, but he also took a pair of pistols that General Lafayette gave as a gift to General Washington. Seems to me John Brown is nothing more than a thief and a scoundrel."

A private posted at the train station: "John Brown's a dead man. That is, unless he surrenders. He don't stand a chance now that federal troops arrived from Washington. John Brown's no match for a West Point man like Colonel Lee. If he knew what was good for him, he'd surrender. Otherwise, he won't walk outta that engine house alive."

"Use your money to buy tickets back to Grafton," Marshall said. He had pulled his three followers to the side of the train station, the only spot he could find that was free from traffic.

Three pair of wide eyes stared at him. The boys' eyes had been that way ever since the farmer had displayed his trophy of severed ears.

"What are you gonna do?" Ira asked.

"I'm not sure," Marshall responded. "Probably wander over to the engine house to see for myself what's happening."

What he didn't tell them was that he would be looking for a way to get inside the engine house.

Ira's eyes narrowed. "We want to go too!" He spoke for all of them.

"No! It's too dangerous. The situation is different than what I thought it would be when I said you could come along. It's best that you go home."

Ira pulled himself up straight. "You can't tell us what to do," he cried. "You're not our father!" Looking to the others: "We're men now, aren't we, boys? And if we want to go see John Brown get hisself killed, then that's what we'll do!"

"Yeah! That's what we'll do!" The others chimed together.

Marshall shook his head. *What was he going to do with them? What could he do?* He realized now that this had been a mistake from the beginning. He should have flat out refused to let Ira join him from the start, just like he'd done with Willy. But it was too late for that now. The damage was done and three defiant boys stood before him. Somehow, he felt responsible. And until he could figure out a way to convince them to go home, he figured that he'd better watch over them.

"All right, we'll go together," Marshall said. "But if you go with me, I'm in charge, understand? It's just like in the army. I'm the general, you're the privates. Whatever I say, you have to do it! Agreed?"

Three silly grins swore allegiance to him.

The Harper's Ferry fire engine house was a brick structure with a peaked roof. A large, white wooden bell tower perched atop it. The engine house was situated just inside a U.S. musket factory compound which was enclosed by a brick wall. A wide dirt road ran the length of the compound, separating the two rows of buildings. It also provided access to the town by way of a wrought-iron gate. Today, however, the road was hauntingly empty of traffic.

Marshall and the boys navigated their way through the river of people to the town square only to find themselves in a much larger sea of humanity. Positioned a safe distance from the armory gate was a mixture of federal troops and militia, behind them a mob of curious onlookers. The spectators were pressed so tightly against the troops that the rear line of soldiers had to be turned around to keep them back. Marshall pushed upward on his toes to get a glimpse of the engine house, but all he could see was the tops of people's heads, a few soldiers' hats, and the engine house bell tower. It was as though the whole world had come out to witness the drama staged by John Brown.

The crowd of onlookers frustrated Marshall. He had not come all this way to be a spectator in John Brown's offensive against slavery. These curiosity seekers were keeping him from joining that offensive. Somehow he had to find a way to get into that engine house!

But to what purpose? Even as he did not come to be a spectator, neither did he come to die a martyr's death in a Virginia armory. This was not the battle he'd envisioned himself fighting with John Brown. That battle was supposed to be against large plantation owners who profited over the enslavement of human beings, not against federal troops. Yet this confrontation threatened to put an end to John Brown's mountain sanctuaries before they had a chance to get started. No! This was the wrong battle.

Suddenly it came to him. *Wasn't this situation similar to his scuffle with slave hunter Frank Toombs?* Had Marshall stayed to fight, needless lives could have been lost, including his own. Instead, he chose to avoid a standoff by escaping. Then, he circled around and engaged Toombs when it was to his advantage. Marshall concluded that was what John Brown needed to do! If he could somehow get inside the engine house and convince Brown to concede this battle, then the plan to establish free Negro sanctuaries still had a chance of succeeding!

Signaling for the boys to follow him, he skirted the back edge of the crowd, weaving around stragglers, making his way toward the heights. He glanced over his shoulder to see if the boys were following. Thomas was on his heels like a faithful dog; Ira's tongue lolled out the side of his mouth as he labored to keep up; and Alfred, who was falling behind, yipped for them to slow down.

Patches of people dotted the hillside. They stood between unevenly spaced houses and under trees, their numbers increasing the closer one got to the engine house. Potomac Street, a canal, and the musket factory's back wall separated them from the armory. Someone had abandoned a wagon in the middle of Potomac Street.

The number of troops was thinner on this side of the compound. The brick wall blocked access to the rear exit of the engine house, making it an unlikely escape route for Brown. Most of the soldiers chatted casually with bystanders. A few of them rested in sniping positions—in trees, atop houses, in upstairs windows. Although they were relaxed, Marshall knew better than to think that they were inattentive.

Marshall pulled the boys aside, huddling them around him. "I'm going into the engine house," he whispered.

"You're what?" Ira cried.

"I came to join John Brown. He's on the other side of that wall. I'm going in. You can do what you want. You can go with me or go back to the train."

Ira, Alfred, and Thomas gaped at each other, each one hoping one of the others would speak first. Marshall allowed them time to wrestle with their feelings. It was one of those moments of passage all boys encounter. Their childhood fantasies were coming face-to-face with reality. This was undoubtedly the first real danger they'd ever faced in their lives.

They were invincible on Grafton's fields of play, no matter how strong the enemy or how large the monster. But this was not play and the battle was no longer imaginary. And from the looks on their faces the boys weren't feeling very invincible today.

"I'm sticking with Mr. Morgan," Thomas said.

Ira and Alfred gawked at him. But only for a moment. Thomas was younger than them. Right or wrong, if Thomas went, they had to go too. It was a matter of manhood.

"I'm in," Ira said.

"I was gonna say it first, but Thomas interrupted me," Alfred said.

Marshall reviewed his troops. Ira's mop of blond hair fell in his eyes. Alfred looked like he was about to cry. And Thomas rubbed his leg nervously. Four words came to their leader's mind. *This is a mistake.* Still, he had to get inside that engine house.

"Listen to me," he said. "I'm the general. You're the privates. Your lives depend on you following my orders, understand? So listen carefully."

The boys drew closer to him. Never before in their lives had they listened to instructions as carefully as they did now.

"See that wagon in the road?"

In unison the three boys looked in the direction of Marshall's pointing finger. Between buildings they could see the old abandoned wagon on the far side of Potomac Street. Eight yards beyond it was the canal, and beyond that the brick wall.

"When I give the word, wander out into the street toward that wagon. Keep walking toward it until someone tells you to stop. Then—whatever you do—don't stop! Run as fast as you can to the far side of the wagon. Stay as low as you can and when you reach it, fall to the ground."

"What if they shoot as us?" Ira glanced nervously around

at the scattered federal soldiers as he asked the question.

"I don't think they will," Marshall said. "By walking, we can get part of the way without alarming them. Then, when we run, hopefully they will be confused long enough for us to reach the wagon."

"Why will they be confused?" Thomas asked.

"The soldiers are watching the building expecting people to try to escape *from* it; they're not expecting people to run *to* it. After all, who in his right mind would try to break into a building under siege?" Marshall chuckled at his own humor. From the sober expressions on the faces in front of him, the boys didn't get it.

"What if Mr. Brown's men shoot at us?" Thomas asked.

"They can't shoot at us, horsehead!" Alfred scoffed. "The wall is too high! They can't even see us!"

"Oh yeah."

"But how are we gonna get into the engine house?" Ira asked.

"Once we reach the wagon, we'll shout over the wall to Brown, tell him who we are, and that we're coming in. Once he knows we're coming, I'll cover the three of you while you cross the canal and scale the wall. Then I'll follow you over. Any questions?"

"You won't leave me out there, will you?" Thomas asked. Without being aware of it he worried the front of his shirt between his thumb and forefinger.

"He's just scared 'cuz he's little for his age," Alfred said in a grown-up way.

"Fighting men like us stick together," Marshall assured him.

With the plan of action understood, the foursome mingled among the bystanders closest to the road. Marshall studied the placement of federal soldiers. He wasn't exactly sure what he was waiting for—a feeling, a sign, something that would indicate to him that it was the right moment for them to run. What he really needed was a diversion. But what? And how?

It was almost as if God were listening to his thoughts. With a cloud of dust, a company of cavalry arrived behind them. Soldiers' heads turned toward the commotion.

"Go now!" Marshall cried in a whisper to the three boys.

Leading the way he casually strolled into the street, his hands in his pockets, at times turning toward the dust cloud of cavalry as though he were trying to get a better view.

A shout came from the back step of a house. "Sarge! Lookee there!"

Another voice. "Of all the. . . . Halt! Halt or we'll shoot!"

"Run!" Marshall yelled. He pumped his arms and legs with all his might. *Were the boys behind him?* He couldn't tell, but he didn't dare look; it would only slow him down. Every muscle within him strained for more speed. They were only halfway there and the wagon didn't seem to be getting any closer.

Suddenly, out of the corner of his eye he saw someone beside him, then run past. Thomas. *That's right, he's the fastest one*, Marshall remembered.

BLAM!

Dirt kicked up a few feet in front of them. Instinctively Marshall threw up an arm to cover his face. Pellets of earth spattered against his face and chest and legs. His lungs burned, his legs ached from the exertion. Still, he ran faster.

"You in the road! Halt! Halt, I say!"

BLAM! BLAM!

There was a scream behind him. Marshall shot a glance over his shoulder. Ira lay facedown in the dirt. Alfred had stopped and was staring at his fallen comrade. Three rifle-toting soldiers were running toward them. Alfred threw his hands over his head. His face was screwed up in terror, his feet did a dance of panic.

"Don't shoot me!" he screamed. "Don't shoot me!"

Marshall stopped just a few feet from the wagon. Thomas had made it. He was cowering safely behind a wheel. Marshall turned toward the remaining two. "Ira!" he yelled. He began moving toward the fallen boy. "Ira! Are you hit?"

While Alfred continued his panic dance, weeping profusely, Marshall watched as Ira Pollard jumped up from the ground.

"Are you wounded?"

Ira looked at Marshall incredulously. His hair and face and clothes were coated with dirt. "No, I just tripped," he said sheepishly.

The rifle-toting soldiers were closing. One of the soldiers had split off from the others and was coming at him. Ira and Alfred were all right for the moment, but far from the wagon. He checked Thomas again.

Don't leave me! The silent words formed on the boy's lips.

The soldier running toward him guessed what he was thinking. "You by the wagon!" he yelled. "Stand where you are!"

No time to weigh pros and cons. He had to act on instinct. Marshall broke toward the wagon.

"I said stand!" the soldier shouted.

Just a few yards to go. Could he make it? The soldier pulled up and planted his rifle against his arm to fire. He took aim.

"NO!" Thomas shouted.

Marshall dug his feet into the earth with all his might.

"Halt, I say!"

Almost there. Just a little more. Marshall dove for cover.

BLAM!

The corner of the wagon exploded into splinters.

BLAM! BLAM!

Two more blasts rocked the wagon. Marshall scrambled to his knees and readied his rifle, poking it through the wooden rungs of the wheel. He grinned. Now he had the advantage.

He had cover while the soldiers were exposed in the open road. Additional soldiers poured out into the road to cover their comrades. A volley of shot hit the wagon like hailstones. Marshall pushed Thomas to the ground, falling on top of him. Bullets whizzed. Patches of dirt exploded around them. Slivers of wood, ripped from the wagon, showered down upon them.

Suddenly, everything was quiet. Marshall lifted his head. Ira and Alfred, their hands over their heads, were being hurried off the road. Alfred's sobs echoed against the heights. As they reached the edge of the road Ira glanced toward the wagon. The soldier escorting him shoved him forward.

A singular voice could be heard among the troops, cursing at the soldiers for firing. "You were ordered not to fire!" he screamed. Then, looking at the wagon. "Of all the fool stunts! In all my years I've never seen anything like this!"

The small body that was pressed against Marshall quivered. "Ira and Alfred will be all right," Marshall said in a soothing, low voice. "The soldiers won't hurt them."

Thomas responded with a weak smile. There was skepticism in the boy's eyes. Marshall couldn't blame him. *Wasn't it just a few moments previous that he assured them that the soldiers wouldn't shoot?*

From their vantage point behind the wagon, the two of them watched through the weeds as Ira and Alfred were marched out of sight. Marshall couldn't help but feel that he was to blame. He should have brought up the rear, kept them in front of him. He scolded himself for not thinking through the possibilities. He'd promised Ira that he'd get him to John Brown's camp. He'd failed, and it gnawed at him. *Would the boys really be all right?* He had to believe that they would be.

"Looks like it's just you and me now," Marshall said solemnly. "Just you and me," Thomas replied. His voice quivered.

While Thomas kept a lookout, Marshall turned his attention toward the wall that separated them from the engine house. The wall was only one obstacle. Scaling it would be the easy part. Scaling it without getting shot was the challenge. He could only hope that the federal officer's order not to shoot had not been rescinded. Still, there was the danger of being shot by one of Brown's men. Somehow he had to initiate contact with Brown and convince him they were friendly.

Just then a movement atop the wall caught his eye. He reached for his gun. His sudden movement startled Thomas. Marshall raised a finger to his lips. Thomas understood. He didn't utter a sound. The two of them watched intently as what looked like a miniature hill of black cotton rose up from behind the wall. It was attached to a black forehead, then a pair of alert eyes which focused beyond them on the federal troops. The dark cotton patch ceased rising once the eyes cleared the top of the wall. Accentuated by a furrowed brow, the eyes moved side-to-side, studying the soldiers' activity.

"Hello there!" Marshall called out.

"Lord Almighty!" The head behind the wall jumped at Marshall's hail. The eyes darted toward Marshall, the head wobbled, then disappeared, followed by a crash.

Voices came from the other side of the wall.

"What did you see?"

"Someone's over dar!"

"Of course there is! That's why you're looking!"

"No, I means thar's someone right over dar!"

"Who?"

"I's don' know who dey is!"

"Are they soldiers?"

"Dey's just a man and a boy!"

"What are they doing over there?"

"Dey's just sittin' dar!"

Marshall called to the voices. "Hello on the other side of the wall!"

Silence.

"We're not soldiers!" Marshall said. "Just like he said, a man and a boy."

This prompted a flurry of low, unintelligible whispers.

"That shooting you heard," Marshall continued. "The soldiers were shooting at us because we want to join you."

Silence.

Marshall and Thomas exchanged glances. "Are you still there?" Marshall said to the wall.

"Who are you?" It was a new voice. Strong, clear. A voice with authority.

"Mr. Brown?" Marshall asked.

"Identify yourself and your purpose," the voice answered harshly.

"I'm Marshall Morgan from Ohio. With me is Thomas . . ." all of a sudden he realized he couldn't remember Thomas' last name, that is, if he'd ever heard it . . . "Thomas from Grafton. We came to join your band."

"Join us?"

"Yes, sir."

"How many are you?"

Marshall looked at Thomas who shrugged. "Like I said, just the two of us."

"Do you bring us news of others?"

Marshall paused. He wasn't sure how to answer. "We can tell you what we've seen since entering Harper's Ferry this morning."

"Do you have weapons?"

"Yes, sir."

"Leave them there. You will be shot dead at the first weapon I see coming over this wall."

Marshall felt uneasy leaving his rifle behind. *He would need it to help defend the engine house, wouldn't he?*

"Did you hear me?" the voice demanded.

"Yes, sir. But won't we need weapons to . . ."

The voice was impatient. "We just seized an armory. We can oblige you with a weapon if you are who you say you are. And if you're not, we'll kill you."

Marshall's face flushed. "No weapons," he said to Thomas.

"Come over one at a time," the voice commanded.

Marshall gave Thomas' leg a reassuring pat. He checked the activity among the federal troops. To his astonishment it looked like no one other than civilians was paying any attention to them! The soldiers were gathered around an officer on horseback. They looked up in concentrated attention at him with only an occasional glance in the direction of the wall. Marshall scanned the trees and houses for snipers. Two. Three. Four of them. Ira and Alfred were nowhere in sight. There would be no better time than now to scale the wall. Still, they would be woefully exposed. And it only took one sniper and one bullet . . .

"Let's go," he said. Crouching low, they used the wagon for cover.

A chorus of shouts came from among the civilians—cheers, shouts, curses, boos. The soldiers, however, held their positions with rifles lowered. Marshall and Thomas slipped into the canal and swam for the wall.

"We're coming over," he yelled when they reached the ledge at the base of the wall, then added, "unarmed." Thomas's eyes were glazed over with uncertainty. Marshall gave him a reassuring nod. Forming a foothold with cupped hands, Marshall boosted him to the top of the wall. The noise from the onlookers grew ever louder. This was the moment they were most vulnerable. Thomas was stretched out completely against the wall. Marshall braced for the report of a rifle. There was none. Hands grabbed at Thomas and hauled him over the wall. There was a muffled cry.

Dropping to a squatting position, his clothes dripping, Marshall called out: "Thomas, are you all right?"

The authoritative voice responded. "The boy's fine. Are you coming or not?"

Marshall checked the snipers again. *Were they waiting for a bigger target?* The federal snipers lounged on tree limbs and window ledges. Not a one of them looked like he had any intention of firing! It didn't make sense.

With as much spring as he could muster, he leaped, pulling himself up until his forearms rested atop the wall. Hands seemed to come from everywhere. They grabbed his arms, clothing, his hair, and jerked him over the wall. His bare forearms scraped nastily against the brick, peeling away the skin in ragged rows. Like a sack of grain, he landed on his back with a thud. Wincing from the pain, he fought to recapture the air that had been forced from his lungs. Through half-open slits, he saw five or six men towering over him with an equal number of rifles pointed at his head.

"Take them inside."

The authoritative voice now had an image to go with it. It was a thin, gaunt face nestled in a mass of gray hair that covered his head and extended down his cheeks to his chin and beyond to considerable length. The mouth showed little sign of ever having lips; it was nothing more than a straight line. His eyes lurked in caves beneath a furrowed ridge. From the recesses they were clear and light, striking in their intensity. It was an image Marshall had seen before in newspaper renderings. He was much older than the renderings depicted and there was more hair, but the man's identity was unmistakable. Marshall was staring up into the face of the notorious John Brown.

Marshall and Thomas were dragged into the engine house and dumped unceremoniously next to a coiled fire hose. The building was shut up, so it was dark inside, but not dark enough to miss the body of a man slumped against a water pump. A dark red oval stained his shirt. His head dropped unnaturally to one side. His mouth hung open, but there was no breath in it.

About a dozen other men, many of them sporting patches of blood on their shirtsleeves or pants were posted near windows and doors, the ones that opened out to the town. In the recesses of the engine house was a small congregation of people, some standing or leaning against the brick wall, others sitting with their backs against the wall. The hostages. Marshall wondered which of them was the relative of George Washington. Without exception, the bloodied watchmen, the hostages, and their leader were all staring at Marshall and Thomas.

"Tell me what's happening outside," Brown demanded.

Marshall attempted to stand. He was shoved down by the Negro whose head had first poked over the wall.

"You can tell me from down there," Brown said.

"We came in on the train this morning." With a nod Thomas' direction, he indicated he meant the boy and him. "From what we observed, you are surrounded by federal troops from Washington. Colonel Robert E. Lee, a West Point man, is in command. They are supplemented by the town militia, I'm not sure exactly how many . . ."

"What are you babbling about?" Brown thundered.

Marshall was taken aback. "You asked me to tell you what was going on outside."

"Not with the federal troops, idiot!" John Brown shook with rage, his voice rumbled. His eyes were an inferno. Brown was clearly a moody man, and his moods were sudden and intense. "Tell me about the uprising!" he shouted.

"Uprising?"

"From the plantations!" Brown roared. "Are they massing

to deliver us? How many are there? Hundreds? Thousands? Surely word has reached them by now. It will take time for some of them to travel all this way, but those who are within a day or two's journey should be arriving by now. How many have you seen? Have you heard anything about their intended plan of attack?"

Marshall's face and mind went blank. "I've heard nothing of such things," he stammered, "nor have I seen any large groups of . . . "

"LIAR!" Brown roared. A bony finger quivered inches from Marshall's nose. "I know who you are! You are hell's servant sent here to deceive us!"

Brown's fiery outburst frightened Thomas so much, he scooted backward on his hands and bottom away from the man.

"Confess it!" Brown raged. "Confess your sin before the Lord God Almighty!"

"You're mistaken. I told you, I came from Ohio to . . . "

"That demon of a colonel sent you in here, didn't he?" Brown screamed. "The boy was included to gain our sympathy, wasn't he? Vile treachery!"

Thomas whimpered at the direct reference to him.

"Confess it! Confess your sin! You're exaggerating the strength of the federal troops, aren't you? And the slaves . . . the slaves!" Suddenly, as quickly as his rage appeared, it dissipated, chased away by a dawning realization. Brown turned a triumphant face upward. His hands stretched toward heaven. "Thank you, Lord!" he cried. Tears stained the small patches of exposed flesh that were his cheeks. "Surely, they are massing in alarming proportions! You have raised up an army of free men to deliver us! Is it any wonder the demonic troops from Washington are unnerved? That explains this deception. But our faith is strong. We will not be deceived. And their plan will be thwarted! For we are the

Lord's army!"

Marshall stared in awe at the figure towering over him. Though he had just been cast in the role of a messenger from hell, he felt no panic rising within him. He felt no fear. On the contrary, this pillar of righteousness overshadowing him caused his skin to tingle. Here was a man who believed so strongly in what he was doing that federal troops could not intimidate him. Marshall had never before witnessed such faith. Though vastly outnumbered, still Brown rejoiced! And what was the source of his confidence? God. And the fact that what he was doing was right. For the first time, Marshall was convinced beyond doubt that slavery was doomed. God would not let a man of such great faith be defeated. Suddenly, Marshall felt ashamed that he had come into the engine house hoping to persuade this great crusader to surrender to the federal troops.

Marshall cleared his throat. "Have not I commanded thee? Be strong and of a good courage; be not afraid, neither be thou dismayed: for the Lord thy God is with thee whithersoever thou goest. Joshua 1:9."

The Scripture verse brought a puzzled expression from the charismatic leader. From the look on his face, he was attempting to discern if the words were spoken in faith, or if this was one more deceptive trick.

Marshall spoke quickly to dispel the crusader's doubt. "Mr. Brown, I'm reminded of an incident in the Bible when the prophet Elisha was surrounded by the armies of the king of Syria. If you recall, God sent the heavenly host to defend His prophet."

A light of recognition sparkled in the crusader's eyes. He was familiar with the passage, enough to be able to quote: "Fear not: for they that be with us are more than they that be with them."

"THEY'RE COMING!"

The alarm was sounded by a bearded man with a raspy voice who was standing watch at the double-door entrance. As he shouted it, he jumped back as if the door had bit him. An instant later the room reverberated with the sound of thunder. The door quaked. Hinges groaned. Dust rose, giving the interior of the engine house a dreamlike setting.

"A battering ram!" the raspy voice shouted.

The first blow had the same effect on the engine house that a stick has on a beehive. At the sound of the impact, everyone jumped. The din inside that followed soon afterward was deafening. Brown shouted orders. His followers simultaneously hollered reports of advancing troops from their positions. Agitated hostages clamored and wailed as they frantically searched for cover.

With the second blow the double doors flew into pieces. The watchman with the raspy voice was thrown backward halfway across the room. Marshall leaped behind the pump wagon, pulling Thomas with him. They found themselves within inches of the dead man. Federal troops poured into the building like sand through an hourglass, overwhelming John Brown's pitifully small army.

Almost as soon as it began it was over. Armed federal soldiers stood everywhere. A hush fell over the room. Now Marshall realized why the federal soldiers didn't stop him and Thomas. What difference did it make if they were captured outside the engine house or inside?

"Mr. Morgan, you are an enigma to me."

Colonel Robert E. Lee sat behind a small wooden table, pen in hand. His eyes squinted against the bright daylight as they worked their way up and down the prisoner standing before him. The gaze halted momentarily when it reached the white streak through the prisoner's hair.

Marshall was flanked by two guards. Their surroundings

were a testimony to restored order. Row after row of evenly spaced tents were arrayed behind the colonel. The occupants of the tents were all dressed orderly in uniforms, they spoke with orderly respect, and they saluted in orderly military fashion. The world was once again safe from the chaos of men like John Brown who would dare challenge the morality of such an orderly world.

"Correct me if I'm wrong," Colonel Lee said, "but as I understand it, you and three other young men entered the engine house while troops were laying siege to it."

"Four of us tried. Only two of us succeeded."

"Yes, that's what this report says." Colonel Lee glanced down at the papers on his desk to confirm that fact.

"Where are the boys now?" Marshall demanded.

His impertinent tone drew a scowl from Lee. "You forget your position, Mr. Morgan. You are under military arrest. You have the right to answer questions, not ask them."

Marshall had interpreted the colonel's gentlemanly demeanor for softness. It was a mistake. Beneath the soft-spoken exterior was a man of rigid authority.

"Forgive me, Colonel," Marshall offered contritely. "It's just that I feel responsible for them. I only want to know if they are being cared for."

"You can rest assured, sir, they are being cared for. Additionally, because of their ages we have notified their families by telegraph." Lee's tone had not softened. Although the gentleman had provided the information, the authoritarian made it clear that he was in control.

"Now then," Lee continued, "what was your purpose in breaking through our lines and sneaking inside the engine house?"

"I had a singular purpose—to join John Brown's band. Having just arrived from Ohio, I expected to find them in Maryland. Instead I found them here. Neither their location nor their situation altered my desire to join them."

"But they were surrounded by federal troops!" Lee said incredulously.

"That fact only made it more difficult for me to complete my journey."

Lee leaned back in his chair and studied Marshall for a moment. Then he said, "Was it your intention to supply Mr. Brown with strategic information regarding federal troop placement?"

"You probably won't believe me, sir, but no. That was not my purpose."

The gentlemanly demeanor returned. "I believe you." The colonel shuffled some papers, found the one he was looking for, read silently for a moment, then said, "Mr. Brown claims that we sent you into the engine house to deceive him and dishearten his men."

John Brown's recorded testimony, if true, was a blow to Marshall. *Had he failed to convince Brown of his sympathies to the abolitionist cause?* True, his attempt to communicate his commitment to the cause was interrupted by the untimely arrival of federal troops. Still through the exchange of Scripture verses Marshall had hoped he'd reversed the charismatic leader's opinion of him. It saddened him to think he had failed.

Colonel Lee continued, oblivious to the effect his words were having on Marshall. "Thus, according to Mr. Brown, you are not one of his men. Hence, the enigma."

Marshall straightened himself as he spoke. "Mr. Brown was only trying to protect me, sir. I am one of his most loyal followers."

The colonel's eyes squinted again. He stroked his neatly trimmed bearded chin. To an aide, he said, "Bring Mr. Brown here."

Moments later the shackled prisoner joined them. In spite

of having received a sword wound during the melee, John Brown walked with dignity and held his head erect. Colonel Lee stood in his presence.

"Mr. Brown," the colonel's tone was courteous, "I would appreciate your help, sir, in the matter of Mr. Morgan's disposition. He claims to be one of your men. On your honor, sir, would you identify him as such?"

The gray-haired abolitionist gave Marshall only a cursory look before replying. "He is not."

Colonel Lee nodded. "Can you tell me then, sir, why Mr. Morgan would claim to be one of your followers when he is not?"

This time John Brown looked at Marshall as he spoke. "No doubt, he shares my outrage over the enslavement of God's Negro children and he will not rest until, like the Children of Israel, they have been set free from their bondage. But until today, I have never seen this man before. However, I would add that he does remind me of another man of a different place and time. I believe his name was Joshua."

"Was this Joshua ever one of your followers?" Lee asked.

"No sir," replied Brown, "he was a follower after God."

Their eyes met. John Brown's and Marshall Morgan's. So Marshall *had* convinced him! For what else could Brown be referring to other than the Bible passage Marshall quoted to him from the Book of Joshua? It was the abolitionist's way of communicating to Marshall in a way he would understand, but one that would remain hidden to the colonel.

Marshall gave a slight nod to show he understood. He not only understood the message, he also understood the significance of the reference. This was his commissioning. Brown was commissioning Marshall Morgan to carry on his work.

"Thank you, sir," Colonel Lee said to Brown. "You have brought clarity to this matter." The colonel then signaled the guards to remove the prisoner. After they had gone, Lee took his seat and turned his attention back to Marshall.

"Sir, it seems you are a follower without a leader."

"So it seems," Marshall replied.

"Furthermore, since you are not a conspirator with Mr. Brown, the only charge remaining is that of interfering with federal troops in the performance of their duty. However, because your interference was negligible and you were a danger only to yourself, I have a mind to drop the charge and release you, provided you promise me that you will leave town by the end of the day. Should I see or hear of you after today, I will have you arrested and punished. Do I have your word?"

"Yes, sir. You have my word."

Colonel Lee silently weighed Marshall's response. Then he leaned forward, resting his forearms on the papers atop the desk. "A word of advice," he said. "Go home, son. Find a girl, if you haven't already, and settle down. Leave the killing and the hatred behind."

"May I go now?" Marshall asked.

Colonel Lee to the guards: "Take him to the train station. Stay with him until he boards."

True to his word, Marshall left Harper's Ferry, but he went only as far as Martinsburg where he awaited news of John Brown's fate. He didn't have to wait long. With Virginian mobs calling for his death and with the eyes of the nation upon the trial, Brown was taken to Charles Town where the Commonwealth of Virginia indicted him for treason against the state and criminal conspiracy to incite a slave insurrection. When Marshall learned of the trial's location, he traveled the short distance south from Martinsburg to Charles Town, avoiding Harper's Ferry. Once there, he worked odd jobs at mercantile stores, livery stables, and blacksmith shops to provide a meager living while he followed the events of the trial.

Emotions ran high. Rumors abounded. Some of the rumors told of abolitionists from the North forming rescue parties to free the accused; others told of Southern lynch mobs who were coming to hang him. Fifteen hundred militia men were brought in to keep order.

Unable to get inside the courtroom, Marshall had to content himself with scraps of news, rumor, and commentary from those who came and went during the trial. Their comments and observations proved so unreliable that he soon found that his best source of information was the newspaper. Although he got the news a day late, and although the Virginia paper was unabashedly biased against Brown, at least it recorded John Brown's court comments and speeches. It was these direct quotes from the charismatic abolitionist that interested Marshall most. In testimony, letters, and interviews, the accused exhibited dignity and fortitude. Throughout the trial, Brown insisted that his object had not been to incite insurrection, but only to free slaves and arm them in self-defense. In the courtroom his words fell on deaf ears. His fate was a foregone conclusion. After all, this was a Southern courthouse.

John Brown's closing speech prior to his sentencing had a particularly profound impact on Marshall. He tore the printed speech from the newspaper and carried it with him wherever he went for years afterward. In part Brown said:

> *I deny everything but what I have all along admitted: of a design on my part to free slaves. . . . Had I interfered in the manner which I admit, in behalf of the rich, the powerful, the intelligent, the so-called great, every man in the Court would have deemed it an act worthy of reward rather than punishment.*
>
> *The Court acknowledges, too, as I suppose, the validity of the law of God. I see a book kissed, which I suppose to*

*be the Bible, or at least the New Testament, which teaches
me that all things whatsoever I would that men should do
to me, I should do even so to them. It teaches me, further,
to remember them that are in bonds as bound with them. I
endeavored to act up to that instruction. Now, if it is
deemed necessary that I should forfeit my life for the fur-
therance of the ends of justice, and mingle my blood further with the blood of my children and with the blood of
millions in this slave country whose rights are disregarded
by wicked, cruel, and unjust enactments, I say, let it be
done.*

The Commonwealth of Virginia found John Brown guilty
and sentenced him to hang on December 2, 1859. On the day
of the execution, Marshall walked around in a daze. For
weeks he had flirted with boyish dreams of rescue attempts.
Surely some miracle would occur and Brown would not die.
But as the date drew closer, and with it the reality of John
Brown's execution, Marshall's optimism died and his mood
soured. By the day of the hanging, he was adrift in a mawkish
black fog.

Along with thousands of others, he was turned away from
the execution site. However, not being an actual witness did
not diminish the impact John Brown's death had on him. Nor
was he alone in this. If John Brown was a controversial figure
in life, he was even more so in death. For weeks following his
hanging, responses filled newspapers all across the country:

Theodore Parker pronounced Brown "not only a martyr,
but also a saint."

A clergyman in Roxbury, Massachusetts, declared that
Brown had made the word *treason* "holy in the American
language."

Henry David Thoreau pronounced Brown "a crucified
hero."

Ralph Waldo Emerson prophesied that Brown would "make the gallows as glorious as the cross."

It was reported that when word of John Brown's death reached the North, church bells tolled, guns fired solemn salutes, ministers preached sermons of commemoration, and thousands bowed in silent reverence for the martyr to liberty.

According to one eyewitness' testimony, Brown said not a word at the gallows. However, he did hand the guard a note which was later read aloud, then printed in the newspaper. It read:

> *I, John Brown, am now quite certain that the crimes of this guilty land will never be purged away but with blood.*

It was a sentiment shared by Marshall Morgan.

Marshall's return to Point Providence was as inglorious as his departure. Three months after he left, he rode the same train and walked the same road, only this time in the opposite direction. There was no one to meet him at the train station. But then, no one was expecting him.

The first thing Marshall noticed as his house came into view was the woodpile. Covered with snow it was still substantial. He wondered how long he would be home before it received its next deposit of freshly chopped wood.

The initial reception from his family was joyous, but the celebratory mood vanished quickly, pulled under by underlying streams of discontent. Paramount among the feelings of discontent was the unresolved argument between himself and his father. Neither man brought the subject up, but it was there between them every time they looked at each other. For Marshall, his father's welcome-home smile and handshake was a thinly disguised gloat of victory, as though the prodigal had come home with his tail between his legs. Marshall pretended the unspoken gloat didn't bother him. Let his father think he had won. Marshall knew that his stay at home would last only until it became clear to him how best to fulfill his commissioning from John Brown. Once determined, he would be gone again just like the first time. And what was also certain, just like the first time, was that his father would probably not approve.

Willy was another stream of discontent. For weeks he'd waited anxiously to receive word from Marshall to join him. After a month with no word forthcoming, it became clear to him that his brother was never going to send for him. Willy's response was to draw up inside himself and sulk. It had taken more than a month of J.D. and Sarah in concerted action to pull him out of his depression. Then Marshall returned. No amount of excuses or explanations from Marshall could satisfy Willy. He hobbled up the stairs and shut himself away in his room.

In the days that followed his return home, Marshall was almost as withdrawn as Willy. He spent the majority of his spare time searching the Bible for guidance regarding his mission. He found the instructions he was looking for in the Old Testament, in passages remarkably dramatic in their passion for righteousness and their lack of hesitation to use force for a righteous cause. Passages like the one that told how God mercilessly drowned Pharaoh's men in the sea when they pursued God's chosen people of Israel. And the one that described how Achan and his entire family were put to death for Achan's sin against God. In the back cover of his Bible, he recorded these and similar incidents. All of them had two things in common: righteous indignation and violent conclusions.

Susanna knew her husband was still awake because he was quiet. Jeremiah was a loud sleeper, sometimes snoring and sometimes simply breathing loudly. "It's good to have Marshall home again," she said into the darkness. "Wouldn't you agree?"

Jeremiah gave a grunt in reply. Susanna took it as an affirmative.

"Does he seem any different to you?" she asked.

"Different?"

"Well, more serious. Somber."

"Marshall has always been that way. He lets his passions overrule his common sense. It will be his undoing someday."

Susanna propped herself up on an arm. She addressed her next comments to the dark lump in the bed beside her. "No, it's more than that. He acts as if he's mad at the world."

"I suppose so. Good-night."

Jeremiah adjusted his pillow and covers, settling in for sleep.

"Well, doesn't that bother you?" Susanna asked.

Speaking through a yawn, Jeremiah answered, "Certainly it bothers me."

"Enough to do something about it?"

"What would you have me do?"

"Talk to him. See what's gnawing at his insides."

Jeremiah snorted. "You know I'm the last person on the earth he'll confide in."

Susanna didn't argue; she knew he was right. With a frustrated sigh she dropped onto her pillow. "Well, we've got to do something!"

Jeremiah rolled over and faced his wife. "If there's one thing I've learned about Marshall over the years it's this: we can help him only as much as he'll let us. Like it or not, he's old enough to choose his own course in life. We can't make his decisions for him. Nor can we force him to do the things we think are best for him. All we can do is trust that the godly upbringing we've given him will take root and produce fruit."

"I suppose so," Susanna sighed. "But there is one thing we can do."

"What's that?"

"We can pray for him."

Jeremiah Morgan took his wife in his arms. In the darkness of their bedroom they prayed. "Dear God in heaven," Jeremiah said, "we don't know all that our son has seen and felt in his recent trip. But somehow he's different and that disturbs us. We trust in the fact that You were there with him all the time. You know what he saw, what he felt, and what he feels now. We pray that You will bring good out of it as only You can. Fill him with Your love. And give us wisdom to do what we can to help him," he paused, then added, "and give us patience to trust You to do what we cannot do. Lord, we give our son to You. Protect him as a little lamb in Your arms. Amen."

While his parents prayed to God concerning their little lamb, Marshall was in his room pacing like a lion. He'd just finished copying a New Testament verse onto the inside back cover of his Bible. For him the verse summarized everything John Brown stood for, and everything he was to do in his mission to eradicate the evil of slavery. While the ink dried, he paced the floor, reciting the verse aloud: "Hebrews 9:22, And almost all things are by the law purged with blood; and without shedding of blood is no remission."

Chapter 7

HENRY Wier, one of Point Providence's lanky young bachelors, was fast becoming the town's most celebrated resident; not for any heroic deed, but because he alone of all the townspeople understood the clicks and clacks of the telegraph machine. And in a day when people craved the latest news with insatiable appetites, Henry Wier determined to make the most of his position. He dispensed the morsels of information as though he himself were creating it.

The young telegrapher's first great performance came following the November 6, 1860 presidential election. It was as though the whole world held its breath as it awaited the announcement of the winner.

The field of candidates was large that year. When incumbent President James Buchanan chose not to run for a second term, the election turned into a four-way race. The Democrat party split, offering two candidates—Stephen A. Douglas for the North and John C. Breckinridge for the South. The remnants of the Whig party nominated John Bell. And the newly formed Republican party fielded a compromise candidate, an Illinois lawyer named Abraham Lincoln.

When the election result first came in, Henry Wier was the only resident of Point Providence to know the identity of the sixteenth President of the United States. With a self-assured air about him, he stood on the porch step outside his closet-size telegraph office and refused to announce the winner until the entire town was represented. When he was satisfied his requirement had been met, he stubbornly waited until everyone was absolutely quiet. Henry wet his lips, swallowed. He unfolded the dispatch and held it in front of him. But before he uttered a sound, a matronly woman standing behind him read the message over his shoulder and shouted:

"LINCOLN WINS!"

The little town on the north side of the Ohio River burst into cheers, with the exception of their deflated telegraph operator. The election of Lincoln was a victory for them, but an ominous one. The winning candidate received not one electoral vote from a Southern state. In fact, his name did not even appear on the ballot in ten Southern states. Nor was he the clear choice among Northern states. He simply had more votes than any of the other three candidates—but just barely.

A story that circulated around Point Providence before the election put things in perspective. It seemed a millennialist preacher was boasting that it didn't matter who won the presidential election because the world was surely coming to an end before 1860 and Jesus Christ would be president of the universe by then. To which another fellow replied, "I'll bet you ten dollars New Hampshire don't vote for him!"

Americans saw the election as a referendum on slavery and the Southern way of life. In the flurry of debates preceding the election, Southern states threatened to secede from the Union should Lincoln win. So when the results of the election were announced, Point Providence, along with the rest of the nation, braced themselves for the Southern states' response. They didn't have to wait long.

On December 20, 1860 Henry Wier stood on his snow-covered step with another announcement, this one carefully concealed so only he could see it. In a somber tone, he read:

By unanimous vote, the South Carolina legislature has

VOTED THAT THE UNION NOW SUBSISTING BETWEEN THE STATE OF SOUTH CAROLINA AND THE OTHER STATES, UNDER THE NAME OF THE UNITED STATES OF AMERICA, IS HEREBY DISSOLVED. In the weeks that followed, Henry repeated this same announcement five more times, each time naming a different Southern state. The unity of the nation had been shattered. On the day Abraham Lincoln was elected there were thirty-three states represented in the United States of America; by the time he was inaugurated there were only twenty-seven states, with more threatening to secede should the federal government attempt to coerce them in matters regarding their domestic institutions.

Henry took to his step again on February 19th. He announced that Jefferson Davis had taken the oath of office the day before as the elected provisional president of the Confederate States. Less than a month later, from the same step he read portions of Lincoln's inaugural speech which had been transmitted over the wires. In a solemn, if not theatrical, tone he read: PHYSICALLY SPEAKING, WE CANNOT SEPARATE. . . . NO STATE, UPON ITS OWN MERE ACTION, CAN LAWFULLY GET OUT OF THE UNION. Henry concluded the last part of Lincoln's speech forcefully: THERE NEED BE NO VIOLENCE UNLESS IT BE FORCED UPON THE NATIONAL AUTHORITY. The gangly telegrapher lowered the paper and stared into the eyes of his neighbors and friends. They were a subdued lot. The implications of the President's speech covered the town like a thundercloud.

At first the townspeople of Point Providence had not been overly concerned with the string of reports that issued forth from Henry Wier's lips. The reports were of events that were taking place hundreds of miles away from their peaceful town. There was a distinct element of detachment about the news, not unlike an ancient history lesson at school. Lincoln's election in Washington, South Carolina's secession vote in

Columbia, and Jefferson Davis's election in Montgomery was significant history, but it had no immediate impact any more than did the battles of ancient Athens or Rome or Constantinople. But that was about to change. Sides had been chosen and with this inaugural address Lincoln had drawn the line. It was only a matter of time until the thundercloud burst. And when it did, none of them would escape its fury.

For Marshall the killing started early. He and Willy and John Hatfield, the giant Negro deacon, were bunched together at twilight with a dozen runaways in the ravine behind the cemetery on the outskirts of Cincinnati when a voice came from on high.

"Nobody move!"

Every eye in the ravine looked up in the direction of the voice.

"Toombs!" Marshall cried.

"Why the surprised look, Morgan? Didn't I tell you I'd come back to get you?" the rotund slave hunter chortled. His rifle was leveled at Marshall's chest. On the opposite side of the ravine was his Toombs' partner, Watkins. He covered the runaways with his rifle.

"Everybody stay calm," Marshall said to the fear-struck runaways. He leaned toward them as he spoke, hoping the movement would conceal his right hand reaching for the rifle by his side.

"Hands in front of you, Morgan!" Toombs shouted.

Marshall froze.

"Don't make me shoot you too soon," Toombs taunted. "I have plans for you first."

Slowly, Marshall brought both hands forward.

"Well, well . . . revenge is sweet! So sweet!" Toombs winked across the ravine at his partner.

"Marshall, what are we going to do?" Willy whispered.

Marshall patted the air with a hand to reassure his brother. "You should have stayed in Canada, Toombs!" he called to the slave hunter.

"Can't speak French," Toombs replied. "Besides I had a debt to repay."

"Nonsense," Marshall said, "as far as I'm concerned, we're even."

Even in the dying light Toombs' flushed face could be clearly seen. "Even! You nearly drowned me in the river, then shut me in a coffin!" he screamed. "Then you so much as sold me into slavery!"

"But I didn't kill you," Marshall said. "And I could have."

"By the time I'm through with you, you're gonna wish *you* was dead!" Toombs said through his teeth. "Everybody stand up! And leave the weapons on the ground!"

The runaways stood uncertainly, not sure what to make of the events. The men on the ridge seemed more concerned about capturing Marshall than he was about them.

Hatfield took his time getting up. The big deacon looked to Marshall for some kind of signal. None was forthcoming. When he rose to full height he towered over the others. His hands clenched and released and clenched and released. It looked as though he was practicing what he was going to do to Toombs' neck should he get hold of it.

Willy too kept his eyes on Marshall. With deliberate poise, Marshall rose, careful not to do anything that would prompt untimely action, which would certainly lead to someone's untimely death.

"You! The cripple!" Toombs shouted.

"His name's Willy!" Marshall said. "And leave my brother out of this, Toombs!"

"You're in no position to give orders, Morgan," Toombs sneered. To Willy: "Pick up the rifles."

Willy looked to Marshall, who nodded his approval. Working

his crutch with one arm, Willy picked up the rifles with the other. Marshall had to give Toombs credit. Willy was the only one among them who, because of his crutch, could not turn one of the weapons on the slave hunters in an inattentive moment.

"Now, everyone out of the ravine." Toombs motioned with his rifle toward the graveyard. With Marshall leading the way, Toombs and a silent, straight-faced Watkins matched their progress along the descending ridge. Upon reaching level ground, both slave hunters were cautious to keep their distance.

"You can't shoot all of us," Marshall said. "All I have to do is give the signal and half of us will come after you and the other half after Watkins. One shot each, that's all you'll have time to get off."

"And my shot will be at your head!" Toombs shouted. Red skin blazed through the patchy beard on his cheeks. Marshall wanted to keep him off-balance, but not push him to irrational action. "Besides, Marshall, I don't want to kill you, I just want to bury you." His wicked laugh echoed in the ravine.

The western twilight had faded to dark. The moon was full and on the rise, casting enough light to make strong shadows. A stiff breeze came from the river. It tumbled leaves across the tops of the graves. The silent Watkins stood so still he almost looked like a cemetery statue.

"Watkins," Marshall said, "surely you can't be in agreement with . . ."

"Shut up, Morgan, or I swear I'll kill you!" Toombs raged. His patchy cheeks puffed up and down in anger. Marshall raised his hands in silent surrender.

Toombs scanned the graveyard with quick, nervous glances. "Over there!" he cried. "That one!" He indicated a grave that was covered with a mound of fresh dirt. "Dig it up!"

Without exception the runaways burst into cries of fear.

"Shut up! Shut up! Shut up!" Toombs waved his rifle at them menacingly.

"They's afraid!" Hatfield cried. "They's afraid of the dead!"

"The dead can't kill them," Toombs shouted, "but I can! I need a coffin. Now dig it up!"

Shoulder to shoulder, the runaways backed away an inch at time.

"I'll shoot!" Toombs yelled. He swung his rifle their direction.

Seeing his chance, Marshall started toward Toombs. The slave hunter was on his guard. The rifle swung back before Marshall could take half a step.

Just then the runaways bolted, going twelve different directions. Toombs shouted and threatened, but he did not dare take his rifle off Marshall. Likewise, Watkins covered the big deacon. Willy fumbled with the rifles, trying to aim one. All of them fell uselessly to the ground. In a matter of moments not a runaway was in sight.

Frank Toombs jawed and spit for nearly two minutes over his loss. "You have been nothing but trouble to me, Morgan. Nothing but trouble! We'll round them up again, but in the meantime I still have you. And believe me, I'm going to make the most of this. Now get over to that grave!"

Prodded with rifle barrels, Marshall and Hatfield dropped to their knees and began digging up the grave with their hands. Willy used his crutch to loosen the dirt.

"Why are we doing this?" Marshall asked.

"Shut up and dig!"

"Toombs, digging with our hands is going to take us all night!"

"I said shut up and dig!"

Still on his knees, Marshall raised up. "Think, Toombs, there's got to be a caretaker's shack around here someplace.

At least let me see if I can find us some shovels."

Seeing the logic in Marshall's request, Toombs instructed Willy to look for the shack with Watkins guarding him. Within minutes a pounding was heard, then the sound of splitting wood. Not long after that Watkins and Willy returned with shovels.

The digging went quickly after that. Before long they hit the top of a wooden coffin and hauled it to the surface.

Standing in the grave, a dirt-covered Marshall asked, "Now what?"

"Dump the body," Toombs said.

"What?"

"You heard me, dump the body! That is, unless you want company when you get buried!"

Hatfield spoke up. "Mas'r Toombs, don't do this."

"DUMP THE BODY!" Toombs screamed.

Offering Marshall a hand, Hatfield pulled him out of the grave. Willy sat on the ground at the head of the grave closest to Watkins.

While Hatfield and Marshall pried the lid off the coffin, Toombs said, "When you shut me up in that coffin, Morgan, I swore I'd do the same to you someday. Only I'm gonna do worse. I'm gonna put you in that coffin and then we're gonna plant you in the ground. And if I feel like it, maybe, just maybe we'll dig you up, say after an hour or two."

Marshall strained at the lid with the edge of the shovel, but his eyes were on Toombs. *His kind was not going to go away easily. No matter what you did to stop them, they would always come back. It was men like Frank Toombs, men who profited from the suffering of others, that prompted John Brown to rise up in righteous anger. And it was men like Frank Toombs who killed him.*

With a screeching groan the lid of the coffin fell to the ground. A white woman, her hands resting peacefully on her midriff and dressed up in Sunday morning attire complete with bonnet, occupied the box.

"Dump the body!" Toombs shouted.

Marshall looked at Hatfield and nodded. Then he glanced at Willy. Marshall gripped one end of the coffin, Hatfield the other. Once again, Marshall caught Hatfield's eyes. With his head he motioned the direction in which they would tilt the coffin.

With all their might, they threw the coffin toward Frank Toombs. The body of the dead woman flew out and tumbled toward the slave hunter. With a shriek, he jumped backward out of the way. At the same moment, Willy threw his crutch at Watkins, catching him soundly in the midsection.

While Hatfield ran to assist Willy before Watkins could catch his breath, Marshall lunged at Toombs. He caught the slave hunter still reeling backwards. The two of them crashed to the ground, the impact knocking the weapon from Toombs' hands.

Watkins was easily subdued by the much larger Negro. Scrambling on his knees, Willy had retrieved the slave hunter's rifle.

Marshall pinned Toombs to the ground. The man beneath him, red-faced and sweating profusely, sputtered murderous threats. *His kind was not going to go away easily. No matter what you did to stop them, they would always come back.* Without letting up, Marshall reached for the rifle. He lay it across Frank Toombs' throat and pressed down.

The slave hunter gagged. Fat hands gripped the rifle as he tried to free himself.

They always come back. They always come back.

Gurgling sounds came from his throat. He tried to speak Marshall's name, but he could barely make a sound.

Only one way to stop his kind.

"Marshall!" Hatfield cried out. "Don't do it! In the name

of God, son, don't do it!"

They only understand one thing.

"Marshall?" It was Willy. "Marshall?"

With all his might, Marshall Morgan pushed down on the rifle barrel until the slave hunter's fat hands fell to the ground, lifeless. Calmly, Marshall placed the rifle on the ground. He stood over the body. He didn't shake. Nor did he feel any guilt. In fact, he didn't feel anything at all.

"Marshall," Willy cried. "You killed him!"

Brushing the dirt from his clothes, Marshall walked away from the body. With a voice that sounded like something he dug up from the grave, he said, "Without the shedding of blood, there is no remission of sin."

"Have you noticed anything different about your brother Marshall since his return?"

"Hmm?" Sarah said, sounding half asleep.

"Sorry if I interrupted your thoughts," Jeremiah said.

Father and daughter rode side-by-side in the family carriage. It was one of those April days when the sky couldn't be bluer, nor the fields greener, nor the air fresher. Spring had come early to Ohio and Sarah was making the most of it. Her eyes closed, she was basking in the sun's warmth, inviting it to penetrate her skin and melt the winter chill in her bones.

The two of them were on their way to Cincinnati, specifically Lane Theological Seminary. Once a year Jeremiah delivered a series of addresses to the ministers-in-training on the importance of the family in parish ministry. For as long as Sarah could remember, she accompanied her father on these trips.

As the family story went—Sarah couldn't remember the event herself—four-year-old Sarah was taken to the porch along with her two older brothers and baby Willy to wave good-bye to Father, who was off on his annual pilgrimage.

However, Sarah refused to wave. With fists wedged against her hips and her lower lip protruding, she complained that she was always waving good-bye to others, but nobody ever waved good-bye to her. To placate his daughter, Jeremiah suggested she ride with him as far as the main road. Lifting Sarah into the carriage, the whole family waved good-bye to her, including baby Willy who was three at the time. But when they reached the main road, Sarah refused to get out of the carriage. There was nothing anybody could do to persuade her. That was the first year Sarah accompanied her father to the seminary. Since then it had become a father-daughter tradition.

During those early visits little Sarah reveled in the opulent attention she received from the all-male students and faculty. After she learned to read, she looked forward to the annual journey to Cincinnati because of the seminary's library. While her father lectured, she would steal away into a corner or under a tree and read. For the last several years, now that she was no longer a little girl, a woman alone under a tree seemed to attract the male students like moths to a flame. She found the interruptions bothersome and each year she determined it would be her last. But then her father would make such a fuss about how much he enjoyed her company on the trips, she didn't have the heart to tell him she didn't want to go with him anymore.

At least the ride there and back was still enjoyable. It was the one time of year it was just the two of them together, without any other family or church members around. In the early days, Jeremiah prompted his daughter with questions just to pass the time. But now that Sarah was older, the conversations were an exchange of ideas, opinions, and dreams. Sarah was exposed to a personal side of her father she never saw at any other time of the year. What was more, her father listened to what she had to say. He seemed to value her opinions and observations.

"Did you ask me something?" Sarah asked. She opened her eyes. At first, everything around her was colorless from the bright light. Then, gradually, the rich colors of the surrounding landscape were restored.

"I was asking about Marshall. Have you noticed any change in him since he returned from Harper's Ferry?"

Sarah chuckled. "I think the whole world has noticed a difference. He's so serious. And moody."

Jeremiah nodded his head in agreement. "I'm concerned about him."

"I'm not defending his moodiness, but how can a person see the things he has seen and not be changed?" Sarah asked.

"We are not who we are because of the people and events around us!" Jeremiah said sharply, perhaps a little too sharply. In a more civil tone but still forceful, he completed his thought. "We are who we are because of our choices. We determine our attitudes and our actions."

With lowered eyes, Sarah replied: "It seems like everyone is angry these days. And frightened."

They rode in silence for a while.

Jeremiah cleared his throat. "I just remembered. I have something for you. Letters. They're in that satchel behind the seat."

Sarah's eyes brightened. Eagerly she turned in her seat and reached for the satchel. Letters from Daniel. It had to be. She had written five letters and had not heard a word from him in return. Grabbing two bundles of letters from the bottom of the satchel, she eagerly turned forward in her seat to open them. Her face recorded her disappointment.

"These are my letters!" she cried.

"The second bundle is mine."

Sarah broke the string on one bundle, then the other, examining the faces of the unopened letters. In hastily scribbled letters the word REFUSED appeared on each one.

"That's Seth's handwriting," Jeremiah said. "On yours as well. I doubt Daniel even knows you have written to him. I'm sorry, Sarah."

Tears blurred her vision, subduing the springtime hues all around her.

"You were speaking of angry people. I fear my friend Seth and your Daniel are among them. I never thought I'd see this day."

Jeremiah blinked back tears of his own. Seeing the hurt in her father's eyes only made Sarah weep all the more. In Sarah's mind, her father had always been an unshakable pillar of resolve. She'd not thought of him needing anyone, besides God, of course. As the pastor of the community, people always came to him when they were hurting. Sharing his strength and wisdom with them, he always made them feel better, stronger. But whom does the pastor go to when he is hurting? Whom does the pastor confide in when his best friend ends their lifelong relationship?

Sarah reached over and lay her hand on her father's forearm. Without looking at her, he smiled and wiped away a tear that had escaped and was making its way down his cheek.

"It seems we have this in common," Jeremiah said in a choked voice. "We both care deeply for someone who is on the other side of this great conflict."

"Daniel still loves me," Sarah said softly. "I'm sure of it."

Jeremiah patted her hand on his arm. "So am I, dear. So am I." Then, inhaling deeply to strengthen himself, he added, "But Mr. Gifford, the postmaster, has advised me to stop writing to Seth, and you to Daniel."

"Why?"

"Well, it seems that a federal official returned these letters to Point Providence. And he was asking a lot of questions about us. Our sympathies toward government figures, loyalty to the country, feelings about the South—that kind of thing. Mr. Gifford suggested that considering the current political climate, it would be wise not to correspond too frequently with people in Virginia. Our friendship with the Coopers might be misconstrued as disloyalty to the government, particularly if Virginia follows the other Southern states and secedes."

"Nobody is going to stop me from writing to Daniel, no matter what happens between the North and South!" Sarah stated indignantly.

"There are forces at work here that are far greater than our two families," Jeremiah replied. "Besides, what good does it do to write if the person you're writing to never receives the letter?"

"I don't care," Sarah said. "I'll find a way to get my letters to him. Even if I have to deliver them myself!"

The carriage passed through the gates leading to Lane Theological Seminary. Their arrival cut off further conversation on the matter.

Sarah had found a book in the library on the parables of Jesus. The subject interested her in ways other than the primary spiritual instruction. Jesus, the master teacher, chose to use simple stories to communicate deep spiritual truths. This was the same kind of thing she wanted to do with her stories.

Searching for a quiet place to read, one that was far away from the regular flow of seminary foot traffic, she thought she found one in a little alcove between wings of a building. Bushes block its view from the walkway, only the end of a stone bench could be seen. However, if she sat on the end closest to the bush . . .

"Oh, excuse me!"

Stepping into the alcove, Sarah discovered another woman had already occupied her hiding place. She was a kindly woman in her mid-fifties with round eyes which were soft and friendly. Black hair parted down the middle of her head and fell to ringlets on both sides. Her nose began thick at the bridge and continued that same width all the way down to full lips. An open book lay in her lap.

"Forgive me," Sarah said, "I didn't know anyone was here."

"Well, this is a pleasant surprise," said the woman. "I'm usually interrupted by young men. It's not often I meet another woman on campus." She saw the book in Sarah's hands and her eyebrows raised in understanding. "You came here to hide too, didn't you? It's a wonderful spot. I found it years ago. Come join me."

"Thank you, no. I'm interrupting you."

"Nonsense. Please join me. I have only a few minutes more, then you can have my spot. Only I don't understand why an attractive young woman like you would want to hide from a campus filled with eligible young men."

Sarah smiled sweetly and sat next to the woman. "I'm not looking for a husband," she said. "I already know who I'm going to marry."

"Does he attend school here?"

"No. He lives in Virginia."

Again the woman's eyebrows raised and Sarah was struck by the absurdity of the times. Just a few months ago no one would have thought anything of the fact that Daniel lived in Virginia. But now, with war so close at hand, the fact raised eyebrows.

"I met my husband here," the woman said. She smoothed the book on her lap with her hands as the memory warmed her.

"Is he with you now?" Sarah asked.

"Yes, he is. We came all the way from Maine so that he could attend the lectures by Jeremiah Morgan. My father has raved about Mr. Morgan for years, but we have been so busy we've never found the time to attend. Until this year."

"Jeremiah Morgan is my father."

One hand went to the woman's chest in surprised delight, the other reached out and touched Sarah on the forearm. "Oh my, what a pleasant surprise! My dear, I hope you appreciate how richly God has blessed you to have a father like him."

"I'm very proud of my father," Sarah said. "I come with him every year for these lectures. It's a special time for us."

"I can imagine it is! And you read while he is lecturing?"

"Sometimes I read, sometimes I like to write."

"You're a writer?"

"Nobody has published my writing yet, but they will someday, God willing."

"What do you write? Poems? Essays?"

"Some poetry, but mostly I want to write books. Novels. I want to write stories that will change people's view of things. Much like Harriet Beecher Stowe has done with her book, *Uncle Tom's Cabin.*"

Again the eyebrows went up. "You have read the book?"

"Oh yes! It is wonderfully written! And you?"

"I'm surprised at the reception the book has received. It's not what I would consider literature, but it's a good story. It could be better. Do you want to write antislavery stories too?"

"No. My stories are based on biblical proverbs. To put it in a sentence, my stories teach people that God's ways are always best."

"How interesting! Do you have any of your stories with you? I'd like to read some if you don't mind."

Sarah proudly produced her novel about Truly Noble which her new friend browsed with obvious interest. At the woman's prompting, Sarah described the plot in detail and answered a myriad of questions about characterization and theme and dialogue.

"You are quite knowledgeable about literature," Sarah said.

"I come by it honestly. My father was an educator. And my husband was professor of biblical literature here at Lane Theological Seminary when we met and married. I've taught a little, and written some myself."

"Oh? What kind of things do you write?"

"Poetry. Novels."

"Have you ever had anything published?"

The woman smiled warmly. "Yes, as a matter of fact, I just had a novel published a little over a year ago, entitled *The Minister's Wooing.*"

A skeptical look crossed Sarah's face. "I've heard of that novel," she said slowly. "Only you didn't write it. It was written by Harriet Beecher Stowe."

"You are partly right," said the woman. "It was written by Harriet Beecher Stowe. But you were wrong in saying I didn't write it, for I did. I *am* Harriet Beecher Stowe."

If Sarah's chin had not been attached to her face at the jaw with bone and muscle, it would have dropped to the ground. But what the woman said made sense. It was Lyman Beecher, Mrs. Stowe's father, who had first enlisted Jeremiah to deliver the family lectures. Lyman Beecher was president of Lane Theological Seminary at the time. Sarah knew that Mrs. Stowe had lived in Cincinnati for a number of years and was associated with the school, but never had she imagined she would actually meet the famous author someday.

"Oh, Mrs. Stowe, can you ever forgive me! I had no idea it was you I was talking to. I feel like such a fool, carrying on about my writing when you are such an accomplished author. I'm so embarrassed!"

"You have nothing to be embarrassed about, child," Mrs. Stowe said, patting Sarah on the hand. "And please don't carry on as though I were someone important."

"But you *are* someone important!" Sarah insisted.

"Nonsense. I am the wife of a poor professor who happens to write. God, in His goodness, has seen fit to use my fledgling efforts to open people's eyes regarding the evils of slavery."

"But you have toured Europe, and had a royal audience in England, and your book has been translated into different languages and read around the world. How can you say that you are not someone important?"

"Simple, child. Because I am not." She chuckled. "You remind me so much of my brother Edward. He wrote me a very concerned letter not long after *Uncle Tom's Cabin* was published in book form. He was disturbed lest all the praise and notoriety should induce pride and vanity, and work harm to my Christian character." Her eyes closed and she smiled sweetly as she thought back on it. "Dear soul, he need not have been troubled. He didn't know that I did not write that book."

"What?" Sarah exclaimed. "You did not write *Uncle Tom's Cabin?*"

"No," Mrs. Stowe said, "I only put down what I saw."

"Had you ever been to the South?"

"No. The story came before me in visions, one after another, and I put them down in words."

Sarah looked skeptical. "Still, you must have arranged the events."

Mrs. Stowe shook her head. "No. In fact a close friend of mine reproached me for letting Eva die. Why, I couldn't help it! I felt as badly as anyone! It was like a death in my own family, and it affected me so deeply that I could not write a word for two weeks after her death."

"And did you know," Sarah asked, "that Uncle Tom would die?"

"Oh yes," she answered, "I knew that he must die from the first, but I did not know how. When I got to that part of the story, I saw no more for some time. I was physically exhausted too. I remember being very tired when we returned to our boarding house for the early midday dinner. After dinner we went to our room to rest. Mr. Stowe threw himself upon the bed; I was to use the lounge. But suddenly arose before me the death scene of Uncle Tom with what led to it—and George's visit to him. I sat down at the table and wrote nine pages of foolscap paper without pausing, except long enough to dip my pen into the inkstand. Just as I had finished, Mr. Stowe awoke. 'Wife,' he said, 'have not you lain down yet?' 'No,' I answered. 'I have been writing, and I want you to listen to this and see if it will do.' I read aloud to him with the tears flowing fast. He wept too, and before I had finished, his sobs shook the bed upon which he was lying. He sprang up, saying, 'Do! I should think it would do!' And folding the sheets he immediately directed and sent them to the publisher, without one word of correction or revision of any kind."

Sarah sat reverently next to Mrs. Stowe, drinking in every word she said. "What a wonderful story! Do you show everything you write to your husband?"

The author nodded. "I value his opinion highly. And what of your Southern gentleman? Does he read your work?"

Sarah blushed at the reference to Daniel. "He doesn't read much, but that's not to say he's illiterate. On the contrary, he's quite intelligent! He does, however, like to hear my stories. Whenever we're together, we'll find a shady tree. He'll lay his head in my lap and I'll read my stories and poetry to him."

With a glint of jesting in her eyes, Mrs. Stowe said, "No wonder the young man doesn't read them for himself with an arrangement like that! I can tell you love him very much, just by the way you talk of him."

Sarah's blush deepened. Her gaze lowered to her lap. "I love him more than my own life." Her voice choked. "Only, I don't know what's to become of us with this cursed crisis between the South and the North."

After a reflective moment, Mrs. Stowe said, "Am I going to get to read your complete manuscript?"

"Oh, would you? You are so kind . . . but that's asking too much of you."

The kindly eyes and gentle smile that appeared on Mrs. Stowe's face were genuine. "I would consider it a privilege." She held out her hands to receive the manuscript.

Sarah extended it as though it were a treasure box filled with the crown jewels of England. She hesitated. "It's the only copy I have, so please . . . oh, listen to me! How shameful. You are so gracious to do this for me, and here I am . . ."

"You are absolutely right to be cautious!" Mrs. Stowe cried. "I promise to guard it as though it were my very own."

"And you'll tell me what you think of it? What you like and don't like?"

"I will give it a thorough critique. And may I share it with my husband? He is quite insightful in literary and biblical matters."

"Of course, you may! O Mrs. Stowe, how can I ever thank you? Just look at me!" Sarah extended a hand. "I'm so giddy, I'm shaking!"

With Sarah's manuscript securely in her lap, Harriet Beecher Stowe pressed Sarah's shaking limb between her own hands. "You know, dear, I almost didn't come with Mr. Stowe on this trip. But his health is so fragile, I thought he might need me. However, these last few days, he has never been stronger, and I was beginning to think I should not have come. Until now. Meeting you and having this chance to read your story has made this trip worthwhile."

Chapter 8

FOR over a decade the dam that held back a nation's rage had held firm. That was not to say it had not suffered cracks. Bleeding Kansas, the trial and execution of John Brown, the Southern states seceding from the Union—each of these had caused rifts in the dam, but it had not toppled. With the attack on Fort Sumter, South Carolina, on April 12, 1861 the dam sprang a leak. A substantial one. Within hours it became apparent that the leak was irreparable. The nation readied itself for the worst.

Throughout the North and South the telegraph wires were hot with news. In Point Providence each new appearance by telegraph operator Henry Wier was greeted with apprehension. These were people living in the shadow of the dam. When the dam burst, it would be their homes, their families, their lives swept away by the flood of released rage.

Henry Wier stood on his step with message in hand. Before unfolding it, he checked behind him to make sure no one was reading over his shoulder. This was his standard practice since his preempted election announcement. This morning he checked twice, a signal that something big had happened. Those assembled shielded their eyes against the bright, early morning sunlight, awaiting the news.

It was Friday. J.D. Morgan stood with his arm around

Jenny Parsons' waist. Willy was next to his mother. Marshall stood alone on the fringe in the shade of a tree. Jeremiah and Sarah weren't due back from Cincinnati until Saturday.

Henry Wier called for everyone's attention. With one last glance over his shoulder, he unfolded the dispatch. The corners of the paper shivered in his hands. With furrowed brow and twitching lower lip, the lanky telegraph operator looked like he was about to announce the end of the world.

AT 4:30 A.M. SOUTH. . . . His voice cracked. With a dry, coughing sound he cleared his throat and began again. AT 4:30 A.M. SOUTH CAROLINA SHORE BATTERIES UNDER COMMAND OF GENERAL PIERRE G.T. BEAUREGARD OPENED FIRE ON FORT SUMTER, A FEDERAL INSTALLATION IN CHARLESTON HARBOR. AT THIS HOUR THE FORT CONTINUES TO BE BOMBARDED. THERE IS NO OFFICIAL WORD FROM PRESIDENT LINCOLN YET REGARDING THE ATTACK. Lowering the dispatch, Henry spoke in his own words. "I've been informed that there will be hourly reports by wire. These I will read to you as soon as they arrive."

Dozens of questions were simultaneously fired at Henry. He waved them off. "I've told you everything I know!" he shouted. "When I hear more, I'll pass it on to you!"

For two hours the town milled around in front of the telegraph office. Then, after the first two hourly reports provided little additional information, the crowd began to dwindle. Essentially the news was that the bombardment continued with heavy damage to the fort. The number of lives lost was not known. The third report sounded almost exactly like the first two. So most people returned to their normal end-of-the-week routines. Only a handful remained. They promised to spread the news should there be any new developments. The Morgans and Jenny were among those who returned to their routine, all except for Marshall. With folded arms, he leaned against the tree and waited for each hourly report. He spoke to no one.

Henry remained faithful at his telegraph office post into the night. More people went home. As late Friday turned into early Saturday morning, Marshall alone was left to hear the reports. Illuminated by the moon, Henry would take his position on the step and read each telegraph aloud to the empty street. He would then look toward the tree. The dark shape of Marshall Morgan was still there, his arms still folded.

The first light of dawn saw Henry's audience increase, only to dwindle again as the reports droned on—fort still under attack, reinforcements stopped at the mouth of the harbor, casualties unknown. By midday Saturday only a handful of people waited in front of the telegraph office.

3 P.M. Lanky Henry Wier fumbled with the door in his hurry to get out. He began shouting—he didn't look over his shoulder, nor did he wait until he reached his step. "Fort Sumter surrenders! Fort Sumter surrenders!" Marshall Morgan walked from under the tree into the sunlight. Within minutes a breathless Henry Wier read the complete text to a full crowd: AT 2:30 P.M. TODAY THE STARS AND STRIPES WERE LOWERED INSIDE FORT SUMTER. IN ITS PLACE ROSE A WHITE BED SHEET SIGNIFYING THE FORT'S SURRENDER. MAJOR ROBERT ANDERSON, COMMANDER OF THE UNION TROOPS, HAS AGREED TO EVACUATE THE FORT TOMORROW, SUNDAY, APRIL 14TH. MORE TO FOLLOW.

Bedlam erupted in the streets of Point Providence. Shouts. Arguments. Questions. Threats of reprisal. Talk of war. Henry Wier glanced toward the tree to see the reaction of the one man who had stayed with him through the night. The shade under the tree was unoccupied. Marshall Morgan was nowhere in sight.

Later that night, among the flood of news reports over the wire, a message arrived for J.D. Morgan. It read: DELAYED IN CINCINNATI. WAR TALK. PREACH FOR ME TOMORROW. WILL RETURN LATE TUESDAY. SARAH HAS GOOD NEWS. It was signed, FATHER.

◆ ◆ ◆

J.D. rose to preach. Every seat of the church was occupied. Men, women, and children jammed the aisles. The crowd was so great, the overflow trailed out the front door and fanned out to the horses and carriages. People bunched together near the open windows to hear the sermon. Everyone was talking war.

The night before when Marshall learned that J.D. was preaching, he pressed his older brother to preach on Hebrews 9:22, *And almost all things are by the law purged with blood; and without shedding of blood is no remission.* J.D. deferred, choosing instead to preach a sermon he titled: "A Psalmist Goes to War."

Two Scripture passages served as the basis of his message: Psalm 120:7: *I am for peace: but when I speak, they are for war.* Developing the text, J.D. proposed that although a man after God's own heart desires peace, sometimes he is forced to go to war. Applying his premise to the present crisis, he said that the North had spoken out against slavery, and rightfully so. That the words of the North had angered the South. And now the Southern states wanted war. "What choice is now left to the man of peace?" he cried. "We have no choice! The man of peace must gird himself for war."

The second Scripture J.D. read described the psalmist's faith on the battlefield. Psalm 27:3-4: *Though an host should encamp against me, my heart shall not fear: though war should rise against me, in this will I be confident. One thing have I desired of the Lord, that will I seek after; that I may dwell in the house of the Lord all the days of my life.*

J.D. concluded: "Though the heart of God's people is for peace, should war come, the Christian warrior will find his strength in God."

It was an even-tempered approach to the national crisis. In

other pulpits, preachers thundered with denunciations of the rebellion. Some preachers argued it was better that the land be drenched with blood than that any further concessions be made to the slaveocracy of the South. At Point Providence the sermon reflected the preacher's nonviolent temperament, leaving those who were hungry for war wanting more.

"Your father would be proud of you," Mother said, hugging her eldest son.

"It's the kind of sermon your father would have preached had he been here," Jenny said, also giving J.D. a hug.

"Exactly like Father would have preached," Marshall chimed in. But from his tone, the remark was not a compliment.

That afternoon, while the people of Point Providence talked and talked and talked of the coming war, Marshall packed his bags. When war came, he wanted to be ready.

He didn't have to wait long.

Monday, April 15, 1861. Henry Wier once again took his position on the step outside the telegraph office. After glancing over his shoulder, he began to read: PRESIDENT ABRAHAM LINCOLN HAS CALLED FOR SEVENTY-FIVE THOUSAND VOLUNTEERS TO JOIN THE ARMY. THEY WILL SERVE FOR THREE MONTHS TO RE-POSSESS THE FORTS AND PLACES AND PROPERTY OF THE UNITED STATES WHICH HAVE BEEN UNLAWFULLY SEIZED. Henry added: "This is it, folks. We're at war."

By late afternoon on Tuesday Point Providence men were marching off to war. Actually, they were marching off to enlist and train for war, but you couldn't tell it by their send-off celebration. Drum and fife music thrilled the air with a stirring call-to-arms. A hastily formed company formed ranks. Hats varied from man to man, as did clothing and weaponry. Some wore old army coats from the Mexican War. Gun barrels and bayonets flashed in the sunlight as they marched. Flags and bunting blossomed everywhere. Pretty young ladies leaned over window sills and waved handkerchiefs and blew kisses. The national crisis acted like an elixir on the people of Point Providence. It brought blood to people's cheeks and spring to their legs. Merchants and clerks and teachers and housewives all came out to cheer on the local volunteers.

The three Morgan boys were among them. J.D. had wanted them to delay their departure until after their father returned home, but in doing so they would have missed the parade. Even so, Willy and Marshall never would have agreed to wait. It was hard to tell which of the two younger brothers was more eager to go to war. Willy was the emotional one, excited to the point of being giddy; Marshall dutifully grabbed his bag and rifle. With lips pressed together in grim determination he walked the road that led out of town.

J.D. caught one last glimpse of Jenny. She was standing beside his mother in front of the church. His thoughts turned to their last moments together the night before.

The porch swing moaned in rhythmic sympathy as the two young lovers swung lazily back and forth. Other than an occasional rattle of dishes in the kitchen, the only sound to be heard was that of the swing. All that could be said had been said. The two of them found greater comfort in the warmth of their nearness and the steady rise and fall of their breathing than words could afford. Her arms draped around J.D.'s neck, Jenny's head rested on his chest.

"It's time for me to go," J.D. whispered. He kissed the top of her head.

Jenny tightened her grip. "If I don't let go of you, you'll have to stay with me."

"Are you taking me prisoner?"

She pulled away. "You make it sound like something unpleasant."

"Not at all! It's just that if I'm to be your prisoner, I want to know what is expected of me."

"That's easy," she said, snuggling against him again. "You will be at my beck and call, fulfilling my every whim."

"I do that already."

"You monster!" she squealed playfully. "You're horrible!"

"Did I say I was complaining?" he defended himself.

She dug her fingers into his ribs where he was most ticklish. He squirmed to get free, attempting to grab her wrists. The swing rocked madly as they wrestled for position. J.D. finally succeeded in capturing the attacking appendages. It was a draw. She couldn't tickle him as long as he held her wrists; he couldn't release her wrists for fear of a renewed attack. Nose to nose they laughed at their stalemate.

"Truce?" J.D. asked.

"Why should I agree to a truce? You can't hold me forever."

"I'd sure like to try."

Her eyes glistened with tears. "Please try," she said.

The next moment they were in each other's arms, holding on with all their might while the porch swing sang its mournful song.

Tents sprang up at the Adams County campground as men and militia poured in from all parts of the state to form the Ohio Volunteers Infantry Regiment. The company from Point Providence, having selected the nickname "Jehovah's Avengers," followed the example of the other arriving militias. They met around a campfire to choose their leader.

"The first thing we do," said a bearded veteran of the Mexican War, "is to elect a captain."

"Elect one?" J.D. asked. "Won't the army send us trained officers?"

The veteran, Vern Hawkins, a big-chested cabinetmaker

and friend of Pastor Jeremiah Morgan replied, "Not likely. You see, the way the army thinks, we's more likely to follow one of our own than some military school outsider."

"Fine. Should we elect a moderator to oversee the election?"

"Not necessary since you will most likely be our only candidate," Hawkins said. Turning to the others he said, "I nominates J.D. Morgan."

"Wait! Wait a minute!" J.D. objected. "I know nothing of military matters. Plus, I don't have any experience in soldiering. We need a candidate who knows what he's doing!"

"Not so." Hawkins stood and addressed the company. "Take it from me, lads. When them bullets start flyin' we need someone leadin' us we believe in. Someone we know won't let us down. As for tactics and that sort of thing, J.D.'s smart. He can learn that stuff right soon enough. That's what military manuals is for. Let me tell you, I found out what war is all about in Mexico. And I want a commander who will do what's right for us and not charge us up some hill into the face of enemy fire just because some fool general's got a notion he wants to see what's on the other side." Hawkins placed a hand on J.D.'s shoulder. "I know'd this boy since he was a tadpole. And he won't be afraid to speak up for us, general or no general. This is the man I wants to follow into battle. Who's with me?"

A small sea of hands rose in affirmation. Willy's hand shot up quickly. Marshall stood in the back off to himself. He didn't raise his hand, but catching J.D.'s eye he nodded his assent.

"Congratulations, Cap'n." The veteran thrust forward a fleshy paw which J.D. shook. "Now I'll go find you one o' them army manuals."

J.D. sat alone by the fire outside his tent. Most of the men had retired. He yawned, rubbed burning eyes, and adjusted his position on a rock so that the light of the fire better illuminated the page he was reading. True to his word, Vern Hawkins brought him not one, but two different army manuals. The older of the two was a French work, translated by General Winfield Scott in 1835. It incorporated a lot of French phrases and obscure jargon with which J.D. was unfamiliar. He preferred the second manual. It was newly revised and updated by William J. Hardee. It included maneuvers that were designed to incorporate the influence of the new rifled musket.

Hardee taught that the line of battle moved in two ranks, one behind the other. Skirmishers moved in advance of the main lines, operating in four-man squads. According to Hardee, the time step for double quick speed was up to 180 steps a minute. The manual claimed that infantrymen with rifled muskets should be able to fire two or three rounds per minute. He also advised target practice to improve marksmanship rather than depend on the old volley method of firing.

J.D. lowered the manual. There was so much to learn, all of it crucial. Lives depended on him knowing this material. Not just any lives—the lives of the men of his hometown. How could he ever return to Point Providence and face a widow or mother knowing that his mistake had cost the soldier his life? He raised the manual to the light and tried to continue. He couldn't. The lines blurred and ran together. "God help me," he prayed.

Reveille sounded at 5 A.M. The volunteers stumbled out of their tents, jarred awake by the trumpet call. They formed a line of sorts in an assorted state of dress. Some of them had only one sock or shoe, unaccustomed to finding their clothes in the dark. A succession of dry coughs ran up and down the line.

The drilling began. With army manual in hand J.D. taught Jehovah's Avengers how to stand with their toes out at an angle of forty-five degrees. Bellies in. Chests out. When their captain was convinced they knew how to stand they were sent to breakfast.

Following breakfast they drilled until dinner, the noonday meal, after which they drilled for two or three more hours as a regiment. Around 5 P.M., after they had been engaged for a full twelve hours, they were dismissed for an hour to prepare themselves and their weapons for dress parade at 6 P.M. — which, admittedly, meant more once they got uniforms. Once that was done, they had dinner from huge boiling cauldrons in front of the mess tents. After eating, their time was their own until lights out at 9 P.M.

Day after day the schedule never varied. They would drill, and drill, then drill some more. The men grumbled, but not openly. Partly because of their leader's tireless example. Every day J.D. was up an hour before them. He retired an hour after them. During his free time he was studying the army manual. Yet still he struggled with all there was to know about being a company commander. There were so many commands to remember. And he knew that during a battle the enemy would not give him time to look up a forgotten command. His fear of forgetting a crucial order weighed heavily on him, so much so that he had nightmares about it.

On the day an army physician arrived, the entire regiment was lined up to be examined. The physician made his way down the rows of volunteers line-by-line. In a droning voice the same litany of questions was asked of each man: "Were you ever sick in your life? Have you got the rheumatism? Have you got varicose veins?" And other questions of like manner. If the answers to the questions satisfied him, he gave the soldier a thump on the chest and a couple of thumps on the back. He then pronounced the soldier in good physical shape and moved on to the next one in line.

After J.D. and Marshall were declared fit, the army physician approached Willy who had tossed his crutch aside. He stood straight as a board, balancing himself on his good foot. Without looking at him, the doctor launched into his litany. He recorded Willy's answers on a sheet of paper. Willy was thumped on his chest and back. The physician pronounced him fit and moved on.

"Yahoo!" Willy whooped.

His response brought a smirk from the physician who then repeated his questions to the next soldier. A freckled-faced boy awaiting examination turned to his buddy behind him and said in a loud voice, "Looks like they's takin' just about anybody, Jeb. That cripple just got in!"

The physician looked up from his form. His litany stopped mid-sentence. He whirled and looked down at Willy's feet. "Is this some kind of joke?" he shouted. Snatching Willy's paper, the physician tore it into pieces. "Well, I'm not laughing! Go home, young man," he ordered. With a snort he returned to the next soldier in line, but not before taking a quick glance at the soldier's feet.

"But I can do anything they can do!" Willy protested.

The physician ignored him.

Willy grabbed the physician's arm. "Let me show you! I can prove to you that I can . . . "

"Young man," the physician thundered. "This is a military camp. Either leave this camp on your own or I'll have you escorted off under armed guard!"

"Come on, Willy." It was Marshall, extending Willy's crutch to him. J.D. stood behind him, motioning for Willy to come with them.

Fighting back his emotions, Willy seized the crutch. With Marshall on one side of him and J.D. on the other, the three Morgan boys returned to their tent.

"Maybe you can't be an infantryman," J.D. said. "But you can be my aide or something like that. We'll find something for you to do so that we can stay together."

Limping along, Willy's response was an irate grunt.

When the physical examinations were concluded, the drilling resumed. Willy occupied himself by sketching. His first pictures were humorous ones of the physical examination process. In each of the drawings the humor was at the doctor's expense. One sketch showed the physician standing on tiptoes peering down a soldier's throat. The doctor's head was completely swallowed up. The caption read: "Feet? Soldiers got feet?"

After a few days he turned his attention to the routine of camp life. His subjects included blurry-eyed soldiers falling into formation at reveille; row after row of soldiers drilling in ragged columns, their chins cocked in pride, the company banner flying proudly; and spirited card games around the campfire at night. He captured the essence of army life—its dreary repetitious side as well as its camaraderie and patriotic sense of determination.

His renderings caught the attention of the soldiers who paid him money for them. Soon he was drawing individual portraits of soldiers standing at attention in their new uniforms or proudly displaying their guns. Some sketches were group portraits. The soldiers willingly paid good money for these individualized portraits which they sent home to their families and girlfriends.

From reveille to taps Willy fulfilled orders for sketches, making more money drawing pictures than he would have as a soldier. Yet he was a tormented man. He cared little for the money, even less for the popularity his talent brought him. All he knew was that he was sketching scenes of an army of which he could never be a part.

J.D. couldn't understand why he was having such a difficult time remembering commands. He studied at every opportunity, but the commands slipped from his memory like feet on a slippery rock. Besides a vast array of voice commands, there were a host of drum rolls and bugle calls to remember. There were fifteen general drum and twenty-six bugle calls, each signaling a distinct order. There were twenty-three more bugle and drum calls for skirmishers. There were calls to open ranks and close ranks, to shift from line of battle to a column and back again. Orders to change the front line of battle to meet a cavalry attack, and so forth. Many times when J.D. needed a specific command, though he'd repeated it in his mind a thousand times, he couldn't remember it. Like right now, for example.

With a row of trees and a stream to his right and a fence fast approaching straight ahead, J.D. couldn't remember the correct command to steer the company around the obstacles. He had seen the obstacles in the distance and figured he'd have plenty of time to recall the proper command. But try as he might, he couldn't come up with it. The fence loomed in front of them. He searched for alternative commands. None came to mind. The eyes of the men on the front line were growing wide with concern. *What to do?* He thought of the manual in his pocket. *Reaching for it now would surely shake the confidence of his men. But how much confidence would they have in him if he marched them into a fence?* They were just a few feet away. *These are good men,* he thought. *They'd probably march into the fence before they'd question my authority.* No matter how hard he tried, he couldn't remember the correct command.

"Company, halt!" he shouted.

The front line halted a foot away from the fence.

"Gentlemen, excellent job! We will now take a recess of ten minutes. Break ranks! And when you fall in, fall in on the other side of this fence."

Behind him the hoofs of an approaching horse could be

heard. "Remain in your ranks!" Reining to a halt was a young colonel. He sat rigid in the saddle. His unwrinkled uniform was so spotless it looked as though it had never been worn. Cold, hard eyes stared down at J.D.

"Report, Captain!"

J.D. saluted. "We were breaking to recess, sir."

"Are your men fatigued, Captain?"

"No sir."

"I should hope not. For if they were fatigued it would merely confirm the rumors I've heard about westerners being indolent puffers."

A murmur rippled though the company. The colonel showed no concern.

"So tell me, Captain, why were you breaking rank if your men are not fatigued?"

A sheepish look covered J.D.'s face. "You see, sir, all of this is new to me. And . . . well . . . I forgot the command that would get us around the fence." He shrugged and smiled.

The colonel did not return his smile. Nor did he appear sympathetic to J.D.'s plight.

"What is your name, soldier?"

"Captain J.D. Morgan, sir."

Upon hearing the name, the colonel's eyes squinted. He cocked his head slightly to one side as he studied J.D. "From Point Providence?"

"Yes sir."

J.D. wondered how the colonel knew where he was from. He looked for some sign of recognition in the colonel's eyes. He saw none. All he saw was a look as hard as iron.

"And I suppose the rank you claim is honorary."

"The men elected me, sir."

The colonel sniffed. "So much for western intelligence. Join your men, Morgan."

"Sir?"

"Fall in, soldier!"

J.D. stepped into line with the rest of his company. For the remainder of the afternoon the colonel drilled J.D.'s company from atop his horse. They marched until 6 P.M., an hour longer than any other company. When they were dismissed, it was time for dress parade. Having no time to change, they were then chastened for being late and unprepared for review. Their punishment was that they would drill in the dark until taps while the other companies ate and enjoyed leisure activities.

At 9 P.M. the dog-tired Point Providence company straggled in from the drill field. Willy met them.

"J.D.! What did you say to get that colonel so mad at you?"

Marshall answered for his older brother. "J.D. did nothing, Willy. That colonel was looking for someone to pick on. J.D. just happened to be the one he chose."

A figure blocked their way to the tent. It was the colonel. J.D. and Marshall came to attention.

"I wouldn't characterize gross negligence on the part of an officer as 'nothing,' soldier." He addressed Marshall. "What's your name?"

"Marshall Morgan, sir."

"I see," said the colonel, nodding his head. "And you are?"

"Willy, sir. Willy Morgan."

"Brothers." The way he said the word made it sound vulgar. He took his time staring at each Morgan. His face twisted into a look of distaste. "Well, gentlemen," he said, "I'm Colonel Benjamin McKenna, the new commander of this regiment. And I will not tolerate incompetence in my officers. What's more, I don't like brothers serving in the same company." To J.D.: "I'll decide later whether or not to replace you. My instincts tell me to break you to private." To Marshall: "Pack your knapsack, you're being transferred to a different company." To Willy: "And where are you staying?"

"With them in the company tent," Willy answered.

"No you're not," McKenna replied. "No civilians in camp."

He called for two guards and ordered them to escort Willy beyond the camp boundaries. Turning on his heel, Colonel McKenna strode away.

For the next two weeks Colonel McKenna closely supervised the daily drills of Jehovah's Avengers. He followed J.D. on his horse, staying so close to him that J.D. could feel the horse's breath down his neck all day long. Whenever J.D. made a mistake or showed hesitation in giving orders, McKenna rose up in his saddle and showered him with profanity-laced sarcasm. Nor was the colonel ever satisfied with the company's performance. According to McKenna they were a company of dolts, the offspring of a town of dolts.

One morning the men's uniforms were drenched with sweat by 9 A.M. and they had not yet begun to drill. For more than an hour Jehovah's Avengers had stood at attention facing the summer sun while Colonel McKenna inspected the other companies in the regiment. He had given J.D. explicit instructions that his company was not to move from the spot until he returned, "lest you injure them by marching them into a fence." So they stood—their faces dripping with sweat, their eyes red and squinting against the sun, their feet burning from the heat of the ground penetrating their shoes. The air was thick and hard to breathe. Insects swarmed around their faces, some of the smaller ones sticking to the corners of wet eyes and on cheeks and necks.

"I see you puffers have been enjoying your little rest," Colonel McKenna chided as he approached them on horseback. "No matter. You'll make up for it. Since you're starting your drill an hour later, you'll do two extra hours tonight. Looks like you're going to miss the evening meal again."

"Sir," J.D. addressed the colonel, "it is my incompetence that has immobilized these men for the past hour. It is only right that I should be punished, not them."

"I didn't ask for your opinion," McKenna barked.

"But, sir . . . "

"SHUT UP, MORGAN!" McKenna screamed. He sounded more like a little boy who wasn't getting his way than an army officer. "Take your men into the field. That's an order!"

J.D. ordered his men about-face and marched them onto the field. He caught a glimpse of Marshall, who for reasons unknown never received transfer orders. Though his brother's face was forward, his eyes were fixed on the colonel. They were overflowing with hatred.

By noon, three men in the company had fainted. McKenna wouldn't allow anyone to attend to them. He ordered the company to continue marching, over their fallen comrades, leaving them to lie facedown in the field.

"Company, halt!" A giant oak tree towered nearby, its arching branches heavy with leaves providing a wide expanse of shade.

"What are you doing, Morgan?" McKenna bellowed.

J.D. to his company: "Take a ten-minute recess. Use your canteens."

Without hesitation the men broke for the shade.

"Come back here!" McKenna growled.

Most of the men halted. Some of them, like horses toward a barn, stepped into the shade and collapsed. To those who heeded the colonel, J.D. said, "Go ahead, men. Ten minutes. I want to discuss something with the colonel."

In a flash McKenna was off his horse. His face purple with fury, the colonel stood toe-to-toe with J.D., the air around them thick with expletives. His arms waved like a broken windmill in a stiff gale. "You've done it this time, Morgan. Countermanding my orders is a court-marshal offense! Just who do you think you are? You're a nobody! A nobody!"

J.D. stood his ground. "I was just looking out for the men, sir. We'll lose enough of them on the battlefield. We can't afford to lose them on the drill field."

"I take it that's your expert military opinion! And on what do you base your expert opinion? Fifteen years of shucking corn? I know men, Morgan! I didn't graduate from West Point without knowing something about men."

J.D. looked over the colonel's shoulder at his company. They were sprawled in the shade like dead men. "I know *these* men, sir. I grew up with them. They're good men. You look after them and they'll look after you. Stepping all over them will not earn you their allegiance."

"Your men couldn't keep their own grandmothers dry in a spring shower!" McKenna roared. "They're not men, they're puffers—spineless blowhards who will assuredly run the first time they hear a gunshot."

J.D. had had enough. He was drenched in his own juices. His head buzzed from the heat. He inched closer to McKenna. The two men were similar. They were both the same height, both had brown hair and mustaches, both had blue eyes, and they were roughly the same age, the colonel being but a few years older. The difference between them was in their uniforms. In this comparison, McKenna had the clear advantage. But J.D. was standing so close to McKenna he could no longer see the insignia on the colonel's uniform.

"I'll put my men up against any other company, anytime, sir!" J.D. shouted.

"Spoken like a true puffer! All hot air and no substance!" McKenna pushed him away.

J.D.'s hands clenched. He charged forward.

"J.D., don't!" Marshall jumped between the two men, preventing his brother from striking.

"How quaint! Brothers sticking up for each other!" The colonel's voice was heavy with sarcasm.

Marshall turned toward his brother and backed him off. "He's not worth it, J.D."

"Haven't you been transferred yet, Brother Morgan? Your timely arrival accounts for the dramatic increase in the stench."

"Just walk away, J.D." Marshall continued to back his brother away.

"So what can I expect next from the Morgan brothers?" McKenna chided. "The cripple to sneak up behind me and hit me with his crutch?"

Marshall whirled around, fists flying. With one blow to the gut and another to the chin, McKenna was flat on his back. Insects swirled happily over the fallen colonel's head.

The flap of the tent wall lifted. J.D. watched as a middle-aged figure in civilian clothes ducked in.

"Father!" J.D. rose from his stool.

"Hello, son."

The two men shook hands. J.D. found his father another stool to sit on. "What are you doing here?" he asked.

Jeremiah lowered himself slowly onto the three-legged stool, not confident it would hold him. Once his full weight was on it, he tested it by bouncing slightly. When he was sure it would hold, he turned his attention to his son. "Pastoral visit," he said. "Thought I'd check on the other half of my congregation. You can imagine my surprise when they told me I had one son in the guardhouse and another confined to his tent."

"And a third son living outside the camp."

"Well, that one doesn't surprise me," Jeremiah said. "Willy was foolish to think he could join the infantry. You wrote me that he was making a living sketching portraits."

"That's right. And he was doing quite well until a couple of weeks ago." A concerned look crossed Jeremiah's face. "What happened?"

"One of those photograph artists set up shop nearby. He's stolen nearly all of Willy's business. The men prefer photographs over sketches."

Jeremiah nodded in understanding. "I'll stop by and see him when I leave. Maybe I can talk him into coming home with me."

"Good luck," J.D. replied.

The implication was unmistakable. For Willy, returning home would be an admission that he was different from all the other boys his age, something he had stubbornly refused to do all his life.

"So tell me what you did to earn the special attention of your regiment commander." There was a glint of humor in Jeremiah's eyes as he asked the question. Of his four children, J.D. had always been the most even-tempered, the most obedient, and the least trouble.

"It's my fault," J.D. began. "I couldn't remember some marching commands. It drew the attention of our new regimental commander, Colonel McKenna. He has ridden me hard ever since."

A shadow of concern crossed Jeremiah's face.

"What?" J.D. asked.

"You said your colonel's name was McKenna."

"That's right."

"Benjamin McKenna?"

"Yes . . . wait, why does that name sound familiar?" J.D. asked.

Before answering, Jeremiah pulled in a large measure of air. He exhaled slowly. "McKenna was my first wife's maiden name."

J.D. slapped a knee. "Now I remember!"

"And if this is the same Benjamin McKenna, he's the orphan boy Caleb adopted following Elizabeth's death. If that's true, your inability to remember commands may have little to do with the treatment you've received. Your colonel may have been taught to hate you simply because you're a Morgan."

J.D. nodded. "That makes sense," he said. "I thought Marshall and Willy were catching the overflow of McKenna's dislike for me. But there have been a couple times he was specifically derogatory about the fact that we were brothers. He doesn't hate just me, he hates all three of us because we're Morgans." With that thought, J.D.'s face soured.

"What's the matter?"

"Marshall's going to feel the brunt force of his anger."

"What did he do? The other men would only tell me there was an altercation."

J.D. nodded. "To put it mildly. McKenna was upset with me for allowing the men to rest during drill. They'd been at it in the heat for several hours. We'd already lost three to the sun. McKenna came down hard on me, and I almost hit him. Marshall stopped me."

"Marshall's in the guardhouse for stopping you from hitting your commanding officer?"

"Well, that wasn't the end of it. McKenna said something derogatory about Willy. So Marshall slugged him."

"Slugged?"

"It's a new term. Hit him. With fists. Hard."

Jeremiah shook his head. "Isn't that just like your brother? Just when things are under control, he explodes."

"Marshall was protecting me from myself."

"He hit his commanding officer!"

"I almost hit him myself!"

"But you didn't. And that's the difference between the two of you. It always has been. Just like coming here. You wanted to wait so that Sarah and I could see you off. It was Marshall who insisted that you had to hurry off."

"And Willy," J.D. added.

"He does whatever Marshall does. Always has."

J.D. decided to let the matter rest. He knew that when his father had made up his mind about something regarding Marshall, further discussion was a waste of energy.

"What will happen to Marshall?" Jeremiah asked.

"That depends on Colonel McKenna. But insubordination is a serious offense. He could be drummed out of the army."

The three-legged stool creaked as Jeremiah shifted his weight uncomfortably. J.D. sat with downcast eyes. "What would that entail?" Jeremiah wondered aloud.

"His head would be shaved; his uniform stripped of all insignia and buttons. Then, while the regimental band plays the 'Rogue's March' he would be led out of camp while the rest of the soldiers shower him with the vilest sort of verbal insults. Sometimes the offender is branded on his cheek, or forehead, or hip with the letter 'I' for insubordination."

Jeremiah cleared his throat. "Maybe I can speak to Colonel McKenna . . . persuade him not to let his personal feelings influence the matter unduly. Do you think he'll listen to me?"

"I wouldn't hold out much hope." Then, in a lighter tone, he asked, "How's Jenny? . . . and Mother?"

A chuckle bounced Jeremiah on the stool, causing it to creak in rhythm with the laugh. "It's a good thing you added that last phrase. I'll tell your mother you asked about her. As for Jenny, she misses you and . . . " He dug in his pocket. " . . . asked me to give you this."

Jeremiah handed his son an embroidered patch. It was circular, nearly two inches in diameter portraying a green frog upon a yellow background. The line for the frog's mouth was downturned at the corners as though it had just experienced something distasteful.

"She said it was for luck," Jeremiah added, sniggering.

"I don't know what's worse," J.D. grinned, "knowing that every man in my company will know what this patch represents, or having to explain it to everyone who doesn't know." He found a pin and secured the patch to his shirt above the left breast. He felt a unique stirring inside him to think that he was holding something that had recently been touched by Jenny's hands.

The tent flap flew open. Bright sunlight splashed all over the interior of the tent and its occupants. Colonel McKenna blew in like a thunderstorm, blocking the sunlight. Two angry-looking armed guards accompanied him.

"Where is he?" McKenna boomed.

J.D. jumped to attention. "Where is who, sir?"

McKenna growled obscenities. "Marshall! Your brother! Where is he?" His pitch rose with each sentence. It was the sound of the frustrated little boy again.

"He's not here, sir," J.D. replied.

"Do you take me for a dunce, Morgan?" McKenna closed the distance between him and J.D. until they were chest-to-chest. "I can see he's not here. What I want to know is where is he?" His face was flushed. Every visible muscle strained. He reminded Jeremiah of a taut violin string being stretched to the breaking point.

"Calm down, son." Jeremiah reached out and touched the colonel's arm. The touch was momentary as the two guards jumped between Jeremiah and McKenna, knocking the preacher's arm away.

"Who is this man?" McKenna roared.

"Sir," J.D. said. "Allow me to introduce my father, Rev. Jeremiah Morgan."

The colonel's rage subsided, only to be replaced by an emotion that was darker and uglier than J.D. had ever seen in a man. McKenna motioned the guards aside so that there was nothing between him and J.D.'s father. Fierce eyes studied the preacher. The colonel's mustache raised and twitched like the snarl of a wolf who had cornered his prey.

"So you are the infamous Jeremiah Morgan," he growled.

"Benjamin, I don't know what you've been . . . "

"Colonel!" McKenna snapped. "You will address me by rank!"

The preacher conceded with a slight bow. "Colonel, then . . . "

"Let me guess," McKenna interrupted. "You have come here to comfort one cowardly son, while the cripple waits outside the camp with a wagon to make good the escape of the insubordinate—and now deserter—son number two. That's quite a family you have here, Reverend. But then considering the rogue stock from which they were sired we shouldn't be surprised, should we?"

J.D. broke in. "Marshall escaped?"

"Oh, haven't you heard?" McKenna turned with a sarcastic expression toward J.D. "His head had just been shaved and the guards were preparing him for his grand exit from camp when an undetermined number of men wearing hoods jumped them. Marshall escaped and so did his accomplices. But I'm told they left behind the distinct stench of Jehovah's Avengers." Turning back to Jeremiah: "But we'll find him and haul him back to camp so that we can give him a proper exit. Oh yes, and a little something on his forehead to remember us by." Back to J.D.: "And as soon as I find the smallest scrap of evidence that you were behind his escape, you will be joining him! You and all the other villains in your company!" He was about to leave when he spotted the frog patch on J.D.'s shirt. "What's this?"

"It's from my girl, sir. She . . . "

Colonel McKenna ripped the patch from J.D.'s shirt and threw it to the ground. "Non-military issue," he said. Then, with a devious grin he added, "That felt good. I'm going to enjoy doing that to all your buttons and insignia when we drum the last of the Morgan brothers out of my camp."

Neither J.D. nor his father spoke until after the tent flap settled behind McKenna. Jeremiah was the first to speak. When he did, it was with a weary tone; the encounter seemed to drain him of all his strength. "He is the image of his stepfather. It's a tragedy that a man would pass on that kind of hatred to his son."

"Knowing his background helps put things in perspective, but what are we going to do about Marshall?" J.D. asked.

"There's little you can do without getting yourself deeper into trouble," Jeremiah replied. "I'll find Willy. See if Marshall's with him. But I doubt it since that's where the army will look for him. I'll ask around a little, then head home. Maybe Marshall will turn up there."

J.D. nodded. From his downcast expression, he clearly wished he could do something to help out.

"If you need me," Jeremiah said, "send for me. I'll come immediately. And J.D. . . . "

"Yes?"

"No matter what happens, your mother and I are proud of you. This is not your doing. It's my fight from long ago, you just happened to get caught up in the storm."

When Jeremiah Morgan reached the spot where Willy was reported to have been, he found the space empty. There was no sign of Willy. According to people in the vicinity, he disappeared suddenly. They claimed he'd talked about leaving for weeks, ever since the photograph artist arrived, but that he showed no real signs of packing up and leaving. Then, suddenly, he was gone. They told him that if anyone knew where Willy had gone, the drunk with one leg would know. He could usually be found milling around the photograph artist's wagon. But when Jeremiah went there to look for him, he could find no person with one leg.

Jeremiah encircled the regimental camp without success. At the completion of his circular course, Jeremiah returned to the photograph artist's wagon. There, lying in a stupor, was a young man of about twenty. He had only one leg. After a quarter hour of trying to talk to him, all Jeremiah could get from the drunk regarding Willy was two words — "gone west."

Jeremiah Morgan sat in the family carriage. For a long time he looked west. Then he urged his horse south toward home.

Chapter 9

MARCHING his company toward Virginia and war, J.D. pondered the future. It wasn't so much that the future concerned him greatly. He did it to keep his mind off his blistered feet. And as his regiment swung south and crossed the Potomac into secession country, he had come to a conclusion. He concluded that if he ever lay dying on a battlefield, his last thoughts in this life would be of Jenny. It was a conclusion based on experience. On any given day, no matter what he was doing, he discovered that at some point he found himself thinking of Jenny. Now, for instance.

Engulfed by the warm stillness of the night, he sat by the campfire. Its pop and crackle was his only company. With his Bible open on his lap and his pencil poised in his hand, he was supposed to be composing his thoughts for the next day's Sabbath services. But the sheet of paper atop his Bible, which doubled as his desk, was blank. His thoughts had drifted to Jenny and her letter which had caught up with him this morning.

With an anguished sigh he gave in to temptation. Abandoning the task at hand, he retrieved Jenny's letter that he had buried in the pages of his Bible. He held up the envelope to the light. Reverent fingers brushed across the pen strokes. Jenny's distinctive cursive lettering had formed his name. The familiarity of her handwriting and the sweet scent of the paper filled him with an ache so strong he was moved to tears.

Carefully removing the letter, J.D. read it again—savoring every syllable, letting the words sound in his mind with the echo of his beloved's voice. His reading pace slowed considerably as he neared the end, in a deliberate attempt to delay the inevitable. He had learned from previous readings that the feeling he felt upon finishing the letter was no less than if Jenny had stepped aboard a train and disappeared over the horizon. The final words sounded: *All my love, forever. Jenny.*

His hand holding the letter fell limp to his lap. The ache of their separation smoldered deep inside him, consuming all thoughts save those of Jenny. *The sermon outline will just have to wait.* Burying the treasured letter in the heart of his Bible, among the pages of King Solomon's own romantic writings, J.D. readied himself to pour out a few love lines of his own.

July 20, 1861

My darling Jenny,

He worked his pencil in his hand, rotating it with a steady motion, as though it were a gear directly linked to his whirling mind. One minute passed. Then another. And another. With a self-conscious laugh he put pencil to paper.

Now that I have written your name, my beloved, I find myself at a loss for words. Several minutes have passed between the writing of the salutation and this line. It is not that I have nothing to say. On the contrary, I have so much I want to say to you. But words fail me. My feelings for you are so rapturous, so overpowering, the words to describe them have yet to be created. O that I were a poet, that I might record my love for you in a panorama of descriptive images! Suffice it to say, my darling, that never a day goes by that you are not on my mind and in my heart. Whenever I contemplate the reality of armed conflict, I do not fear death; I fear the thought of passing from this life without ever having the chance to hold you in my arms one last time, to feel your lips against mine. I fear that my final proclamation of love to you will be reduced to mere marks on paper. How I long to breathe life into these printed words, to whisper them in your ear — I love you, my darling Jenny. I will always love you, no matter how great the distance between us which, by the way, has increased considerably since my last letter.

Since I wrote you last, our regiment has left Ohio. We are in Virginia now. "On to Richmond!" is the phrase repeated a thousand times a day. We have joined a host of other regiments near Centreville. If there is any truth to the rumors we will all "see the elephant" before too many days pass. The phrase means to see all there is to see. In our case, to experience war firsthand.

All of Point Providence should be proud of their men in this company. They have trained well and are ready to fight. Everyone is confident this is going to be a short war. I pray they are right for that would mean I will be home soon. In fact, many of the men are so confident in a quick Union victory that some of them are afraid the war will be over before they get a chance to fight.

That's why most of the men were glad we were called up to Virginia, even if it was sudden-like. From what I heard, we have Colonel McKenna to thank for that. Apparently he has political aspirations and being a war hero will do him good. Rightly so. Nobody would want to vote for a candidate who showed up after the war was over. As for me, I wouldn't mind showing up late.

Thinking of Colonel McKenna reminded me of something I need to tell you. Remember the incident I told you about, how the colonel ordered me to remove the frog patch from my uniform, the one you sent me? Well, when the rest of the company heard about it, they felt the colonel didn't fully appreciate the symbolism of the frog for our company. So they took a vote and unanimously decided that our company flag should bear the image of a frog! When the colonel saw the flag, he fussed and fumed, but there wasn't much he could do about it. So from now on, whenever we go into battle a frog will lead the way on our company standard. And you are to thank for that.

I was distressed to read in your last letter that no one has heard from Marshall or Willy yet. I pray for them nightly. Marshall, especially, has been on my mind of late. He is the one who most wanted to join the army and fight. Yet I'm here and he isn't.

It's getting late, my dearest, and I must close though I hate to. Whenever I write to you, somehow you are closer to me. But tomorrow is the Sabbath and I must finish preparing an inspirational message for the company. Remember, darling, whatever happens, I will always love you. Nothing can ever stop my love for you. Not separation. Not war. Nothing.

Pray for me. I pray for you.

Your friend and devoted lover,
J.D.

J.D. cringed as he checked his pocket watch. He'd stayed up much later than he'd intended. But he didn't regret the time spent. Tucking his letter next to Jenny's in the Bible, he returned to the blank sheet of paper that was to be his Sabbath message.

He read again his chosen text from the psalmist: *The Lord is my light and my salvation; whom shall I fear? the Lord is the strength of my life; of whom shall I be afraid? When the wicked, even mine enemies and my foes, came upon me to eat up my flesh, they stumbled and fell. Though an host should encamp against me, my heart shall not fear: though war should rise against me, in this will I be confident. One thing have I desired of the Lord, that will I seek after; that I may dwell in the house of the Lord all the days of my life, to behold the beauty of the Lord, and to inquire in His temple.* —Psalm 27:1-4.

Then he outlined a message that addressed the growing cockiness he had observed among his men regarding the coming conflict. He had specifically searched for wisdom to guide his thoughts from among the writings of this ancient warrior. Using King David's words, J.D. prepared himself to remind his men that the confidence of a Christian soldier was in nothing else save the Lord of hosts.

When he had a rough outline, enough to guide his thoughts, he retired to his tent.

With less than half a night's sleep, J.D. was awakened. It was 2 A.M. The regiment was moving out. For two days Brigadier General Irvin McDowell had made feints at a stone bridge crossing Bull Run near the town of Manassas. Now, leaving one division to occupy the Confederates at the bridge, McDowell marched two divisions by night in a looping maneuver north and west to cross the stream at Sudley Ford and surprise the enemy by attacking their left flank at dawn.

In the darkness of the tent J.D. pulled on his clothes. His light blue trousers and dark blue flannel sack coat looked the same dark gray in the dim light. The rustle of clothing and creak of cots were the only sounds in the tent as the other soldiers donned their uniforms. The mind fog of the recently awakened kept conversation to a few nearly incoherent mumbles.

"Where's my left shoe? Anybody got two left shoes?"

"I'll help you find your shoe if you help me find my pants. Can't go to war without pants."

J.D. snatched up his haversack which contained rations, half of a shelter tent, his knapsack, 160 spare rounds of ammunition, a change of uniform, and his personal effects. Next he grabbed his rifle-musket, cartridge box with its 40 rounds of ammunition, percussion cap-pouch, and canteen. "Let's go, men," he said with a thick voice. "Can't keep the rebels waiting. Wouldn't be polite."

As the Ohio volunteers marched to battle, wave after wave of rifles sparkled in the night like moonlight on the ocean. By daybreak they were still woefully shy of Sudley Ford. The six-mile maneuver proved to be twice as long. But no one seemed unduly concerned. They hadn't planned on taking all day to whip the Confederate army anyway.

John Brown's body lies a-moulderin' in the grave.
John Brown's body lies a-moulderin' in the grave.
John Brown's body lies a-moulderin' in the grave.
Glory, glory, hallelujah!
Glory, glory, hallelujah!
Glory, glory, hallelujah!
His soul is marchin' on!

He's gone to be a soldier in the army of the Lord.
He's gone to be a soldier in the army of the Lord.
He's gone to be a soldier in the army of the Lord.
Glory, glory, hallelujah!
Glory, glory, hallelujah!
Glory, glory, hallelujah!
His soul is marchin' on!

We'll hang Jeff Davis on a sour apple tree.
We'll hang Jeff Davis on a sour apple tree.
We'll hang Jeff Davis on a sour apple tree.
Glory, glory, hallelujah!
Glory, glory, hallelujah!
Glory, glory, hallelujah!
His soul is marchin' on!

The Ohio volunteers sang lustily. They were feeling good about themselves and the coming battle. The long months of drill were finally over. Now it was time for them to show the nation, especially the rebellious Southern states, what they could do. It was time to whip Johnny Reb's hide all the way to Richmond.

From Centreville to Sudley Ford the Union soldiers' high spirits were expressed in song after song. They sang everything from hymns to songs of their girls back home to songs of army life. To the tune of "The Sweet Bye and Bye" they sang:

There's a spot that the soldiers all love,
*   The mess-tent is the place that we mean,*
And the dish that we like to see there
*   Is the old-fashioned, white Army bean.*

'Tis the bean that we mean,
*   And we'll eat as we ne'er ate before.*
The Army bean, nice and clean;
*   We will stick to our beans evermore.*

Other times they sang in competition with the other companies in their regiment, each company boasting superior bravery and marksmanship:

Of our company we will sing,
Bully boys!

Join and make the chorus ring,
Bully boys!
Jehovah's Avengers is our name
And we will sustain its fame,
With our cool and deadly aim,
Bully boys!

By early morning the troops were not alone on the road. A growing number of civilian carriages accompanied them to the battlefield. Senators and congressmen and their lady friends rode alongside the Union troops to see the battle firsthand. They carried picnic lunches and bottles of champagne with them. One top-hatted man stood in his open carriage waving a pair of tickets high in the air as he passed by.

"Whatcha got there?" a soldier cried.

"Tickets to a Union ball in Richmond for tonight," the man with the hat exclaimed. "Can you get me there on time?"

"Guarantee it!" the soldier shouted gleefully. "We'll get you there in time for dinner if you promise to introduce us to some pretty girls."

"Guarantee it!" the man with the hat shouted back. With a huge guffaw, he fell to his seat as his carriage lurched forward.

Scattered among the civilians was a large contingent of the press, largely from Boston, New York, and Washington. New York's *Times* and *Tribune* reporters scurried after each other in the haunting fear that one would get a quote or angle the other missed. *Harper's Weekly* illustrators sat on rocks and tree stumps sketching the officers on horseback and the rows of troops passing by, their unit flags flying. An occasional photographic arts wagon appeared here and there, but they had to wait until the troops stopped before they were able to do business. Movement appeared as a blur on their plates.

Nearly half a dozen men with pads and pencils surrounded Colonel McKenna who sat erect on his horse, looking noble. The reporters recorded his every word as though he were the tablet-laden Old Testament prophet descending from Mount Sinai. One of the men with a pad, an artist, asked the colonel to turn his face slightly away from the sun for a more dramatic lighting. He obliged.

"Soldier, come here!" McKenna bellowed.

A private pointed to himself questioningly.

"Yes, you. Come here."

The private broke ranks and ran to the colonel. The reporters parted like the Red Sea so that the soldier could stand before his superior officer. The private saluted smartly.

"Give me your canteen," the colonel ordered.

The private dutifully obliged, handing up his canteen to the man above him on the horse.

Colonel McKenna filled his mouth with water and made a face. He swallowed. "Warm," he said. "But at least it's wet." This drew a chuckle from the reporters. Several of them recorded the quote. The colonel took another swig. "Answering all your questions creates quite a thirst," he said. "Hopefully, my quotes aren't as dry as my mouth." Another chuckle from the men with pads.

The colonel handed the canteen back to the private without gratitude and dismissed him. The private hustled up the parade line to catch up with his company.

"Do you not carry a canteen of your own, Colonel McKenna?" one reporter asked.

"Not necessary," came the reply. "These men are here to do two things. First, it is they who will drive the Confederates back to Richmond—that is, if they obey the commands of their officers. Because they are new recruits, our greatest concern at this point is their lack of experience. We don't know how they will react under fire. It will be up to us officers to lead them by our example. Second, they are here to service their superior officers. So why should I be burdened with a canteen when there are so many canteens readily available to me?"

"Is that something you learned at West Point?" a *Tribune* reporter asked.

"The first part I learned at West Point. The second part I learned from my father."

More chuckles from the reporters as they scratched on their pads.

Suddenly, Colonel McKenna raised up in his saddle and shouted. "You men! What are you doing?" To the reporters: "You'll have to excuse me, gentlemen. I have a problem company to deal with." The reporters parted and Colonel McKenna urged his horse up the line of marching columns. He didn't go far, so the reporters chased after him.

"Get out of those bushes and back in ranks!" McKenna shouted.

Skinny Henry Wier and stout Vern Hawkins jumped, startled by the sudden shout. Then a stained grin crossed Henry's face. He held out his cupped hand. "Look, sir!" he exclaimed. "Blackberries! First of the year! Plump ones too. Want some?"

"This ain't the time for berry picking!" McKenna roared. "Get back in line!"

Henry's grin faded. He looked beyond the colonel at the parade of men. "Don't worry about us, sir. We can catch up with our company. They ain't movin' that fast!"

Just then the reporters caught up with them. McKenna drew his saber and leveled it at Henry Wier's throat. "Hand me those berries, Private." Henry gulped hard and dutifully obeyed, doing his best to stretch his hand towards the colonel without getting any closer to the point of the saber. "Now join your ranks, or I'll give you a taste of my blade."

Henry ran up the road instantly. Vern was not as quick. With a scowl, he saluted McKenna, then ambled up the road. McKenna slid his saber back into its scabbard.

"They're not regulars," he said distastefully to the reporters. He munched on a few berries. "Volunteers. Next to useless. Especially that company. Crude westerners from Ohio. No discipline. When we win this war, it will be in spite of companies like that one." He threw a few more berries in his mouth.

"What company was that?" one reporter asked.

"They call themselves Jehovah's Avengers. They're from Point Providence."

"What kind of avengers?" another reporter asked.

"Jehovah's."

"Point where?"

"Exactly," replied McKenna.

The reporters laughed at his joke.

The sun was blazing overhead by the time they reached Sudley Ford. Trees bunched together tightly on both sides of the river, slowing the advance. Unit after unit crossed the stream and organized themselves in the forest on the other side.

"Guess this is it. Ain't that so, J.D.?" Point Providence's lanky telegraph operator whispered to his company commander. He didn't mean to whisper. Nerves choked his voice. Henry rubbed the barrel of his rifle with his thumb. Up and down. Up and down.

J.D. looked away before speaking, not wanting to call attention to the telegraph operator's nervous mannerisms. He focused instead on the soon-to-be battlefield beyond the trees. An open grassy expanse rose gently toward a plateau. A two-story wooden house was the only structure in sight. "Yep, Henry. Guess this is it."

"SILENCE IN THE RANKS!"

Colonel McKenna leaned forward in his saddle, looking down upon them from behind.

J.D. glanced at the colonel, acknowledging the command. The sight of McKenna sparked a strange sensation in him. The colonel's menacing presence, so prominent during their drills in Ohio, prompted a peculiar feeling of familiar comfort in this unfriendly forest.

"Prepare to move out!" Word was passed from company to company. The order caused thousands of pairs of feet to shuffle back and forth. Throats were cleared. Some of the men closed their eyes and mumbled prayers. Others clenched their jaws and stared at the field before them with unblinking eyes. Pulses raced.

The men from Point Providence were lined up behind a company of Michigan volunteers. When the command was given, they would follow on the heels of the Michigan boys into their first battle.

A leaf fluttered to the ground in front of J.D., where it lay still. Standing among the trees it was moist and cool, almost cold. It wouldn't be that way for long. A wave of heat from the field penetrated the perimeter of the forest, hot and dry. Then the leaves of the trees shooed the heat back and it was cold again. The alternating temperature caused J.D. to shudder involuntarily.

"Scared, Morgan?" McKenna jeered. His eyes rolled skyward. "How did I ever get linked up with the likes of you? You shouldn't even be here. You're a farmer, not a soldier. I just hope you don't get us all killed."

Drums beat. Trumpets sounded the charge. With a yell, the first row of units charged into the field. At Colonel McKenna's orders, the Ohio volunteers stepped forward to follow them.

The wind ripped overhead. A blinding, thunderous boom

followed. Nearby a stout tree trunk exploded, reduced to splinters. Its massive limbs, no longer supported, crashed down upon a company of Indiana regulars. Their startled cries echoed in the recesses of the forest.

"The Rebs know we're here!" McKenna screamed.

It was an understatement. Several more ripping sounds were followed by loud cracks and booms and more human cries as the Confederate army poured shell after shell into the forest.

J.D. heard it coming. A long tearing sound, followed by a deafening explosion. Pieces of wood and leaves and dirt flew past him, then showered down from above. He was knocked to the ground. When he opened his eyes, he saw tree and human limbs scattered indiscriminately around him. Other than a ringing in his ears, he felt no injury. He moved his legs, his arms. No pain. A tree limb held down his legs. He pushed it aside and stood. There was a taste of blood in his mouth. He probed his mouth and lips with his tongue. A split lip. If that was the only injury he suffered, he could count himself fortunate indeed.

"Henry! Are you all right?"

The telegraph operator was buried under a leafy branch. He was groggy, but uninjured. One by one, the fallen men of Jehovah's Avengers rose from the ground. Other than scrapes and splinter wounds, no one was hurt seriously. The troops that had been arrayed behind them rushed past on both sides, yelling and whooping their way onto the field of battle.

Just then J.D. spotted Colonel McKenna's horse. Charging into battle. Riderless. J.D. scoured the ground for the colonel. He found McKenna sitting at the base of a tree. Blood poured down his right cheek from a gash on his forehead at the hairline. His uniform and hands were splattered with wood splinters. With arms clasped around a tree trunk, he sat with his eyes clenched tightly closed. Sweat mingled with blood as it poured down the crevices of his cringing face and dripped from his jaw and chin. His shaking rattled the leaves overhead.

J.D. knelt down beside him and laid a hand on his arm. "Colonel?"

McKenna jumped at the touch. But that was his only response. His eyes remained closed. Union soldiers poured past them as though they were not there. More trees exploded around them. Smoke and the screams of the wounded filled the forest.

"Colonel, are you hurt bad?"

No response. Just shaking and sweat.

J.D. tried to pry McKenna's hands loose from the tree, hoping to see if the colonel was injured anywhere other than his forehead. McKenna's hands refused to be moved. When J.D. exerted stronger force, the shaking colonel growled incoherently, refusing to let himself be freed. Never once did McKenna open his eyes.

"J.D.? Is the colonel dead?"

Henry Wier and Vern Hawkins stood at a distance. It was Henry who had asked the question.

"I only see a head gash. He won't let loose of the tree to let me check. Vern, you have more experience in this than the rest of us. Come here and see what you think."

The Mexican War veteran knelt down beside J.D. He eyed the colonel on one side, then the other. "No wounds that I can see," he said. Then he tried to pry the colonel's hands free from around the tree, just as J.D. had done. He got the same response. A closed-eyed growling sound. Vern stood.

"He's just scared. Seen it afore. There'll be no movin' him until his strength gives out."

"So what do we do?" J.D. asked.

"Leave 'im here."

Another shell ripped the air overhead and exploded behind them.

"We can't just leave him here!"

Vern shrugged his shoulders. "Nothin' else we can do. The best we can do is to fight back these Rebels. If we don't, they'll be takin' care of him soon enough."

At a loss for any other course of action, J.D. took one last look at the colonel and nodded. "Any casualties among our men?"

"None," Vern replied. "At least not that I know'd of. They went on without us. Didn't want to get left out of the battle since they figure this will be the only one there is."

J.D. grinned. The Ohio volunteers would have nothing to be ashamed of on this day, of that he was sure. "Let's see if we can catch up with them," he said.

The three remaining members of Jehovah's Avengers ran out of the forest in search of a company flag with a frog on it. They were greeted with the blazing light and heat of the midday sun and new sound. In addition to the air-ripping sound of artillery, they could hear bullets whistling over their heads. Occasionally, one would find its mark. And a soldier would fall. Sometimes there was a scream. Other times there was only a heavy thud as the body hit the ground. With bodies falling around them, the three men of Point Providence pressed forward, crouching as they ran up the grassy slope.

They caught up with their company at a split-rail fence which ran beside the Sudley Road. Other than a few minor wounds from the artillery blasts in the forest, the entire company was still intact. J.D. chided them good-naturedly for charging into battle without their company commander. In return, they goaded him for lagging behind. Some expressed their surprise to discover, halfway across the field, that he was not with them. In all the excitement, when the charge sounded, they charged. They never stopped to consider that they might be leaving their commander behind.

Their brief reunion took place under a hail of Confederate bullets. They talked as they reloaded. The Rebels had stopped the charge, but only momentarily. As more and more troops emerged from the forest, the outnumbered Confederate army took a severe pounding. Then they broke.

After firing a volley, J.D. ordered his men to cease fire. Clouds of smoke and dust paraded across his line of vision, obscuring the enemy. He waited for the smoke to clear, catching what glimpses he could through the breaks.

"They're running!" he shouted.

As though to confirm his observation, a trumpet sounded an advance. With the other companies, Jehovah's Avengers chased after the running Rebels with great glee.

"We've whipped 'em! We've whipped 'em!" Vern shouted.

All around them Union soldiers ran and shouted.

"We'll hang Jeff Davis to a sour apple tree!"

"Bully for us! Bravo! Didn't I tell you so?"

Henry whooped and hollered and jumped, waving his cap over his head. "The war is over! The war is over! The war is ... " He spun around and collapsed face first into a bush of flowering dogwood.

"Henry!" J.D. saw him fall. Rushing to his side, J.D. pulled him out of the bush. He turned him over and lay him on the ground. Henry's neck was half gone. One side of his face and the chest of his uniform were sprayed with blood. The lanky telegraph operator's eyes were fixed open in a look of surprise. His lips were stained with blackberries.

Henry Wier, who had proudly announced to the citizens of Point Providence the events that had led up to the war, was now the town's first loss. The lanky bachelor who had announced the war's beginning did not live to see its end.

J.D. cradled Henry in his arms. The pink petals of the dogwood flower lay about them on the ground. Some lay on Henry's still body. The air was heavy with their scent. As bullets whistled over his head, J.D. prayed a prayer, commending Henry's soul to its Maker. Then, gently, he lowered Henry's head to the ground beside the flowering dogwood. From that day on, J.D. Morgan always associated the scent of the flowering dogwood with Henry Wier and death.

Atop the plateau the Rebel line stiffened and held. Jehovah's Avengers settled in near the Warrenton Turnpike. A wooden two-story house shielded them from the Confederate artillery. The house was pounded mercilessly. Some of the balls entered one side and came out the other, showering the Avengers with shingles, boards, and splinters. Another company that had arrived before the Avengers called it the Henry house. They claimed the widow Henry still occupied the house. An elderly woman and bed-ridden, she refused to leave. If that was true, J.D. concluded, she was dead now. No one could survive in a house as shot up as the Henry house.

During a lull in the action J.D. called for reports from his men. Henry Wier was the only fatality of the battle so far. Several others had fallen to leg and arm wounds. With sweaty hands, he fumbled for his canteen. Rolling over onto his back, he drank. The water was hot. Still, it relieved the scratchy, sticky feeling of his throat and mouth, and washed down the taste of smoke and dirt and blood.

It was after three o'clock in the afternoon. They had been on the march or in battle for more than twelve hours. J.D. was feeling the fatigue of the long day. From the half-closed eyes of his men, he knew they were feeling it too. The intensity of the sun and the heat had drained them as well.

Turning back over onto his belly, he surveyed the plateau. Before him lay a scene of smoke and dust and wild shouting and moans and hissings and howlings and explosions. Black smoke rose from the Henry house. The air was acrid with the smell of gunpowder and body sweat. Fallen horses littered the plateau, as did broken and mangled bodies. Soldiers from both sides. J.D. had never entertained grand illusions of war. But this was worse than he ever imagined it would be.

Then he noticed a stirring on the Confederate side. In the distance, out of range, men were cheering. *For what? Because they had held? Or possibly because reinforcements had arrived?* And if that was the case, the strategic question was this: *Were they fresh?* J.D. felt confident that his men could outfight and out-endure any other unit on an equal basis, Union or Southern. But if fresh troops had indeed arrived, it would be a mismatch.

His suspicions were confirmed soon enough. A banshee cry issued forth from among the Confederate armies. It was an unnerving sound followed by wave after wave of Rebels running onto the plateau. A fresh volley from the Union troops did little to stop them. A few Rebel soldiers fell, but that didn't slow the ever-arriving troops streaming over the hill onto the plateau.

J.D. ordered his men into position. All around him rifle-muskets thundered and spit fire and smoke. The Rebels kept coming. The Avengers loaded and fired again. All around them Union companies broke ranks and fled down the side of the plateau. This only served to encourage the onslaught of Rebels. They yelled louder and ran faster. J.D. ordered another volley. Half of his company turned and ran, ignoring his order to hold their ground. As he yelled after them, another quarter turned and fled. To those that remained, he directed them to load and fire, and they did.

Vern plopped down beside him. "J.D.," he said, "there's a time to fight and a time to retreat. Look around you."

Everywhere J.D. looked Union soldiers were abandoning their positions on the hillside.

"We can't defeat the whole Southern army ourselves," Vern said. "I'm saying this friend-to-friend. You're my commander. If you think we should hold our position, with God's help, I'm with you."

Their position was hopeless. J.D. knew it. He just didn't want to admit it.

"Let's get out of here," he said.

The remnant of the Avengers followed their leader down the hill. The slopes swarmed with retreating, disorganized forces. Riderless horses and artillery teams rushed past them. By many soldiers, every impediment to flight was cast aside — rifles, bayonets, pistols, cartridge-boxes, haversacks, canteens, belts, and overcoats.

All these things weighed heavily on J.D.'s back, yet he resisted the panicky urge to shed them. His legs and feet felt like lead; he was barely able to put one foot in front of the other. His throat and lungs were on fire. He wanted to look over his shoulder to see if the Rebels were closing, but he dared not look back. He fully expected to feel a hot rifle bullet hit him in the back at any moment.

He saw a bridge ahead of him. The passage across was slowed by the congestion of carriages and artillery wagons and ambulances trying to get across. An artillery shell passed overhead. A second later the earth beside the road erupted like a geyser. Another shell and another geyser, this one closer to the bridge. Horses reared in fright. Drivers fought to keep their wagons under control.

One shell found its mark on a wagon crossing the bridge. The horses were lifted off the ground, then fell in a heap, never to move again. The wagon overturned, blocking the passage across the bridge. Those who could jumped from their wagons and waded across the river on either side of the bridge. J.D. and his Avengers followed them.

Although the water cooled his legs and lower torso, J.D. had little to feel refreshed about. The water proved to be one more obstacle to slow his aching, exhausted legs. It was the kind of running that occurred in bad dreams. He knew he had to run, had to get away, but the harder he tried, the harder it was for him to move.

For three miles hosts of Northern troops fled from the field of battle. They didn't stop until they reached Centreville. The procession was a mixture of military wagons and civilian carriages. J.D. saw the man who had earlier waved in the air tickets to a ball in Richmond. He sat glum and sweaty in the back of his carriage as it ambled along beside the straggling, defeated Union army.

At Centreville, J.D. and the Avengers rejoined the rest of their regiment. Without exception the soldiers trudged along, heads lowered, feet dragging. Physical exhaustion was only part of it. A Union victory had turned to a Confederate rout. And they found that fact difficult to live with.

With his tent pitched, J.D. walked with ax in hand to gather some firewood. On the edge of the camp, surrounded by reporters, stood Colonel Benjamin McKenna. He was removing his hat so that the reporters could get a look at his bandaged head.

"Artillery shell," J.D. heard him say.

A reporter asked the colonel to explain how the Union forces could be so close to victory only to be pushed back by the Confederate troops.

"The blame lies with our green, inexperienced volunteers," he said matter-of-factly. "They turned coward and ran. There was nothing we officers on the front line could do to stop them. We ordered them to hold their ground. We even pulled out pistols on them and threatened to shoot them if they ran. As you can see, it did little good. Our tactics were sound and we have superior military leadership. It was the volunteers who let us down."

J.D. bit his lip, opening the split. A trickle of blood made its way down his chin. He wiped it off angrily and stalked away. With aching arms he chopped enough wood for the entire company. A couple of times he thought of Marshall and the woodpile back home and chuckled. Now *he* was doing the chopping! It didn't solve anything, but it did make him too tired to care anymore.

Chapter 10

YOU'VE checked that bag at least a dozen times," Jeremiah complained. "Susanna, you've packed everything I'll need. Come to bed."

He lay with his hands behind his head watching his wife lift shirts and trousers from his travel bag, study the contents beneath them, plop them back in place, and dig down the other side, all the while checking things off her mental list.

"Susanna! If it's not in there, I'll get along without it."

Her head popped up. "Without what? What am I forgetting?"

"Nothing!" Jeremiah insisted. "I just meant that you've packed everything. Anything that is not in that bag, I won't need."

His wife's brow furrowed. Her unfocused gaze indicated she was reviewing the list again. From beyond their bedroom wall came the lilt of feminine giggles. The furrowed brow turned toward the wall separating the two bedrooms.

"That's what is really bothering you," Jeremiah said.

With a sigh of frustration, Susanna dropped the travel bag at the foot of the bed and crawled under the covers next to her husband. "Are we doing the right thing?" she asked.

"I've asked myself that same question a hundred times this past week."

"And what answer do you get?"

Jeremiah laughed. "A different one every time!"

Susanna didn't laugh with him. The cloud of concern that swirled around her was impervious to the encroachment of levity. Another round of giggles penetrated the bedroom wall.

Jeremiah scooted over to his wife and extended his arm. In response Susanna lifted her head and cuddled next to him, lying her head in the crook of his arm. Hers was a reflex reaction to nearly three decades of sharing a bed with him. They stared at the ceiling as they talked.

"I tell myself that she's a grown woman," Jeremiah said. "That this is a wonderful opportunity for her. That she is better off there doing something worthwhile than here pining away after Daniel."

"But New York?" Susanna cried. "It's so big. And so far away!"

"It's too late to change our minds now! We already gave our consent."

One of Susanna's hands appeared from beneath the covers. It wiped an eye, then the other. "She's the only one left! It's been a hard enough adjustment for me to lose the boys all at one time. With Sarah gone, this place will be like a tomb."

"We haven't lost the boys!" Jeremiah protested. "They're just gone temporarily. They'll be back!" It was a leaky attempt at consolation, failing to hold any comfort, and he knew it.

With the news of Henry Wier's death at Bull Run, Point Providence had its first taste of war's bitter fruit. Unlike other groves where they planted dead seeds and reaped living fruit, on the Virginian battlefield they had given a living son and reaped the fruit of death. Families braced themselves for a long, bitter harvest.

As for the Morgan family, they had still not heard a word from Marshall or Willy. And the letters from J.D. provided enough grisly detail of modern warfare to cause his mother to have nightmares.

Another series of giggles erupted from beyond the wall.

"Sarah! Jenny! Go to bed!" Jeremiah shouted. "It's late! Get some sleep!"

The response was muffled giggles, then silence.

Susanna rolled off her husband's arm and punched her pillow. "You'd better get some sleep too," she said with her back to him. "You have a long trip ahead of you."

"Will you be all right?"

"What choice do I have?" she answered. "Come tomorrow all of my children and my husband will be gone and I'll be left alone. What more could I ask for?"

"Susanna. . . . " Jeremiah reached over and placed his hand on his wife's shoulder. She shrugged it off. "I'll be back in a couple of weeks at most," he said.

Susanna gave no indication she heard him, so he reached over beside the bed and put out the light.

Sarah Morgan's world changed forever the day she received the package from Maine. Above the return address there was a single name, STOWE. Ripping the package from her father's hands, who had received delivery at the post office, Sarah rushed over to the sofa in the sitting room. Brown wrapping paper flew in every direction. She uncovered her manuscript, neatly tied with string, and a letter from Harriet Beecher Stowe.

The letter began with warm greetings, expressing a sincere fondness for the manuscript's author. Mrs. Stowe wrote that she felt she knew Sarah more intimately after having read her story. The following review was encouraging. Mrs. Stowe said Sarah's novel was a much needed moral tale, that it had an intriguing plot with contrasting characters, and that for the most part it was clearly written. The only area for improvement, according to Mrs. Stowe, was that the dialogue was "a bit bumpy," as she put it.

Sarah reveled in every word.

The second page of the letter were comments made by Mr. Stowe as dictated to his wife. "He reads everything she writes," Sarah explained to her parents. They had pulled two chairs close and eagerly watched their daughter read the letter. Jeremiah was certain that when word spread around town that Sarah had received a letter from Harriet Beecher Stowe there would surely be a line of people wanting to see it.

Mr. Stowe's remarks were not as favorable as his wife's, though they weren't unkind. Using words that made him sound like a New York reviewer, he pronounced Sarah's story "a fledgling effort by an author that shows promise." In particular, he criticized the motivations of her characters, especially the wealthy villain. He concluded that Sarah had evidently not been around wealthy people, for she seemed to know little of their attitudes and mannerisms. As the story stood, he saw Sarah's villain as an unreasoning mad dog. Instead of rabies, however, he was afflicted by simple greed.

Before closing the letter, Mrs. Stowe emphasized that her husband truly liked the story, but thought it needed more work. Then she expressed her sincerest wishes for Sarah's literary success and offered to pass the manuscript along to her publisher after Sarah had reworked it.

Sarah lowered the letter. Her head was swimming. Joy bubbled inside her like a geyser about to erupt. She could hardly contain it. Warning spurts involuntarily escaped her lips in the form of giggles.

"We're so proud of you, dear," her mother said.

"You have a God-given talent," her father added. "This letter confirms it."

Sarah's head fell backward. With eyes closed she clutched the letter to her bosom and smiled at heaven.

"What's that on the back, dear?" Her mother pointed at the letter.

Turning the letter over Sarah discovered a postscript. As she read it silently, all expression drained from her face. Her wide eyes grew even wider. Then the geyser erupted.

"I can't believe it!" she screamed with ecstasy. "I can't believe it!"

Jeremiah and Susanna were on the edge of their chairs.

"Listen to this!" Sarah could hardly contain herself to read Mrs. Stowe's postscript aloud. "Recently the Christian Tract Society in New York City contacted me," Sarah read, "inquiring if I knew of any women writers who would be interested in writing tracts for them. It seems that all of their male writers have gone off to war. So they have converted a portion of their building into a dormitory and are looking for six unmarried women who can write for them full-time. They feel there is an urgent need for tracts that will minister to the spiritual needs of our soldiers. The six writers will work closely with an editorial board to produce the tracts. According to my information, the hours will be long but the rewards eternal. They are looking for young ladies who can work for a period of one year or until the war ends. I hope I am not being presumptuous, but I forwarded to them your name and address. If you are available, I know you will do an exemplary job for them.—HBS"

Sarah let out a high-pitched squeal of delight. Her parents' response was not as enthusiastic.

A few days later Sarah received a personal invitation to come to New York from a Mrs. Thomasson of the Christian Tract Society. The way the letter was worded, Sarah was a world-renowned author, on the same level as the woman who had recommended her. Mrs. Thomasson apologized for not being able to pay Sarah the wage she was undoubtedly worth. Then she went on to say she prayed Sarah would accept the invitation to work for the Christian Tract Society as her part in the war effort. The letter outlined the proposed writing schedule and described in detail the precautions that were being taken to ensure that no harm would ever come to the ladies in their employ.

If Sarah had her way, she would have been out the door heading East that same day. Her parents balked. They were against the idea of Sarah moving to New York, no matter how many precautions were taken by the Society. And it looked like the issue was settled until Jenny dropped by. She sided with Sarah. Not only that, she offered to go with her to New York.

It took several months of parent-child negotiations, but finally everything was settled. Sarah's parents agreed to let her go. Jenny's parents agreed to let their daughter go. And the Society agreed to house Jenny for the duration of Sarah's stay. This they did only because Mrs. Stowe had recommended Sarah so highly.

A dry, bitter wind whipped around towering New York City buildings. It was late October; too early for snow, but not for frigid temperatures. Like a turtle withdrawing into its shell, Jeremiah ducked down into his coat. His gloved hands held loosely the reins of the carriage as his tired horse plodded down Broadway, following a congested line of vehicles in front of them. Vehicles of every sort jammed the streets — carriages large and small; ice wagons; wagons hauling dry goods, crates of vegetables, and hay; photographic art wagons; and horse-drawn buses. The brick street upon which they rolled was rutted and rough. Uprooted bricks lay broken and scattered. Pot-shaped holes gave the vehicles a bone-jarring jolt now and then. However, none of this — the cold, the crowds, the jolts — seemed to dampen the spirits of the two girls sitting behind him.

"I can't believe it!" Sarah cried over and over. With one hand she held fast to Jenny's arm without ever taking her eyes off the buildings that stretched skyward all around her. It was as though her hold on Jenny was a grip on reality. "Look at that building! Four, five, six stories high! I can't believe we're actually here! We're in New York! NEW YORK! Can you believe it?"

Jenny was oblivious to Sarah's hand on her arm. Though she was a bit more subdued, still her insides were racing. Like Sarah, other than Cincinnati, she had never been to a big city before. She was taken aback by the sheer number of carriages and horses and pedestrians that were pushing, yelling, and squeezing in all around them. People of every description occupied the streets, well-dressed men and women in black suits and full skirts; sailors from a variety of nations; ragged beggars in the alleys and gutters, many of them children.

"Look!" Sarah squealed. "There's Barnum's Museum! And over there, St. Paul's Cathedral! I've seen sketches of St. Paul's in magazines. I never dreamed I'd see it myself! This is . . . this is . . . what can I say? This is so . . . "

Jenny smirked. "You writers have a way with words," she teased. Sarah seemed not to hear her; neither did her slump-shouldered father in the driver's seat. "Mr. Morgan," Jenny called, "has the city changed much since you lived here?"

Jeremiah glanced back over his shoulder and mumbled, "A little. Not much." He had grown quieter and quieter the further away from Point Providence they traveled, and had not spoken a word until now since they entered the city.

He pulled up his coat around his ears and sank back into the collar again. He hoped the girls hadn't noticed his deepening depression. If they did, he hoped they would conclude that his withdrawal was due to arthritis, which was partially true. It wasn't unusual for him to withdraw whenever it flared up. It was his way of battling the pain.

The carriage hit a deep rut knocking Jeremiah several inches to his left. The chill of the previously exposed seat penetrated his pants. He repositioned himself onto the spot he'd already warmed. The sudden jolt threw the two girls together, causing them to bang heads. It must not have hurt them too badly. They rubbed their heads and giggled.

Jeremiah flexed one gloved hand, then the other. The cold weather had enflamed his joints. But it wasn't the arthritis that had brought on his black mood. The city of New York was responsible for that.

Street after street was riddled with visual triggers that set off mental images of his past life. The pond at Central Park—where he and Elizabeth first kissed. The pedestrian bridge spanning Ann Street—where they stood for hours watching the carriages pass beneath them. From the appearances of the couples, they used to guess what first attracted her to him and vice versa. Of course, since the people they saw were strangers, they never knew if they were right. But they liked to think they were fairly accurate with their guesses. The most devastating New York memory came when the carriage passed 57th Street.

Jeremiah was determined not to look down the street. Yet when the moment came, he found himself helpless to resist. There it was. The McKenna mansion. The home of Jeremiah's first and greatest love; also the home of his most formidable enemy.

Even though he'd anticipated an emotional response upon seeing the mansion again, Jeremiah was surprised at the strength of the feeling that stirred inside him. He thought he had hardened himself against these memories years ago. Yet here they were again. Resurrected. Alive and well and as strong as ever. A single glimpse of the mansion brought to mind all his youthful passions—his hopes and dreams, his fears, his inhibitions and insecurities. It was as though these emotions had been at the end of the street all these years waiting for him to pass by.

Jeremiah fought the feelings with thoughts of the present. He wasn't unhappy with the way his life had unfolded at Point Providence. He loved his life there. His family. His church. His friends. His ministry. *It's a good life,* he reasoned. *Any man would be proud to have such a life.*

His words lacked persuasive power. Shot from a worn-out bow, they fell short of the target. When Jeremiah Morgan ran away from New York he lost something. A measure of self-respect. He felt he'd betrayed his Morgan heritage. Those who had gone before him were a passionate people living in a passionate land—unafraid to take great risks, to make great sacrifices, to face great evils. Jeremiah, on the other hand, had settled for a small church in a quiet town. A place with limited opportunities, little risk, and no danger. He'd sacrificed the high ideals of his forefathers for personal safety.

Jeremiah's stomach ached horribly. The reins in his hands shook, but not from the cold. His breathing was ragged. He swayed in his seat.

Enough! he scolded himself. *You're acting like a fool!* Straightening himself in the seat, he took a glance over his shoulder to see if the girls had noticed his pitiful display. They had not. They were still moving from one side of the carriage to the other taking in all the sights of the city.

Good. There was no reason for them to know what he was thinking or how he was feeling. That's the way it had always been. Jeremiah had never told his children the details of his life in New York. They knew he attended school there, that he was previously married to Elizabeth McKenna, and that she and their son died in childbirth. But that was all they knew, nothing else. They knew nothing of Caleb McKenna's crusade against him, nor of his fleeing New York in fear. As far as they knew, he moved to Ohio in answer to God's call to evangelize the West.

Nor did Jeremiah talk much with his wife about his life in

New York. He tried once. It was on one of those deep summer evenings when the heat of the day had at long last been run off by a cool breeze from the river. The children were in bed. Jeremiah and Susanna sat on the front porch. A star-spangled sky stretched to the horizon. For some reason, the subject of Jeremiah's New York courting days came up and he described to Susanna some of the antics that took place when he and Elizabeth and Seth and Emma went ice skating on the frozen lake in Central Park. Maybe it was the gleam she saw in his eyes when he spoke of Elizabeth, or the thick warmth of his voice. But when Jeremiah glanced over at his wife, hurt bathed her eyes. He'd said too much and he knew it. For Susanna realized that though she held first place in his life, she would never hold first place in his heart. That place was forever set aside as a monument to Elizabeth.

Jeremiah never again spoke of his first wife. Neither did Seth and Emma speak of her when they visited. They pretended as though Jeremiah's life began the day he entered Point Providence.

"There it is! There it is!" Sarah was hanging halfway out of the carriage. She pointed to a sign etched in stone over an arched double door. The sign read: CHRISTIAN TRACT SOCIETY.

With a long sigh Jeremiah guided the horse to the curb. While Sarah and Jenny bounced onto the walkway, Jeremiah trudged to the back of the carriage and untied the luggage. Had anyone been watching him, they would have thought he moved with the weight of two lifetimes upon his shoulders.

O for a thousand tongues to sing
My great Redeemer's praise,
The glories of my God and King,
The triumphs of His grace!

He breaks the pow'r of canceled sin,
He sets the pris'ner free;
His blood can make the foulest clean,
His blood availed for me.

Jenny sang soprano; Sarah sang alto. Their voices blended naturally, reaching all the way to the domed ceiling of the sanctuary. Blue and red and green sunlight fell on the pages of their hymn books, colored by an enormous stained-glass window at the end of their pew. As the final strains from the enormous pipe organ echoed throughout the sanctuary, the congregation took their seats. All eyes focused on the ornate, raised pulpit in the front.

The first Sunday of November, 1862 had dawned crisp and fresh. For Sarah and Jenny, it was their first Sunday in New York City without Sarah's father. It was also the first worship service they attended in New York's famed Heritage Chapel, the largest congregation by far in the Heritage Churches of America denomination. The two previous Sundays the girls had attended church services with Jeremiah at a small church near the waterfront. Both he and Seth had preached frequently at the church during their school days, and when the congregation learned that Jeremiah was in the city they invited him to preach their again. However, now that Jeremiah had left for home, the two girls attended services with the rest of the ladies of the Society.

Jeremiah headed back to Ohio satisfied that the Christian Tract Society had made adequate arrangements for the care of the two girls. Sarah was one of six girls who had been recruited by the Society to write pamphlets. Jenny was hired on as Mrs. Thomasson's assistant, with some cleaning duties besides. She was paid only room and board for her work.

The arrangements included mandatory attendance at church services at Heritage Chapel. As with every other part of their regimen, guidelines were strict. The girls traveled to church together in the same carriage; they sat together in the same pew; and they traveled back to the Society together. There was no allowance for exceptions.

Sarah looked over at Jenny and smiled. The smile was returned. The excitement of their adventure had yet to wear off.

Having ascended the pulpit, the senior pastor raised a hand to his mouth and cleared his throat. His clerical robe slid down the upraised arm revealing a thin, bony appendage. An elderly man, Rev. Charles Evans was tall and thin. His hair, gray and thinning, was combed straight back on all sides. There was a green pallor about his skin, accentuated undoubtedly by the stained glass lighting. After a brief prayer that sounded more like a warning to those who didn't listen, he began to preach.

He spoke without passion. Seldom did he fluctuate his voice. Reading from a printed manuscript, he droned on and on, rarely looking up. Other than his dry, raspy intonation, the only sound to be heard was the occasional rustle of a page as he sifted his manuscript.

The thing that struck Sarah as most peculiar was that his sermon was not based on a Scripture text as were all the other sermons she'd heard from Heritage preachers. Rev. Evans' sermon was more like a political statement praising the Democratic candidates in the upcoming elections. With Election Day just two days away, Rev. Evans called on his congregation to let their voices be heard at the polls, especially in favor of Horatio Seymour, the Democratic candidate for governor.

For Sarah, who was not the least interested in politics, the entire sermon would have been without any redeeming value had it not been for the antics of a bearded man on the second pew. He sat alone on the aisle. The pews immediately in front of him and behind him were vacant. Shocking-white hair fell

gracefully down the back and sides of his head, then drew
under in tight curls. His top hair curled likewise, making his
forehead look like a beach with foaming surf. A full growth
of beard, also of the purist white, covered his cheeks and
chin. His upper lip, however, was clean shaven. The elderly
man had an eagle's beak for a nose, and he sat in his pew fully
erect with self-dignified importance.

What made his presence in the worship service humorous
to Sarah was the fact that of the hundreds of people within
her line of sight, he alone was captivated with the sermon.
More than captivated. He was a participant. It was as though
the preacher and this one listener were performing a duet.

Rev. Evans would make a point, and the white-haired man
would shout, "Amen!" Another point was made, then "Praise
the Lord!" Still another point and "Tell 'em! That's a fact!
Tell 'em again!" It went back and forth like this throughout
the sermon. As for the preacher, instead of being distracted
by the interaction, it seemed to please him.

With the sermon concluded, the ladies of the Society filed
out of the pew and made their way down the aisle. Since most
of the young men their age were off at war, and since the
majority of the young ladies had been in town only a short
time, Mrs. Thomasson's job was made easier. The older men
in the congregation were either married or too old for the
ladies, and the younger men—still boys—were too unsure of
themselves to approach a gaggle of girls. Both groups merely
stood in the distance and stared.

At the front door the Rev. Evans greeted the parishioners
one by one as they ushered out into bright sunshine. In spite
of the sun, the wind was chilly enough to warrant coats and
gloves, the donning of which created a logjam. Sarah and
Jenny shuffled along patiently in the stream of people. Just
then Sarah's stomach made a loud grumbling noise which set
Jenny and a couple of the other girls to giggling. No sooner

would they regain control of themselves, when her stomach would growl again. The girls' giddy behavior brought disapproving looks from Mrs. Thomasson. Sarah could only hope that her stomach would behave itself as she approached the minister.

"And you are?" The preacher's cadaverous hand stretched out in greeting.

"Sarah Morgan," she said.

Thin eyebrows raised. "Of the Boston Morgans? The wealthy merchant family?"

"Distant relatives," Sarah replied. "My father is a minister at Point Providence, Ohio."

The eyebrows lowered. "Oh, that Morgan."

A recently familiar voice came from behind her. "You're one of Jeremiah Morgan's children?"

Sarah turned to face the voice and found herself standing before the white-haired man. He was of average height, and favored his left side with a gold handled black cane.

"Yes, I'm Jeremiah Morgan's daughter." Sarah smiled sweetly.

Hard eyes looked her over. "You have your father's nose . . . and stature," he said. "And that's a fact."

"So I've been told," Sarah replied. "I'm also told I have his stubbornness."

"Is that so?" He wasn't smiling.

Sarah had mentioned the stubbornness in an attempt to be humorous. Now she wished she hadn't said it. "Do you know my father?" she asked.

A wry smile creased the man's face. His lips were almost nonexistent. "I most certainly do know your father," he said. "At one time he was my son-in-law."

"Miss Morgan," the pastor stepped in to perform the introductions, "this is Mr. Caleb McKenna." The way the preacher said McKenna's name Sarah would have thought he were introducing the President of the United States.

"Yes! I've heard of you!" Sarah exclaimed. "Mr. McKenna!"

McKenna's face wrinkled with suspicion. "Good things, I hope," he said.

"When I said I'd heard of you, I meant I've heard my father mention your name. You're a banker, aren't you?"

"Mr. McKenna is sole owner of New York City's largest bank," the preacher said.

For a long moment the banker studied Sarah like he would a ledger. She returned his scrutiny with a friendly smile. Then he extended his hand. Sarah took it. It was cool and wrinkled. He bowed slightly, then turned to leave. He hadn't taken many steps when he swung around and said, "Come to lunch today."

His abruptness took Sarah by surprise. "That's very kind," she stammered. She looked back at Mrs. Thomasson. "But I don't think I can."

"Why not? Of course you can!"

"You see, sir, I'm with the Christian Tract Society and . . . "

"Do they own you?"

"Of course not, it's just that . . . "

"If they don't own you, you can come." He pointed his cane at Rev. Evans. "See to it that the arrangements are made. I'll have the carriage brought around."

"Of course, Mr. McKenna," Rev. Evans replied. But from the irritated look on his face, it was clear the preacher did not appreciate being ordered around in front of his own church.

"Mr. McKenna?" Sarah called after him.

"Yes?"

"Excuse me for being so forward, Mr. McKenna," she said. "But can my friend Jenny Parsons come along? She came with me all the way from Ohio."

"A relative?" The old man shot a lingering look at Jenny.

"Not yet." Sarah replied.

"Not yet? What does that mean?"

"It means she's promised to my older brother, J.D. As soon as he gets back from the war, they plan to get married."

"J.D." The man sounded out the letters.

"It's short for John Drew."

"You plan to marry this fellow?" The question was directed to Jenny. She flushed at such a personal question in front of strangers. "Yes," she said quietly, "that is, if he'll have me."

To Sarah, McKenna asked: "Do you have other brothers and sisters?"

"Yes, sir. Other brothers, at least. There's Mar . . . "

"Tell me at dinner!" McKenna cut her off. He pivoted on his cane and walked away. Over his shoulder he cried out, "And see that she gets released or covered or whatever it is she needs, Evans."

"Yes, Mr. McKenna," the minister replied.

"What about Jenny?" Sarah called after him. "Can she come?"

Without looking back, the old man raised an open hand as though he were waving. "Yes, yes. Bring her along," he said.

Taking Mrs. Thomasson aside, the Rev. Evans entered into negotiations. He had a tougher task than he'd anticipated. Little did he realize he was attempting to exempt Sarah and Jenny from one of the Society's newly formed "no exception" rules. An animated but quiet discussion followed. The only thing Sarah actually heard was the minister's voice straining at one point when he said, "He's not just any man. He's Caleb McKenna!"

The next thing Sarah knew, she and Jenny sat in the largest, most ornate carriage she had ever seen in her life. Pedestrians actually stopped and stared at them as they rode by. Oblivious to the attention they were drawing was the white-haired banker sitting opposite them. He said not another word to them until after they turned down 57th Street, pulled past huge iron gates, and stopped in front of a mansion that looked large enough to house the entire population of Point Providence.

Chapter 11

THE moment Caleb McKenna walked through his front
door an amazing transformation overcame him. As the
doorman removed the banker's cloak and hat it was as though
a butterfly had emerged from his cocoon.

"Beatrice! Beatrice, dear! We have guests!" he called cheer-
fully up a curved stairway that was so wide ten people could
easily ascend it walking abreast. Catching the doorman, he
said, "Alfred, gather the staff. I want them all to meet our
guests."

Sarah and Jenny exchanged flabbergasted expressions. Their
host was nothing less than bubbly.

"You must forgive a foolish old man," he said to them. "It
is not often we have such lovely guests."

To the sound of clicking heels on polished hardwood
floors, the staff arrived—two maids, a cook, and Alfred, the
doorman. Shoulder to shoulder they formed a straight line.
Their host introduced them by name and informed them that
the girls were staying for dinner. With each introduction the
girls received a glassy-eyed nod, nothing more. Then they
were dismissed to their duties. Clicking heels signaled their
departure.

"Here she is, the love of my life!" McKenna motioned to a
matronly woman descending the staircase. "This is my beloved Beatrice!"

The woman on the staircase looked ancient. Never had Sarah seen so many wrinkles on a face. The woman's hair was gathered in a swirl on top of her head and adorned with a red plume. A simple yet elegant red dress with straight lines covered a plump figure. As she drew closer, Sarah noticed that her powder had been applied none too carefully. Splotches of powder were caked on her cheeks; crevices were filled with it. As for her eyes, the wife of Caleb McKenna wore the same glassy-eyed expression as the servants. She stopped four steps shy of the landing.

"Come, come, my dear. I want you to meet two beautiful young ladies." McKenna extended a hand toward his wife. When she didn't respond, he hobbled up the four steps, took her by the arm, and led her down, all the while smiling like an excited schoolboy. Pressing close to her, he whispered in her ear. Her response was a smile. It wasn't a great smile. It looked like someone had carved a smile out of wood and glued it to her face. The change in her expression caused some of the caked powder to fall from her cheeks onto the front of her dress.

"Ladies, I would like to introduce my bride, Beatrice McKenna."

"So nice to meet you, Mrs. McKenna," Sarah said, extending a hand. Mrs. McKenna looked at her hand a moment as though she weren't sure exactly what to do with it. Then she raised her hand and placed it limply into Sarah's.

"Delighted to make your acquaintance," Jenny said. The limp hand swung over toward her.

"And you're never going to guess who these ladies are," McKenna said to his wife excitedly. "This is Jenny . . ." He looked at Jenny questioningly.

"Parsons," Jenny offered.

"Forgive me for not knowing that, my dear. Jenny Parsons. These young ladies have come all the way from the frontier—Ohio to be exact—to write for the Christian Tract Society. They attended our church this morning."

"Actually, Sarah is the writer," Jenny corrected him. "I'm simply accompanying her as a friend."

Delighted surprise registered on McKenna's face. "What a wonderful thing to do for a friend," he exclaimed. "The two of you must be very close!"

The girls looked at each other and nodded.

Turning his attention to Sarah, McKenna said, "And this lovely flower is the real surprise, dear. When I overheard her introducing herself to Rev. Evans, I could not believe our good fortune. Do you know who this is?"

Sarah smiled warmly at the attention she was getting and looked to Mrs. McKenna to see if she would guess. Vacant gray eyes stared back at her.

"This is Sarah Morgan!" McKenna exclaimed. "This young lady is the daughter of Jeremiah Morgan!"

As quick as lightning there was a flash of recognition in the eyes of Beatrice McKenna. Recognition and something else. Fear? Hate? Pain? Then it was gone. Her eyes were vacant once more and her smile was attached firmly to her face.

Beatrice McKenna did not complete her dinner. After a few sips of soup she excused herself and left the dining room. Her husband offered his apologies for her, explaining that she had not been feeling well of late. To make up for her absence, he doubled his efforts to be a genial host.

The dining room, as with all the other rooms Sarah had seen, was extravagant in every way—in spaciousness, in wealth, and in cleanliness. In fact, it was this last characteristic that struck her the most. Everything was polished and shiny. The hardwood floors reflected windows and furniture like a mirror. She saw the reflection of her hand on the mahogany table whenever she reached for her goblet. The china plates reflected her face. The silver service sparkled. There was not a smudge, or fingerprint, or scuff to be seen anywhere.

This cleanliness extended to the servants as well. Their clothing was beyond clean. It was free of wrinkles or stains of any kind. And if their clothing was smooth, their duties were performed in kind. They were present when needed, absent otherwise.

"You have a lovely home, Mr. McKenna," Jenny said. "I've never been in anything this grand."

McKenna eyed the room. "It's an accumulation of many years," he said.

"So immaculate," she continued. "I was raised in a clean home. But nothing like this. This is beyond clean."

McKenna dabbed his mouth with a napkin. Instantly a maid appeared to remove his soup bowl.

"The funny thing about our house," Jenny said, "is that it is most clean whenever Mother is angry or upset about something. She takes out her frustration by cleaning." She chuckled, then said. "She has this pewter pitcher that was given to her as a wedding present. I always know that my mother and father have been fighting when that pitcher is shining like silver."

While McKenna laughed, the maid shot a glance at Jenny.

"I assure you such is not the case in this house," McKenna boomed. "I have a very efficient staff. We're like a loving family. They know there's nothing I wouldn't do for them. In return, they do their best for me."

Jenny watched the maid as she moved behind her employer carrying the soup dish. A sneer appeared on her lips. It was gone by the time she moved back into McKenna's field of vision.

"Sarah, tell me about your family," McKenna said warmly, his hands folded in front of him on the table as he leaned toward her. "It's been so long since I've seen your father.

And so many things have changed. How is he?"

Sarah placed her spoon beside the soup bowl and dabbed her lips with a napkin. The maid came to take her bowl. "Father is doing well," Sarah said. "It's too bad you couldn't have seen him while he was here."

"Next time, Lord willing," McKenna said. "Is he the pastor of a church?"

Sarah nodded. "A small church compared to Heritage Chapel, but then we live in a small town. It is nothing like New York City."

"A Heritage church?"

"Yes. There wasn't one in Point Providence, so Father began one."

"How wonderful!" McKenna said with a pleased expression. "Tell me about your brothers and sisters."

"As I was saying at the church, I have three brothers. But I'm the only girl."

"Are they all older than you?"

"Two of them are. J.D. and Marshall. Willy is the youngest."

"They're all old enough to be in the army, are they not?"

"Oh yes, they're all old enough. But Willy was born with a clubfoot, so he couldn't pass the physical examination."

"Understandable."

"Besides, he and Marshall are missing."

"In battle?"

"Not exactly. There were some problems at the training camp. I wasn't told the nature of the problems, but the result was that Willy and Marshall went further west. We haven't heard from them since."

"How awful," McKenna said.

Jenny fidgeted in her seat. She dabbed pursed lips with a napkin. Her soup bowl was instantly taken away.

"And what about J.D.?" McKenna asked.

"Well, you already know that he and Jenny are promised to

each other."

McKenna nodded approvingly at Jenny.

"He is in the army. His company elected him captain," Sarah said with pride. "He was at the Battle of Bull Run."

"Was he?" McKenna started with surprise. "So was Benjamin, my son!"

"We know," Jenny said. "Your son commands J.D.'s regiment."

A dumbfounded McKenna straightened in his chair "Why, of course!" he exclaimed. "Now why didn't I put that together for myself? Do Ben and J.D. know each other?"

"Oh yes," Jenny replied. "They know each other."

Turning his attention to Jenny, McKenna asked, "Are they friends?"

"They're not close," was all that Jenny said.

McKenna's eyebrows descended. "You're not telling me something," he said. "I can see it in your face."

"It's not my place to say anything," Jenny said. "You're our host."

"What kind of host would I be if my guests were afraid to speak freely? Please, dear. Tell me what you know."

Jenny looked to Sarah who nodded. "Your son has been hard on the entire Point Providence company, particularly J.D."

"For what reason? Do you know?"

Jenny lowered her eyes. She spoke hesitantly. "J.D. and Mr. Morgan think it has to do with you and the past."

McKenna closed his eyes and sank back in his chair. "I was afraid of that," he moaned. "I never should have told him about that time. I did a lot of things which I regret. But it's past and there's nothing we can do about it now, except try to make amends. That's why I was so happy to meet you today. It gives me a chance to make amends. As for Benjamin . . . "

He paused when the kitchen door swung open and waited until each of them was served a large portion of venison with white bread and carrots on the side. Not until the servants were gone did he continue.

"As for Benjamin, you have to understand that he is a driven man. He wants to make his mark in the world, and he has the brains and the willpower to do it. His goal is to become a politician—specifically, the governor of New York. And after that, who knows? Maybe even President. Lord knows we need someone with intelligence in that office." With a chuckle, "You can imagine how frustrated he must feel right about now with gubernatorial elections this week and him playing soldier in the army."

Sarah and Jenny smiled politely.

"Anyway," McKenna continued, "he takes himself too seriously. Always has. I guess that's my fault. I used to be that way until I learned better. You see, I used to think you had to step over people to get to the top of your chosen profession. I was born in poverty and I grew up hating it. I concluded that there were two kinds of people in the world—the haves and the have-nots. And I was determined to become one of the haves. Only I thought in order to do that you had to take everything you got from someone else." Sheepishly he said to Sarah, "That's the way I was when your father knew me. But since that time, I've learned that the more you help people, the more you have in return. So, to put it briefly, I changed my ways. I find no greater delight than in helping people achieve their dreams." He sighed deeply. "Unfortunately, Benjamin has not learned that lesson yet."

A light flamed in Sarah's eyes. "You used to be poor?" she asked.

"You have no idea how poor we were," he replied. "The house I was raised in was nothing more than a shack. We could look outside between the slits in the planks. In the winter, we'd find paper or cloth, anything to stuff in the cracks to keep the wind out. Our only source of fuel was corn husks that we would burn to keep warm."

"Oh, this is delightful!" Sarah exclaimed.

"There is nothing delightful about being cold," McKenna said.

Sarah turned red. "Please excuse me," she pleaded, "I didn't mean to make light of your poverty. It's only that you are exactly the person I need to talk to! You see, I'm writing a novel. And Harriet Beecher Stowe's husband said I needed to . . ."

McKenna held up a hand to stop her. "You know Harriet Beecher Stowe?"

Sarah spoke breathlessly. "I met her at Lane Theological Seminary . . . she's such a delightful woman . . . not anything like you would think with her being so famous and all . . . anyway, we were talking about writing . . . only when I was talking to her, I didn't know who she was . . . and she looked at some of my writing . . . then I found out she was Harriet Beecher Stowe and you can imagine how I felt! Then she offered to read my novel and give me some suggestions . . . and her husband too . . . he has a literary background . . . well, they read it and he said I needed to talk to someone who had gone from poverty to riches because one of my characters wasn't realistic . . . the character is a wealthy man and in this case, the villain . . . which isn't to imply that all wealthy people are villains . . . anyway, when you said that you were raised in poverty, it was like God was answering my prayer . . . you're exactly the person I need to talk to . . . that is, if you would be willing."

A smirk formed on McKenna's face halfway through Sarah's soliloquy and remained there until after she finished. "I'd feel privileged to be interviewed by you," he said. "Did Mrs. Stowe think it was good? Your book, I mean."

"Both she and Mr. Stowe found it promising," Sarah said, beaming as she spoke.

"Then after you interview me, maybe I can help you get it published. Several of the larger publishing houses in New York do business with my bank."

"You would do that for me?" Sarah squealed.

"It would be my pleasure."

"But you haven't even read my manuscript!"

"What do I know of manuscripts? I'm a banker. If Harriet Beecher Stowe likes it, that's good enough for me."

"This is unbelievable!" Sarah cried.

"Unbelievable," Jenny said.

McKenna stabbed a piece of venison. "Like I said, my new-found joy is making people's dreams come true."

Soft sobs mingled with the sounds of rhythmic breathing. The women's dormitory was dark except for a small patch of moonlight on the floor, an elongated replica of the room's only window.

"I thought you were my friend!" Sarah whimpered.

"A true friend isn't afraid to speak up when someone she cares about is about to make a serious mistake," Jenny whispered back from the bed next to Sarah's.

"I don't care what you think," Sarah said. "I'm keeping my appointment."

"Can't you see he's lying?"

"No, I can't. What I see is a man who is sorry for the way he acted in the past and is trying to make up for it."

Jenny flopped onto her pillow with an exasperated sigh. "He was lying about his son! Knowing how much Ben McKenna hates J.D., don't you think he would have written his father about him?"

"Maybe Ben McKenna doesn't write letters," Sarah said lamely.

"Sarah!"

"You heard Mr. McKenna say that his son was a driven man. Maybe he has so many enemies, if he wrote about them all, he wouldn't have time to do his duties!"

"WILL YOU TWO GO TO SLEEP!" An angry voice leaped out of the darkness at the far end of the dormitory.

"What about the servants and his wife?" Jenny whispered more softly.

"What about them?"

"He kept telling us how wonderful everything was in his house, how much the servants loved him and were like family, that sort of thing. But things didn't look very warm around there to me. The maid even sneered at him behind his back!"

"You're making that up!"

"I am not!"

"I can't believe how rude you're being, Jenny. Mr. McKenna was very gracious to us. He was kind and generous. And what was that nasty remark about your mother cleaning when she is angry? Really, Jenny, that was uncalled for!"

"Maybe I was rude, but I'm not blind! I just don't like that man and I don't trust him. And neither should you."

"I don't care what you say," Sarah sniffed. "I'm going to keep my interview appointment with Mr. McKenna. And, who knows, he might just help me get my book published."

"That's what this is all about, isn't it? You're going there for no other reason than to get your book published, no matter what this man has done to your father. If you ask me, that's pretty selfish, Sarah Morgan."

The room was quiet for a few moments. The only sound was an occasional sniffle from Sarah. "I can't believe you said that," she whimpered.

"That's the way it looks to me."

"Then I guess we have nothing else to say to each other."

"I guess not."

"THANK GOODNESS!" cried the voice in the dark.

The following Friday evening, after receiving special permission from Mrs. Thomasson, Sarah went alone to interview Caleb McKenna at his mansion. He was in particularly good spirits. Tuesday's election results not only had seen Democrat Horatio Seymour elected governor of New York but the party make up ground in the House of Representatives.

"All in all, a good election," pronounced McKenna as he walked Sarah to the door. "Anything, even a Democrat, to keep that well-meaning baboon in the White House from ruining this country."

"President Lincoln?" Sarah said with a startled tone.

"Don't get me wrong," McKenna said. "He's an admirable man, but he's weak in the head. With the proper men in the proper places, we can keep him from doing something foolish. Everything is under control."

"I want to thank you for taking time to talk with me, Mr. McKenna."

"It's the least I can do. And when you finish rewriting, let me know. I'm serious about getting that manuscript into the hands of a publisher."

"I'd be ever so grateful," Sarah said.

"Grateful enough to dedicate the book to me?"

Sarah's face went blank. She didn't know how to respond.

"I'm joking, my dear," McKenna laughed.

Sarah laughed with him. "If you could help me get this published, you would deserve to be in the dedication," she said. "Oh, I only wish Daniel knew about this!"

"Daniel?"

Sarah blushed. "Daniel Cooper. He's very special to me."

McKenna scratched his beard in thought. "Cooper. Cooper. Didn't your father have a friend named Cooper? Let's see, his first name was . . . "

"Seth."

"That's right!" McKenna beamed. "Your special friend isn't related to Seth Cooper, is he?"

"My Daniel is Seth Cooper's son."

"You don't say!" McKenna exclaimed. "And your two families have been close all these years?"

Sarah's shoulders slumped forward. "Until recently. The Coopers are Confederates."

"That's right! I do recall hearing that Seth Cooper took a church in Virginia." The banker mirrored Sarah's look. "I'm so sorry. This war must be very hard on you then."

"It is. I guess it wouldn't be so bad if I could at least get a letter to him now and then."

Again McKenna stroked his beard in thought. "There might be a way . . . " he said.

"Really?" Sarah struggled to keep from getting her hopes too high. "O Mr. McKenna, if you could do that, you would be the most wonderful man in the world!"

"Well, I'm not saying it would be easy," he replied. "But there are diplomatic couriers going back and forth across the lines all the time. And I'm not without resources, you know. Do you know what regiment he is in and his company?"

Sarah was crestfallen. "I haven't heard from him since before Harper's Ferry. All I can tell you is that they live in Manchester. It's south of Richmond, across the James River. Does that help?"

He placed a tender hand against Sarah's cheek. "Well, it would be easier if I had the name of his company, but don't despair. I'll see what I can do."

Sarah took his hand and kissed the palm. "I would be forever in your debt," she said.

Caleb McKenna opened the door for her.

"I can walk home," Sarah said. "The Society is only three

or four blocks distant."

"You have lived in a small town too long," McKenna replied. "It is not safe for a young lady to walk unescorted in New York in the daylight, let alone at night."

With one more expression of gratitude, Sarah stepped into the night and the awaiting carriage. The banker stood in the doorway until the carriage was gone from sight. Then he reentered his house and closed the door behind him.

On the side of the street opposite the mansion, a dark figure clung tightly to the shadows watching the departure. After the carriage passed by, the figure hurried after it on foot, cutting through alleys and back streets to keep it in sight. When Sarah emerged from the carriage, the figure ducked into another shadow and watched, noting the name and address of the Christian Tract Society.

On the road leading home Jeremiah Morgan was waylaid by his fears. They ganged up on him, attacking in concert. No sooner had he left New York behind when the feeling of insignificance descended upon him again. It assaulted him with the thought that everyone was caught up in the war, all except him. While the whole country wrestled with the greatest crisis to face its young existence, he was retreating to Point Providence to hold the hands of half of his tiny congregation — the half that was left behind.

Then, while insignificance launched its frontal assault during his waking moments, unsubstantiated fear attacked him with a flanking maneuver while he slept. The Job dream returned, in which messenger after messenger appeared to him announcing the death of his children and the destruction of everything he cherished.

"Traveling is not good for me," he muttered angrily to himself, his carriage clipping along at a steady pace. "Too much time to think. Far too much time to think."

Having spent the night at Harrisburg, Jeremiah journeyed toward Hagerstown, below which he would catch a road heading west. He'd done everything he could to escape his attacking fears. He prayed. He made mental lists of the things that needed to be done once he arrived home. He concentrated on the passing landscape with its farms and fences and fallow fields. But inevitably the fears returned. He thought of Sarah and Jenny in New York, regretting that he ever agreed to let them go there. He thought of Marshall and Willy. The two renegade runaways. *Where on God's earth were they? Couldn't they at least write and ease their mother's anguish?* He thought mostly of J.D. He had no reason to believe any harm had come to his son. But he didn't need a reason to fear the worst. Only the relatives of the confirmed dead or missing were notified. The photographs of battle he'd seen knew nothing of systematic or orderly processes that could give an accurate accounting.

Photograph artist Matthew Brady had arranged a showing of photographs in his New York gallery. It featured the carnage of the one-day battle at Antietam. Newspaper accounts had described the strategy of the generals, the three-front battle, the outcome with both sides claiming victory, and a list of dead, wounded, captured, and missing. In short, the news account was textbook material. However, Mr. Brady's photographs, like never before in history, brought the battle's aftermath to life—or more correctly, to death in all its grisly horror.

The photographs showed men—boys really—Union and Confederate, piled on top of one another three and four deep on a sunken road. One picture portrayed a soldier on his back, his eyes staring lifelessly toward heaven. Jeremiah could hear the flies buzzing over him. Another picture showed bodies scattered thickly across the remnant of a cornfield, their pockets turned outward or their shoes missing—the victims of after-battle scavengers. Jeremiah found himself compellingly drawn from picture to picture. He approached each with a fresh attack of anxiety as he scanned the faces of the dead, expecting at any moment to see the twisted face of J.D. staring back at him.

From one end of the exhibit to the other, Jeremiah prayed for his son. All of the Morgan family hopes and dreams rested on J.D. Surely God would not let the Morgan line end in this grotesque manner on some farmer's cornfield.

Jeremiah had never felt more helpless. He ached horribly. For the first time in his life, all of his children were out of his reach. Beyond his help, beyond his counsel.

Previously when demons of doubt assailed him, Jeremiah would occupy himself with a task or project of some sort. He found that if he kept himself busy, the demons eventually grew tired of waiting for him and disappeared. But today that tactic was impossible. With miles of road before him and nothing else to occupy his mind, all he could do was ride in misery as his twin fears launched attack after attack.

As the road wove through wooded ridges with open farms in between, carriage traffic increased for no discernible reason. Soon Jeremiah found himself hedged in all around by a line of carriages that equaled any logjam he'd encountered in New York. The carriage occupants wore church clothes and solemn expressions. Little talking was done except between drivers and horses.

"Excuse me," Jeremiah said to the hollow-cheeked driver next to him. "Where is everyone going?"

The driver of the carriage looked Jeremiah over suspiciously. Peering cautiously around him was a young woman wearing a black bonnet. She also scrutinized Jeremiah. "Memorial service," came the curt reply, then the other driver fixed his eyes forward.

"Thank you," Jeremiah said. *Apparently not the talkative*

type, he thought.

The hollow-cheeked driver leaned toward the woman as she whispered something in his ear. When he straightened up, he said to Jeremiah flatly: "A public service. For the fallen Pennsylvania regiments at Antietam. You're welcome to come if you want."

"Thank you, again," Jeremiah said, adding a smile and a nod to the woman.

It wasn't the kindest invitation he'd ever received, but hoping the diversion would subdue his attacking fears at least for the day, Jeremiah followed the line of carriages into a field in which a platform had been erected. He anchored his horse among a small clump of trees on the edge of the field, stretched aching muscles, and rubbed inflamed knuckles. A crowd of several hundred people had gathered in front of a platform skirted with red, white, and blue bunting. Jeremiah ambled toward the crowd, choosing a place along the outside edge since he wasn't one of the mourners.

As a minister he'd grown accustomed to, but never comfortable with, funerals. It was his observation that most funerals and memorial services were very much alike. Death was the great humbler. Heads were bowed. Feet were heavy. People spoke in whispers. As a young minister, he had tried to prepare people for death. But no matter his method, families always greeted death with surprise. Jeremiah gave up trying to prepare them against their wills and stuck to ministering to them when death touched them, as it always did.

From the cluster of trees next to his carriage came the sound of angry voices. Two men in top hats were going at each other furiously. They both shook index fingers under each other's noses—one reaching up to do so, the other bending over—and both were shouting at the same time. The taller of the two men backed the smaller man into Jeremiah's horse. Doubling his effort, the smaller man gained back some ground only to lose it again, resulting in another bump against the horse.

Heated words at such a time were nothing unusual. Jeremiah had observed that no matter how great their faith, death frightened people. It put their nerves on edge. And it didn't take much to push teetering nerves too far. He also noticed that on those occasions when nerves spilled over the edge, people often felt contrite afterward, but also better that their mounting emotion had found a release.

Still, Jeremiah thought it best to wander over toward his horse. Not that he thought his horse was in any danger, but to be cautious he went anyway. After all, it was the only horse he had and Ohio was still a long way off.

Acting like his only concern was the horse, Jeremiah took the bridle in hand, patted the horse's neck, then checked the harness. His presence effectively altered the flow of the argument but didn't stop it as the two men cast furtive glances at him. Jeremiah continued about his business which was really no business at all. From what he could gather from his late arrival to the argument, each one was blaming the other over the absence of a scheduled speaker. Once again the shorter man was backed into the horse. Annoyed, the horse swung its head toward the offenders.

"Can I be of any help, gentlemen?" Jeremiah asked.

The taller man, who had an elongated face and a long, thin neck, replied sarcastically, "Not unless you're a minister."

"I am a minister," Jeremiah replied.

The way the two men looked at him, Jeremiah felt like the pearl of great price and that these two men would willingly sell everything they had to acquire him. The smaller man was at his side in a flash. His round cheeks were beet red from the exertion of his argument with the man with the long neck. Looking up at Jeremiah, two uneven rows of teeth stretched between the scarlet cheeks.

"Surely God has sent you, sir," Red Face said with whimpering excitement. "You see, we are in a desperate plight. We were to have a chaplain address the crowd on this occasion, but he has either been detained or . . . " he shot a murderous look over his shoulder at Long Neck, " . . . he was not given the proper date and time. Good sir, would you be so kind as to help us? We need someone who can bring a word of encouragement to these good people who have come from all over the county to remember their dead. And you, being a minister and all, surely have done this sort of thing hundreds of times. Could we prevail upon you to address them?"

Long Neck added, "We know what we are asking you to do is a daunting task, since you've had no time to prepare. But we have mayors and elected officials waiting for some kind of memorial service to begin. And neither one of us is a speaker." He looked to Red Face with pleading eyes to agree with him on this point.

For the first time since Jeremiah spotted them, they agreed on something. "We are definitely not public speakers," Red Face insisted.

"Nor is anyone else on our committee," Long Neck added. "Tell us what me must do to persuade you, kind sir, to offer just a few words to these good people. If you consent, we will be forever in your debt."

Two pairs of tired, anxious eyes pleaded with Jeremiah, one from on high, the other from below.

"I'm afraid, gentlemen," Jeremiah replied, "that I'm not dressed for such an occasion. You see, I've just come from New York and I'm traveling to . . . "

Red Face grabbed Jeremiah's arm in desperation. "It matters not how you are dressed," he cried. "These people are not ones for finery. They are farmers and their wives. But we can explain your attire, sir, if it bothers you. Though I am confident it makes little difference to them in their grief. Sir, if there is any compassion in your heart, please say you will give them a word from the Lord."

Jeremiah could understand how the two men felt. It is a meeting planner's nightmare to have everything prepared and the speaker not arrive. Then he looked past them at the gathering of mourners. What these men said of the assembly was true. These people needed a word from the Lord. *And was not this the very ministry he had been called of God to do?*

"I'll get my Bible," he said.

Long Neck—Jeremiah never did learn the names of the two men—introduced him to the gathering as a New York City pastor with a large congregation who had been enlisted for this specific occasion. He added that due to other pressing engagements in New York, the good pastor had just recently arrived and thus did not have time to change from his traveling clothes.

Jeremiah made his way to the front center of the platform, unsure how to respond to his introduction. He decided it would do more harm than good to challenge the introduction point by point. He simply said offhand that although he had just arrived from New York, he was currently the pastor of a church in Ohio. Then he paused a moment to measure the needs of the people who stood before him.

They were a sea of mourners. Mothers and fathers whose sons had gone off to war, never to return. Maidens who had promised to be faithful to someone now dead. Wives who would wake up alone every morning, their empty beds memorials to slain husbands. Children, backed against their mothers' legs, not understanding why their mothers were so sad, not understanding why their fathers couldn't come home.

They stood in clusters looking up to him. Their eyes were hollow; their lives broken; their hearts drained. Some, who in their grief could not yet bear to stand with strangers, secluded themselves in closed carriages, listening in private.

Jeremiah brought them a word of comfort from God. He spoke to them with the tenderness of a pastor; he spoke to them with the empathy of a father whose son was also in the army.

"The psalmist reminds us," he preached, "of that which is abundantly clear to us at this moment—life is uncertain. It is fragile. And on any given day, any one of us may be called home. In what is probably the most familiar passage in the Bible, the psalmist writes, 'Yea, though I walk through the valley of the shadow of death, I will fear no evil: for Thou art with me; Thy rod and Thy staff they comfort me.'

"You must understand, the psalmist was not unacquainted with the uncertainties of life. He refers to the valley of the shadow of death. As a shepherd, it was his task to guide his sheep safely through the gorges and canyons surrounding Bethlehem. He knew that predators often lurked deep in the shadows. He knew that without warning any one of those predators could leap from its hiding place and kill his sheep. But he also knew that it was his responsibility as the shepherd to protect his sheep.

"Then it dawned on him. When he faced the dark uncertainties of life, he was not alone. That is why he cries out with joy, 'The Lord is my shepherd!'

"Dear friends, neither are you alone in your dark valley of grief. God will shepherd you through the valley.

"Listen to another passage of Scripture. This time from the prophet Isaiah: 'Hast thou not known? hast thou not heard, that the everlasting God, the Lord, the Creator of the ends of the earth, fainteth not, neither is weary? there is no searching of His understanding. He giveth power to the faint; and to them that have no might He increaseth strength. Even the youths shall faint and be weary, and the young men shall utterly fall: But they that wait upon the Lord shall renew their strength; they shall mount up with wings as eagles; they shall run, and not be weary; and they shall walk, and not faint.'

"With these words the prophet describes three levels of living. One level is a high level of exaltation—'with wings of eagles.' This level describes those times when life doesn't get any better. When our hearts are overflowing with young love. When we hold our newborn offspring in our arms for the first time. When we sit arm-in-arm on the front porch swing with our spouse of several decades and watch the sunset. This is life. But it is not the only level of life. There is another level in which we 'run, and not grow weary.' This phrase describes the day-in, day-out existence of life. When the work is done at the end of long, satisfying day. This too is life. But there is a third level of existence when we 'shall walk, and not faint.' If we are honest with ourselves, there are times when it is a struggle to get out of bed in the morning. When we wonder if we'll be able just to put one foot in front of the other. Times when we want to give up, to drop out of the race. Times when the pain of life seems too much to bear and we don't know if we can continue on.

"It is upon this third level of existence that we find ourselves today. The predators have struck. Our losses are real. Our grief seems unbearable. But God is here with us. He is our shepherd, and He will see us through this valley."

Following the service, Jeremiah made himself available to any family who wanted him to pray with them. He wept as Mr. Brady's disturbing pictures came to mind. He couldn't help but wonder as he prayed if that was their son, their betrothed, their father he had seen in those pictures.

Afterward, preparing to leave, Jeremiah felt warmed by the turn of events. This unexpected diversion from his trip had given the day some meaning. What's more, the Scripture passages he'd read had been an encouragement to him as well. His personal demons would not be bothering him anymore today.

"Rev. Morgan?" A firm hand rested on his shoulder.

"Yes?" Turning, Jeremiah looked into the unsmiling face of a sturdy man with a firm jaw.

"Your presence is requested at that carriage." The man pointed to a carriage off by itself on the far side of the field. It was a large carriage. Its owner was evidently wealthy. The messenger added: "I was instructed to tell you that a grieving father requests your counsel."

Jeremiah was by now anxious to get back on the road. But the life of a minister is not his own and he determined to finish what he had begun. He followed the messenger across the field to the carriage. Theirs were the only two carriages left in the field. The platform was empty. The last of the mourners were making their way home down the road.

Jeremiah did not see who was in the carriage until after the man with the firm jaw had opened the door and Jeremiah had stepped halfway in.

"Thank you for coming," said the carriage's sole occupant.

Jeremiah was so stunned at who he saw, he almost fell back out the door. Long fingers motioned for him to have a seat. So Jeremiah Morgan stumbled into the carriage seat opposite the President of the United States, Abraham Lincoln.

Chapter 12

T HE Confederate major general was a comical sight. His arms flailed dramatically. His saber flashed in the late autumn sun. His head bounced side-to-side like a rag doll. Stomping behind a company of soldiers hunkered down in a trench, the major general did all he could to get them to advance. He shouted. He kicked dirt on them. He slapped some of them on their backsides with the flat of his blade. Nothing he did could make them budge.

To demonstrate to his men that they had nothing to fear, he stepped over them. Atop the defense works he shamed the soldiers for their lack of courage. "See?" he screamed. "We're out of range!" Turning forward with arms outstretched, he said, "They couldn't hit an elephant at this dis . . . "

BLAM!

The major general collapsed into the trench, dead. From eight hundred yards away the sniper coolly watched from his treetop perch. He pushed the hair out of his eyes, combing his fingers through a streak of white. In a voice so low it was barely audible, he said, "Without the shedding of blood, there is no remission of sin."

The Confederate trench came alive. Marshall Morgan had poked a hornet's nest. "That made 'em mad, Willy," he yelled to his brother on the ground. "Here they come."

A dozen soldiers stormed over the ridge of the trench,

screaming at the tops of their lungs. Marshall's deadly shot had crossed a tree-studded ravine. For the soldiers to get to him, they had to circle around to his left along a ridge. That gave Marshall and Willy a little extra time, but not much.

Willy slipped on some leaves as he positioned himself directly under the limb that supported his brother, his arms stretched high. Marshall dropped the heavy rifle to him. Willy caught it as he had done so many times before. Swinging on a branch, Marshall hit the ground with a thud.

"Let's go!" he cried. Grabbing the rifle from Willy, he bounded over the far side of the ridge. Just then he heard a cry behind him.

"Ahhhh!"

Marshall slid to a stop. Willy was on the ground at the base of the tree. "What happened?" Marshall cried.

"Sprained my ankle!"

Marshall ran back to his brother. "Is it bad?"

"Yeah."

"Try to stand on it." Marshall yanked Willy upright and positioned the crutch under his brother's arm. "How's that?"

Willy took one step and crumbled. Through the trees Marshall could hear the Confederates coming.

"Go on without me!" Willy cried. "Go!"

The fir tree that had served as Marshall's perch was situated on the top of a ridge that fell away on two sides—a side that sloped away from the Confederate trench, the one Marshall had started down; and a side descending into the ravine that separated them from the Confederates.

"Go!" Willy insisted.

Marshall kneeled down next to his brother. "Hold on and don't make a sound!"

"What are you going to . . ."

Before Willy could finished his sentence, Marshall shoved

his brother down the ravine closest to the Confederates. Willy rolled over and over down the ravine, stopping only when he rammed against a fallen log. He moaned. Marshall then tore a snatch of material from his shirt and snagged it on the trunk of a tree a few feet down the opposite side of the ridge. Coming back over the ridge, he vaulted down toward Willy. The screeching of the Confederates was getting louder.

"Stop moaning or we're dead!" Marshall whispered upon reaching Willy. He covered Willy with leaves, then hid behind the fallen tree trunk just as the Confederates reached the fir tree.

Peering around the end of the log, Marshall watched as a Confederate private spotted the snatch of cloth. He waved it like a flag. "Down this way!" he cried. Then he disappeared over the far side of the ridge. The others followed him, screaming as they went.

Willy moaned.

"Be still!" Marshall whispered.

"For how long?"

"What's your hurry?" Marshall asked. "Do you have some pressing appointments I should know about?"

The Morgan brothers didn't stir for the rest of the afternoon and into the night. Marshall watched as the scout troop returned to their trench by way of the ridge. They shuffled back dejectedly for not having caught the sniper. Not one of them even bothered to explore the other side of the ridge.

Under cover of darkness, Marshall pulled his bruised and injured brother out of the pile of leaves. Lifting Willy onto his back, Marshall carried him up the ridge then down the other side to safety. They didn't stop until well after midnight. When they did, Marshall collapsed from exhaustion. The two brothers slept at the base of a small bluff without a fire and without having anything to eat.

After escaping from the Ohio regiment guard house, with the cloaked assistance of his company, Marshall grabbed Willy and the two fled into the wilderness. Since the Union army had cast them both aside, they decided to form a militia of two and do battle against the South on their own.

They stayed alive by foraging for food at night from farms. Along the way they managed to pick up a rifle, a few rounds of ammunition, and an old Mexican War haversack at an abandoned house. Since their army consisted of only two soldiers, they concluded that their offensive would have to be one of stealth with hit-and-run tactics. Ambushing a couple of scouts, they picked up more ammunition. Marshall used it for target practice. Hour after hour, day after day, he aimed and fired until he could hit anything in his sight. Although he tried hard, Willy never was any good with a rifle. His contribution was his artistic attention to detail. He had the ability to scan the scenery and locate the hiding places of their enemies. He did this by noticing manmade disturbances in the natural order. He would spot the landscape anomalies and Marshall would get into position and pick off the Confederate in hiding.

At first they had to sneak up dangerously close to their victims because of the limited range of Marshall's Sharp's rifle. With Willy's limited maneuverability, they had their fair share of hairbreadth escapes. One lucky day they got the best of a Confederate sharpshooter, and the army of two came into possession of a British-made Whitworth rifle with a mounted scope. It was a heavy piece, weighing over thirty pounds, but its hexagonal bullets were deadly from a much greater distance. The rifle was believed to have a range of one mile.

As summer turned to fall, the Morgan brothers worked their way deeper and deeper into Southern territory, each brother contributing according to his abilities. Although Willy felt a rush of excitement each time his landscape analysis proved accurate, still he longed to be in a real army. And it wasn't unusual for him to sink into a depressed mood which lasted several days whenever his clubfooted slowness risked their lives.

Marshall was methodical and determined in everything he did. He was on a religious crusade and wouldn't be satisfied until every slave in the South was freed, even if that meant he would have to kill every Southerner to free them. Taking his cue from the Old Testament, he dedicated himself to his crusade by taking a Nazirite vow. He swore to abstain from all products of the vine, to abstain from using a razor, and never to touch a dead body until his mission was fulfilled. The first part of his vow was easy to keep since he had never been one to drink wine or ale. Observance of the second part brought about a change in his appearance as his hair and beard grew. And the long range of the Whitworth rifle made the third part of the vow easier to keep since he could kill from a great distance.

After each kill he recited his verse: *Without the shedding of blood, there is no remission of sin.* His targets were mainly officers. The higher the rank, the better. He even dreamed of the day when he could get General Robert E. Lee—that self-righteous colonel at Harper's Ferry who captured John Brown—in his rifle sights. He reasoned: Chop off the head of the snake and the serpent is harmless.

"Weather's turning cold." Willy held his hands up to the fire. Four eggs crackled in a frying pan. Marshall had appropriated them earlier from a nearby hen house. Now, while he cleaned the Whitworth, Willy cooked breakfast. They were encamped on the edge of a small clearing in a forest. For Marshall, the smell of eggs frying in the cold morning air had become one of life's greatest sensations.

He replied to Willy's weather comment: "As soon as the Rebs get their winter coats, we'll have ours. Of course, they'll probably have a brand new hole in them. But we can patch that."

"I don't want a Confederate coat!" Willy whined. "We'll get shot at by our own side!"

"Maybe we can get some that aren't military issue," Marshall said. "Then again, I've rather enjoyed using Confederate equipment." He patted the Whitworth. "Gives their deaths a touch of irony, don't you think? Rebs being killed by their own bullets. Are those eggs ready yet?"

"Marshall, look!" Willy whispered urgently. "A scouting party!" He pointed across the meadow. Five, no six, soldiers entered the clearing. They hadn't spotted Marshall and Willy yet. At first sight it wasn't clear whether they were Union or Confederate. A diversity of clothing was still the norm for the Western armies on both sides. Consequently, the Morgan boys had found it a prudent practice to hide first and determine which side the soldiers represented second.

Marshall snatched up the pieces of the Whitworth, the haversack, and his cartridge. He slipped into the woods quickly and noiselessly. Willy reached for his crutch and the Sharp's rifle. In his haste he kicked the handle of the frying pan. The frying pan clanged to the ground, dumping the eggs in the dirt and grass. Willy looked up. Sure enough, the scouting party had spotted him. As fast as he could move, he hobbled into the trees. The crack of a rifle was followed instantly by flying wood splinters from a tree next to his head. Willy froze and raised his hands.

An adolescent voice from behind him cried, "I told you I smelled eggs! Didn't I tell you? There they are! Eggs! Just like I said."

Slowly, Willy turned around. Six soldiers ran toward him. Five kept an eye on him while scanning the trees behind him

for Marshall. The sixth soldier, a pudgy-faced boy s44freck-
les, had eyes only for the frying pan. As they got closer, Willy
breathed easy. He'd been captured by five privates and a corporal. The corporal wore Union insignia.

"What a relief!" Willy cried. "We thought you were Rebs!'

The soldiers kept their rifles trained on Willy, their eyes
still searching the forest. All except for the pudgy private. He
dropped to his knees next to the fire.

"Oh, look at them eggs!" he lamented. "Them beautiful,
beautiful eggs!"

"Who are you?" the corporal asked as he scrutinized Willy,
following the length of the crutch down to his clubfoot.

"Name's Willy Morgan. From Ohio."

The corporal had a large, bushy brown mustache that
drooped well past his chin.

"Them beautiful, beautiful eggs!" the pudgy private cried.

"Dimick!" the corporal shouted. "Will you forget about
your stomach for one minute?" To Willy: "There were two
of you. Where's the other one?"

"Right here." Marshall emerged from the forest to the
right of the soldiers. Two of them swung their weapons nervously toward him. He walked forward with the Whitworth
pieces held high, barrel pointed toward the sky, and his other
hand up and open, from which dangled the strap of the haversack. One of the soldiers relieved him of the Whitworth and
immediately set to examining it. With relish, he began piecing
it together.

"Identify yourself," the mustached corporal ordered.

"Just like my brother said. We're Morgans from Ohio."

The corporal's eyes bounced back and forth from one
brother to the other looking for similarities. "How do we
know you two ain't Johnny Rebs?" he asked.

"Look at this, Corporal," the private with Marshall's rifle
said. "It's a Whitworth. The kind used by Reb sharpshoot-

ers." The private held the weapon reverently. His eyes caressed it inch by inch. He was obviously a lover of guns who was getting his first look at the British-made piece.

The corporal glanced at the weapon. "So it is," he said. "So it is." To Marshall: "Care to change your story?"

"No," Marshall replied. "I got if off a Confederate soldier. It was better than mine."

"You kill him to get it?"

"That's the only way he'd part with it."

The corporal's mustache twitched in irritation at the answer. "You got any proof you're not Johnny Rebs?" he asked.

"Just our word," Marshall replied.

"All right, let's move out," the corporal said. "We're taking them back to camp." To Marshall: "You can tell your story to my captain. Let's go, men." He glanced over at the pudgy private by the fire. The boy was gathering pieces of the fried eggs from the ground, dusting off the dirt and picking off the grass before eating them. "Dimick! You're making me sick!" he cried. "Come on! Let's go."

The scouting party ushered Marshall and Willy through the trees to a dirt road that took them south. The corporal led the way with Marshall and Willy surrounded on all sides by soldiers. The Morgan brothers exchanged glances. Marshall gave Willy a confident nod. There was nothing to worry about. He was sure he could convince the corporal's superior they were not Confederate spies. In fact, the very thought that anyone would even suspect him of being a Confederate was downright ludicrous when one thought about it. Dimick and the soldier cradling Marshall's rifle trailed behind them. The pudgy private licked egg from his fingers.

"Dimick, you're disgusting!" the corporal shouted back to him. "You'd better not complain that you got sick over them eggs! You have picket duty tonight, and you've managed to weasel out of it the past two . . . "

BLAM! BLAM!

A bullet caught Dimick in the forehead, killing him instantly. He collapsed to the ground, his fingers still in his mouth. The soldier carrying Marshall's rifle dropped the weapon and fell to his knees, his hands clutching a growing red stain on his chest. He fell face forward in the dirt.

"Take cover!" the corporal cried. It was an unnecessary order, for the remaining scouts were already scattering for protection.

Marshall grabbed Willy by the shirt with one hand and had the presence of mind to scoop up his rifle with the other. With all his might, he pulled Willy with him to the side of the road, plunging headlong behind a cluster of boulders. The corporal was right there with them, scurrying to stick his rifle barrel in Marshall's ribs.

"Friends of yours?" he said. Cautiously he pulled the Whitworth from Marshall's hands.

The three remaining privates managed to find cover on the far side of the road behind some trees.

"Willcox!" the corporal called. "Anyone else hit?"

"No!" came the reply. "What do we do?"

The corporal scanned the landscape in the direction of the shots. The road was clear. There were trees of various sizes scattered here and there on both sides. A gully to the left. But no sign of snipers. He raised up slightly to get a better view.

BLAM! Ping!

A bullet struck the rock and ricocheted off.

The corporal pulled his head back with a curse. "Can you see anything?" he shouted to the others.

"Nothing!" came the reply times three.

The corporal cursed again. "Great!"

"Corporal," Marshall said in a low, calm voice, "if my brother and I can clear the area of snipers, will that convince you that we're not Rebs?"

The mustache sneered at him. "And just how do you propose to do that?"

"It's what we do best," Marshall replied. "Will you believe us?"

"I don't trust you."

"You don't have to," Marshall said. "Keep your rifle in my ribs. If at any time I do something you don't like, pull the trigger."

The corporal eyed him suspiciously. He scanned the area again, weighing the possibilities. From the rising anger in his face, Marshall could tell he was concluding he had little choice. "If you breathe funny," the corporal said, "I'll shoot you, then your brother."

"Agreed. I'll need my rifle."

Reluctantly, the corporal handed over the Whitworth rifle. At the same time he gave Marshall's ribs an extra jab just to remind him it was there.

Marshall took the rifle and looked it over. The gun-loving scout knew what he was doing. The Whitworth was ready to load. He reached for the ammunition pouch. "How many are there, Willy?"

"Two." There was no hesitation in Willy's voice.

The corporal stared at Willy in skeptical wonder, much like he would if trying to figure out how a magician was performing a sleight-of-hand trick.

Marshall calmly rested the barrel in a crevice between two boulders. "Where are they?" he asked.

"The first one is on the far side of the road. The fir tree with the broken lower branch about 500 yards distant."

"Got it," Marshall said.

Willy continued: "If the tree were a clock, the sniper would be in the two o'clock position."

Marshall squinted at the tree. "Got it," he said. He pressed his cheek against the rifle stock and took aim, squeezing his left eye shut. He waited and waited and waited. Then, taking a slight breath, he held it.

BLAM!

Five hundred yards in the distance a Confederate sniper fell from the tree.

Marshall mumbled: "Without the shedding of blood, there is no remission of sin."

"If that don't beat all!" the corporal exclaimed.

"Where's the other one?" Marshall asked. Willy located him. Marshall took aim. A minute later a second Confederate sniper tumbled from his perch.

"The area's cleared," Marshall said.

"You stand up first," the corporal ordered, poking Marshall in the side.

Marshall laid his weapon down and stood. Willy stood too. After a quick glance around, so did the corporal. He stared at the brothers in admiration.

"How did you spot them snipers?" he asked Willy.

"The trees were wrong," Willy answered.

"Trees were wrong? What do you mean by that?"

"Just what I said. They were wrong. I've been drawing trees all my life, so I know how they're built. Snipers have a bad habit of rearranging the limbs of the trees to give them something extra to hide behind. I simply show Marshall where the leaves are wrong. He does the rest."

"Incredible!" the corporal exclaimed.

The scouting party buried their dead. Leaving the Confederate snipers where they fell, they returned to camp. Marshall and Willy went with them, not as prisoners, but as breakfast guests. The corporal felt he owed them at least that much.

Following breakfast the corporal took Marshall and Willy to his captain. Leaving them there, he went to make the necessary changes in the picket-duty schedule. Pudgy Private Dimick would be missing his turn for the third and final time.

"Marshall?"

"Yeah?"

"I've been thinking."

The Morgan boys had been given a two-man tent to use while they were in camp. This was their third day there. Marshall dozed away the afternoon, his hands behind his head and a smile on his lips as he listened to company after company drill in a nearby field. Willy sat on a stump near the tent opening. He sharpened a pencil with his knife. Both were enjoying the feeling of security that came from being surrounded by so many other soldiers, a security they hadn't felt in months.

"So you've been thinking. Are you telling me this is a new experience for you?" Marshall teased.

Willy grinned, but it quickly vanished. "I've been thinking that you ought to take the position that Captain Hill offered you."

"Not without you. We're a team."

Following their breakfast, Captain S. Wilbur Hill had interviewed the Morgan boys. He was clearly impressed with Marshall's marksmanship and had inquired if he or Willy had any previous record with the army. Marshall told him that they had gone to enlist with all the other men from their town, but when Willy was rejected because of his feet, the two of them struck out on their own. No other details were offered. Hill came right out with it. He needed good sharpshooters. *Would Marshall be interested in joining the army?* Marshall's answer was immediate. *Not without Willy.* So Captain Hill expressed his regrets and the Morgan boys were dismissed.

"The money would come in handy," Willy said. "You wouldn't have to steal to survive."

Marshall raised up on one elbow. "You know, that just might work, Willy. I could take the position and since I'd be off by myself most of the time, you could just join me. Great idea, Willy. And you're right about the pay. It will come in handy."

"That's not what I was thinking, Marshall," Willy said. He kept his head lowered as he spoke, concentrating on sharpening a pencil that was by now already sharp.

"Something's bothering you," Marshall said.

Willy didn't say it directly. After a few attempts to get it out, he said, "I almost got us killed the other day. Twice. And that wasn't the only time. It's happened before."

"Nonsense, Willy! Did you see the way that corporal looked at you after you picked out those Rebs in the trees? He was impressed. Mighty impressed."

"You had to pull me out of the road to keep me from getting shot. And if that scouting party were Rebs, we'd either be dead by now or on our way to Andersonville Prison."

"Willy, we each have our strengths and our liabilities. Together we make a good team. We're the Morgan brothers army—the best two-man army in the world."

Again Willy grinned, but it soon became clear to Marshall that brief moments of levity were not about to change his mind. "There's a photographic wagon just outside camp," Willy said. "I talked to the photographer yesterday. He's looking for an assistant. I'm thinking about taking the position."

The news pulled Marshall from the tent. He hovered over his brother. "You don't know anything about photography," he said.

"He's willing to train me."

"I thought you hated photographs."

"I hated photographers because they stole all my business. But, the way I see it, photographs are here to stay. And if people want photographs rather than sketches, why starve to death fighting it when I could be making money by taking pictures?"

"But you're an artist!" Marshall insisted.

Willy nodded. "That's why the photographer wants me. Seems he knows how to develop pictures but has no concept of balance and contrast and composition. The photography business is getting competitive and newspaper editors want more than just a picture of the battlefield."

Marshall studied his brother. "You're serious about this, aren't you?"

"How often do we get two job offers in as many days?" Willy asked.

"If this is what you want to do," Marshall said, "then take the position. I just don't want you going off because you think you're putting us in danger. After all, we're at war. People get killed every day and most of them have two good feet."

"That just got me to thinking," Willy said. "Fact is, I can't pass up this chance to become a photographic artist."

Marshall slapped his brother on the back. "I'm going to miss you," he said.

"Are you going to tell Captain Hill you've changed your mind about becoming a sharpshooter for the army?"

Pulling on the tip of his beard and crinkling his nose, Marshall said, "I don't know. I'll have to think about it."

Three days later Marshall Morgan rode out on his first reconnaissance mission for the Union army. Willy waved to him from the side of Zeke Custis' Photographic Arts wagon. A bag of horse feed lay at his feet. Once his brother was out of sight, Willy picked up the bag and attended to one of his many duties, none of them having anything to do with the art of photography.

"God be with you, Marshall," Willy whispered as he fit the feed bag on the fly-infested horse.

Chapter 13

MARSHALL was content to wait. He had learned that patience was a sharpshooter's greatest virtue, especially at a time like this when it was sharpshooter against sharpshooter. He lay belly-down behind a log, staring at a mammoth fir tree. There was a Confederate soldier in the tree, of that he was sure. What he wasn't sure of was his exact location. He had a general idea, but the area was too large for certainty. So he was waiting for the Reb to make a mistake, to grow restless and shake a tree branch or, better still, to climb out of the tree.

It was by accident that Marshall had spotted the other sharpshooter. Marshall liked to think of it as a gift from God. He caught the movement in the tree out of the corner of his eye just as he was about to step from a small thatch of trees onto a forest path. His horse was a tied to a tree several hundred yards distant. Marshall had left him there to take a look around on foot and was returning when he spotted the foot in the tree.

The foot appeared only briefly. Actually, it was the bending motion of a branch that caught Marshall's eye. The foot stepped onto the branch, which bent down far enough for Marshall to see a gray pant leg. Then the foot disappeared. Apparently the other sniper had been getting into position. A moment later everything in the tree was still, but by then

Marshall was concealed behind the log. There was no indication he'd been spotted. The way Marshall figured it, the sniper was now waiting for someone to return to the horse. Hence, the gift from God. If Marshall had not seen the swaying branch, he surely would have been picked off by the sniper the moment he approached his mount.

Willy, where are you when I need you? Marshall thought as he scrutinized the sniper-laden tree for the hundredth time. *If the tree were a clock, he'd be at nine o'clock, halfway between the tip of the hand and the stem*, Marshall guessed, using Willy's terminology. Looking through the rifle scope, he focused hard on the spot—looking for a patch of gray, or a glint of metal, or a slight movement. But he saw only green. He waited.

Willy threw a blanket over the snoring Zeke Custis, who had passed out by the fire, and went to bed. This was typical for Zeke. If he wasn't printing photographs or selling them, he was drinking. The photographer usually roused himself from bed by noon, spent the afternoon making prints, sold them in the evening when the soldiers had a couple of hours of free time, then drank himself to sleep. Rarely did he ever take photographs. He was content to sell prints he made from a set of "very special" glass negatives he'd purchased from a New York photographer. Whenever Willy inquired when Zeke would be taking some photos of his own, he always replied, "Too much time, too little profit."

Occasionally there was enough time and profit to get Zeke to haul out his camera. If a newspaper or magazine agreed to pay him enough, Zeke would photograph the aftermath of a battlefield in all its gruesome glory. But it was a cumbersome process. After setting up his camera he would have to sensitize a glass plate with a collodion solution, load the plate in the camera, shoot the picture, then process the plate while the emulsion was still moist. From the negative image on the glass he would make a couple of prints that might or might not ever appear in a publication. It was the same with portraits.

"One, maybe two prints per negative for the portraits," Zeke complained. "It's not cost efficient. The key to success in the photography business is to print the kind of pictures that a lot of people want. Then you can sell hundreds of prints from just one negative!"

And if the line behind his wagon every night was any indication, Zeke knew what kind of pictures soldiers wanted. He never told Willy the subject of his pictures. But it wasn't hard for Willy to find out. He couldn't remember how many times soldiers had come up to him to ask him if Zeke was the one selling the "provocative" pictures. His employer was selling pictures of French girls posing in lingerie.

Willy found Zeke Custis to be crude, insulting, and obnoxious; and his pictures disgusting. But being with Zeke allowed him to stay close to the army camp and battlefields. And while he fed Zeke and his horses, and picked up after him, and cooked his meals, and occasionally learned something about photography, Willy still dreamed of someday finding himself in the midst of a raging battle, his rifle blazing away, his saber flashing gloriously in the sun.

It's time to see if I've learned anything from Willy, Marshall said to himself. He aimed at a patch of needles that looked out of place. With a short intake of air, he steadied himself. Gently, he pressured the trigger.

BLAM!

Branches in the tree shook in a cascading series as a gray-clad form tumbled down. The Confederate sniper hit the ground with a thud. His rifle fell out of the tree after him.

Got him! Marshall congratulated himself. Then, as was his practice, he said, "Without the shedding of . . . "

But his quotation was premature. The sniper in gray rallied. Scrambling to his feet, he grabbed his rifle and sprinted into a thick patch of trees. He was an odd sight. An old man, judging by his full gray beard and mustache; yet the man had no hair on top of his head. It looked to Marshall as though all of the man's hair had slipped from his head, down the sides of his face, and was now dangling under his chin. Still, he was spry for having gray hair. He skedaddled as quickly as a young man.

Marshall grimaced. "Guess I'm just not as good at spotting them as Willy," he uttered to himself. He considered chasing after the retreating sniper, but decided against it. The lucky Reb was either halfway to Atlanta by now or his regiment lay just beyond the trees. Either way, he wasn't worth the chase. So Marshall gathered his things. He decided it was time to return to camp, at least two day's ride away. He mounted and got underway.

His report to Captain Hill would be that Vicksburg was girding its defenses for attack. The city was being fortified on the northern and eastern sides. The western perimeter was heavy with cannon in anticipation of a naval attack from the Mississippi River. Marshall would recommend that the sooner the Union armies strike, the better. By spring, Vicksburg would be prepared for a siege. However, he knew it was unlikely that the Union armies would launch an offensive before spring. It would take that long for them to gather and coordinate the necessary forces on land and river.

BLAM!

A bullet whistled by his head.

BLAM!

His horse staggered and fell. Jarred from the fall, Marshall had enough presence of mind to roll against the horse and use it for cover. He reached for his Whitworth. He was fortunate that his horse fell to the right. Had it landed on its other side,

Marshall's rifle would have been pinned under the horse. Pressed up against him, Marshall could feel the animal breathing in labored fashion. It was the only movement the horse was making.

Marshall readied his rifle, took a deep breath, and swung the gun over the top of the horse. He hoped to be able to pick out his target quickly. If not, he'd pull back, wait a minute or so, and try again. As it turned out, he only needed one try. The bald pate and gray beard of a Confederate sniper peered from behind a tree. Marshall squeezed off a quick shot.

BLAM!

Wood chips flew from the center of the tree. The Rebel sniper jerked back his head. A moment later Marshall heard the crunching of leaves and branches. The sniper was running! This time Marshall took off after him.

It was all Marshall could do to keep up with the fleeing sniper. The thought that kept coming to his mind as he labored to keep the sniper in sight was: *This fellow is spry for a gray beard!* The Confederate sniper darted this way and that, indiscriminately; not allowing Marshall time to stop and take a shot. However, neither did the tactic allow the Confederate time to turn and shoot, which meant that Marshall was safe as long as the Reb kept running. Concentrating fully on closing the distance between them, he figured that should the Reb slow to fire he, himself, would have ample time to get off the first shot. Marshall was content with this advantage; now if he could only keep up with the running Reb.

His chest was heaving. His throat and lungs burned. His legs begged for him to slow down. But Marshall was determined that no bald-headed, gray-bearded Rebel was going to outlast him in a foot race. He urged his legs to move faster.

The Rebel sniper broke into a clearing of mounds and scrub brush. *Excellent!* There was no longer anything for him to dodge behind or between. Marshall ran to the edge of the clearing. Slamming against the trunk of a tree to steady his heaving chest, he raised his rifle. The way the Rebel scurried this way and that over a series of shallow mounds, Marshall found it next to impossible to keep him sighted in the scope. Marshall tracked him with the cross-hairs, panning left, right, then left again. He applied pressure to the trigger.

The Rebel disappeared!

Raising his head from the scope, Marshall stared in amazement. *What happened?* One second the bald-headed rebel was in his sights, and the next it was as if the earth had swallowed him up! *Unbelievable!*

The Rebel had to have jumped into some kind of hole or ditch that Marshall couldn't see—camouflaged by the mounds. He lowered his rifle. It would be foolish for him to step out into the open. The Rebel sniper could pop up from just about anywhere. Marshall would be an easy target.

But then, Marshall wasn't about to let the Rebel go either. He had an idea. *Let the old man think I gave up! Patience. Patience is the key!* He formulated a plan. Cautiously, covertly, Marshall moved parallel to the unseen ditch for about half a mile. He stayed well inside the woods. His plan was to flank the rebel and sneak up on him from behind.

Of course, there was the possibility that the sniper had kept on running. But Marshall thought it unlikely. This man had come back once already. It was a matter of pride now. The Rebel would be looking for Marshall. Of this, he was confident, because that's exactly what he would do if the roles were reversed.

Staying low to the ground and keeping a sharp eye to his right, Marshall wove around the dirt mounds, never crossing over the top of one. Then, several hundred yards from the woods, he saw it.

I knew it! he cried under his breath. A ravine. Fifty, sixty yards wide. A gap so wide it was hard to believe anything could conceal it. He slid down the steep side, crossed the bottom—guarding his right—then, up the other side. Now he backtracked his parallel course, staying far enough away from the ridge so as not to be seen by anyone in the ravine.

He began to imagine the look he'd see on the Rebel sniper's face when the Rebel realized—too late—that he'd been outmaneuvered. Staying low, he measured his distance by the woods in the background. When he was in alignment with the place where he'd begun his circling maneuver, he got down on his stomach and inched his way toward the edge of the ravine.

He peered over the edge.

Nothing!

Had he overshot his mark? Marshall checked the woods. *No. This was the spot. He was sure of it.* The ridge of the ravine opposite him was steep and heavily eroded. Small shrubs dotted the side. Nothing anyone could hide behind.

The sniper was nowhere to be seen.

Marshall was disappointed, but cautious. He lay still for a long time. *Had the sniper returned to the forest? No. Marshall would have spotted him crossing the mounds.* Nervously, he glanced behind him thinking that he might have been outmaneuvered himself. But no one was in sight. Not in the ravine. Not among the mounds. He could come only to one conclusion. The sniper had run off.

I guess I gave him too much credit, Marshall said to himself. *A good lesson to learn. Not everyone is as stubborn as me.*

Marshall raised up and dusted himself off. Again he scanned the ravine, still finding it hard to believe that the Rebel sniper had run away. In this battle of wits, the old man had won. One thing, though. He had to give the old man credit for strategy. It was a brilliant move for him to come back after having been knocked out of that tree. Completely unexpected. As for the chase, Marshall also had to give the Reb credit for using his knowledge of the terrain to make good his escape. This man was a worthy adversary. If it weren't for the fact that the rebel sniper was a poor shot, Marshall would be . . .

BLAM!

Marshall's right leg exploded in pain. The force of the bullet spun him halfway around. His rifle tumbled near the ravine's edge.

BLAM!

It felt like someone smacked him on the left shoulder with a branding iron, spinning him again. The two shots had turned Marshall completely around. He collapsed facedown on the ground. Spitting dirt and gravel from his mouth, he searched for his rifle. His eyes clenched involuntarily from the pain in his leg. He could feel life's liquid draining from his thigh. A blackness crept over his mind. He fought it off. Mustering all his inner strength, he fought back the inferno.

Pushing with his left leg and pulling with his good arm, he crawled toward the edge of the ravine and his rifle. It was dangling halfway over the ledge. No sooner had he touched the stock of the rifle when another shot kicked up dirt on the lip of the ravine. He pulled back, checked his rifle, then crawled toward the edge. He was going to get that old man once and for all!

Cautiously, he peered over the edge. To his astonishment, the view into the ravine was unchanged. The far wall. Scattered shrubs. The bottom. All were clear of any activity. The old Rebel was nowhere to be seen!

BLAM!

Another bullet buried itself in the lip of the ravine, kicking dirt and pebbles into Marshall's eyes. He rubbed them out. Blinking uncontrollably, he searched for the sniper's position. Bush by bush. Inch by inch. There was simply no place to hide!

Marshall's leg began to throb unbearably. His shoulder complained every time his shirt rubbed against it. His eyes stung from the dirt. Grit ground between his teeth.

O Lord, Marshall prayed, *give me Willy's eyes, if just for a moment.* He raised up slightly to get a better view of the bottom of the ravine.

BLAM!

A bullet whistled overhead.

There it is! Marshall quickly rubbed one eye, then the other. He looked again. There was no mistake. He saw smoke. Gunpowder smoke. It rose from behind a small bush.

That doesn't make sense! That bush isn't large enough for a grown man to hide behind. Yet there it was. Smoke from the last shot. How . . . of course! A cave! The bush hid the entrance to a cave! It couldn't be more than a few feet across, but there was no other explanation for it.

Marshall maneuvered himself as best he could into his familiar shooting position. He refused to acknowledge the pain in his leg or arm. He raised the Whitworth, aiming at the dead center of the bush. He took his time.

BLAM!

Another bullet whizzed past his head. Marshall pressed his eye against the scope. Through the scope he could see black behind the leaves and branches of the bush. An opening in the earth. He smiled and eased back on the trigger. He fired.

BLAM!

The bush shuddered. He waited. There was no sound coming from the bush. No movement either. He waited some more. *Did he hit the sniper? Or was the sniper waiting for him to come and investigate?*

Marshall could ignore the pain no longer. He rolled over in agony. Then, keeping an eye on the bush, he bandaged his leg with a spare shirt from his haversack. Also, he inspected his shoulder. It had a burned crease on it, much like one would expect to see if a fireplace poker had been applied to it.

Still, there was no movement or sound from the ravine. Marshall held up his hand. He shouted at the bush and waited for a response. None was forthcoming. Slowly, he raised up, ready to fall to the ground should he see or hear anything. Nothing happened. No shots rang out. He stood. Still nothing.

Using his rifle for a crutch, he made his way down the side of the ravine and across the bottom. He approached the bush from the side. He poked his rifle into the branches. No response. Moving toward the front, he stared into the bush, looking past the branches. At first, all he saw was darkness. Then there was a flicker of light coming from inside the bowels of the earth. Pulling the bush aside, he found a small opening about three feet deep, large enough for an adult male to crawl through. As the sunlight penetrated the opening, he saw the top of a bald head. The old man's face lay in the dirt. Reaching inside with the butt-end of his rifle, Marshall rolled the head first to one side, then the other. It flopped freely, showing no sign of life.

Just then an uneasy thought crossed Marshall's mind. *Was anybody else in the cave? Maybe the sniper was protecting someone!* Marshall yelled into the opening. He got no response. The only way he could tell for sure would be to drag the old man's body out of the way. He hesitated. There was the matter of his Nazarite vow in which he committed himself to abstain from touching dead bodies.

The pain from his wounds stirred an awful recipe in his stomach. His head grew light, his vision blurred. It was a convincing argument to ignore the vow this one time.

Reaching into the hole in the ravine wall, Marshall grabbed the Rebel sniper by the shirt and dragged him out. The Rebel rolled down the side of the ravine, coming to a stop at the bottom. He lay face-up. Marshall's bullet had hit him square in the forehead.

Marshall turned his attention to the opening. He realized he was vulnerable to crawl through the opening; he chose to do it anyway. Grasping his rifle, he crawled into the cave—pushing with his left leg only, the right leg dragged as if dead.

Once inside, he found a small room with earthen walls. Apparently the opening had been larger at one time, because inside was a bed, a travel chest, a small desk, and a chair. A candle was lit and resting on the table. The way Marshall figured it, the cave was dug out, the furniture moved in, then the opening was reduced to a one-person passageway.

Marshall limped over to the bed and sat down. His whole body ached from his wounds. The loss of blood and fatigue pulled at him with invisible hands.

No! Got to get rid of the body first.

Marshall dragged himself back through the opening. He pulled the body of the Rebel sniper about a hundred feet away, made a shallow grave, and covered it with rocks. There was no eulogy, only his customary recitation: *Without the shedding of blood, there is no remission of sin.* Marshall buried him only to conceal the body, not to pay homage to him. He left no clue that might lead someone to discover the nearby cave.

With the Rebel body hidden in the earth, Marshall crawled back into the cave and collapsed on the bed. He never knew for sure if he passed out or simply fell asleep. All he knew was that everything went dark and for a while the pain stopped.

He awoke chilled. The dampness of the cave and his loss of blood set him to shivering, and he could do little to stop it. He clawed at the blanket on the bed and wrapped it tightly around him. Still he shivered. His leg was stiff and throbbing; his shoulder was tender. The seared stripe on it was taut, like a stretched animal hide set in the sun. The shoulder was bearable; the leg was not. Its throbbing set off a pounding in his head so unsparingly harsh, he had to strain to focus his eyes. All of this was compounded by the shivers and all he could think about was getting warm.

Clutching the blanket in place with one hand, he grabbed his rifle with the other and stumbled toward the hole that led outside. With a fair amount of grumbling, he realized that in order to crawl out he was going to have to let go of either the blanket or the rifle. He tossed the rifle out the hole. It clattered in the ravine. Any other time he never would have parted with his rifle. But he was so cold, he figured that if someone was waiting for him in the ravine, he'd rather be shot with his own gun and put out of his misery than give up the blanket.

He emerged on the other side of the dirt wall to a gray, cold, blustery day. His rifle lay undisturbed on the ground. No one was around. Pulling the blanket higher and tighter around his neck, he retrieved his weapon. The wind seemed to cut right through the blanket and his clothing. He gave considerable thought to crawling back through the hole into the cave. The thought of a fire kept him outside.

He decided to relocate in the forest. Before leaving, he concealed the cave opening with the sagebrush. Then he made his way across the mounds toward the forest in a direct line, as much as the terrain and his stumbling would allow. It was difficult for him to determine the time of day from the sky. Thick, gray clouds formed a low ceiling, obscuring the sun. His watch ticked in his pocket, but with the shivers and the blanket and the gun, it was too much trouble to retrieve. Besides, the hour made little difference to someone who didn't know what day it was. *How long had he been in the cave? One night? Two? More?* He didn't know. And, at the moment, he didn't care. All he could think about was getting warm and easing the aching pain in his leg and head.

Limping around, he collected firewood. Before long he was cuddled close to a good-sized fire. The fire was larger than was prudent for a scout, but he was willing to risk the possibility of detection for the certainty of warmth. For the remainder of the day and through the night, he never wandered more than a few feet from the fire.

The next morning dawned bright and crisp. Marshall awoke and rose. His leg was stiffer than ever, his shoulder too. But his head was clear and the shivers were gone. For that he was grateful. In their place was a roaring hunger. He hadn't eaten since the morning of the encounter with the Rebel sharpshooter, however many days ago that had been. His thoughts turned to the provisions he brought with him. They were with his fallen horse.

Making his way to the site of his ambush, Marshall hoped to recover his provisions. He held out little hope that the wounded horse would still be alive. Or if it was, that it would be of any use to him. When he reached the place where the horse had fallen, it was cleared. There was no horse. There were no provisions.

Had the wounded horse gotten up and wandered off? Or had someone removed the dead carcass? He searched the immediate area. It was well-trampled, making it difficult for him to solve the mystery. But there was one thing of which he was certain. He would find no provisions here. His stomach grumbled loudly.

He remembered seeing a few small plantations to the north of Vicksburg. Marshall set out in that direction hoping to find some unattended chickens who would be willing to share their eggs with him.

The closest plantation was farther away than he remembered. By the time he reached it, it was nearly noon. His leg burned something awful. He was weak and lightheaded.

Marshall observed the house from a distance. Odd. For the longest time there was no discernible activity around the house or barn. And there was no one in the fields. If it weren't for the mooing of cows in the barn and the strutting of a few roosters, Marshall would have concluded the plantation was deserted. He circled around back so that the barn would conceal his approach to anyone in the house.

He made his way across the hardened rows of a cornfield that were littered with dry, brown withered stalks, the remains of an autumn harvest. His wounded leg was pounding worse than ever. It made him nauseous.

Get the eggs first, he told himself. *The leg can rest while you cook them. You'll feel better after you've eaten something.*

His leg argued with him. It was a convincing complaint. Twofold. Pain and rising nausea. Marshall had to stop halfway across the field and lean on his rifle to keep from passing out. He rested again when he reached the barn.

Cackling chickens called to him. Poking his head around the corner of the barn, he spied a wooden chicken coop. *Take two eggs for what ails you,* he murmured. *You'll feel better in the morning, so says old Doc Morgan.*

Reaching the coop he pressed on the door and let himself in. His fear was that someone had already gathered the eggs and left him nothing. Steadying himself with his rifle, he reached under the first hen. His fear was dispelled. He felt two warm eggs. Taking them, he grabbed a third egg from another nest. He was extra hungry.

The door swung open. "Put them eggs back, you Yankee thief!"

Marshall wheeled around. The sudden motion sent his head spinning, almost knocking him off his feet. He fought to focus his eyes. Blurry images took shape. He didn't like what he saw. He found himself staring down the unsteady barrel of a Confederate rifle. At the other end of the weapon was a young private. The boy couldn't be more than sixteen years old. He was nervous to the point of shaking.

"Put them eggs back or I'll blow your fool head off!"

"Easy with that rifle!" Marshall cried. "I'll put the eggs

back." Slowly he reached toward the closest nest.

"Wait!" the boy yelled.

Marshall froze. His head was swimming in pain.

"Don't put the eggs back!" the boy ordered.

"What?"

"You heard me."

"You're going to let me keep them?" Marshall asked.

"Didn't say that. Follow me out of the hen house. Come on, move!"

As Marshall moved toward the door, he understood what the boy was doing. With his one hand clutching the barrel of the rifle and his other hand occupied with eggs, he was less likely to make any sudden moves with his weapon. Clever. He had to give the Rebel boy credit for that one.

Leading the way, the boy backed out of the coop, cautiously keeping the door open with the rifle barrel until Marshall could catch it with his shoulder. Then the boy jumped back to regain some distance.

Twin pains greeted Marshall at the door. The spring on the door slapped it against his wounded shoulder at the same instant the sunlight hit his eyes. In this instance two straws plopped on the proverbial camel's back. Marshall's knees weakened. A wave of nausea rose from his gut and passed before his eyes like a white sheet. It was a curious sensation. The boy with the rifle spun out of view; Marshall could feel the eggs fall from his hand; then he saw his hand grasping for the side of the door, finding nothing but air. The next thing he saw was the underside of the chicken coop eaves.

The Confederate private danced around him, pointing the rifle and yelling, "Don't move! Don't move or I'll shoot!"

Marshall couldn't have moved if he wanted to. Darkness engulfed him.

Chapter 14

MARSHALL moaned. There was a metal clanking sound and the pungent smell of soiled hay. He winced. His mouth tasted like sweaty flannel. "Ohhhh," he moaned again. The pain was returning. His leg—stiff and burning. His arm—cramped and tight. There was that clanking sound again. *What was it?*

Marshall raised his eyebrows, but the eyelids refused to follow. He tried again. With a fluttering movement, his eyelids blinked back the light until his pupils could adjust.

He was in a barn. Seated on the ground. A stall of some sort. The walls were solid, about four feet high. He looked to his left. The backsides of three cows greeted him from the far side. Then he noticed his own fingers. They were level with his shoulders. That didn't make sense. He tried to move his hands. They swung in a strictly controlled arc accompanied by the clanking sound. *Shackles!* Black bands circled his wrists. Chains fastened him to the side of the stall. His ankles were fastened with black bands too, linked together with a chain.

"Southerners!" he murmured. "They'll enslave anyone."

As his faculties returned little by little, he explored his surroundings, which didn't take long. He was in a barn with cows and, from the sound of it, a rooster or two. A few yanks on his shackles met with unyielding resistance. From the angle the light was streaming through the cracks in the side of the barn, he figured it was late afternoon. He listened for sounds outside the barn. As he was straining to hear far away, he heard the creak of a large door nearby. A moment later, a gun barrel poked around the opposite edge of the stall. The Confederate boy followed close behind.

"You're awake," the boy said. Even though Marshall was shackled, the boy approached him as he would a wild beast in the forest. "You fainted. You sick or something?" the boy asked.

Marshall looked the boy over. He was small, a little over five feet tall. His uniform was too large for him, and he hadn't seen much action in it. Other than dirty knees, it looked new. A brown shirt and gray vest were stuffed under his coat. They were large for him too. His forage cap was pulled down to his ears; brown hair protruded from the edges. His hands and face were fair-skinned. A thin nose with a hint of freckles separated blue eyes.

The boy's brown hair and timid personality reminded Marshall of Thomas from Grafton, the "fastest one" of the three boys that accompanied him to Harper's Ferry. From Marshall's inferior position, the thing he noticed most—besides the rifle that was continuously pointed at his face—was a large rectangular belt buckle. It featured three capital letters— C.S.A.—Confederate States of America.

"I said, are you sick?" the boy asked again.

"I'm wounded," Marshall replied sarcastically, nodding toward the bloody rip in his trousers.

The boy took offense. "I can see that! I'm not blind. But you fainted out there."

"Loss of blood. Hunger. Those things have that kind of effect on people. You'd know that if you'd seen any action."

"I've seen plenty of action," the boy insisted.

Abruptly, the boy left only to return a while later with a plate of bread and meat which he slid toward Marshall from a safe distance. He turned to leave.

"Is this some sort of torture?" Marshall asked.

The boy turned back, puzzled.

"I can't reach the food." Marshall rattled the chains.

The boy looked at Marshall's hands, then at the plate. It was true. He picked up the meat from the plate and placed it in Marshall's left hand as deftly as he would if he were placing it in the mouth of a crocodile. The bread he stuffed in Marshall's mouth, then jumped back.

Marshall transferred the bread from his mouth to his other hand. "Is there someone who can attend to my wound?"

The question seemed to puzzle the boy. He mulled it over then said, "I'll ask around."

A couple of hours later the boy returned with a water basin and some bandages. Using a shovel, he pushed the sloshing basin next to Marshall. "You'll have to do it yourself," the boy said. "Everyone else is busy."

"Your camp surgeon is too busy to treat the wounded?"

"He said Yankees get treated last," the boy replied. "Best if you do it yourself."

"How?" Marshall asked.

"Clean the wound, then wrap the leg," the boy replied.

"Do we have to go through this again?" Marshall rattled his chains. "Or are you going to stuff the bandages in my mouth?"

This proved to be another puzzle for the boy. Marshall's suspicions grew. This boy wasn't slow-minded like Ira, the tavernkeeper's son at Grafton. The chicken coop incident was proof of that. Making Marshall hold the eggs to keep his hands off his rifle had demonstrated intelligence. Ira never would have thought of something like that. *So why were these simple requests proving to be such a puzzle to the boy?* Marshall considered the fact that most young boys, abruptly separated from all that is familiar to them and thrust into an army role, experience a fair amount of disorientation. But somehow this situation was different.

The boy left and returned with the key to the shackles. He studied the situation a while before concluding that he had no other choice. He would have to unlock Marshall's wrists himself. He inched forward as though Marshall had a contagious disease. Holding the rifle on Marshall with one hand, he bent over and fit the key into the left shackle. It was a clumsy effort. After the third try, the shackle slid open.

Immediately, the boy jumped back. A look of relief appeared on his face as he gripped the rifle tightly with both hands. The key had fallen into the hay next to Marshall. "You can do the other one yourself," the boy said. "But not the leg shackles." He waved the rifle barrel at Marshall as a warning.

Marshall unlocked his other wrist. He stretched, rubbed his wrists, then proceeded to unbuckle his belt.

"What are you doing?" the boy cried.

"The wound is on my upper thigh," Marshall retorted, stating the obvious. "I have to drop my pants to get to it. Unless you have a better way."

Another puzzle for the boy. He blinked several times, then said, "No sudden movements."

The contortions Marshall had to go through to drop his pants to his knees reminded him of times he'd removed soaking wet trousers. It took a while, but he finally managed to do it. Using a piece of bandage as a sponge, he dipped it in the water and proceeded to clean the wound. The sniper's bullet had ripped away a fair piece of flesh. The area was red and black and extremely tender. He tossed a soiled bandage aside for a fresh one. As he did, he glanced at the boy. The boy's head was turned away. Furtive glances were taken sporadically to check on Marshall's progress. Marshall grinned at the boy's squeamishness.

"I want to speak to your commanding officer," Marshall said.

"He doesn't speak to prisoners."

The quick reply intrigued Marshall. "Surely, one of your superiors is available—a sergeant or maybe a corporal."

"I'll see what I can do."

Marshall wrapped his leg, then pulled his trousers back up. "Done," he announced.

The boy seemed relieved. Standing, he waved the rifle in the direction of the right shackle. "Put it back on your wrist," he said. Marshall shackled his right wrist. "Now toss me the key." Marshall obeyed.

As cautious as the boy was to unlock the wrist shackle, he was doubly cautious in securing it around Marshall's wrist. Once it was locked, the boy let out a sigh. Tossing the water from the basin, he piled the bandages in it and proceeded to leave.

"Hey, Reb," Marshall called after him. "Do you have a name? What do I call you?"

"You don't," came the answer.

Marshall heard the barn door close and the latch fall. "Guess I'll just call you Reb."

The night was long and uncomfortable. By morning the muscles in Marshall's back and neck were knotted and cramping. He heard the door open. A moment later the private appeared with a plate of scrambled eggs and a fork.

Marshall laughed. This brought a suspicious frown from the private. He stopped well short of his prisoner.

"What are you laughing at?" the boy demanded.

"I've never been spoon-fed by a Confederate soldier before," Marshall said. He rattled his chains.

"And you never will be," the boy said.

He dropped the plate next to Marshall. Producing the key

to the shackles, he unlocked Marshall's left hand. With sighs of relief, Marshall stretched his arm and rubbed his neck. "Look, if I promised not to . . ."

"No. The other hand stays shackled." The determination on the boy's face signaled that this was not a matter that could be negotiated.

Right-handed Marshall balanced a fork-full of eggs. Half of them fell off. He couldn't help but remember that it was eggs that got him into this predicament in the first place.

"Tell me something, Reb," Marshall said. "Why are you the only one to look after me?"

"It's my job."

"Sorry, Reb, but that doesn't make sense. It's customary for men to take turns at guard duty. You're the only guard I've seen."

"Eat your eggs. I have other duties to perform."

Marshall scooped some eggs. Only half made it to his mouth. He spoke as he chewed. "Am I going to get to talk to one of your superiors today?"

"They're busy."

Marshall grinned. "Busy?"

"That's what I said."

"Or nonexistent?"

The boy's eyes narrowed. "Shut up and eat your eggs," he said.

"You're not in the army, are you? At least not anymore."

The boy said nothing.

"There are no army sounds around here," Marshall said. "No reveille. No orders. No sounds of men drilling. I never hear you talking to anyone; taking orders from an officer, that sort of thing. No sound of horses coming or going. And when I stumbled in here a few days ago the place looked deserted. There's no army around here. You know what I think, Reb?"

"I don't care what you think," the boy said sharply.

"I think you're a deserter."

"Think what you like."

"I think this is your farm. Mom and Pop are in the house. From the way you turned your head while I dressed my wound, I figure you got a glimpse of battle and it turned your stomach. You got scared and ran away. Must have been your first battle considering how new your uniform is."

"I'll come back for your plate when you've finished eating."

Marshall called after him. "And you'd better get someone to milk these cows. They're ready to burst!"

A short time later the boy returned. He tossed the key at Marshall. It was followed by a milking pail. "Unlock your other hand," the boy ordered. "You're going to milk some cows."

Marshall freed his right hand and lowered it with a groan. He reached for the leg shackles.

"Not them!" shouted the boy. "They stay on. Toss me the key."

Marshall threw the key to the boy. "Can I stand up?" he asked.

"Unless you know of another way to get over to the cows."

With no small amount of effort, Marshall stood. He stretched luxuriously. His leg was as stiff as ever, but it felt like it was healing. His shoulder was sore, but improved.

"Come on, we don't have all day!" The boy stepped back and motioned with the rifle toward the cows.

"Beg to differ with you, Reb, but I do have all day," Marshall replied. "That is, unless there's going to be a shooting or a hanging I don't know about yet."

His statement seemed to surprise the boy. "Just milk the cows," the boy ordered. "They do teach you boys in the

Union how to work, don't they?"

Once the cows were milked, Marshall was promptly placed in shackles again. "Hey, Reb!" he said.

"What?"

"I'll help out with other chores just for the chance to get up and move around. It gets awfully sore just sitting here."

The boy looked at him suspiciously. "I'll talk it over with my superiors," he said.

The creak of the barn door woke him. All was dark except for a few shafts of blue light streaming in through cracks in the plank wall. Marshall heard a rummaging sound. The cows heard it too. They mooed at the disturbance. Marshall listened as farm tools were tossed aside, things overturned. Whoever it was, they were making their way toward him stall-by-stall.

A dark form rounded the side of the stall. The silhouette was that of a soldier, much larger than Reb. A shaft of moonlight glinted off the barrel of a pistol.

"What the?" The form jumped back when he spotted Marshall.

"Don't shoot! Don't shoot!" Marshall cried. "I'm chained to the wall."

The intruder leaned into the stall to get a better look. "Why so you is," the husky male voice said. "And you're a Yank too!"

Marshall squinted into the darkness. He saw a soiled Union uniform with corporal chevrons filled by a black-bearded soldier with a bulbous nose and one eye that strayed to the left.

"You're in a fine mess," said the corporal.

"Hurry!" Marshall cried. "I don't know where he keeps the key, but maybe you could pry the shackles off the wall with something. We can figure out how to get them off once we're out of here."

"Sorry, can't do that, Yank," said the corporal. He bent over Marshall, rifling through Marshall's pockets. The man's breath and body odors were suffocatingly strong. "Don't suppose you have any coins on you," he said.

"You're a deserter," Marshall concluded.

"Like to think of meself as a one-man nation who has declared independence," the corporal grinned.

"Look, I have no problem with that," Marshall said. "Just help me get free and you can go your way and I'll go mine."

"As a one-man nation, I makes me own laws," said the corporal. "Law number one is: Look out for yourself. Law number two is . . . well, there is no law number two. It takes all me effort just keeping law number one. Which brings me to a point of business." He cocked the pistol and placed it against Marshall's temple. "Let's negotiate. You tell me how many people are in the house, and I won't pull this trigger. Do we have a deal?"

Just then the barn door swung open. Light from a lantern filled the interior of the barn.

"Who's there?" It was the boy's voice.

The corporal held a finger to his lips, gesturing Marshall to be silent. Then he stood slowly, keeping his pistol low against his leg where the boy couldn't see it. "Don't shoot!" he said. "I was just looking for a place to rest me achin' bones."

From his position Marshall couldn't see the boy, but he was sure the boy had his rifle and that the rifle was shaking.

"You're a Yankee," the boy said.

"You're a Rebel," the corporal replied.

The corporal's right hand gripped and regripped the pistol. In a conciliatory voice, he said, "Look, son, I don't want to be any trouble. I just want a place to sleep. If you don't want to share your barn with me, I'll just be on me way." The gun hand began twitching.

"He's got a gun, Reb!" Marshall cried out.

Fury distorted the corporal's face. He raised his pistol over the stall.

BLAM!

The Union corporal flew backward, stumbling over Marshall. The pistol plopped in the hay. The corporal made a couple of wheezing sounds, then he was still. Marshall stared at the pistol. Instinctively he tried to grab it. Chains held him back.

The boy was quickly over them both, his rifle at the ready. His lips were set in grim determination. He was in full uniform, complete with cap. Cautiously, he poked the corporal.

"You got him in the neck," Marshall said. "He's dead."

The boy cautiously stepped around Marshall and the dead corporal. As he retrieved the pistol, he looked like he was about to cry. Placing the weapons off to the side, he pulled the corporal's body to another stall. "In a few hours it will be morning," the boy said. "We'll bury him then." He picked up the weapons, his lantern, then all was dark again.

Marshall didn't sleep any more that night. It wasn't so much the excitement as it was the boy; the way he fought back his emotions yet still managed to move the bloodied body of the dead corporal. Marshall had been wrong about him. The boy had shot the intruder without hesitation. And he showed no squeamishness when it came to moving the body. For Marshall, it was a mystery.

The next morning was overcast and gray. The boy unshackled Marshall's arms, handed him a shovel, and led him behind the barn.

"We'll bury him here," the boy said. "Dig."

The leg shackles clanked as Marshall dug. It took him a while to grow accustomed to the restrictions on his leg movements. By the time he did, his ankles were chafed. The experience gave him a greater appreciation for the number of freedom celebrations he'd witnessed as he ferried slaves across the Ohio River. All the more so when he compared his brief time in captivity to a lifetime of theirs.

"Just like the good old days, isn't it, Reb?"

The boy sat on a stump, his back against the barn, the rifle across his legs. Next to him was a dwindling pile of chopped wood. The boy's uniform was wrinkled and getting more wrinkled every day. Marshall guessed he was sleeping in it at night.

"What are you talking about?" the boy asked.

"You, a Southerner, sitting there while you watch someone else labor. Only difference is, I don't have black skin."

"Shut up, Yankee. You don't know what you're talking about."

"Morgan. My name's Marshall Morgan. Not once have you asked me my name."

"Keep digging."

"And your name is?"

The boy hopped off the stump. "That's deep enough. Let's get the body."

While the boy guarded him, Marshall dragged the body from the barn to the grave, then proceeded to cover the corporal with dirt. With a few pats of the shovel and a swipe of the back of his hand across his dripping brow, Marshall declared the job finished.

"Not yet," the boy declared. From inside his coat he produced a small Bible. Propping his rifle against the barn—still within reach—he opened the Bible and began to read: "For as in Adam all die, even so in Christ shall all be made alive. . . . And as we have borne the image of the earthly, we shall also bear the image of the heavenly. Now this I say, brethren, that flesh and blood cannot inherit the kingdom of God; neither doth corruption inherit incorruption. Behold, I show you a mystery; we shall not all sleep, but we shall all be changed, in a moment, in the twinkling of an eye, at the last trump: for the trumpet shall sound, and the dead shall be raised incorruptible, and we shall be changed. . . . O death, where is thy sting? O grave, where is thy victory? The sting of death is sin; and the strength of sin is the Law. But thanks be to God, which giveth us the victory through our Lord Jesus Christ."

In the middle of the Bible reading, Marshall realized he was standing with his mouth wide open. The boy's funeral service was totally unexpected. It was a courtesy Marshall never once extended to the Confederate soldiers he had killed.

"Let us pray," the boy said. He bowed his head, but didn't close his eyes. "Dear God in heaven, please accept this soul we send to You. Receive him as Your little lamb. I pray that his life was more pleasing to You than his death. But more importantly, I pray that his sins were covered by the blood of the cross of Jesus Christ. I forgive him for the evil he intended for us. Thank You for Your protection. And I pray that You will give us victory over those who invade our land. This we pray in Jesus' name. Amen."

"Hey, Reb. Too bad your fellow soldiers couldn't have joined us for this occasion," Marshall said sarcastically as he was led back to the barn. "Or your parents," he added with a glance at the house.

"We each have our duties," the boy said. "This was mine."

That night Marshall sat in the stall stewing. It angered him to think the Southern boy had prayed to God. *What did God have to do with anyone in the South other than to condemn them for the immorality of their slavery? The boy was speaking blasphemy! And then for the boy to ask God to give the South victory against enemy invaders! Of all the gall! It was clear that God was using the Union army as His instrument of righteousness to punish the South for their wickedness! How dare that boy pray in the name of Jesus for the Union's defeat!*

Yet no matter how worked up Marshall got over the boy's audacity, there was one thing the boy said that Marshall couldn't get out of his mind. The boy had forgiven the man who was his enemy. This was something Marshall could never do. Never.

The next day Marshall and the boy were behind the barn again. This time Marshall was chopping wood. The sun was out and, regardless of the leg chains, it felt good to work up a sweat. Besides, the activity allowed him to release some of his frustration over the boy's prayer at the funeral.

Marshall chuckled to himself. *Here I am, down South, chopping wood. Didn't I do enough of this in the North?*

He kept a watchful eye on the boy. Sitting on the same stump as yesterday, his back against the barn wall, the warmth of the sun was working on him. The boy was dozing off. Marshall would halt his chopping every so often to see if he'd fallen asleep. Every time he paused, the inactivity would rouse the boy awake. But each time it was taking longer.

After a couple more logs, Marshall paused. The boy didn't stir. He rattled his leg chains. The boy's head was tilted awkwardly to one side. Quietly, but with due speed, Marshall lay aside the ax. He crossed over to where the boy was sleeping and snatched the rifle from his lap.

The boy awoke with a start. A grinning Marshall pointed the gun at the boy's chest. He never realized until now how much more comfortable it was to be on this end of the rifle. The boy's eyes were wide. He looked like he was about to cry. Yet he said nothing.

"I don't want to hurt you, Reb, but if you cry out or resist, I'll have to shoot you. Nod if you understand."

The boy nodded slowly, never taking his eyes off the hole at the end of the rifle barrel.

"Hand me the key to these shackles," Marshall said.

The boy fished around in his vest pocket and produced the

key. He held it out to Marshall.

"Better yet," Marshall said, "you unlock them."

The boy took back the key and kneeled down. Marshall had to back away a step to give the boy room, being so close to the woodpile. The boy fumbled with the shackles nervously. As he did, Marshall looked around for a way of escape. It was a mistake.

Grabbing a piece of wood from the woodpile, the boy swung it with all his might, hitting Marshall's wounded leg. The pain shot all the way to his head. A second blow struck his hands, sending the rifle flying. Before Marshall could recover, the boy launched into him with his shoulder, knocking him to the ground. The uninjured, younger boy beat Marshall in the scramble for the rifle.

In the battle of the barnyard, the victory went to the South.

Marshall lay on his back in pain. The boy was on his knees, once again pointing a rifle at his captive. As soon as Marshall was able to get up, he was taken back into the barn and once again shackled to side of the stall.

The boy slumped down against the other side of the stall. Panting. After a few moments, he said, "I suppose I should thank you."

"Thank me?"

"For not killing me with the ax," the boy said. "You could have split my skull real easy."

Truth is, Marshall had never thought of it. He chastened himself for missing his chance to escape. But even had he thought of it, for some reason he couldn't have brought himself to taking the ax to the boy. Now that he thought of it, he didn't think he could bring himself to shoot the boy either, which wasn't a healthy attitude to have toward one's enemy. He only hoped that given the opportunity, the boy would be unable to shoot him too.

"If you're so grateful," Marshall said, "let me go."

"Can't."

"Why not?"

The boy sighed. "If I let you go, would you promise to go back to the North and never return to the South again?"

"I couldn't make that promise," Marshall said.

"That's why I can't let you go." The boy stood up to leave. "I can tell you this, though. You were right about the army. I'm not attached to any company. But I'm no deserter either! This is my home and I'll protect it with my life." He turned and took a few steps.

"What about your parents? Are they in the house?" Marshall asked.

The boy answered without turning around. "They're both dead. My father was a major general. He was killed at Sharpsburg. About a month ago my mother took sick with malaria. She died too. I'm the only one left to protect our farm." Once again, he started to go.

"Reb, wait!" Marshall called. "Look what this war has cost you! Is it worth it? Is slavery worth the lives of your father and mother?"

The boy wheeled around, his face red. Tears spilled down his cheeks. "Is everyone in the North as dense as you?" he yelled. "My father set our slaves free over five years ago! He did it because he thought it was the Christian thing to do; he did it even though it caused many of the townspeople to hate him. He even convinced some of his friends to follow his example. You've got it all wrong, Yank. Most of us in the South aren't fighting for slavery! That's nothing more than a Northern excuse to come down here and conquer the South!"

"Then if you're not fighting for slavery, what are you fighting for?" Marshall asked.

"We're fighting because you're down here on our land."

◆ ◆ ◆

It sounded like rolling thunder. The blast rattled the barn, shaking loose dust and bits of hay from the rafters that floated down through the beams of moonlight like snow. There was an interval of peace, but it didn't last long. Thunder rolled again followed by a bone-rattling quake as Union cannons shelled Vicksburg.

With each blast, the stall quivered. The barn's frame creaked and groaned. Marshall stared upward into the darkness looking for cracks in the beams. He was rewarded with dust in his eyes. He spit out bits of straw that fell in his mouth.

Marshall pulled on his chains, hoping the blast had weakened their hold on the wall. They were as solid as ever.

The next blast sent a wooden pillar tumbling over on the cows. They complained loudly, trying to pull out of their stalls.

BOOM!

A corner of the barn collapsed. Dust was dense. As it slowly dissipated, Marshall could see jagged planks jutting out at odd angles. There was also a ragged hole in the upper corner of the barn, and the flickering of flame.

The fire ran across the dry hay on the barn floor. Smoke and light and heat and dust swirled around him. One of the cows broke loose, but had nowhere to go. It danced in horror around and around looking for a way out. To keep from being trampled Marshall yelled and screamed at it every time it came near.

Just then he saw a bobbing lantern coming toward him. It was the boy. With all the commotion around him, he hadn't heard the barn door open. The cow saw its way of escape and bolted past the boy who had to dodge to one side to keep from being knocked down. The boy let loose the other cows, then approached Marshall.

Setting down the lantern, but still holding the rifle, he unlocked one shackle then handed the key to Marshall to get the other. Marshall reached for his leg shackles.

"No!" the boy yelled.

"How can I run with these on?" Marshall yelled back.

"You'll manage! Give me the key!"

The boy had that stubborn, determined look on his face. Marshall handed him the key. With the boy covering him from behind, Marshall hobbled out of the burning barn. The blaze lit up the front of the house with an eerie, orange light. The light from the boy's lantern was lost in the brightness of the blaze.

"In the house!" the boy shouted.

Forgetting his chains, Marshall tried to take the porch steps two at a time. He dropped like a falling tree, his ribs crashing against the steps.

"Inside! Inside!" the boy behind him yelled.

"I'm doing the best I can!" Marshall pushed himself up and stumbled into the house. It was dark. All he could see were dim shapes of furniture and lamps and tables. Even in the darkness there was a well-to-do air about the room. When the boy cleared the doorway with the lantern, Marshall's impressions were confirmed. The lantern splashed light on polished mahogany, red velvet, and glistening crystal in an elegant cabinet.

Thunder rolled. The blast shook the crystal roughly.

"Straight back and to the left!" the boy yelled.

Marshall crossed the room and entered a hallway. As light and shadow danced on the walls he saw paintings and photographs of smiling people. A man and woman shoulder-to-shoulder. *The boy's parents?* A pretty young woman. *A cousin? Girlfriend?* Images of a happier time. A boom shook the house. The pictures jumped. The picture of the man and woman crashed to the floor when the boy fell against it.

At the end of the hallway, Marshall turned left. He paused in the darkness until the light caught up with him. It was the dining room.

"The shelling is coming from the river," the boy said. "This room is farthest away."

Marshall nodded. It mattered little which room they hid in. A shell could hit any one of them. But at times like this the mind uses logic to try to gain a measure of control over the madness. Marshall studied the room. A crystal chandelier dangled over a solid mahogany table with eight matching chairs. A matching china cabinet was pressed against one wall.

"Help me push the table into the corner," he yelled. "We can huddle under it."

The boy agreed. Chairs were tossed carelessly aside. The table slid easily across the polished wood floor. Marshall climbed under. The boy handed him the lantern, then joined him, keeping a distance between them and the rifle pointed at Marshall.

They sat and waited. But not for long. A shell screamed overhead.

BOOM!

The chandelier rocked crazily from side to side. The cabinet leaned forward like it wanted to fall, then righted itself. The boy's eyes were closed tightly. His jaw was tense. He was shaking.

"Better extinguish the lantern," Marshall said. "If it gets knocked over, we're in bigger trouble."

The boy nodded. He extinguished the flame. The early light of dawn shone through the windows. The sun wasn't up yet, but the light sky provided a soft, blue glow to the room. The boy returned to his huddled position and closed his eyes. "I never liked thunderstorms when I was young. This is worse."

That was something they could agree on. Marshall found himself shaking. There was something wicked about the sound of shells. And the uncertainty of where they landed cheapened life, reducing it to a game of chance. *Would this one crash down upon you, or wouldn't it? How about the next one?*

A series of shells thundered and boomed as if to confirm his fears. Each one grew closer. Louder. With the first one, the chandelier shook; the second shook the walls; the third one shook the floor and the very foundation.

Marshall could hear the boy whimpering in fear. He couldn't help but think how odd was the moment. Here he was hunkered under a table with a Confederate private, complete with coat and forage cap and rifle. But he no longer felt feelings of anger toward the boy or the uniform. The boy's eyes were wide, his brow furrowed. Marshall had seen that look before. On Thomas. Under the wagon just outside the engine house. It was the look that said, "You won't leave me here, will you?"

BOOM!

The whole room rocked. Marshall was knocked over on his side. So was the boy. The table pitched back and forth over them. The chandelier crashed to the floor followed by the cabinet. As Marshall tried to right himself, he found himself in a cloud of dust and smoke so thick he could barely see past the legs of the table. Strange, though, everything was lighter than it was a moment ago.

As the smoke cleared, Marshall understood why. Half the room was gone!

Beside him, the boy was sobbing convulsively. Marshall grabbed him by the shoulders. "We can't stay here!" he yelled.

The boy shook his head, eager to get as far away as possible.

"I think I know where we will be safe," Marshall yelled. "Do you want me to take you there?"

The boy nodded again.

"I need the key to remove these shackles!" Marshall said.

The boy hesitated, but only for a moment. He fumbled for the key.

Seconds later, they were out from under the table. Strangest thing. Marshall's first instinct was to leave by the front door. Then he realized the ridiculousness of it all and jumped outside the house from the dining room. The boy was right behind him, with his rifle trained on Marshall's back.

Good. Marshall thought. *At least he still has his wits about him.*

With shells screaming overhead, Marshall led the boy through the cornfield. He backtracked the route he'd taken to get to the farm from the forest.

Marshall heard a grunt and a clatter. He looked back. The boy had tripped and was sprawled on the ground. The rifle was several feet away. Marshall raced backed to him, picked up the rifle, then the boy. Marshall handed the rifle to him, "Are you all right?"

"Where are you taking me?"

A shell exploded near the trees, sending dirt and rocks skyward. The forest leaves shook at the sight.

"There's a ravine just beyond the trees," Marshall yelled. "A cave. We'll be safe there."

Marshall took off running. The boy was right behind him. They crisscrossed their way over the mounds and down the side of the ravine. Marshall ran slowly down the middle of the ravine, scanning the walls. He'd only been there once before and was having difficulty finding the cave again.

"Where is it?" the boy called.

"Wait right there!" Marshall cried. He had an idea.

There was that look again. On the boy's face. The Thomas

look. *You're not going to leave me here, are you?*

"I'm just going up the side to get my bearings!" Marshall cried. "I'll be in sight the entire time." His leg began complaining as he strained up the side of the ridge. With one last agonizing push he reached the top. He looked back toward the forest. This was the view he saw when he was tracking the sniper. *There it was!* About a hundred yards farther up the ravine. "I see it!" he yelled to the boy.

Favoring his injured leg, he slid down the wall of the ravine.

BOOM!

A geyser of dirt and dust erupted between him and the boy. When it cleared, Marshall saw the boy facedown on the bottom of the ravine. When Marshall reached him, he was breathing, but unconscious. There were no visible cuts or wounds.

He bent over and scooped the boy up to carry him to the cave. The boy was surprisingly light. In fact, the uniform sank several inches against Marshall's arms. It had made Reb look bulkier than he was.

Gently laying him down near the mouth of the cave, Marshall removed the bush that concealed the entrance. He tossed the rifle in first. Then he backed in. Halfway in, he grabbed the boy by the shoulders and dragged him through the entrance. Inside, he lifted the boy to the bed and fumbled to light the candle on the stand.

A shell burst nearby. The earth cushioned its blow. Of course no place was completely safe, but this was definitely better than the house.

Marshall leaned over the boy to check for wounds. He removed the boy's hat.

"I don't believe it!" he cried.

Long brown hair spilled out.

The boy was a girl! Or more precisely, a young woman.

Chapter 15

"PRESIDENT Lincoln's been shot!"

When J.D. heard the news from the ridge behind him, his head snapped up. He had been staring down the deadly end of a Springfield rifle musket barrel, checking for any powder residue his cleaning cloth might have missed.

The words numbed him. For a moment, he sat there, immobile, as a thousand irrational thoughts bounced around his mind, each one offering a reason why the news couldn't be true.

It was too nice of a day for something like this to happen. Bad news should only come on dreary, overcast days. Not like today when everything was so peaceful. Perched on the heights opposite Fredericksburg, Virginia, he had watched the late afternoon sun descend upon quiet streets, stretching the shadows of the buildings across the meandering Rappahannock River. From his vantage point, he could see the pickets of both armies, each on their own side of the river. Soldiers leaned lazily on their weapons and shared the news and gossip from their respective sides, even though they'd been expressly ordered not to socialize with the enemy.

For early December, it was a warm day. Still, the air had a little nip in it and the chill of the rock had penetrated his pants when he first sat down. It hadn't taken long for the trickle of a nearby brook and the sight of fallen leaves turning cartwheels down the slope to lull him into a comfortable, sleepy mood.

"Captain! Did you hear me? Lincoln's been shot!"

This time, J.D. whirled around. It was Wheelright, a gap-toothed practical joker.

"Not funny, Corporal," J.D. said after identifying the news bearer. "I'm not as gullible as the privates."

"Really, Captain! I'm not kidding!"

"Yeah, I know," J.D. sighed. "And you weren't kidding last week when you had the whole company believing that Napoleon III was coming to review the troops." J.D. shoved the ramrod down its tube, irritated at Wheelright's intrusion into his peaceful world.

J.D. could hear the corporal slipping on fallen leaves as he descended the slope behind him. "Captain, that thing about Napoleon, that was a joke. This isn't!" Wheelright grabbed J.D.'s arm and looked him in the face. "Lincoln's carriage just skidded into the compound. It has bullet holes in it and the driver was shouting for a surgeon!" Wheelright's eyes never blinked as he spoke; his pupils were tiny islands surrounded by a sea of white. Perspiration formed on his bare upper lip and the muscles in his neck were strained and red. The nineteen-year-old corporal's chest heaved for air.

Still, J.D. hesitated. "All right," he said finally, laying his weapon against the rock, "let's go see."

As the captain and corporal crested the ridge, J.D. saw men of every rank and description running toward a monstrous cloud of dust in the compound. It was as if they were drawn to it, like iron shavings to a magnet.

J.D. could feel the tug of unfolding tragedy pulling him to the scene. A sour feeling formed in his gut. If what the corporal said was true, this tragedy would do more than ruin a comfortable, lazy Saturday afternoon; it would change history forever. It was Lincoln who held the Union factions together. It was Lincoln's vision of an undivided nation that fueled the Union forces. Could Vice-President Hannibal Hamlin complete what Lincoln had started? Not from what J.D. had heard of the man; Hamlin didn't have the strength of character of an Abraham Lincoln. If Lincoln was dead, the Army of the Potomac might as well pack up and go home.

A small open field separated him from history. J.D. closed the distance as fast as he could. As he ran, his boots beat a rhythm for his prayer:

Lord, no;
please, no;
not Lincoln;
dear Lord.

When he reached the edge of the crowd, he could barely see anything over the sea of blue uniforms in front of him. There were too many of them, each one straining to get a glimpse of what was happening. The dust had dissipated enough that, standing on his toes, J.D. could see the top of a carriage, but that was all.

"Captain!"

The voice was Hawkins'. *But where?*

"Captain, up here!"

J.D. looked up. Hawkins was draped over a tree limb above the crowd.

"What do you see?" J.D. called. "Is it really Lincoln?"

Hawkins looked like he was about to cry, a disturbing sight for a veteran of his age and experience. "The surgeon just went into the carriage," he said, his voice cracking. "It's the President's carriage, all right. I seen it plenty of times before when I was in Washington."

J.D. looked around. He had to find a way to get up higher so that he could see what was happening. *The water barrel!*

He ran to the barrel and tipped it over. The water rushed out, forming a miniature river between two rows of tents. J.D. rolled the empty barrel to the edge of the crowd, turned it upside down, and stood on it.

"Is there room for me?" Wheelright asked.

"Give me your hand." J.D. reached down and grabbed the corporal's hand as Wheelright planted his foot on the edge of the barrel. With one pull, J.D. was face-to-face with the corporal. The two had to grab each other's waists to keep from tumbling off.

"I'm taller than you," J.D. said, "so you turn around in front."

The two men on top of the barrel looked like they were dancing in slow motion, but soon they were both facing the compound. J.D. had to hold on to Wheelright's shoulders to keep from falling off the back of the barrel. But at least he was able to see.

The first thing he saw was the back of a dark brown carriage, its door hanging open. J.D. could see a painted "L" in an oval on the door panel, and a small window on the back of the carriage allowed him a tiny glimpse inside. At first, there wasn't any movement. Then, he saw a figure stand and a moment later a surgeon stepped out. The surgeon shook his head, said something which J.D. couldn't hear, and gestured to two sergeants who walked to the carriage and climbed in. The carriage rocked back and forth in a crazy manner as the figures of the sergeants—or was it just one sergeant moving back and forth?—passed in front of the back window. Then, the carriage tilted radically and the first sergeant stepped out. He was carrying a man's feet.

An eerie hush gripped the crowd. It was a terrifying silence. No one spoke. No one coughed. No one cleared his throat. It was as if everyone stopped breathing. To have that many people crammed into a small compound without a sound was unnatural and unnerving.

The midsection of the wounded man appeared, his face still shielded by the carriage door. There was a dark red stain near the waist of the man's white shirt.

Then, the second sergeant stepped out of the carriage, his arms hooked under the wounded man's shoulders.

"That's not Lincoln!" someone shouted.

The crowd that had been as still as death now surged to life. Everyone tried to see who had emerged from the President's carriage, to guess his identity.

"It's Vice-President Hamlin!" someone shouted.

"It's not Hamlin, Hamlin's fatter than that!" There was a spattering of laughter.

Some said it was J.D. Breckinridge; others said it was Secretary of State Seward.

"Who do you think it is?" Wheelright asked without turning around. There was no answer. "Captain?" Wheelright craned his neck to see behind him. J.D.'s mouth was hanging open stupidly. "Captain, are you all right?"

J.D. shouted, "That's my father!"

When Jeremiah Morgan stepped into President Lincoln's personal carriage, it never occurred to him that someone might mistake him for the President of the United States. For Jeremiah this was the chance of a lifetime. He wasn't stepping into a carriage, he was stepping through a doorway that led to his destiny.

Lincoln's secretary, J.D. Nicolay, had escorted him from the President's office to the red brick stable which was situated between the White House and the Treasury Department. He waited as Nicolay spoke to a man who was not pleased with the conversation. Nicolay was insistent and the man stomped into the stable.

"The man you saw me talking to," Nicolay explained when

he returned, "is Patterson McGee. He will be your coach-man."

"He doesn't seem to relish the assignment," Jeremiah noted.

"That's just his nature. He'll deliver you safely to General Burnside." Then, handing Jeremiah a folded piece of paper, Nicolay said, "Here's your pass. It's signed by the President himself." A pause and a smile. "I'm glad it's you and not me. Anyway, best of luck." Nicolay held out his hand and Jeremiah shook it.

A few moments later, the President's carriage emerged from the stables. It was a modest carriage, considering its owner, but Jeremiah had never ridden in anything like it before. When Lincoln offered to let Jeremiah use it, the President explained it was one of three carriages available to him. It wasn't the most elegant of the three, but it had simple lines and a light, graceful structure. It was a dark brown "Clarence"—a closed, four-wheeled carriage with a driver's seat high in front with two double seats inside facing each other. The mountings were silver-plated and the wheels were black with broad, dark-brown stripes and edged with canary stripes.

McGee reined the horses to a stop as a stable hand scampered out and opened the door for the minister. Jeremiah thanked the boy and stepped into his carriage of destiny.

Jeremiah could hardly contain his glee as the coachman urged the team down Pennsylvania Avenue. He ran his hand along the brown, silk-corded material that lined the carriage, then along the black leather seat. The front of the coach was curved and lined with glass, offering a panoramic view of the nation's capital. Jeremiah jumped over to the other seat and rode backward for a while.

As the coach turned right, heading south on 14th Street, a distinguished-looking man tipped his hat at the carriage. The man's lips formed a simple greeting, "Mr. President." Then, as the carriage passed closer and the man saw that Jeremiah was not the President, his surprise and embarrassment were obvious. Jeremiah slid to the backseat.

As the carriage crossed the Mall, Jeremiah could see the red stone towers of the Smithsonian and unfinished Capitol through some trees on his left. There were sheds, stacks of lumber, and marble blocks scattered around the construction site as workers completed the wings and dome of the Capitol building.

The carriage lumbered across Long Bridge and Jeremiah was reminded of his mission. The bridge was guarded by sentries who snapped to attention and saluted as the carriage passed. On the far side of the span, cavalry officers sat on horses with rifles across their thighs and artillery men cleaned the cannon that protected this vital artery to the nation's capital. The task the President had given him was to encourage young men just like these—boys, really. Boys who should be growing up at home, not dying on battlefields.

The carriage picked up speed as it skirted the Potomac River. Traveling the road leading south to Falmouth, Jeremiah chuckled and settled back for the ride. "Lord, I was beginning to think this day would never come," he said aloud.

For the first time in his life Jeremiah felt worthy to be a Morgan. Here he was at fifty years of age, fresh from a meeting with the President of the United States in which the President sought *his* advice, riding in the President's personal carriage, carrying a pass signed by the President authorizing him to preach to the Army of the Potomac. This was an assignment worthy of a Morgan. If only Susanna could see him now.

Susanna!

Jeremiah bolted upright so quickly, McGee glanced back to see if anything was wrong. Susanna had no idea where he was! As far as she knew, he should be arriving in Point Providence any day now. He would write her a letter tonight. Hopefully, it would reach her in a couple of days.

As McGee urged the horses onward, Jeremiah sat back again and wondered what the next few days would be like. He saw himself preaching to Union soldiers, lonely boys far from home. He would teach them about the comfort of Christ. He saw himself reporting back to the President, counseling the Commander-in-Chief to hold on to his vision of freedom and equality. Perhaps if things went well, he might even be asked to address the reunited houses of Congress following the war—senators and congressmen eager to implement the ways of God into the laws of the nation. He saw himself leading them in a prayer for national healing. He saw himself . . .

Jeremiah didn't hear the first shot. The wood behind the silk lining exploded beside his head. He stared at the splintered wood stupidly, unable to comprehend what it meant.

"Tst! Yah! Get up now!" McGee screamed at the horses.

The carriage bolted forward, sending Jeremiah's head crashing against the back of the carriage.

The second shot was a loud crack. The front left glass pane shattered, spraying the interior with glass. Jeremiah felt a hot claw tear at his right side near the waist.

"Hya! Get amovin'!" The coachman's voice was a frightened cry. He swore at the horses and prayed to God in the same breath.

The horses picked up more speed. There were times when it seemed like the whole carriage was thrown in the air, only to come crashing down.

Glancing down at his side, Jeremiah could see a growing red stain. He reached for the wound with his left hand, hoping to stop the flood pouring out of him.

The carriage rocked back and forth crazily, knocking Jeremiah to the floor. He could feel the effects of the wound begin to spread throughout his body; his head fell back against the seat as he fought to remain conscious. Out the window Jeremiah saw a blur of bare treetops against a background of high winter clouds.

He closed his eyes. "No, Lord. Please, don't let it end this way. Not now. Not now." His breathing came in short gasps.

The carriage turned sharply and threw Jeremiah against the side. There was a fresh jab of pain.

"How bad are you hurt?" McGee had glanced back and saw him sprawled on the floor.

Jeremiah tried to respond, but all he could manage was a weak smile.

For the next few moments Jeremiah remembered bouncing violently as the carriage jumped in and out of ruts and holes in the road.

Then, the carriage slowed, but only slightly. "President's carriage! Wounded man!" Jeremiah heard McGee calling over and over. A moment later, the carriage was flanked by two soldiers in blue on horseback.

Jeremiah bounced like this for several minutes, then, with exaggerated movements, the coachman pulled the horses to a stop. The carriage skidded to the right and stopped in a cloud of dust, throwing Jeremiah against the forward seat. Another jab of pain shot through his side, this one so strong it almost pushed him over the edge. As Jeremiah fought to hold on to his senses, he could hear men shouting and running from every direction. The door flew open and a major burst into the carriage. The surprised look on his face was so comical, even half-unconscious, Jeremiah had to suppress a chuckle.

"You're not the President!" the major shouted.

Jeremiah merely shook his head. The major looked around the interior as if Jeremiah were hiding the President somewhere.

"Sorry to disappoint you, Major," Jeremiah managed to say. "But it's just me."

The major turned toward the open door. "Get a surgeon in

here! He's been hit in the side."

Jeremiah had logged hundreds of hours beside the injured and dying during his pastoral ministry. To him, the strangest part of any emergency was the waiting time. And while Jeremiah waited for medical assistance he could hear the whispers of men surrounding the carriage.

"Is Lincoln really in there?"

"Is he dead?"

The carriage bounced as the major left and a man with a medical bag entered. The doctor visibly started when he first saw Jeremiah. "You're not the President!" he said.

"So I've been told," Jeremiah replied.

"Well, let's take a look at you anyway." The doctor placed his bag on the seat just above Jeremiah's head and gently pulled the pastor's hand away from the wound. The doctor couldn't resist commenting on Jeremiah's swollen hands.

"Arthritis?"

Jeremiah nodded.

"How old are you?"

"Fifty."

"Pretty young to have it this bad," the doctor said as he focused his attention on the wound.

Jeremiah chose not to look at the wound with the doctor, so he concentrated on the freckles dotting the top of the doctor's head as they bobbed up and down a few inches from his face. As the doctor poked around the wound, the pain rose to new levels. Jeremiah concentrated harder on the freckles, trying to see if he could recognize constellation patterns in them. He managed to spot one—with a little imagination, three freckles aligned to form Orion's belt. Then, the skin-and-freckled universe rose from his sight, replaced by the doctor's face.

"Not a serious wound. Actually, quite clean." He turned toward the door. "Let's get him to a bed." Jabbing a bloodied finger toward two soldiers, he said, "You, grab the legs and you grab him under the arms." Then, without even looking back at his patient, the doctor crawled out of the carriage. He had to part a sea of boys in blue uniforms to make a pathway for his patient.

One boy grabbed the doctor's arm. "Is the President going to be all right?"

"Relax, boy." The doctor pulled his arm free. "That ain't the President."

Two huge forms filled the carriage doorway. They performed a curious dance around Jeremiah as they maneuvered for position to complete their task. Jeremiah felt himself rising above the carriage floorboard.

As the trio emerged from the carriage he heard a familiar refrain, "That's not the President!" Which was soon replaced with, "Who is he?"

The trio waddled across the compound toward a row of white tents. Midway there the soldier carrying Jeremiah's legs stopped abruptly. He shifted the feet in his hands back and forth as if he didn't know what to do with them. A moment later, Jeremiah understood the soldier's dilemma. He was trying to salute.

Four heavily decorated figures emerged from both sides of the lead soldier, two on each side. Jeremiah recognized the first man immediately by the characteristic whiskers cascading down the man's jowls. It was General Ambrose Burnside, the commanding general of the Army of the Potomac. He also recognized Generals Sumner and Hooker. The fourth general remained a mystery.

So this was to be his grand entrance, Jeremiah thought as he looked around him. Four generals and what looked like the entire Union army staring down at him while his feet pointed skyward and his backside almost dragged on the ground.

"Who the devil are you and what are you doing in the

President's carriage?" Burnside thundered.

The other generals crowded in to get a closer look at Jeremiah. None of them looked pleased to see him.

"General. . . ." It was the doctor. "Let's get his wound dressed, then you can shoot him."

General Burnside snorted, shook his head as if Jeremiah was the strangest thing he'd ever seen, and marched back from where he'd come. Two of the three other generals followed him. The fourth, Hooker, stood his ground and stared at Jeremiah with suspicious eyes. As long as he stood there, the soldiers carrying Jeremiah didn't dare move.

"If he remains here much longer, the man's gonna bleed to death." It was the doctor again. The lead soldier looked at Hooker for permission to continue on. Hooker motioned the soldier forward with a nod of his head, never once taking his eyes off Jeremiah. As the trio maneuvered Jeremiah through the tent opening, Jeremiah was turned in such a way that he got one final look at the compound. Hooker hadn't moved. Hands on hips, he watched Jeremiah until he could see him no more.

The hospital tent was a large walled structure, filled end-to-end with cots, but there were just a few patients. The doctor removed Jeremiah's shirt, cleaned and dressed the wound without ever saying a word to him. Then he was gone. A few moments later the flap of the tent flew backward and Generals Burnside and Hooker approached the bed, followed by an entourage of orderlies. There wasn't a friendly face among them.

Burnside stood on Jeremiah's right, closest to his head. He was slightly paunchy, tall, and very hairy, all except the top of his head which was a smooth extension of his forehead. His facial hair, which had become his trademark, flowed full and unhindered down the sides of his face—muttonchops, they were called—then curved upward to form a mustache. His chin was cleanly shaved. Burnside's eyes were dark and vulnerable, the wrinkles at their corners indicating that they enjoyed a good laugh. But the general's eyes weren't laughing now.

On the other side of the bed, closest to his head, was General Hooker. He stood perfectly straight. His hair was short and sculpted, looking like the hair on a marble statue of a Roman emperor. His eyes were sharp and humorless. His lips were thin, almost to the point of being nonexistent. The thin line turned downward at the edges.

"Let's have it," Burnside bellowed. "Who are you and what are you doing in the President's carriage?"

Jeremiah answered briefly. "I have a pass from the President in my coat pocket," Jeremiah motioned toward his coat which was draped over a chair beside the bed. "It explains everything."

Burnside retrieved the paper from Jeremiah's coat, unfolded it, and read silently.

"Read it out loud!" Hooker demanded.

Burnside shot a warning glance at Hooker. Jeremiah sensed this wasn't the first time Hooker had tried to give an order to his commanding officer. But Hooker didn't back down.

Looking back at the paper, Burnside read aloud, "Major General Burnside, My dear sir: The bearer of this letter, Rev. Jeremiah Morgan, is my trusted spiritual advisor. Please treat him kindly, while I am sure he will avoid giving you trouble. . . ." Burnside peered over the note at Jeremiah, who smiled and shrugged. The general continued, "I have found him to be of valuable assistance and comfort in spiritual matters and have charged him to equip our troops spiritually for the demanding task set before them. A. Lincoln."

"Let me see that!" Hooker shoved a demanding hand toward Burnside. The belligerent general's arm held rock-steady just a few feet above Jeremiah's nose. Jeremiah's gaze traveled up the outstretched arm, past the shoulder insignia of a major general, and up Hooker's thin, sharp nose to glassy, cold eyes. Hooker's expression was that of a parent to a troublesome child who came home with another disciplinary note from the schoolmaster.

Burnside chose to ignore Hooker's impertinence. He slowly and deliberately folded the note and slipped it into his side coat pocket. "So you're the President's parson?"

"Not exactly." Jeremiah tried to pull himself up in bed a little. He felt uncomfortable with two generals hovering over him. But as he pushed himself up with his arms, a sharp pain punched his wound and he decided it was best to lay still. "I just met President Lincoln a week or so ago. I'm the pastor of a small church in Ohio."

"Which church?"

"The Heritage Fellowship Church in Point Providence, Ohio. Just east of Cincinnati along the Ohio River."

"Point Providence, that's where Grant was born, isn't it?" Burnside asked.

Jeremiah shook his head. "You're thinking of Point Pleasant. Not too far from us, actually."

The commanding general sighed and turned to leave, then came right back. "Why didn't Lincoln inform us you were coming?"

Jeremiah shrugged. "My coming happened rather quickly. In fact, other than Lincoln and the people in this camp, no one knows I'm here."

"Lincoln could have telegraphed," Hooker said. "That's just like him, always doing what he wants to do without consideration as to how it affects us. He dispatches the presidential carriage with no notification and no armed guard."

Burnside addressed Jeremiah. "Do you know who shot you?"

Jeremiah shook his head no.

"Do you have any personal enemies that want to see you dead?" Burnside asked.

The question took Jeremiah by surprise. It never occurred to him that someone would be targeting him. Until this moment, in his mind the incident had been a case of mistaken identity. Yes, he had enemies—Caleb McKenna was angry enough with him to want to see him dead and the powerful New York banker certainly had the connections and resources to hire someone to do the dirty deed—but Jeremiah couldn't bring himself to believe that he was the intended target of any gunman. "My enemies don't use guns," he replied. "Their weapons are more subtle. I believe a sniper shot at the President's carriage hoping to kill someone important."

Burnside stroked his whiskers as he weighed Jeremiah's words. "Probably a scout," he said. Turning to an orderly who had been standing at a discreet distance from the interrogation, Burnside ordered, "Send a detachment up the road. Tell them to look for a Confederate scout or sharpshooter." The orderly saluted and scurried out of the tent.

"Waste of time," Hooker sneered. "He's long gone."

"Just the same, it's best to check," Burnside responded.

Burnside's words hit Hooker in the back. He hadn't waited for any response. As soon as Hooker had delivered his criticism of Burnside's order, he had turned and marched out of the tent, his assistants trailing him. Now, the only people left in the tent besides Jeremiah were General Burnside, a corporal, a few sick soldiers, and their wide-eyed nurses who had gone to great effort to pretend they had not been eavesdropping on the unusual events between a preacher and two generals.

"I'm afraid I haven't made a very good first impression on General Hooker," Jeremiah said to Burnside.

"It's not easy to impress a man who believes he is always

right," Burnside responded. As soon as the words were spoken, Burnside seemed to regret making such a statement to a stranger. Addressing the corporal, he said, "As soon as the doctor releases him, put the parson in the VIP tent." Looking back at Jeremiah, but still talking to the corporal, he added, "He arrived in a VIP carriage, might as well put him in VIP quarters." The corporal held his place as the general moved in front of him toward the exit.

"General?" Jeremiah asked.

The general turned back toward him.

"I have son here. J.D. He's a captain. Would it be possible for me to see him?"

Burnside looked at the corporal: "Locate Captain Morgan and deliver him to his father." Then back at Jeremiah: "You said no one knows you're here. Are you married?"

"Yes, sir."

"I suggest you write your wife." With that, General Burnside pushed aside the tent flap and was gone.

Chapter 16

JEREMIAH dozed on the hospital cot. He heard the soft flap of the tent as it rose and fell, but the sound got lost somewhere between his sleeping and waking moments. The sound played in his mind as part of an image of a sunny summer day at Central Park, long ago. He and Seth were young then. The flapping was a tablecloth sailing in the wind, anchored to the ground by Elizabeth and Emma. Elizabeth was striking. Adorned in a brilliant white summer dress, she flashed a carefree smile at him. Nearby some children laughed and screamed with delightful abandon. The breeze was cool, the grass warm as he and Seth . . .

"Father?"

The image faded to black. Central Park, Elizabeth, Seth, Emma were gone. But if this wasn't Central Park, where . . . ?

"Father? I can come back if you're too tired to talk."

The darkness became light as Jeremiah's eyes opened a crack. White canvas stretched overhead, peaking at the top of a pole.

"Father?"

Jeremiah turned his head. His eldest son stood beside him in a captain's uniform. Instinctively, Jeremiah attempted to rise to greet him. His right side reacted to the attempt as if hit by a fist. "Ohhh. . . . " His hand moved quickly to his burning side's aid, but there was nothing it could do but rest gently near the wound in sympathy. The pain reminded Jeremiah where he was.

"Don't try to get up, Father," J.D. said. He held a hand with slender fingers over his father, motioning for him to remain in bed. His neck seemed lost in his collar. His cheeks were hollow. He was tall and stiff.

"You look thin," Jeremiah said. His face spread wide with a grin. "But it's good to see you, son." Memories of the photographs of Antietam flashed in his mind. J.D.'s lively pink hands and face, the dark blue of his coat, the yellow brass of his buttons—all these were a strong contrast to the colorless photos of the war dead. Jeremiah couldn't stop himself from grinning. His son was alive.

"Are you hurt bad?" J.D. asked.

"Actually, I think your mother's cooking saved my life." J.D.'s forehead pulled up in a puzzled look.

Jeremiah chuckled. "That extra layer of fat around my waist," he explained. "I think it stopped the bullet from doing any serious damage."

The humor seemed to relax J.D. His shoulders fell to a more natural position. "Can I ask you a question?" he asked.

"Anything."

"What were you doing in the President's carriage? I couldn't believe my eyes! Everyone was expecting to see Abraham Lincoln. Then, all of a sudden, instead of the President, there you were!"

"It made for a dramatic entrance, didn't it?" Jeremiah said.

"So how did you get into the President's carriage in the first place?"

"The President loaned it to me."

One side of J.D.'s mouth curled up in a wry half-grin. He wasn't sure whether his father was telling the truth or pulling his leg.

"That's what happened!" Jeremiah insisted, enjoying the

moment. "President Lincoln sent me down here to preach to the army. He gave me his carriage, his driver, and a handwritten message to General Burnside for the assignment. When I'm finished, I'll report back to him."

"When . . . how long . . . I didn't know you knew President Lincoln." J.D. stammered.

"Just met him. Pull up a stool and I'll tell you all about it."

As J.D. retrieved a short three-legged stool, Jeremiah noticed that the other six or seven patients in the tent were also adjusting themselves to hear the story. Some propped themselves up on an elbow. Others cocked a listening ear his direction. Jeremiah didn't mind. As the pastor in a small town he was used to everyone knowing his business. Besides, it would provide a needed distraction for them; help them get their minds off their wounds if just for a short time. He began by describing his sudden invitation to speak at the memorial service.

"Afterwards, this man—a secret service agent as it turns out—told me that a grieving father wanted to talk to me. Imagine my surprise when the carriage door opened and there sat President Lincoln! Naturally, it didn't take but a moment to recognize him."

"Is he really as tall as they say?" J.D. asked. "I've heard he's six-foot-four."

"He's every bit that tall, and thin too," Jeremiah replied.

"So what did you talk about?"

Jeremiah's face sobered as he thought back to the conversation. "We need to pray for our President," he said. "Whether they agree with him or not, everyone knows how great this national crisis weighs upon him. How could it not? But what many people don't know is that he bears personal burdens that are just as great. The President still has not gotten over his son's death earlier this year. A sadder face than his I have rarely seen."

"I remember reading about the boy's death," J.D. said.

"His name was Willie. Just like our Willy, only spelled different." Jeremiah's eyes rolled upward as he recalled the details of the conversation. "The President told me of an incident shortly before Willie's illness. He and his brother were playing with two playmates—from Cincinnati, mind you."

J.D. shook his head in disbelief. "Cincinnati! So close to us. Do we know the family?"

Jeremiah shook his head. "I didn't recognize their last name. But it seems the boys took rags and old clothes and made a doll. They named him Jack. He had red baggy trousers, with a light-blue jacket and red fez on his head."

"Like a Zouave!" J.D. laughed. Having adopted the dress and drill of the French Algerian infantry, the Zouaves were one of the more colorful military units.

"As it turns out," Jeremiah continued, "the boys sentenced their doll Jack to be shot at sunrise for sleeping on picket duty. They were about to carry out the sentence when the gardener suggested they ask the President for a pardon for Jack. Racing into the White House, the four boys made their request to President Lincoln. He listened to their plea, then soberly wrote on a sheet of Executive Mansion stationery:

The doll Jack is pardoned.
By order of the President.
A. Lincoln.

Jeremiah and his son shared a laugh over the doll Jack's brush with death. "Apparently the President's Willie had a remarkable mind," Jeremiah continued. "The President told me that Willie had memorized all the main railroad stations from New York to Chicago. He would walk around the house calling them off—Troy, Schenectady, Utica, Rome, and on and on. The boy would spend hours drawing up time-tables, then conducting imaginary train rides with perfect precision."

"How did he die?" J.D. asked.

"He went riding in a chilly rain and fell sick with cold and fever. A few days later he was dead."

There was silence for a moment. Jeremiah glanced around the tent. The other patients were lapping up every word.

"I wish you could have seen him," Jeremiah said, speaking of the President. "You would better understand the depth of this man's compassion. At one point, he said to me, 'It is hard, hard, hard to have him die!' "

There was silence in the hospital tent for the President's sorrow.

Softly, J.D. asked, "Did the President travel to Hagerstown to attend the memorial service?"

"I don't think so," Jeremiah replied. "Nobody seemed to know he was there. They didn't announce his presence, or refer to him in any way. It was my impression he was just passing by, saw the service, and stopped to listen a while."

"And who did he get to hear? My father!" J.D. beamed with obvious pride.

"After we talked about Willie for a while, he asked me to ride along with him." A sheepish look covered Jeremiah's face. "Who am I to say no to the President of the United States? Naturally, I consented!"

His side began to burn. Jeremiah repositioned himself. A glance toward the other patients showed they were still with him. *What better activity did they have to do?*

"McClellan was on his mind a great deal," Jeremiah said of the President. "This was just before he replaced McClellan with Burnside. The President kept saying over and over, 'The man's got the slows.' " Looking at his son, Jeremiah added, "Then he inquired about you."

"Me? The President inquired about me?" J.D. said, astonished.

"Well, I told him you were in the Army of the Potomac, and he asked how you were faring. Then, he returned to McClellan. He said, 'I regret to inform you, Morgan, that your son is not serving in the Army of the Potomac.' I replied, 'I'm sure he is, Mr. President.' The President replied, 'No sir, he is not. He and all the others are serving as nothing more than General McClellan's bodyguards.' "

This anecdote brought a frown from several of the other patients.

"Anyway," said Jeremiah, "two days later, at the White House, I learned that McClellan had been replaced."

"You mean to tell me you rode with the President all the way back to the White House?"

"And stayed there as his guest," Jeremiah beamed. "Our President is a very spiritual man and he likes to gather opinions. He would call upon me at odd times for just a few moments. He'd ask my opinion on something. As I spoke I could almost see him mentally compare my opinions with other opinions he'd stored in his head—sort through them, judge them worthy or unworthy, toss away the dross, keep the gold, then seek another opinion. And this man has no small number of people wanting to tell him what he should be doing. I've never seen such a parade of personalities!"

J.D.'s eyes were wide with interest as he listened to his father. "You said he sent you down here to preach to the troops?" he prompted.

Jeremiah nodded. The exertion from talking was taking its toll on him. He was tiring. He saw this as an opportunity to let J.D. do the talking for a while. "The President is convinced he did the right thing in replacing McClellan, but he's concerned about the morale of the army. He asked me to evaluate the situation and do what I could to lift the soldiers' spirits. So tell me, how are things in camp?"

Shifting uneasily on the stool, J.D. studied the dirt floor a moment before answering. "The President is right to be concerned," he said. "Many of the fellows are strongly devoted to McClellan."

This brought scattered verbal approval from the other patients in the tent.

"It's not that they don't like General Burnside. He's a friendly, personable fellow. But he's no McClellan."

Cries of "Little Mac" sounded in the tent.

"I've heard him compared to Napoleon," Jeremiah said.

"No matter what President Lincoln thinks of him," J.D. said, "the Army of the Potomac loves him. He was cheered greatly when he rode out of camp. And I heard that Burnside apologized to him for being the one to replace him."

Jeremiah nodded in understanding. His eyelids were growing heavy. He fought to stay awake, not wanting this time with J.D. to end.

"In a word, the men are discouraged. Many of them want McClellan to form his own army and march on Washington."

Jeremiah was astounded. "Is there any possibility of that?"

"The men are serious, if that's what you mean," J.D. replied. "They think McClellan can do a better job running the country than Lincoln and the Congress. Whether McClellan would ever do that, I can't say."

Jeremiah tucked away that piece of information. He'd be sure to include it in his report to the President.

"Besides the change in command," J.D. continued, "we've had eight months of mud and drill and more mud and more drill. Illness is rampant."

Jeremiah looked around at the vacant cots.

"This is an officer's tent." J.D. saw what his father was thinking. "The enlisted soldiers' hospital tents are just about full and we haven't seen action in a long time. The men keep saying they came here to fight for their country, not to die of malaria."

"How is Ben McKenna treating you?" Jeremiah asked.

Before replying, J.D. glanced up at the other officers in the tent. His reply was formed to fit the situation. "About the same."

Jeremiah was beginning to drift off. "Sarah and Jenny are in New York," he said groggily.

"Jenny told me so in her last letter."

"They're fine . . . fine." Jeremiah's words were coming out between moments of shallow sleep. "Of course, I didn't bring word from Jenny . . . didn't know I was coming . . . so how could . . . she . . . "

"And Mother? Is she all right?"

"Fine . . . fine . . . "

"Have you heard anything from Marshall or Willy?"

Jeremiah's answer was a shallow snore.

They stood in rows, shoulder-to-shoulder, stretching back almost as far as he could see. From a raised platform, Jeremiah contemplated his Sunday-morning congregation as J.D. introduced him. The soldiers' faces were solemn, young. Too young to be soldiers in Jeremiah's opinion. *Why do nations send their young to war?* He had his opinion on the matter. Nations send their young because young men lack a healthy sense of fear that comes with age. If you tell young men they're invincible, they'll believe you. If you order them to charge up a hill into a storm of bullets, they'll do it because you told them they could do it. Unlike men Jeremiah's age. If an officer told him to charge up a hill, he'd tell the officer that if he wanted the hill taken, take it himself. Not these boys. They'd charge up the hill and get themselves killed. He could tell by their faces.

One other thing he could tell by the faces massed in front of him. They didn't want to be there. Not just here at Sunday services, they didn't want to be in the war any longer. Gone was the we'll-whip-them-in-ninety-days bravado. These men were tired. Tired of the mud. Tired of drills. Tired of living in tents. Tired of eating hard tack, salt beef, and pork. Tired of fighting. Tired of waiting to fight. Tired of being so far from home. There was no grand cause driving these men. If someone were to tell them they could go home, the place would be empty in a minute.

Jeremiah had his work cut out for him with this congregation. It would take a miracle to effect a change of heart in these boys. Luckily for Jeremiah, he represented Someone who specialized in miracles.

As he rose from his seat and approached the lectern, all eyes were on him. Officers sat on horseback under cover of trees, looking as though they were there to prevent a riot. Their jaws were set and hard, their eyes were weary, just like the men they commanded. From the looks of things, the whole regiment was inflicted with a terminal case of depression and despair.

Jeremiah cleared his throat. It was a bad habit for a speaker, he knew. But he always did it. It annoyed his wife. For her sake, he'd tried to stop, but he never remembered until he was doing it. *How does one stop a throat-clearing halfway through it?* Maybe he did it to give himself one last moment to consider what he was going to say.

Lord, look at these boys, he said to God silently. *What can I possibly say that will get their attention? What can I say that will lift their spirits and give them hope?* Jeremiah walked away from the lectern to one end of the platform. He said not a word; he simply looked the boys over. Their eyes followed him. Then he walked to the opposite side of the platform and stood there in silence. The eyes of the boys followed him.

With every eye on him, he said, "Boys, your mothers are praying for you." He crossed the platform one more time.

The only sound to be heard was the clomping of his shoes. "Did you hear what I said?" he asked the other side. "Your mothers are praying for you. This is the Sabbath, and if there is one thing of which I am certain, it is this: Today, at this very minute, your mothers are in church and their thoughts and prayers are for you. In Boston, mothers are praying for you. In Trenton, mothers are praying for you. They're praying in New York, and Philadelphia, and Cleveland."

"In Woodbury?" one soldier cried out.

"Mothers are praying in Woodbury!" Jeremiah yelled back.

"In Logansport?" another cried out.

"Mothers are praying in Logansport!"

"In Danville?"

"Yes, son! Mothers are praying in Danville! All over the country, mothers are praying. Just like Hannah, who prayed for Samuel when she dedicated him to the Lord at the temple, so your mothers are praying for you, dedicating you to the Lord. Just like Mary who prayed for her son Jesus as she watched Him die on the cross, knowing that He was doing what He had to do, so your mothers pray for you, knowing some of you will die, but also knowing that you are doing what you have to do."

Gone was the sea of despair that had stretched before Jeremiah when he started. In its place was a rising tide of interest as the boys' hearts were turned toward thoughts of home.

"You see, boys, your mothers pray for you because they know who you are. They know you better than your superior officers know you. Better than the men you share a tent with. Better than your closest friend. So it is only right that they should pray for you. Who better to pray for you than the one who knows you best? And when they think of you, they don't see a corporal or a lieutenant or even a general. They see their boy who still takes orders from them no matter how old he is." Laughter rippled through the ranks. "They don't see infantry or cavalry or gunners. They see their boy doing chores around the house. There is no pretense when it comes to mothers. No matter what your rank or accomplishments in life, you will always be their boy."

Jeremiah removed his handkerchief and wiped his face. For a cool day, he was working up a considerable heat.

"I once heard a story about George Washington, a man who had a pious mother. As the story goes, immediately following the surrender of the British troops at Yorktown, General Washington headed for home. A runner preceded him to inform the general's aged mother. The runner announced with great flourish, 'His excellency, General Washington, will be arriving shortly.' To which Washington's mother replied, 'Tell George when he arrives that I will be glad to see him. Oh, and remind him to wipe his feet before entering the house.' "

While the soldiers laughed, Jeremiah mopped his brow again.

"Knowing your mothers are praying for you," Jeremiah continued, "don't you think you ought to do something for them? At the conclusion of this service I want each of you men to go immediately to your tents and write your mother a letter. Tell her you're thinking of her. Tell her you love her. Tell her you will be home as soon as you complete your task for your country. Tell her she would be proud of you if she could see you now; then, live in such a way to make your statement true. Boys, your mother is praying for you and it's time you told her how much you love her."

Jeremiah was beginning to wonder if he would make it to the end of the service. His head was getting light. Perspiration poured from his forehead. He had to steady himself by leaning on the lectern.

"With this story, I'll conclude," he said. "There once was a little, ragged newsboy who lost his mother. Out of love for her, he wanted to do something in her memory. He determined to buy her a tombstone for her poor grave. This would be no easy task since his earnings were barely enough to provide himself with food. Nevertheless, he went to the stone yard looking for a tombstone. To his dismay he discovered that even the cheaper ones were beyond his financial abilities. He had to settle on a broken piece of stone, the remains of a stonecutter's accident. The next day the boy carted the stone to the graveyard and managed to maneuver it in place. Kneeling in front of the stone, he used an old file to carve his mother's epitaph. Every day he would come by and work on the inscription, letter by letter. After a few days, the man who sold him the piece of stone became curious about the little boy and went to the graveyard to see what had become of the boy and the stone. Finding the stone in the graveyard, he saw letters scratched on the surface, all in capitals. The words read:

MY MOTHER
SHEE DIED LAST WEEK
SHE WAS ALL I HAD
SHE SAID SHEAD BE WAITING FUR

"The stonecutter came back a week later, but the inscription still had not been completed. He asked the groundskeeper if he had seen the boy. The groundskeeper said, 'Didn't you notice the fresh little grave beside the grave with the stone? That's where the boy is. It seems the little fellow was hurrying down the street, coming here to finish his mother's tombstone when he was hit by a runaway wagon. The way I heard it, he had an old file in his hands when he died. He was thinking of nothing else other than finishing his task. The boy kept saying, "I didn't get it done. I didn't get it done. But she'll know I meant to finish it, won't she?"

He died with those words on his lips.' When the stonecutter told the story of the boy to the men at the stone yard, they took up a collection and purchased a large tombstone and placed it at the head of the boy's grave. It read:

HEAR LIES A BOY
WHO LOVED HIS MOTHER."

Jeremiah moved to the side of the lectern so that nothing separated him and the rows of soldiers. He leaned heavily on the lectern to keep from falling over.

"Boys," he cried, "your mothers are praying for you. Don't disappoint them. Do the work you've come to do, so that when this war is over you can march home with your heads held high. This will make your mothers proud of you."

The service concluded with a prayer of benediction, after which J.D. assisted his father back to the officers' hospital tent.

After just a few minutes in a reclined position, Jeremiah's strength began to rally. The tent flap rose and General Burnside entered followed by his ever-present line of aides who looked like ducklings following in their mother's wake.

J.D. jumped to attention and saluted.

"As you were, Captain," Burnside said. Then, to Jeremiah: "Superb job, preacher. Absolutely first-rate! Have you seen what's happening outside?"

Jeremiah shook his head. "No, sir, I haven't. I was feeling a little weak and came straight here."

Burnside said, "On every rock and log and stool, they're writing letters. Many with tears. But that's good. You can see it on their faces. You've given them hope, preacher! And you've given them a positive task to help keep their minds off their misery. Well done! Well done!"

"Thank you, sir," Jeremiah said.

"Hooker was impressed too," Burnside said, noticeably pleased.

Jeremiah's eyebrows raised.

"At his recommendation, I have a request to make of you."

"Yes, sir?"

"We'd like you to conduct a series of meetings this week. Revival-type meetings every evening. Can you do that? It would be good for the men."

"I would be honored, General."

"Excellent!" Burnside boomed. "Excellent!"

By Wednesday a person couldn't walk down a row of tents without hearing a hymn sung, or seeing a group of eager soldiers gathered around a Bible, or seeing men huddled together on their knees praying. The air crackled with spiritual excitement. Revival was sweeping through the Army of the Potomac, and beyond. From neighboring towns and villages civilians lined the roads to attend the evening service—mothers and young children, older folks, sometimes entire families.

Soldiers volunteered to use their talents at the worship services. Lieutenant George Logan of Detroit, Michigan, a fair-haired, blue-eyed voice teacher, led the singing and sang solos. With head tilted backward, his face heavenward, his eyes closed, George Logan's tenor voice sounded forth the call of God as clearly as Gabriel's trumpet. A thirty-voice volunteer choir and a band of sorts assisted Logan with the congregational singing. The band consisted of a few trumpets, a clarinet, a flute, and a fiddle. The music was lively, if not always on key.

During the day, Bible studies were held in every company. One battalion organized a 'round-the-clock prayer vigil for revival. For a week in early December, 1862 the Union army became a church and Rev. Jeremiah Morgan was their pastor.

◆ ◆ ◆

"The hand of the Lord was upon me, and carried me out in the spirit of the Lord, and set me down in the midst of the valley which was full of bones, and caused me to pass by them round about: and, behold, there were very many in the open valley; and, lo, they were very dry. And He said unto me, Son of man, can these bones live? And I answered, O Lord God, Thou knowest."

People drank in every word as Jeremiah read from his Bible. Soldiers perched on sturdy branches of every tree. They stood on wagon beds and rain barrels. So tightly packed together were they that Jeremiah could not see a blade of grass or a patch of ground between them. As he read to them, his heart pounded with a sense of urgency. He was God's prophet for this hour.

"Again He said unto me, Prophesy upon these bones, and say unto them, O ye dry bones, hear the word of the Lord. Thus saith the Lord God unto these bones; Behold, I will cause breath to enter into you, and ye shall live: And I will lay sinews upon you, and will bring up flesh upon you, and cover you with skin, and put breath in you, and ye shall live; and ye shall know that I am the Lord."

His Bible lay proudly open. His hands clutched the lectern's wooden edges as he read God's Word to them. Thousands gathered before him, yet no other sound was heard other than his voice. The people listened so intently, that even his intake of air between paragraphs was audible. Never before had Jeremiah witnessed so great a thirst for spiritual things. Never before had he felt the moving of God's Spirit as he did now.

"So I prophesied as He commanded me, and the breath came into them, and they lived, and stood up upon their feet, an exceeding great army."

To address his congregation, Jeremiah moved to the side of the lectern. He moved as though he were walking on holy ground. "Ezekiel's valley resembles a battlefield, doesn't it?" he asked. "A forgotten battlefield. A battlefield whose only monument is the bleached bones of those who have fallen. Did this battlefield have a name? If it did, no one remembers it. For what cause did these soldiers fight and die? What flag rippled over their heads when they breathed their last? No one remembers. The prophet hears no hurrahs. No victory songs are sung. Did the deaths of these men gain their side a victory? Or are these the vanquished? There is no way for Ezekiel to know. He sees only bone stacked upon bone. And they are very dry.

"It would appear that all is hopeless in this valley. It is a visible reminder that we all are mortal; that this is the way of all men—we live and then we die. But God did not bring His prophet to the valley of destruction that he might mourn the dead. The prophet was led to the edge of this valley to witness the power of God. At God's command, the bones assembled. With God's breath they came to life. And they were an exceeding host. Imagine it! One minute they were nothing more than a pile of bleached bones; the next minute, they are a regiment of living, breathing human beings with hopes and dreams and desires. How is this possible? It is possible because God is the giver of life.

"This whole dramatic demonstration was to impress upon Ezekiel an essential truth that—in the midst of our daily tasks—we tend to forget. God gives life.

"This truth is as true today as it was in the prophet's day. God gives life. Without God there is no life. God is the source of all existence. Upon this truth rests everything in which we believe. As the Apostle Paul reminds us, 'For if the dead rise not, then is not Christ raised: And if Christ be not raised, your faith is vain; ye are yet in your sins. Then they also which are fallen asleep in Christ are perished. If in this life only we have hope in Christ, we are of all men most miserable.'

"God gives life. This is our hope! Long after names like Bull Run, Shiloh, Seven Pines, and Antietam are forgotten, those who have fallen on those battlefields, those whose bones are bleached white as snow, will live and breathe and have their existence in Him. 'For the Lord Himself shall descend from heaven with a shout, with the voice of the archangel, and with the trump of God: and the dead in Christ shall rise first: Then we which are alive and remain shall be caught up together with them in the clouds, to meet the Lord in the air: and so shall we ever be with the Lord.' "

On Friday, Jeremiah preached on light and darkness using two Scripture passages from the New Testament:

And this is the condemnation, that light is come into the world, and men loved darkness rather than light, because their deeds were evil — John 3:19.

Let your light so shine before men, that they may see your good works, and glorify your Father which is in heaven — Matthew 5:16.

"The darkness of hatred and gloom of war are covering our land," Jeremiah preached. "How shall we fight it? With rifles? If you shoot at darkness, does it flee? With swords? Do you think for a moment that darkness can be cut, or jabbed, or stabbed to death? Can an army outmaneuver, outflank, and overrun darkness? So then, how do we defeat this dark evil that has invaded our land? Simple. We light a candle and the darkness flees. There is no darkness black enough that cannot be conquered with the smallest candle.

"The early days of Christianity were some of the darkest days ever witnessed in history. Godly men were hunted down, tortured, imprisoned, and crucified. Among them was the Apostle Peter. For nine months Peter's home was the horrible, fetid prison at Mamertine. The dungeon in which he was placed was without equal for its horror. Mamertine was a deep cell cut out of solid rock, consisting of two chambers, one over the other. The only entrance was through a hole in the ceiling. The lower chamber was called the death cell. Light never entered it and it was never cleaned. The awful stench and filth generated a poison fatal to the inmates of the dungeon. It is said that the number of Christians that perished within that diabolical cell is beyond computation. How Peter survived those nine, long, dreadful months is beyond our comprehension. Yet history records for us that while the Apostle Peter was imprisoned there, forty-nine men were converted by his witness. Two of them were his jailers! Light in darkness! It's a wonder to behold."

"Excuse me, sir, may I come in?"

Colonel Ben McKenna was seated on a stool next to a small table. Upon seeing J.D. standing outside his tent, he folded a piece of paper, slipped it into the pages of a book that J.D. thought was a Bible, and shoved the book under his cot. Crossing his legs casually, he said, "What do you want, Morgan?"

Taking a hesitant step inside the tent, J.D. said, "May I sit down?"

"You won't be staying that long," McKenna replied. "State your business."

"It's of a personal nature, sir." J.D. paused for a reaction.

"You come to light a candle in my face, Morgan, to see if you can make me go away?"

J.D. caught the reference to his father's sermon. He ignored it. "I saw you at the service tonight," he said.

"All commissioned officers have been ordered to attend."

"I see. I didn't know that." J.D. looked around the tent nervously, thinking this would be easier to do if he were sitting. McKenna glared up at him impatiently, so he got down to business. "What I came here for, sir, is to try to make amends. We have not gotten along well. I'd like to change that. And, if it's agreeable to you, I'd like us to get off to a fresh start."

McKenna rose. "You want to be my friend?"

"Very much," J.D. replied.

"Out of the question."

"May I ask why, sir?"

"I'm your commanding officer. It would not be appropriate for us to be friends even if I wanted us to be, which I don't. Is there anything else, Morgan?"

"Yes, sir, there is. I was watching you tonight at the revival service . . . "

J.D.'s confession didn't sit well with McKenna. He obviously didn't like the thought that someone had been watching him.

" . . . and you seemed to be receptive to my father's message."

"Your father's message," McKenna smirked. "You two are quite the models of an ideal father and son, I must say. You've made an impression on a lot of important people. Not bad for a preacher and his nobody son from an insignificant town."

J.D. tensed. McKenna was goading him and he was determined not to respond in kind. But the colonel wasn't making it easy for him. "As I was saying, at one point you seemed to . . . "

"You misread my reaction," McKenna snapped.

"But surely you believe in the things about which my father was preaching."

For a moment there was a softening in the lines of McKenna's face. Then, just as quickly as they softened, they hardened again. "Your father's beliefs are irrational. Christianity, like sentimentality, is a weakness."

"How can you say that?" J.D. cried. "Considering the way you were raised."

"I was raised to be a national leader," McKenna snapped. "A leader's strength comes from within himself, not from some outdated concept of invisible powers bestowed by invisible beings to those who grovel before them. You are dismissed, Morgan."

J.D. turned to leave, stopped, and said, "Excuse me for saying so, sir, but you're wrong. I only pray you'll realize it before it's too late."

"Save your prayers for other weak-minded men like yourself, Morgan."

J.D. bid his colonel a good-night and left.

McKenna waited a few minutes. Then he retrieved the book from under his cot and opened it to the place marked by the folded piece of paper. He unfolded the paper. It was a letter from New York. His stepfather. The first part of the letter told of the older McKenna's amusement with Jeremiah Morgan's daughter. He claimed to have interesting plans for her, but didn't specify what the plans would be. At the end of the letter, the banker made reference to a passage of Scripture—2 Samuel 11:15—followed by the words, "You know what to do."

Returning to the Bible passage, McKenna read: *And King David wrote in the letter, saying, Set ye Uriah in the forefront of the hottest battle, and retire ye from him, that he may be smitten, and die.*

Chapter 17

THE fog that lay heavy on the river's surface dissipated as the mid-morning sun made its presence felt. From atop Stafford Heights Jeremiah and J.D. watched as teams of engineers scurried below them to assemble three pontoon bridges. It was the tardy arrival of the pontoons that had allowed time for the revival services to be held. Jeremiah couldn't help but think that God had caused the delay so that the soldiers would have a chance to put their lives in order before battle. Many of them did just that. Several hundred had responded to Jeremiah's preaching by either making a first-time commitment to God or by renewing their commitment to Him.

On the river, engineers slipped the pontoon boats into the water, arranged them side-by-side in a line that stretched toward the opposite shore, then linked them together with planks to form a walkway. The hammering sounds they made were drowned out by the constant booming of cannon from the Union-held heights. A steady bombardment of Fredericksburg's waterfront had pushed back the Rebels, allowing the engineers to start their work. However, no sooner had the first of the pontoons been set in place when Rebel sharpshooters began firing at them from windows and rooftops. Jeremiah and J.D. watched as one-by-one the engineers clutched at their bodies and collapsed onto the bridge or splashed into the river.

"Can't something more be done to give them the cover they need?" Jeremiah asked.

"The increased artillery barrage doesn't seem to have helped, has it?" J.D. replied, analyzing the situation. He scanned the structures across the river. The outlying buildings were riddled with hits, yet the sniper fire hadn't diminished. A series of fresh, thundering booms echoed through the river valley. Across the way new holes appeared in walls as bricks and wood flew into the air. On the bridges, two more engineers collapsed, hit by sharpshooters' bullets. The incomplete pontoon bridges were strewn with the bodies of the men building them.

As Jeremiah watched the men fall, he felt guilty for feeling thankful that it was someone else's sons on those pontoons. He glanced over at J.D. His son's eyes were focused intently on the action below. The boy had aged since he left home. Susanna would be surprised at how much. Then Jeremiah wondered if Susanna would ever see her son again. He shook the thought off. J.D. would survive this war. The future of the Morgans rested on him. God would protect him. God would surely protect him.

"Captain Morgan?"

J.D. turned toward the voice. "What is it, Wheelright?"

The corporal's face was sober. All business, an unusual state for the company prankster. "Colonel McKenna sent me to fetch you."

J.D. nodded. "Inform the colonel I'll be right there." Wheelright turned on his heel. "Do you know what he wants?" J.D. called after him.

Wheelright shrugged. "Can't say for sure. But I overheard they're looking for companies who will knock out them Rebel sharpshooters. I believe Colonel McKenna done volunteered us."

"Thank you, Corporal. I'll be along shortly." Turning to

his father, J.D. said, "Looks like I have to go. I just want you to know how much I enjoyed having you in camp this week. Even if you did pop in sort of sudden-like."

"Look, J.D.," Jeremiah said. "I don't know how much longer I can stay. I have to get back to Washington before I return home. But considering the fact that I was shot at coming into camp, I was thinking I might request an escort back to Washington. I'm sure if I spoke with General Burnside, he would consent for you to . . . "

"I appreciate what you're trying to do, Father," J.D. answered, smiling warmly. "But you can't protect me from the war. Besides, my company depends on me. Not too bright, are they?"

Jeremiah felt ashamed that his effort to protect his son was so transparent, and so selfish. J.D.'s refusal made him all the more proud of his eldest. "May God go with you, J.D.," he said.

The two men stood awkwardly apart, unsure how to leave each other. Jeremiah decided for both of them when he opened his arms and embraced his son.

"Give my love to Mother," J.D. said.

"I will."

Jeremiah remained atop Stafford Heights and watched as Jehovah's Avengers rushed to the riverside and loaded into several pontoon boats. He watched breathlessly as they pushed onto the river. Puffs of gunfire could be seen coming from the town's buildings. Tiny geysers of water erupted all around the pontoons.

The splashes in the water reminded J.D. of hail pummeling the Ohio when he was boy. Only this wasn't a carefree day on the river and the hail splashing around him were miniballs. Keeping everyone low in the boat, he urged the rowers to dig deep. Two of his best marksmen returned fire. It was ineffective. He scanned the river's edge. There was no cover to be found. Between the river's edge and the town was a sloping stretch of open field. They had only one option. Storm the buildings.

J.D. hated tactics based solely on numbers. The theory in this situation is that the enemy with his inferior numbers can't stop a charge of superior numbers. The superior force will suffer losses, but the objective eventually will be attained. J.D.'s problem was that while his superiors talked of numbers, he knew those numbers had names and wives and families waiting for them back in Point Providence.

The boat wedged onto the shoreline. J.D. ordered everyone out. A withering shower of rifle fire greeted them. One man fell. Then another. And another.

"Haul this boat on shore!" J.D. cried. "We'll use it for cover."

The urgency of the moment gave the men extra strength, for the boat literally flew onto the shore. Tipped on its side, the bottom facing the town, the wooden hull gave them a temporary reprieve from the storm of bullets. Packed tightly, their faces inches from one another, J.D. evaluated the situation.

"We lost Shepherd," one man said.

"And Smith."

"And Taylor."

J.D. nodded. Their bodies were floating facedown in the river. Beyond them more boats were completing the crossing. Further beyond that J.D. could see a silhouetted figure standing beneath a tree on Stafford Heights. His father. Watching.

"Chase. Wheelright." The two men looked toward him. "Work your way to the edge, one on one side, one on the other. See if you can eliminate some of those Rebel sharpshooters before we cross that field."

While the others watched, the two men, lying prone on the

ground, poked their heads around the edges of the boat and searched for targets. The reports of their rifles indicated they found something to shoot at.

Chase laughed.

"What is it?" J.D. asked.

Crooked teeth grinned from behind a forest of hair that surrounded Eli Chase's mouth. He was an older man. A relative newcomer to Point Providence, having lived there only ten years. He'd moved to Ohio from Mississippi following the death of his wife. All of his children were grown. When the former Mississippi native first joined the Union army, some men in the company were skeptical about his loyalties. But Eli Chase proved himself to be a dependable asset to the company and a superior marksman.

"One of them Rebs ain't thinkin'," Chase said.

"In what way?"

"Got himself into a pattern. He's on the roof of that red brick building. Pokes his head up for three counts, fires, then disappears for a minute exactly. Pops up, counts three, and fires. Deadly predictable."

From behind the cover J.D. heard a bullet whistle overhead. Eli Chase counted softly to sixty. "Fifty-seven, fifty-eight . . ." he closed one eye and aimed the other down the rifle barrel, "fifty-nine, sixty!" With a grin, "Now . . . one, two . . ." BLAM! "Got 'im!"

"Are you sure you got him?" J.D. asked.

"Tumbled clear off the roof," Chase said, pleased with himself. "That's one dead Reb."

By now the other boats had landed. A wave of Union soldiers washed ashore. Like a rising tide they stormed the city of Fredericksburg.

"Let's go, men!" J.D. shouted.

Emerging from cover, he led his company into the face of scattered arms fire. Sheer numbers. There would be losses.

Losses with names. Shepherd. Smith. Taylor. But they would gain their objective.

The amount of gunfire directed at them decreased the closer they got to the buildings. The Rebel sharpshooters were retreating. From here on out it would be street fighting to gain control of the town.

A scream caught his attention. It was an awful sound, like that of a wounded animal. To his right he saw Eli Chase standing over the body of a dead Rebel lying next to a red brick building. Chase's rifle was on the ground next to the fallen soldier. His arms hung limp, his tear-stained face raised in anguish.

"I've killed my own son!" he wailed. "I've done killed my own son!"

No amount of consolation could persuade Chase to leave his son. J.D. called to Wheelright and instructed him to stay with Chase until the town was secured.

Within hours Fredericksburg was under Union control. The pontoon bridges were completed and regiment after regiment filed across them into the town. Soon, a small city accustomed to a population of 5,000 people bulged with 30,000 Union soldiers. J.D. and Wheelright assisted Eli Chase in the burial of his son. But the man's grief would not be appeased.

Friday, December 12th. Jehovah's Avengers huddled in the darkness on the floor of a milliner's shop. Silver moonlight projected a rectangular patch of illumination on the hardwood floor. This was the company's only source of light. Fires and lanterns were prohibited since they were so close to the enemy. Outside the window, wild shouts and revelries could be heard up and down the mud streets as Union soldiers looted the town.

In the milliner's shop were gathered those who wanted no

part of the looting, many of them the product of the recent revival. They sat in a circle around the silver patch of moonlight much as they would if it were a campfire. The mood was quiet, but upbeat. The dozens of hats that lined the walls reminded J.D. of the host of heaven looking down upon them.

Seated next to J.D. was Lieutenant Logan, the tenor. He led them in singing, "Rock of Ages," "Amazing Grace," and "All Hail the Power of Jesus' Name." Then he sang for them, "Home, Sweet Home." The sound of their voices was occasionally interrupted by breaking glass, swearing, and threats from outside the shop.

Following the singing, some of the men told their stories as an encouragement to the others. As each man spoke, he was granted everyone's undivided attention. Some spoke for a short time, others longer, but each man's testimony was treated with a holy reverence.

Big-chested Vern Hawkins spoke of the time when he was a soldier in the Mexican War. "I want you boys to know what a merciful, forgiving Lord we have. And I oughta know. 'Cause I was the most mean-spirited liar that ever was. One time, I remember, my brigade was in a real tight spot. Bullets was swarmin' like bees to honey. Shells was burstin' all around us so that I coulda swore it was rainin' dirt and rocks. I was scared. More than that, I was sure I was gonna die. So I up and told the Lord that I was real ashamed of myself, and that if He'd cover my head this time we'd settle the thing as soon as I got out."

J.D. looked from face to face as the soldiers listened to the veteran. Without exception, they stared at Hawkins with unblinking eyes. Most of them had lived with this man for well over a year now. They knew him to be quiet, but strong. Not a man given to emotion, and certainly not a man that one would expect to ever be scared of anything. But neither would they have thought him to be the deeply spiritual type. He wasn't one to go around saying, "Praise the Lord," for every little thing. Nor was he quick to point a finger at someone or quote Scripture at the slightest provocation. Tonight, though, they were seeing that deep inside this big, quiet man was an unshakable love for the Lord.

"Then I got to fightin'," Hawkins continued, "and forgot all about it. We got outta that scrape and I never once remembered the promise I made to God. That is until we got into an even bigger mess. We was hopelessly outnumbered and surrounded. Pinned down in this little canyon. And when the bullets started a-hissin' all around and shells sent wagons and carts flyin' into the air, my broken promise came back to me. And I've got to tell you, my coward heart stopped beatin' and pretty nigh fainted. I tried to pray and found that I couldn't. So I just said, 'Lord, here, Lord, if You will look down here; I know I lied to You and have no right even to be talkin' to You. And I know You shouldn't believe me, 'cause if a man lied to me like I've lied to You, I wouldn't believe him for a second. But I don't want to go to hell. And I'm serious and honest this time, and if You hear me now, we'll meet just as soon as I get out safe, and we'll settle things.' "

Vern Hawkins raised a hand to his mouth and cleared his throat as the emotion within him rose. Outside the window a piano could be heard belting out a bawdy tune. In the street two men were arguing over the divided portions of a leg of lamb. Inside the milliner's shop, everyone in the circle paid little attention to anything other than Vern Hawkins' story.

"Well, you probably could have guessed, but God did all I asked Him to do. But what did I do? Boys, I'm ashamed to say it, but I lied again. I never thought one thing about it at all until another day when I was pinned down by sniper fire. Everyone else around me was lying dead. Picked off, one-by-one. Hell gaped before me, and at the entrance were my two lies I had told. Of course, I couldn't pray. Why would God waste His time listening to a man like me? Finally, I managed to cry out, 'Lord! I deserve it all if I go to hell right now. And I can't pray that I won't lie to You no more, because You know I can't keep my promises. All I can say, Lord, is that it's in Your hands. Hell or mercy. I've got no time to talk about it. But, O Lord!—no, I dare not say it.' And so it was, I cowered behind a thin tree knowin' that I would feel a hot Mexican bullet at any moment. But, brethren, He did it. He did it! A scout troop came from nowhere and picked off that sniper! And the moment the thing was over, I didn't give myself time to lie again. I just took out and ran as deep into the woods as I could, where God and me could be alone together. I threw my musket onto the ground and then I joined it. I couldn't stop crying and thanking the Lord for saving me. That night I settled everything with the Lord. And the Lord forgave a miserable lying wretch like myself. That's how I know we have a good and a great God."

A smattering of low-voiced "Amens" and "Praise the Lords" provided benediction to Hawkins' testimony. J.D. smiled warmly at him. He'd come to admire the steady spirit of the big cabinetmaker.

"Look at that!" Wheelright shouted. Everyone in the millinery shop followed his line of sight out the window and skyward. To the North, ribbons of color adorned the heavens, the aurora burealis. The celestial show was brighter than J.D. had ever remembered seeing it.

"God's smilin' down on us," a baby-faced private said. "A sure sign of victory tomorrow."

"How do you know He's not smilin' down on the Rebs?" another private challenged him. "They can see it too, you know."

"I know they're for us 'cause they're in the North!"

After several more testimonies, the informal meeting broke

up with each of the soldiers staking out a place on the floor to sleep for the night. Wheelright provided some levity when he showed everyone an embalmer's card that had been thrust in his hand as he was just about to board the boat to cross the river.

"Hey! I got one too!"

"Me too! This man just shoves it into my hand as I'm crossing the pontoon bridge!"

"Did he look like an undertaker?" Wheelright asked. "Tall, skinny, dark circles under his eyes?"

"That's the one!"

Wheelright laughed. "The fellow must have practiced embalming on himself. He's got no brains! How are we gonna call on him if we *do* need his services? We'll be dead!'

The soldiers laughed at the morbid absurdity of the undertaker's business cards.

Smoke from smoldering buildings combined with a persistent fog to give the streets of Fredericksburg a particularly eerie look on Saturday morning. The vapors were stirred by soldiers tromping through the muddy roads. Their companies filled the unpaved streets from side-to-side. Despite the early morning fog and mud, the men were cheerful, optimistic. Officers worked their way through the formations informing the men that they had the Rebels outnumbered. Lee himself was on the top of Marye's Heights and they were going to knock him off of it.

"You gonna lead us into the battle, Colonel?" Wheelright asked McKenna.

"Not today, Corporal. I will be coordinating your movements with the other commanders from atop that church steeple. But believe me, I'd rather be charging up that hill with you. We're gonna teach Johnny Reb a thing or two, aren't we?"

"Yessir!"

To J.D. the colonel said, "I have placed you as the lead company in the regiment. Yours will be the greatest glory in today's victory. No matter what happens around you, keep pressing forward. Do you understand? Keep pressing forward."

"Yes, sir," J.D. said.

McKenna locked eyes with him. J.D. saw something in them that wasn't right. A lingering regret, perhaps? Then the colonel was gone.

As it did the day before, the fog burned off by mid-morning. J.D. found the inactivity just before a battle to be maddening. He wasn't alone. Soldiers shifted constantly from one foot to another, bantered incessantly, cracked jokes, and checked to see if there was any movement by the troops in front of them every three or four seconds. Eli Chase joined in none of this. He stood sullenly still, his gaze distant, his face downcast.

"Are you all right?" J.D. asked him.

"Will be once the fighting starts," Chase said without looking up.

"Eli, there's no way you could have known that was your son."

Chase stared silently at the muddy ground.

Rifle fire broke out beyond the buildings. Then cannon fire. A wave of apprehension worked its way from company to company the length of the street. The Battle of Fredericksburg had begun in earnest.

Jehovah's Avengers emerged from the town in formation. Crossing a dirt road they stepped onto a broad field that sloped upward toward Marye's Heights and General Robert E. Lee's army. The field was marshy and streaked with shallow ditches. The road they'd just crossed curved up the hill then crossed in front of them. It was here, behind a stone wall, that the Confederate infantry had taken up their position. Behind them, on the crest of the hill, was their artillery. The Rebels had superior position; the Union had superior forces. *Knock Lee off the hill.* That was the order. Drive the Army of Northern Virginia back to Richmond.

J.D. and the men of Point Providence followed Lieutenant Logan's Michigan volunteers onto the field. Commanders of both units ordered their men to face right so that they were shoulder-to-shoulder facing the enemy. J.D.'s unit had a drainage ditch directly in front of them about a hundred yards distant. He'd have to maneuver them around it. The necessary commands came to his mind automatically. He grinned at the memory of training camp when those same commands were elusive.

There was no grand strategy for today's battle. Storm the heights. Charge into the face of the Confederate rifles and cannons. Send wave after wave until their hilltop position was overrun.

The units that had gone before them had been hit hard. Already, the rise leading to the stone wall was strewn with men and horses and weapons. The Confederates awaited the next wave. They were stacked four deep behind the wall. It was nearly noon. The December air still had a bite to it, enough to redden men's cheeks.

"This is it," J.D. said to his company. "There are some who say we're puffers. It's time for us to prove them wrong. So that after today, should anyone call us that again, no one will believe him."

J.D. looked on his company with pride. They were good men. Eli Chase gripped his rifle tightly. He hadn't smiled since they buried his son. He stood solemn, yet eager to charge. Wheelright, the practical joker, and Willis, his favorite target, stood side-by-side. There was a look of determination on both their faces. Vern Hawkins, the old veteran, wore a let's-get-on-with-it expression. These and the other men of the company had become his family away from home. There wasn't a single one of them that he didn't feel he could count on for his life.

Raising a hand high in the air, J.D. cried out, "Psalm 18:3. 'I will call upon the Lord, who is worthy to be praised: so shall I be saved from mine enemies.' " Then he prayed, "God in heaven, this is a day You have made. We rejoice in it. Give us Your strength for this battle. When the day goes hard and cowards steal from the field, may everyone know which side we're on. We are Jehovah's Avengers, and today we take a stand for freedom! Amen."

A chorus of Amens joined his.

"Corporal!" The corporal holding the company flag snapped to attention. "Hold that flag high! We want our enemy to know who it was who defeated them on the field of battle!"

"Yessir!" In response to the challenge, the boy inched the flag up higher than normal. On the flag were the names of the battles in which the company had fought, accompanied by the image of a green frog. The flag fluttered proudly in the breeze. J.D. thought of Jenny. And of home.

The bugle charge echoed against the stone wall, followed by the cries and screams of hundreds of men. With a whoop, J.D. Morgan signaled his company to follow him.

The going was easy. Across the drainage ditch. Up the hill. The wall and the Rebs grew larger as he got closer. Previously nondescript Confederate uniforms took on human characteristics—a private fumbled his rifle, a corporal wiped sweat from his brow, a major stroked his mustache as the wave swept toward them. *Nothing can stop us*, J.D. thought. *Too many of us. Too few of them. They won't be able to shoot and reload fast enough.* His breathing labored.

Eli Chase burst past him. Screaming wildly, he deliberately

threw down his rifle. With arms stretched out to his sides he ran at the wall, looking like he wanted to be crucified. A miniball obliged him. Hit in the face, he shrieked, covering the wound with both hands. But still he ran. Another ball spun him around. A third ball arched his back. A fourth felled him.

They were halfway up the hill.

J.D. jumped over Eli's body. The number of dead on the ground grew thicker. Pressed in on both sides, J.D. found it impossible to avoid them. It was an unnatural feeling, flesh and bone under his boots. An arm. A hand. He wanted to stop and apologize, as though they could hear him. He pressed onward.

A sheet of miniballs charged over the wall, mowing down Union soldiers like a scythe through grain. Lieutenant George Logan caught one in his throat. He lay on his back making a wheezing sound, the kind organs make when they have a hole in their bellows. Then he fell limp, his tenor voice silenced.

J.D. heard a louder, heavier sound. Cannons. Artillery shells cut paths through the wall of soldiers. One moment Wheelright was running next to him. The next moment he was gone, blown out of existence. The force of the blast lifted J.D. off his feet and threw him against the soldiers behind him, knocking three of them to the ground. Another sheet of rifle fire passed over him, leveling a row of men behind him.

One of the soldiers J.D. had landed on was Vern Hawkins. The two men struggled to roll over on their bellies, all the while keeping low.

"Thoughtful of you to knock me down like that," Vern said wryly. "But you can't keep saving me. The rest of the company will think I'm your favorite."

"I was about to thank you for catching me," J.D. replied. "I'd hate to be knocked all the way back to the foot of the hill and have to start all over again."

They were a little more than hundred yards from the wall. The last volley had stopped the wave. Most were falling back and regrouping.

"Has anyone tried talking with these fellows?" Hawkins said. "Maybe we could work this out peaceably."

"Right about now, I'd be willing to lay down my rifle if they'd lay down theirs," J.D. replied.

"Ah, but then there's that age-old dilemma," Hawkins said. "Who's going to lay down their rifle first?"

J.D. looked over his shoulder behind him. "For the time being, I'm content just to lie here until some of those fellows behind us decide to join us."

"Always knew you'd make a smart commander," Hawkins said.

Another volley of artillery whooshed over their heads. One shell caught a private lying on the ground cleanly on his knapsack. Underwear, clothing, and personal effects went flying. The private was startled, but unharmed. Soldiers on both sides of the wall fell to laughing.

Another Union wave rushed up the hill.

"Here they come," J.D. said.

"Don't know which would be worse," Hawkins said, "getting shot by the enemy or stomped to death by your own army."

"Think of it this way," J.D. replied. "Which would be easier to explain to your grandchildren—a bullet wound or a footprint on your back?"

As the wave approached them, the two men jumped to their feet and rushed forward. They got no more than three steps when they were greeted by a volley of rifle fire.

Vern Hawkins dropped to his knees. His rifle clattered to the ground. With a moan, he fell forward.

J.D. dropped to his side. "Vern! Vern!" he cried. He rolled the veteran over. The cabinetmaker's eyes were wide and unfocused. There was a black hole in his chest, rimmed with blood.

With his forehead touching the dead man's forehead, J.D. wept bitterly. With bullets whizzing around him and dead soldiers lying all about, he told himself this was no time to mourn. But Vern Hawkins deserved better than this. He was a good man. A gentle, down-to-earth man. As J.D. wept, a void grew inside him with amazing speed. It took on cavernous proportions in seconds. It was more than just an empty space, it was a space that demanded to be filled. And if it couldn't be filled with grief, J.D. would fill it with anger. Someone was going to pay for Vern Hawkins' death. A life for a life. Or better still, because of the quality of Vern Hawkins' life, a whole lot of lives. And J.D. knew just where to find sacrificial lives.

The Union tide was pushed back again. So J.D. rolled to his back to await the next rush. His chest was heaving. His jaw hurt from being clenched so tightly. He checked his weapon. No use in wasting time. He was going to eliminate as many of those Rebs as he could until the next wave came. Then, he was going to charge that wall and kill them all. His weapon ready, he rolled over on his belly and took aim.

There were so many to shoot at, he really didn't need to aim. *Officers. Kill the officers,* he thought. *With no one to lead them, maybe the rest will go home.* J.D. searched the back row for officers. He spied two talking to each other. A colonel had his back to J.D., partially shielding a major general. J.D. would have preferred the major general, but he had to take the clearest shot. If he was lucky, maybe he could get two officers with one bullet. Pressing his cheek against his weapon, he rested the rifle sight on the back of the colonel's head. *This one is for you, Vern,* he thought. J.D. applied pressure to the trigger.

Just then, the colonel swung around and pointed at something beyond J.D. The Confederate's face with its square jaw came clearly into view. It was Daniel Cooper!

J.D.'s hands flew from the rifle as if it had been struck by lightening. His heart pounded in his chest. His hands shook. "O Lord!" he sobbed. "O Lord!" Conflicting emotions rose and fell inside him until he thought he'd burst. Anger over Vern Hawkins' death; love for Daniel Cooper; terror over the thought that he almost killed his best friend; relief that he didn't. Lowering his head, he cried into the dirt.

The sound of another Union wave swept over him. Someone trampled on him. What was it Vern said? *Get shot by the enemy or stomped to death by your own army.* He had to get up. Grabbing his rifle, he struggled to his knees, but was quickly knocked back down. He tried again. Swept up by the wave, he was carried along by the other soldiers. The wall was nearly fifty yards away. They ran headlong into a line of rifles pointed at them.

J.D. couldn't keep his eyes off Daniel. Cooper was still explaining something to the major general, fashioning a box with his hands, then pointing toward the river.

"Daniel!" J.D. cried.

Artillery shells screamed overhead.

"Daniel!"

There was too much noise. Screams. Whoops. Shells exploding. The rattle of equipment. Commanders shouting orders. The dying calling from below for medical help.

"Daniel!"

The entire line of Confederate guns erupted simultaneously. J.D.'s left leg exploded. Screaming in agony, he fell on two soldiers. Neither man complained. They were beyond complaints, beyond feeling. J.D.'s eyes rolled in pain. He reached for his leg. A jagged bone protruded through the skin. He heard a scream. A private, shot in the face, fell on him. Then another. And another.

He tried to push them off. Too heavy. Or he was too weak. Either way he was buried beneath the weight of the fallen men. The pain in his leg was excruciating. Unbearable. *Why didn't he pass out?* It would be a welcome relief. Concentrating on the pain, he tried to will himself to faint. After a while, he gave up. He screamed for help. Either no one heard him, or no one could do anything to help him. Still he screamed and pleaded as men trampled over him, then back, then over, then back. He could hear more men falling. Moaning.

J.D. lay in a pile of dead men. Unable to move. He fought for breath. His senses began to fail, as did his strength. Lying his head back, he saw the stone wall upside down. Confederate soldiers loaded and fired, loaded and fired as quickly as they could. Some of them were draped over the wall. Behind the lines of infantrymen, Daniel Cooper came into view. The major general was with him, nodding.

"Daniel!" J.D. cried. It was barely a whisper.

They were gone from sight.

"O Daniel!" J.D. cried. The sounds of the battle were all around, muffled by the bodies that lay on top of him. As the day wore on, the frigid December air reached through the bodies and touched him with cold fingers. He began to shake uncontrollably. As the light of day faded, the discharge of guns lessened in intensity until they stopped altogether. With the darkness came silence, except for the moans of the wounded and dying stacked two and three deep in the field.

J.D. Morgan's voice was among them. Throughout the night he slipped in and out of a restless sleep, too weak to rescue himself. Whenever he managed to drift off to sleep, either pain or a blast of icy air woke him. But in those moments that he did sleep, he dreamed of Jenny and summer days and home.

From the church steeple Colonel Ben McKenna watched as the Jehovah's Avengers fell under a hail of bullets and artillery fire. Using a telescope he followed J.D.'s progress up the slope, J.D.'s brush with death when the artillery shell hit Wheelright; and he watched emotionlessly as J.D. collapsed, his leg shattered by a miniball. McKenna stood transfixed as soldier after soldier fell on Jeremiah Morgan's oldest son. With a vacant look in his eyes, he lowered the glass.

When the sun went down and the temperatures dipped, McKenna descended the church steeple's spiral stairs. He said not a word to anyone. Walking as though in a trance, he trudged through the muddy streets of Fredericksburg, crossed the pontoon bridge, ascended Stafford Heights to his tent, entered, and closed the flap behind him.

Jeremiah Morgan spent the day on Stafford Heights at the same spot where he said good-bye to J.D. He strained to see as much of the battle as he could, but saw mostly smoke. By twilight he was tired and sore.

"The reports aren't good."

Jeremiah turned to see General Ambrose Burnside. His eyes were fixed on the battlefield across the river as he spoke. "We broke through on the left offensive briefly, but they called up reserves and sealed the breach. Marye's Heights was a disaster. There's no other word for it. We sent fourteen brigades up that insignificant incline. Never got within fifty yards of it. It's all my fault."

"General, I'm sure you acted in the best interests . . ."

Burnside waved him off. "When the pontoons arrived late, allowing Lee to entrench on the heights, I should have pulled back. Instead, I bowed to pressure to do something before we go to winter quarters. It's a mistake I'll live with the rest of my life. There wasn't a moment today that I have not grieved for the men who fell charging up that hill. Countless numbers of them. And it's my fault."

As a pastor, Jeremiah had learned that there were times of

grief when words were inadequate for the situation. This was one of those times.

"Have you been to my headquarters?" Burnside asked.

"The mansion just up the way?"

"Chatham Mansion," Burnside replied. "Do you know who used to live there?"

Jeremiah shook his head.

"Mary Custis. The wife of Robert E. Lee. He courted her under the trees in the yard."

A wry smile crossed Jeremiah's lips. "I didn't know that."

"These are strange times, Rev. Morgan. Strange times," Burnside said. "May God help us all."

"That is the one certainty in this whole affair," Jeremiah replied.

A rustle of leaves behind them prompted both general and reverend to turn around.

"There you are!" It was Nicolay, President Lincoln's personal secretary. The normally meticulous Nicolay looked exhausted and disheveled.

"Looking for me?" Burnside said.

"Actually, I'm looking for both of you," the out-of-breath secretary said. "The President is anxious for a report regarding today's encounter."

"I sent him a telegraph," Burnside said rather testily.

"And that's what prompted the President to dispatch me," came the reply. "He's asked me to get a detailed report from you. I'm to deliver it to him in the morning. And Rev. Morgan . . ."

"Yes?"

"The President requested that I bring you back to Washington with me."

Jeremiah glanced over his shoulder past the Rappahannock where the smoke was still rising from the battlefield. Facing Nicolay again, he said, "I was hoping to see my son one more time before I returned to Washington."

"The troops are pulling back tonight," Burnside said. "He should be in camp shortly." The words, "if he's still alive" were left unsaid.

"I leave at daybreak," said the President's secretary.

"I'll be ready," Jeremiah answered.

General Burnside marched off abruptly. "If you want that report . . ." he said to Nicolay without waiting for him. He didn't finish the sentence.

Jeremiah watched as Burnside and Nicolay departed. He'd hoped to be able to say something to the general to ease the man's conscience. But the opportunity never presented itself.

The Rev. Morgan stood beside the pontoon bridge as company after company of the Army of the Potomac limped back across to camp. He saw no sign of the Jehovah's Avengers, let alone his son.

It was after midnight when he left the bridge and returned to the company camp. Row after row of tents were dark, not because the occupants were sleeping, but because they never returned from the battlefield. J.D.'s tent was among those that had no light.

Jeremiah went to a lighted tent and knocked on the tent pole. A scared eighteen-year-old private invited him in. Jeremiah didn't recognize him. He learned the boy was from Point Pleasant, the town just down the river from them. He'd just been assigned to the company. With tears, the boy did his best to stop himself from shaking as he described the day's events. He said he knew J.D., but hadn't see him after the initial charge. Jeremiah prayed with the boy and agreed to stay with him until the boy fell asleep.

It was just an hour before dawn when Jeremiah returned to his son's tent. He lifted the flap and entered it. Kneeling beside J.D.'s empty cot, in the dark he prayed for his son until sunrise. Then he rose from his knees, stepped into the dawning day, and after taking one last glance across the river, climbed into the carriage with President Lincoln's personal secretary and rode back to Washington.

President Lincoln looked as downhearted as he did the first time Jeremiah met him when he had described to Jeremiah his son Willie's death. He was taking the Fredericksburg defeat hard.

Lincoln called Jeremiah into the Oval Office the moment he arrived. Abandoning his position behind the desk, he sat in an upholstered chair identical to the one Jeremiah was sitting in and positioned at a friendly angle to his. "So you don't know the fate of your son?" the President asked.

"No, sir. As I was leaving, I learned that a hospital had been set up in one of the town's buildings. I didn't have time to check there before I left."

Lincoln rang a bell. Instantly a secretary entered. "Send a messenger to Fredericksburg immediately. Tell him he is to learn of the status of one J.D. Morgan." Lincoln turned to Jeremiah.

"Captain?"

"Yes, sir," Jeremiah replied. "Captain John Drew Morgan."

"Have the messenger report directly back to me when he returns," Lincoln concluded.

The secretary didn't have to be dismissed. He knew his orders and left sharply to carry them out.

"Thank you, sir," Jeremiah said.

"It's the least I can do for you," the President said. "From one father to another."

"Thank you."

"Now let me do for you the most I can do." Lincoln reached over and lay his huge hand over Jeremiah's hand. Jeremiah had never felt a hand so large since when as a little boy he held his father's adult hand. With head bowed, Abraham Lincoln began to pray, "Dear Lord and Father of us all, never should we forget that this great national crisis is daily spawning thousands of personal and family crises in houses both North and South. And so I join my heart with my brother as we pray for his son, Captain John Drew Morgan. Carry him as a little lamb in Your arms safely to the bosom of those who love him best. Amen."

Jeremiah unsuccessfully fought back tears. But never for a moment did he get the impression that the President thought less of him for it.

"Forgive me for changing the subject abruptly," the President said, "but I understand you know Dr. Seth Cooper."

The sound of his best friend's name startled Jeremiah. *What possible connection could Seth have with President Abraham Lincoln?* "We were quite close before the war," Jeremiah said.

Lincoln nodded in understanding. "Jefferson Davis has enlisted your friend to try and win British support for the Confederate cause."

"Excuse me, sir, but that doesn't make sense. Seth is no politician."

"Seth Cooper was not sent as a politician or a diplomat. The South has no shortage of either one, but they have been unsuccessful so far. No, this is a new tactic. Dr. Cooper has been enlisted to raise popular support for the Southern cause by preaching in the churches of England. And from the reports I've been receiving, he is making astonishing headway."

Jeremiah nodded. "Seth is one of our nation's greatest preachers."

"Rev. Morgan," Lincoln said earnestly, "England must not give aid to the South. We must prevent it at all costs."

A perplexed look crossed Jeremiah's face. "What can we do?"

Tall and erect even while sitting, Lincoln said, "I want you to go to England and neutralize him."

"You're not asking me to kidnap or . . . kill him, are you?"

Lincoln burst into laughter, his eyes twinkling with merriment. "No, my friend, I would never ask such a thing of you. I want you to go to England and preach. Show them that the North has a great preacher too, and that preacher is opposed to slavery in any form."

Jeremiah shook his head. "I'm no match for Seth when it comes to preaching."

"You don't have to be," Lincoln said. "From the reports I received from Fredericksburg, you're a better preacher than you claim; but more importantly, you open the door for God and invite Him in to do the real work. That's all I'm asking you to do in England."

Jeremiah lowered his head in contemplation. A battle of pulpits, that's what he was being asked to engage in. And his opponent was his best friend. On the one hand, he was flattered beyond belief. The man asking him to do this was not only the President of the United States, but a man who understood the power of words. It was Lincoln's public debates with Stephen A. Douglas that made him a household figure.

Then a thought occurred to him and he knew he would go to England. He was a Morgan. All his life he had prayed for a chance to do something worthy of the Morgan name. Now, here he was, sitting next to the President of the United States wondering whether or not he should respond.

"I'll go to England, Mr. President," Jeremiah said.

"And be assured that as soon as I hear word from Fredericksburg, I'll send it to you by special messenger. Father to father," said Lincoln.

Chapter 18

S ARAH Morgan spent every Sunday afternoon at the Mc-
Kenna mansion on 57th Street. As each week drew near
its end, she looked forward with heightened anticipation to
her visit with the New York banker. Her work at the Christian Tract Society was proceeding satisfactorily, but her
dream was to write stories of love and danger and espionage
and battles between good and evil. At the Society she wrote
scriptural warnings to soldiers about the evils of alcohol, card
playing, and low morals—a noble work but not on the same
level as that of a novelist. That's what made Sunday after-
noons so special. At the McKenna mansion, she was no longer an anonymous writer of pamphlets, but a budding novelist
on the verge of a great career.

Sarah's Sunday trappings added to her anticipation of notoriety and fame. Whereas at the Society, she was one of several
writers sharing dormitory facilities, at the McKenna mansion,
she was one-of-a-kind, surrounded by the finest things city
life had to offer—large and lavish rooms adorned with
artwork and tapestries, meals served upon silver and china
settings, and the pampered attention of servants. And then
there was the attention heaped upon her by one of New
York's wealthiest bankers. Always the consummate host, Caleb McKenna was generous with his praise regarding the
revised chapters of her novel which she delivered to him

weekly. This was at his bidding. Two copies would be needed by the publisher, he had been told, at such time they would submit the novel. So at his expense he hired a copyist to make the necessary reproductions. It would be a waste of talent, McKenna insisted, for Sarah to make the copies herself. Her time was best spent creating stories.

The size of the Sunday gatherings at the McKenna mansion varied from week to week. Beatrice McKenna never joined their company. Not since Sarah's first visit to the mansion had she seen the woman of the house. Polite inquiries yielded identical responses, "Please excuse Beatrice, she's not well." After the third week, Sarah stopped asking. Jenny attended the Sunday dinners sporadically. Although invited weekly, she accepted the invitation on the average of every third Sunday. Following her visits, she and Sarah would inevitably argument over Caleb McKenna's motives and true nature. It usually took Jenny two weeks to calm herself sufficiently to accept another invitation. Most Sundays it was just Caleb McKenna and Sarah Morgan. And that was the way Sarah liked it.

Occasionally Sarah's Sunday visits were soured by intruders. At least that's how she characterized the unexpected business callers who showed up on McKenna's doorstep. The intruders were men of all descriptions. Some were dressed fashionably and spoke well-polished prose, others wore nothing more than rags and spoke with grunts and incomplete sentences. But regardless of their appearance and manner of speaking, they always brought with them some sort of emergency. Caleb McKenna would whisk them off to another room. He never transacted business in front of Sarah. Sometimes her host would disappear for a few minutes, other times he was gone for nearly an hour. It mattered little, for when he returned his good nature was always spoiled. When the intruders came to the door, the day was never the same and Sarah resented them.

"I received two letters this week," McKenna said, tossing his napkin onto the remains of a beef steak on his plate. The plate and napkin were swept away seconds later by one of the servants. "Both letters bear good news. Very, very good news. And that's a fact!" He sat back in his chair, his hands folded across his middle, looking like a little boy who was mighty pleased with himself.

Sarah and Jenny exchanged glances across the table. It was a third Sunday; two weeks had passed since the girls' latest and greatest argument. The weekdays preceding this Sunday had been friendly and cordial because they had both deliberately avoided saying anything about Caleb McKenna. Still, their relationship was strained and the closeness they once felt for each other was gone.

"You look like you're about to bust," Sarah giggled. "Are you going to share the good news with us?"

Leaning his snowy locks against the back of the chair, McKenna stared at the ceiling as though he were in a quandary. "Well . . . " he said, deliberately stalling, " . . . one of the letters has to do with you," he nodded at Sarah.

Sarah stopped chewing. Swallowing quickly she said, "Me?"

McKenna smiled, but didn't answer. He knew just how to get her attention.

Jenny sat straight-faced. She refused to be caught up in the old man's dramatic buildup.

"But first, let me tell you about my letter," he said.

"Oh! You're so cruel!" Sarah pouted playfully.

"I know, I know. It's a gift," he replied. "But I did receive good news. Ben wrote me from Fredericksburg and he's doing fine. He wasn't hurt in that awful debacle."

Jenny bolted upright in her chair, mightily interested now. "Did your son say anything about J.D.?" she asked.

A smug smile appeared on the banker's lips at her reaction. "That's right," he toyed with her, "your J.D. was at Fredericksburg too, wasn't he?" McKenna paused, pretending to remember what was written in the letter. In fact, he was enjoying the fact that he had something Jenny wanted, even if it was just a bit of information. "No," he said slowly, "wait, let me think . . . no, I don't believe Ben mentioned anything about J.D. in his letter. I take it by your interest, dear, that you haven't heard from your intended since the battle?"

Jenny's head lowered in disappointment. Her eyes were moist. She shook her head slightly to answer his question.

"I'm so sorry, for the both of you. And that's a fact," McKenna said.

Sarah too had sobered at the lack of news regarding her brother's fate.

McKenna cleared his throat. "But I just might have something else here that will brighten your mood a little." He reached into his vest pocket and produced an envelope. "I said I'd received two letters this week. The second one is addressed to a Miss Sarah Morgan." He extended the envelope Sarah's direction.

Just as her fingers touched it, McKenna pulled it back playfully. Smiling, he extended it again. Sarah snatched it from his hand before he could pull it back a second time.

"It's from Daniel!" she squealed.

"What?" Jenny cried, genuinely surprised.

"It's from my Daniel!" Sarah cried again. She placed the envelope against her chest, and tears fell down her cheeks. "Mr. McKenna, how did you ever manage it?"

With a self-satisfied grin, he said, "I told you I had my sources."

"How can I ever thank you?" She gripped the envelope as though she couldn't believe it was real.

"Why don't you go into the library where you can be alone when you read it?" McKenna offered.

Pushing her chair back, Sarah bolted from her seat. She rushed to Caleb McKenna's side and kissed him on the cheek. "Thank you, thank you!" she whispered. Then she ran from the room.

Closing double doors behind her, Sarah raced to a sofa situated in front of an eight-foot-wide fireplace. As a small friendly fire kept her company she ripped open Daniel's letter.

February 12, 1863

My dearest Sarah,

I write this letter with the hope that it will somehow reach you, however impossible that seems. But when a man is as desperately in love with you as I am, he will do most anything given the chance to express his feelings. I do not pretend to understand the circumstances that have led to the penning of this letter, but I will trust that our God who guides everything according to His good pleasure has some part in these events and that He will see this letter reaches you.

Following the Battle of Fredericksburg, I was quickly reassigned for reasons that have never been explained to me. O Sarah, my beloved, I sincerely hope that neither J.D. nor Marshall nor Willy were on that hellish field at Fredericksburg. You would not believe the carnage even if I had adequate words to describe it to you. Near the end of the day, after more than a dozen charges up the hill had been repelled by our troops, the bodies of the Union dead and wounded were stacked in rows like cords of wood. As the final troops withdrew I was standing within earshot of General Lee as he surveyed the scene. He said, "It is good that war is so terrible, lest we should become fond of it."

Then, turning to leave, he said, "Why don't they just leave us alone?" Sarah, I have never seen anything like it and pray to God that I never will again. There is no cause on earth that is worth the sacrifice of so many human lives.

A few days after the battle, I was sent to Norfolk. Although I am not at liberty to tell you my duties, I was informed that I have diplomatic privileges which include the sending of private letters. I know this sounds unbelievable, but not only was I told that I could reach you by way of a New York address, but I was almost ordered to write to you. Although I've rarely seen or heard of circumstances stranger than this, who am I to question this opportunity to communicate with the one I love?

My darling, darling Sarah. I pray for the day when these hostilities cease and I can once again hold you in my arms. I do not fear dying in battle. My greatest fear is that in my absence you will fall in love with another man. If that were to happen, I would welcome death, for life without you would not be worth living.

I know I'm rambling, my darling, but recent horrors of war have deepened my appreciation for life and family and love. Sarah, may the days fly swiftly by until we are reunited. And may God Almighty keep us both safe until that hour.

I will love you forever,
Daniel

In Caleb McKenna's mansion library, Sarah read the letter from Daniel four times over with tears.

"You don't like me, do you, Miss Parsons?"
With Sarah absent from the table, Caleb McKenna struck up a conversation with his remaining dinner guest.

"I think I understand you," Jenny replied noncommittally.

"A measured, if not ambiguous response," McKenna observed with an amused tone. "Do you think it is wrong of me to take an interest in Sarah?"

Jenny looked toward the doorway through which Sarah had exited. She did not want to be having this conversation. She replied by saying, "I'm not concerned with your interest in Sarah, as much as I am concerned with the motive behind your interest."

With palms pressed together, McKenna drummed his fingertips each one against its opposite. He had turned in his chair toward Jenny, giving her his complete attention. A servant girl appeared in the doorway with a silver platter of cookies. The banker waved her away. "So you doubt my motives are sincere?" McKenna asked his guest.

Jenny pondered a moment before saying, "Let's just say I have observed that your interpretation of your relationships is not always shared by the other party in that relationship."

The finger-drumming ceased. "I'm not sure I understand what you're saying, Miss Parsons."

Jenny wasn't sure what she was saying either. She felt frustrated that she did not have any evidence, other than the man's past, to support her distrust of him. And her inherent faith in the ability of people to change weakened even that argument. To date, her only evidence was the passing sneer of one disgruntled maid, her suspicions about the reclusive Beatrice McKenna, and a general feeling of dislike for the man.

"Why don't we just get to the heart of the matter," Jenny said. "What do you want from Sarah?"

McKenna's hands spread apart innocently. "I want nothing more than to be able to say that I helped a fledgling novelist take flight. Is that so hard for you to believe?"

"A man doesn't elevate himself to your position without expecting something in return for his favors," Jenny said.

"It's precisely because I have risen to this position of affluence that I *can* do things for others without expecting anything in return, Miss Parsons," the banker replied.

She was getting nowhere. She glanced again at the doorway.

"All I ask, Miss Parsons, is that you reserve judgment of me until I can prove to you my good faith by introducing Sarah to a prominent publisher. Could you find it in your heart to do that for me?" McKenna was playing on her sympathies and it angered her.

"Until I have evidence to the contrary, I suppose I can give you the benefit of the doubt," Jenny said.

"That's all I ask!"

Having deposited the girls in a carriage that would return them to their dormitory, Caleb McKenna stood before the library fireplace. He unceremoniously dumped Sarah's manuscript in the fire. At first the bulky papers nearly smothered the flame, but as McKenna lowered himself onto the sofa the edges of the manuscript curled, turned black, and were soon waving orange and yellow flames like flags in a stiff breeze. In a matter of moments Sarah's latest revisions were beyond recovery.

The banker sat back on the sofa, his legs crossed, and pulled from a breast pocket the letter from Ben. Donning spectacles, he read the letter again:

December 13, 1862

Father,

A major battle was fought today just outside the city of Fredericksburg. It did not go well for the Union army. We suffered a staggering defeat with significant losses. In the stillness of the night we can hear the wounded crying to us from beyond the river. It makes sleep difficult.

On a personal note, the day was not without its victories. In an Old Testament sense, we fared well.

Ben

The carriage bounced merrily as it passed through the iron gates of the McKenna mansion and into the street. The darkness of the night couldn't dim the glow on Sarah's face. Jenny tried not to look at her; Sarah's happiness only seemed to make her misery that much more unbearable.

"Isn't it a glorious night?" Sarah hugged herself and squealed.

Jenny grunted.

"Why so glum?" Sarah asked. The delight faded from her face. "Oh, I'm sorry. How inconsiderate of me. I'm so caught up in my own good fortune that I forgot you haven't heard from J.D. yet. Please forgive me, Jenny."

"That's only part of it," Jenny replied.

"What else . . . oh. . . . " Anger wrinkled her brow. She recognized the familiar path this conversation was taking. "Don't you dare say anything unkind about Mr. McKenna," she warned, "not after all he has done for me!"

"He's up to something and it's not good!" Jenny blurted. "I can sense it! That man is evil!"

"How can you say that?" Sarah cried. "Why would he help Daniel and me if he were evil? Why would he help me get my manuscript published if he were evil? Mr. McKenna is the kindest, most unselfish man I've ever known!"

Jenny held up a hand. "I'm in no mood to get into this tonight."

"How can you enjoy a man's hospitality . . . "

"I said I was in no mood for this tonight!" Jenny insisted.

"Well, I don't care if you're in the mood for it or not! I can't stand by when you attack the very man who has acted so unselfishly . . . "

"Driver! Stop!" Jenny shouted.

At the driver's command, the horses pulled up and the carriage slowed.

"Jenny, what are you doing?"

"I'm getting out." She reached for the latch and swung open the carriage door.

"Don't be foolish!" Sarah said. "Driver! Continue on!"

"I'm getting out!" Jenny gathered her dress around her and climbed out of the carriage. She slammed the door behind her. Sarah's face appeared behind the glass. A look of worry replaced the anger.

"Jenny, don't do this!" she yelled. "You're just being stubborn and it will get you into trouble! The streets aren't . . . "

"Continue on, driver," Jenny said.

"But, Miss, it's not safe for you . . . "

Pulling her hood over her head, Jenny marched away from the carriage without looking back.

"Miss? Miss!"

A moment later she heard the clop, clop, clop of horse hoofs fade into the distance, then all was silent. She stopped. Her hands hung heavy at her sides. She wanted to cry.

The city street upon which she stood was lighted. The soft glow of lamps lined the way at regular intervals. But to a woman alone on a New York street the lights only served to make the shadows that much darker and deeper. The air was dry and biting cold. Already Jenny could feel her skin beginning to chafe. She wanted to get out of the dark and the cold, but she hated the thought of returning to the dormitory. It had been a mistake coming to New York. She wasn't needed here and Sarah didn't want her. Tomorrow she would tell Sarah she was going home, the sooner the better. First thing in the morning she would inquire into the price of train ticket. If she didn't already have enough money, somehow she'd get it. Maybe her parents could ...

A scrape interrupted her thoughts. More like a scuffing sound. Shoe leather against brick. Jenny looked all around her. The street was empty. Eerily empty. No carriages. No people. No movement of any kind, not even a moth around the street lamp.

Her heart pounding, Jenny started walking.

Another scrape.

She looked behind her. This time she saw something. A dark figure emerging from a tree shadow. Wide shoulders. Tall. A man's gait. Jenny walked faster and crossed the street. The figure matched her stride, staying in the shadows.

She was still three blocks from the Society building. If she cut through an alley, she could reduce the distance to two blocks. Pausing at the alley entrance she considered her chances. The light from the street failed just a few yards into the alley. From there all was black until the exit at the far end.

No. Stay on the street, she told herself. *Stay in the light.*

She glanced behind again. The man was crossing to her side of the street. Passing under a street lamp revealed a bulky, woolen coat and wrinkled, stained trousers. He wore no hat. Thick black hair, uncombed and dirty, covered his head and face. He was looking at her. Following her. Behind him another figure emerged from the shadows, this one smaller and stooped, covered with clothing from head to toe.

Jenny pressed on frantically. Her eyes darted this way and that, searching for a coach. A policeman. Another human being. But there was no one else. Just her and her two pursuers. She looked for a friendly doorway. Windows in all the buildings were dark. She tried one latch, then another. Both locked. This was Sunday. Businesses were closed.

"Miss Morgan! A moment! A moment, please!" a gruff voice beckoned.

Without stopping, she looked behind her. The man was lumbering toward her! *O Lord, please help me!* Jenny prayed. She picked up her skirt and began to run.

"No, wait! Miss Morgan, wait! I won't harm you!"

Jenny didn't believe him. She ran harder. She could hear the sound of his hulking footfalls. His labored breathing was getting louder, closer. She was still two blocks from the Society building and safety.

A hand grabbed her shoulder, pulling her to a stop. Jenny screamed. A sweaty, hairy hand clamped over her mouth. She came face-to-face with a husky man whose head looked like an explosion of black hair with eyes and a nose. His hands and arms were huge. Jenny struggled to break his grip on her. He was too big, too strong.

"Miss Morgan! Miss Morgan! I won't hurt you! I won't hurt you!" His voice was raspy, his eyes earnest. "Please don't scream. I won't hurt you!"

"I'm not Miss Morgan!" Jenny screamed into his hand. The sound that came out was a muffled protest.

Her captor turned her into the light. "You're not Miss Morgan!" he exclaimed, but he didn't release her. "You're the other one!" Jenny twisted and turned. She tried to bite his hand. He cupped it before she got hold of flesh. She screamed a muffled scream. Nothing had any effect. "Please don't scream!" her captor said, his tone almost a whine. "I don't like screaming."

"Then let me go and I won't scream!" she said with muffled voice.

"I can't let you go yet," said the man apologetically.

"Why not?"

From behind the oversized captor came a hard, feminine voice. "Because we have business with you, Miss Morgan."

"I'm not Miss Morgan!" Jenny screamed into the hand.

"This ain't Miss Morgan, Ma," said her captor. He turned

her face into the light. As he did, not only did the woman get a good view of Jenny, but Jenny got a good look at the woman. Every inch of the woman was covered except for her hands and face. From the appearance of these, the woman was past middle age and she'd lived a hard life. Her hands were rough, callused, sinewy. Her facial skin was thick and leathery, not adorned with cosmetics of any kind. Her eyes were brown and piercing, her lips thin and pursed. When she spoke, she displayed yellow, overlapping teeth.

"What's your name, Miss?" the woman asked. Her voice was as cold as the winter wind.

The hand over Jenny's mouth loosened slightly. "Let me go!" Jenny screamed. Instantly the hand clamped down on her mouth, tighter than before.

The woman moved closer to Jenny until she was just inches from Jenny's face. Jenny had never seen eyes as hard as hers before. A callused finger stretched toward Jenny's nose. "I'm trying to do you a favor, Missy; that is, if you are a friend of Miss Morgan. Are you?"

A favor? Jenny was perplexed. *What kind of people do favors in the dead of night by taking someone hostage? Yet if these two had wanted to harm her, they could have already.*

"We don't have all night, Missy." The woman was growing visibly disturbed. "Are you a friend of Miss Morgan's or aren't you?"

The man's hairy hand moved up and down with Jenny's nod.

"And your name?" the woman asked.

The hand on Jenny's mouth loosened. "Jenny Parsons," she said weakly.

The woman seemed satisfied with Jenny's cooperation. She backed away a step. The man holding her relaxed. Jenny's instincts shouted at her to shove an elbow into the man and run. But before she could do it, the woman said, "Sarah

Morgan. She is Jeremiah Morgan's daughter, isn't she?"

"Yes," came the tentative reply.

"Then what's she doing with Caleb McKenna?"

"I don't see that that's any of your business."

"I'M TRYING TO HELP HER!" the woman shouted. The outburst was sudden, explosive, unnerving. The man holding Jenny let loose of her and covered his ears. Jenny understood why he didn't like screaming.

Jenny could have run. She didn't. It was the mention of Jeremiah's name that stopped her. This wasn't a random robbery or assault. The woman had piqued her interest. Before running away, Jenny had to know what business they had with the Morgans. "Mr. McKenna is helping Sarah get a book published," Jenny said.

"What kind of book?"

"A novel." A quizzical look on the woman's face prompted Jenny to add, "A long, made-up story."

"What's McKenna getting out of it?"

"He claims he's getting nothing out of it."

The woman shook her head from side to side so hard Jenny feared the woman might knock herself over. "McKenna doesn't do anything for anybody that's free, least of all for a child of Jeremiah Morgan. You mark my words. Miss Morgan is in danger. McKenna's scheming. He wants something. The devil always wants something. You sup with him and you'll pay. You'll pay with your life."

"Tell me what you know!" Jenny pleaded. All thoughts of trying to escape were gone for the moment, replaced by her concern for the Morgans.

"I know who you're dealing with," the woman said. She focused hard on Jenny. Then she cursed. "I was hoping you were Miss Morgan. I have something for her father. A matter of life and death, you might say."

"You can give it to me; I can see that he gets it," Jenny

replied. "I'm close to the family. Jeremiah's oldest son, J.D., and I are pledged to each other."

A wry grin crossed the woman's face. "J.D.?" she asked. "Short for John Drew."

The woman nodded. "Heed my words, Missy. You and Miss Morgan get out of the city, as far away from Caleb McKenna as you can get. Tomorrow. Tonight, if possible. Your lives are in danger and I won't be to blame should something happen to you." Reaching under her folds of clothing, the woman pulled out an envelope. She extended it to Jenny. "With all haste, Missy. With all haste!"

A moment later the woman and her hulking son were gone, leaving Jenny standing alone under a New York street lamp holding an unmarked envelope.

Jenny reached the Society building without further incident. She sneaked past the hallway leading to the dormitory and proceeded to the writers' workroom. A row of carrels lined a wall, separated by partitions. She lit a lamp and pulled out a chair from one of them. Turning the envelope over in her hands, she examined it. The envelope was thin and wrinkled, there were no markings of any kind on it. Jenny searched the darkness behind her. Satisfied she was alone, she opened the envelope. It contained a single page. Unfolding it, she read the hastily scribbled lines that sloped downward as they reached the edge of the page.

When she finished, she sat there staring at the lamp. Numb. For nearly two hours, she sat there, unable to decide what she should do. Then, she grabbed a blank sheet of paper and a pen and wrote a lengthy letter to J.D., praying that he would know what to do.

Hiding both letters under her coat, she sneaked into the dormitory. Sarah lay on the bed next to hers, her back to Jenny. Jenny could tell Sarah was awake by the restless way she squirmed to get comfortable. Neither girl said anything.

Jenny hid the two letters in a book under her bed. She undressed and climbed between the bedclothes.

A candle appeared at the end of the dormitory and glided between the beds. Stopping at the foot of Jenny's bed, the candle illuminated the stern face of its bearer, Mrs. Thomasson. The Society's matron hovered over Jenny in silent judgment for several moments. Then she said, "We will talk in the morning." The light glided back out the way it came and soon all was dark again.

Jenny lay on her back staring at the ceiling. After a time, Sarah's soft, rhythmic breathing indicated she was asleep. But there would be no sleep for Jenny this night. She couldn't get the contents of the woman's letter out of her mind.

"Sarah, please don't go!"

"We have nothing to say to each other, Jenny Parsons."

Sarah secured the bow in her hair. She smoothed and straightened her dress, fussing over every detail until it was just right. Jenny watched in exasperation. It had been a long, horrible, frustrating week. Mrs. Thomasson's punishment for Jenny's "total disregard for the clearly established rules of the Society and lack of common sense" was a doubling of her workload. "I'll keep you so busy you won't have time to get into trouble," the matron had promised. It was a promise well-fulfilled.

Jenny didn't mind the extra work, most of it physical—scrubbing floors, waxing, and polishing. The work gave her an outlet for the tension and frustration building up inside her, frustration stoked by Sarah Morgan.

Jenny didn't tell Sarah about her late-night encounter during the walk home, but it wasn't for lack of trying. The information in her possession proved beyond doubt McKenna's duplicity. But every time Jenny tried to say anything, Sarah walked away from her. When Jenny followed after her to make her listen, Sarah would cover her ears with her hands. It had been that way all week.

On Thursday Sarah had received an engraved message from McKenna informing her that he had arranged a meeting "of great importance" for her on Saturday next. A carriage would deliver her to the place of meeting and she was to dress formally. No mention was made of the substance of the meeting, only that Sarah would be "delightfully surprised." The message made no mention of Jenny.

"If you insist on going," Jenny said, "then I'm going with you."

"You weren't invited," Sarah said huffily.

"I'm inviting myself."

"Jenny Parsons, you weren't invited and you're not going."

Throwing on a cloak, Jenny replied in as stern a voice as she could muster, "Sarah Morgan, I came to New York for one reason and one reason only—to protect you. It's a promise I made to your parents and I intend to keep it. If I have to do it in spite of you, I will. But I'm going. If I have to steal a horse and follow you—I'm going!"

Sarah's response was an icy stare.

When the carriage arrived, the driver was the same man who drove them home Sunday night. A genial, older man with gray hair, he rolled his eyes when he saw Jenny. "I'm sorry, Miss," he said, "my instructions were to take only Miss Morgan."

"That's all right, driver," Sarah replied. "Miss Parsons came to see me off."

While the driver held open the door, Jenny elbowed her way past him, following Sarah into the carriage. Plopping down onto the seat opposite Sarah, she crossed her arms and said: "I'm going with you." To the driver: "I'm going with her."

The driver looked helplessly at Sarah, who grudgingly nodded. Pulling away from the Society building, the carriage made its way toward the hotel district. Neither girl looked at the other.

"You're going to feel pretty foolish when we reach a hotel restaurant and you're not allowed in," Sarah said at last.

"What makes you think we're going to a hotel restaurant?"

"*We're* not going anywhere. But I know what this is all about tonight."

"You do?"

"Yes, I do. It's quite clear when you think about it. We're heading toward the hotel district, right? And I was instructed to dress formally. Who frequents the hotel district at night? High-society people, like bankers and publishers. Mark my words, Mr. McKenna and a prominent publisher will be awaiting my arrival. For what purpose? To inform me that the publisher wants to publish my book. After all, how many publishers invite authors to an elegant setting just to reject them. So, you see, it's quite simple. What else could it be?"

"What else, indeed," Jenny replied dryly.

"Really, Jenny Parsons! It's hard for me to believe I have misjudged you all these years. Well, I'm glad you came, because now you will be proved wrong once and for all. That is, after you sit in the carriage all night while I dine in an elegant restaurant. But of one thing you can be sure: When this carriage takes us home tonight, you will be riding home red-faced sitting opposite a soon-to-be published author!"

No more was spoken for a time as McKenna's carriage glided past one fashionable hotel after another. With the hotel district behind them, the carriage emerged onto a street paralleling the wharf. Crossing over the East River, the disappointment on Sarah's face was pronounced. She stared in bewilderment at the moonlit ships in the harbor. The sea-heavy air worked its way into the carriage interior with its distinctive odors of salt and sand and seaweed. Drops of moisture made jagged tracks on the window as the carriage picked up speed.

Jenny made no comment. The passing seascape had deflated Sarah's dream; she did not need a reminder. When the carriage passed the last of the city lights and barreled onto a bayside road, Jenny's thoughts turned to their safety. She had never before been in this part of New York. The landscape was dark and treacherous.

"Driver! Driver!"

Either the driver couldn't hear her or he was ignoring her. He urged the horses to pull harder as the carriage climbed upward along a cliffside road. To the right of the carriage the land crumbled into a mass of rocks upon which the bay water lapped. As they climbed the hill the sparkles of the moonlit bay grew smaller and smaller. In the distance she could see the dark silhouette of a sloop at anchor. To the left of the carriage a wall-like ridge of dirt passed them in a blur. The carriage ride that had begun with the gentle rock of city streets was now a wildly bouncing escapade as its wheels jumped in and out of the road's ruts.

"Jenny?" Sarah's voice was soft and frightened. "Where is he taking us?"

Shaking her head slowly, Jenny replied, "I don't know, but stay calm." She succeeded in keeping her voice steady, but wide eyes betrayed her confidence for the fraud that it was. She searched the interior of the cabin for something she could use as a club.

The road descended to sea level again. The bay narrowed, then opened up to a seemingly endless expanse of water. It was all Jenny could do to keep from jumping out of the carriage and pulling Sarah with her. *But what then?* They were in unknown territory. *To whom would they run for help?*

"Lord, help us," Jenny prayed aloud.

"Amen," replied Sarah.

The carriage slowed. Jenny reached over and took Sarah's hand. "Whatever awaits us, if I tell you to run, you run as fast as you can," she said.

"No!" Sarah cried. "I'd never leave you. Besides, it's my fault that we're in this predicament."

"We don't know that it's a predicament . . . "

" . . . yet," Sarah finished Jenny's sentence.

The carriage pulled to a halt. Jenny scanned all around the carriage, looking for a way of escape. To the one side they were cut off by a tiny cove; the door side opened to a grassy knoll with a forest beyond it. *Which way to go? Stay on the road and risk recapture or flee into the unknown dangers of the forest?* She resumed her search for a club.

"Driver!" Sarah called out. "Why have we stopped here?"

The gray-haired driver climbed down casually from his seat and opened the carriage door. "Miss Morgan," he said, "would you kindly step out. Your party awaits you."

Still holding hands, the two women stared out the door, neither one making a move to get out. The silhouette of a lone male figure stood in the center of the grassy knoll. Moonlight traced his form, but failed to highlight any identifiable features such as his age or the expression on his face.

"I'm not getting out until I know who it is I'm meeting," Sarah said to the driver.

"My apologies, Miss, but I was not informed of the gentleman's identity," said the driver. "My instructions were to bring you here and, after you have completed your business, to drive you home."

"Then, driver, you may consider Miss Morgan's business complete," said Jenny. "Please, take us home now."

"No, wait," Sarah said. "I can't leave without knowing who it is. What would I say to Mr. McKenna?" She moved toward the door. "Jenny, you stay here. If anything happens to me, ride away and get help."

"Sarah, don't be foolish," Jenny cried.

"I trust Mr. McKenna," Sarah replied. "He would never do anything to harm me."

Jenny grabbed hold of Sarah's dress and wouldn't let her out. "Sarah, Caleb McKenna is not who you think he is!"

Sarah brushed Jenny's hand aside. Referring to the man on the grassy knoll, she said, "He's just standing there! If he'd wanted to harm us, he could have done so already. Let me find out what he wants!"

Jenny attached herself to Sarah's dress. With an exasperated grunt, she capitulated. "All right, but we're staying together. I just can't understand how anyone can be so optimistic and stubborn at the same time!"

The women climbed out of the carriage and, hand-in-hand, moved across the grassy knoll. The figure remained as still as a statue. Dew from the grass coated and chilled their feet as they walked. Jenny shivered from the sensation. Her fingers hurt from gripping and being gripped. The pale moonlight colored the knoll with a silver-blue light, which faded quickly to deep black among the trees.

The girls stopped midway between the carriage and the man. Sarah spoke: "Sir?"

His head cocked, nothing more.

"Sir, this is indeed an unusual setting to transact business. Please state your business with me."

"Sarah?"

That voice! Sarah's hand broke Jenny's grip and flew to her heart.

"Daniel?"

"Sarah? And Jenny! Is that Jenny with you?"

Daniel and Sarah closed the distance between them, their feet barely touching the ground. As the two intertwined, the only sounds to be heard were the muffled cries of their names and Sarah's happy sobs.

Jenny felt faint. The sudden turnabout of emotion from intense fear to relief and happiness for Sarah and Daniel was nearly too much for her. With her hand against her bosom, she strolled about the grass trying to regain her composure. She wanted to keep an eye on Sarah and Daniel, but didn't want to stare. As she circled the couple, she was amazed how differently things had suddenly become. The place that had a short time previous had been a sea trap on one side and a forest trap on the other was now a moonlit rendezvous for lovers. The moon and stars shined happily overhead; a peaceful, sparkling cove lay in the distance with the carriage and faithful driver standing nearby. It was the kind of scene Sarah would portray in her overly sentimental novel.

Then too, Jenny had to fight off feelings of resentment. How she wished she could lose herself in J.D.'s arms. How she longed to lay her head against his chest; to feel his arms squeezing her tightly; to hear him whisper her name; to feel his warm breath on her neck. It wasn't fair. J.D. was a Union soldier, and Daniel was . . . Daniel was a Rebel! A Rebel on Union soil! He could get shot for being here! They all could get shot as spies! In the excitement of the moment, political differences had somehow been conveniently set aside, but if anyone saw them, it could mean their lives.

Jenny strode over to the lovers. A sheepish, friendly face raised and greeted her. "Hello, Jenny," Daniel said. "It's good to see you again." His large, boxlike jaw was prominent even in the dim light.

"Daniel, it's good to see you too . . . it really is, but do you realize how dangerous it is for you to be here?"

Sarah didn't seem to mind the interruption. In fact, she didn't even seem to notice it. With her hands around Daniel's waist and her head against his chest, she seemed content to stare up at him and watch him talk.

"It is thoughtless of me," Daniel said, looking down at

Sarah, and kissing her again. "And yes, I realize the danger. But given the opportunity to see Sarah again, it was one I couldn't pass up."

"Caleb McKenna arranged for this rendezvous?" Jenny asked.

Daniel nodded.

"How? Why?"

"I can't answer that," Daniel said. "I'm as perplexed as anyone. In fact, I thought for sure it was a trap. But like I said, I considered the chance of seeing Sarah again worth the risk. I don't trust the man."

"We have something in common," Jenny said.

"You mean beside our love for this gorgeous woman?" Daniel replied.

Jenny looked aside as the two lovers engaged in a second round of furious kissing. Daniel was the one who broke it off.

"The longer I stay, the more dangerous it is for us," he said. "It breaks my heart, my beloved, but I must go."

"Go where?" Sarah asked.

A shrug of the shoulders. "I can't say," Daniel replied.

"Will I see you again?" Sarah cried.

"I don't know," Daniel replied. "It's not for me to say."

"Daniel, I'm glad to see you too," Jenny said, "but I must admit, all this mystery disturbs me."

Moving away from Sarah, Daniel embraced Jenny tenderly. "Thank you for being such a faithful friend. I love you for it. Have you heard from J.D. recently?"

Tears came to Jenny's eyes. "Not since Fredericksburg."

Daniel's eyes lowered. "I'm so sorry. I'll pray for you both."

He embraced and kissed Sarah one last time. "I will always love you, Sarah. Always."

"And I you."

"And when this blasted war is over, I'm coming for you."

Their hands lingered, fingers outstretched, wanting to make the touch last as long as possible.

"I'll be waiting," Sarah said.

Daniel Cooper disappeared over the edge of the road leading down to the cove.

Sarah rode all the way back to the Society with her head back against the carriage interior. A perpetual smile was planted on her face. "I can't believe it! I can't believe it!" she said over and over again. "It was like a dream! A fairy tale dream come true! And I owe it all to that blessed man, Mr. Caleb McKenna!"

Chapter 19

ON Sunday Sarah couldn't wait for the church service to end so she could thank Caleb McKenna for arranging her late-night rendezvous with Daniel. She hardly heard a word of Rev. Evans' sermon. Neither was Jenny paying attention, but for different reasons. She spent the hour staring at the back of Caleb McKenna's head.

He is up to no good. But what? What? she pondered.

If it was difficult to reason with Sarah before, it was impossible now. There had been a moment in the carriage the night before when Sarah's faith in McKenna was shaken. She might have listened then. But not now. Once Sarah saw Daniel in the field, the battle was over. Caleb McKenna had been elevated to the status of a saint in Sarah's mind. And one does not speak sacrilege regarding a saint to a true believer. Even when one knew that the saint was a rascal and a traitor.

Jenny had pieced it together in the darkness of the dormitory the night before. While Sarah slept the contented sleep of a young woman in love, Jenny wrestled with the evening's turn of events. She concluded Daniel had arrived by boat, probably the one that she had seen darkly anchored off the coast. She knew that somehow McKenna had arranged his arrival. *What was it he'd told them?* Something about diplomatic connections. *But if that were the case, wouldn't they have met Daniel at some diplomatic function or at a diplomat's of-*

fice? Would a diplomat smuggle a Rebel behind enemy . . . that was it! Of course!

Jenny's realization made her heart race. This, along with what she already knew about McKenna, made him an exceedingly dangerous man. He was a smuggler! He was playing both sides of the war for profit. While his radical Republican friends pressed for a total blockade of all Southern ports, he was running his own blockade! His Southern contacts weren't diplomats at all. They were smugglers! She knew she had to tell Sarah, but she also knew Sarah wouldn't listen to her.

"Jenny! Stand up!" Sarah whispered harshly.

Everyone around her was standing. The sermon was over and the congregation was grabbing hymnbooks. Standing several pews ahead of them was the white-haired banker. He leaned silently on the pew in front of him while the congregation sang:

Jesus, still lead on,
Till our rest be won;
And, although the way be cheerless,
We will follow, calm and fearless . . .

As soon as the hymn was over and before the final organ strains had time to echo in the vaulted ceiling, Sarah burst into the aisle. Throwing her arms around the old banker, she planted a kiss on his cheek that nearly sent him tumbling.

A clearly pleased Caleb McKenna sat in his usual place at the head of the enormous, polished mahogany dinner table. Sarah sat on his left as she did every Sunday. Jenny sat across from her, her usual place during her infrequent visits.

"So, you enjoyed my little surprise last night?" McKenna said to Sarah.

Her hands pressed together, her eyes closed with delight,

Sarah exclaimed, "It was heavenly! How can I ever thank you enough?"

"And you, Miss Parsons—even though you invited yourself along last night—was I finally able to convince you of my noble intentions?"

Jenny dabbed her mouth with a napkin. "What can I say? Daniel's presence took us completely by surprise."

Sarah reached across the table and took McKenna by the hand. "A question, though. Why did you have me dress formally? A diversionary tactic? If so, it worked masterfully. I was convinced I was being taken to an elegant hotel restaurant!"

McKenna looked at Sarah's hand in his and squeezed it. "No, my dear, not a diversionary tactic. I confess—I'm a romantic. I put myself in your young man's place and asked myself how I would want to see my beloved after a long absence. So I arranged for you to wear your finest dress. I wanted Daniel's first glimpse of you to be one he would remember until his dying day. Tell me, was he pleased?"

Without letting go of McKenna's hand, Sarah rose from her chair and kissed him again on the cheek. Jenny looked away.

"How would you like to see your young man again?" McKenna asked.

"Tonight?" Sarah squealed with delight.

"And . . . " McKenna motioned to a servant who delivered to him a four-inch-thick package wrapped in brown paper and tied with string which he handed to Sarah saying, " . . . after which, you will personally deliver this manuscript to Mr. Clarence Edwards, the senior editor of Brown & Brown, who has agreed to publish it once he has met the author. And that's a fact."

Sarah was stunned. Her mouth gaped open in a very unladylike way. She stumbled back to her chair and collapsed, her hands caressing the brown package. Printed in neat, bold letters, Sarah read: Brown & Brown Publishers, Mr. Clarence Edwards, Senior Editor, 769 5th Street, New York, New York.

"Is this too much for you, my dear?" McKenna asked, leaning forward with concern. With an apologetic tone he continued, "I'm truly sorry if it is. It was not my intention that both events take place on the same day, but circumstances being what they are demand it. You see, my diplomatic favors have run out and I cannot keep Daniel in the area after tonight. As for the book, Brown & Brown wants to publish it with their fall line. They are anxious to finalize the transaction so they can begin working on the manuscript."

Sarah's mouth moved, but she found herself unable to say anything. She clutched the package to her bosom with tears rolling down her cheeks.

Jenny eyed the package suspiciously. "They want to publish the book without having read it first?" she asked.

McKenna laughed at her. "Always the skeptic, aren't you, Miss Parsons? Mr. Edwards has been reading the manuscript all along. It was his suggested revisions I have been passing along to Sarah. However, he was unwilling to commit himself until after the revisions were completed to his satisfaction. So, for Sarah's sake, I thought it best not to mention his involvement until he made a clear offer. I didn't want to elevate her hopes needlessly. This manuscript . . . " he indicated the package held by Sarah, " . . . is the final copy. Mr. Edwards insisted that the author deliver it to him herself. Does that meet with your approval, Miss Parsons?"

No, it did not, but for fear of angering Sarah, Jenny kept her thoughts to herself. Instead, she said to Sarah, "It seems we suddenly have a very busy night ahead of us. I suggest we leave immediately to prepare ourselves for it."

"For once, Miss Parsons and I agree!" McKenna banged

the table with his hand. Rising quickly, he pulled out Sarah's chair for her. Covering her hand with his, he said, "I have instructed my driver to wait for you at the Society. He will take you to your romantic rendezvous; following that, to meet your publisher. My dear Miss Morgan, please give my best to your Daniel," he kissed her hand, "and to Mr. Edwards."

Her eyes heavy with tears, Sarah pleaded, "Won't you please accompany us? It would mean so much to me if Daniel could meet the man who has done so much for me."

"My dear, I would like nothing better than to accompany you," he replied. "Unfortunately, pressing business matters prevent me." He chuckled self-consciously. "You see, one of the ironies of being successful in business is that once you attain that which you've worked so hard to build, you discover that no longer are you in control of the business, the business controls you! And that's a fact! But let's not allow a little thing like my absence spoil the moment. This is a day we have both been waiting for! You can tell me all about it next time we meet!"

"I promise to regale you with every exquisite detail!" Sarah stood and bid him good-bye with one last kiss. Then she joined Jenny who was already standing at the front door.

Following the same route as the previous night, the carriage left the city behind them just as the sun was slipping behind the western profile of the New York skyline. It was twilight as they crossed the East River. And as darkness descended upon the Upper Bay it struck Jenny as odd that the same road that had instilled such fear in them the night before could appear so ordinary one night later. The coach lights, so deficient in their illumination the night before, tonight glowed with a soft, casual radiance.

Sarah hummed happily most of the way. The packaged

manuscript rode on her lap. Jenny could not afford to share Sarah's carefree attitude. One of them had to stay on guard. Jenny refused to allow herself to be lulled into complacency, though she had to admit it was getting harder for her to maintain a constant vigil. Every time she had anticipated danger, every time she had warned Sarah of danger, something good had happened and she felt like a fool. But she wasn't going to give in now. Not with the things she knew of Caleb McKenna. To keep herself from relaxing, she closed her eyes and remembered the night she was accosted by the leathery-faced woman and her son. *What was it the woman said?* "You sup with the devil and you'll pay!"

They found Daniel in the same place as the night before. Sarah was running up the knoll into her lover's arms before the carriage stopped rolling. Jenny chose to allow them their privacy. She remained behind in the carriage with the manuscript. "It's a beautiful night, Miss," the gray-headed driver said to her, holding open the carriage door. "We may be here a while. Wouldn't you like to get out and walk around a bit? It's a long drive back to the city."

Jenny looked around outside the carriage. The sea was sparkling, the sky was awash with stars, the air was crisp and fresh. She glanced toward the knoll. Sarah and Daniel were oblivious to anything but each other. "Thank you, no. I think I'll sit in here," she said.

"Are you sure, Miss? It's a very long ride back."

"I'm sure."

Slowly, almost reluctantly, the driver closed the carriage door. "Maybe in a few moments, then?"

"Maybe."

The driver walked to the front of the carriage, leaving Jenny alone. The manuscript sat on the seat opposite her—a mysterious, silent companion. There was something odd about the way McKenna insisted that the publisher had to have it on a Sunday night. Certainly he wasn't going to do anything with it tonight. *Why couldn't Sarah deliver it to the publisher's offices Monday morning?*

Jenny reached across the carriage and pulled the package onto her lap. It was weighty and flexible within the confines of the string. It felt like a manuscript. *Isn't it odd*, Jenny thought, *that Sarah is delivering a manuscript she has not seen in its final form? What if changes had been made which Sarah would not approve?*

Jenny looked outside again, this time to see if anyone was close by. Daniel and Sarah stood face-to-face, hands clasped between them, smiling frequently and talking. The driver was not in sight. She guessed he was up front with the horses. The carriage lamps provided enough illumination for her to read the address on the package.

Using her fingernails, she pulled at the string ties on the package, careful not to break the string. Once the string was removed, she worked the edges of the brown wrapping paper, opening one end of the bulky manuscript.

"How about now, Miss?"

A small scream escaped Jenny's throat. The driver had startled her, and she him in return. He jumped back a foot. Hastily smoothing down the edges of the brown paper, Jenny exclaimed, "You frightened me!"

The driver apologized, but he sounded more agitated than apologetic. Something was bothering him, and it wasn't the fact that she was opening the package. Not once did he even look at it. Taking a swift glance up the road, he said, "I really think you should get out now, Miss."

"Not now!" Jenny said in as calm a voice as she could produce. She wanted to see what was in this package and get it rewrapped before Sarah and Daniel decided they should be sociable and insist that she join them.

"There's a stream up the road a bit," the driver said nervously. Perspiration trickled down his cheeks. "I thought I'd water the horses . . ."

"We can do that on the way back," Jenny insisted. "That will be all."

Another glance up the road. He didn't move away from the door.

"I said, that will be all!"

Muttering something incomprehensible the driver rejoined the horses.

Once he was gone from sight, Jenny returned to the package. Peeling back a layer of brown packaging, the white edges of a stack of papers appeared. With a little more effort, the top of the first sheet appeared. It was a disorderly page with handwriting, scribbles in the margins, and official-looking stamps. "This isn't a manuscript!" she cried softly. Lifting the package closer to the carriage lamps to get a better look, she gasped at the name she saw on the top page. It read:

Edwin M. Stanton   *February 25, 1863*
Secretary of War
ARMY OF THE POTOMAC
Official Records, War Department

Summary of First Corps preparedness:

Without removing the papers from the wrapping, Jenny hastily flipped through them, scanning the top portions. The entire stack was a hefty collection of documents detailing Union troop strength, maps of regimental positions, and reports on artillery and ammunition supplies.

A feeling of panic grew in the pit of her stomach. Like an icy hand it reached upward and gripped her throat. *These are not the kinds of papers two women should have in their possession while meeting a Rebel soldier behind Union lines!*

"Miss, I really must insist you get out while I . . . " The driver appeared in the doorway again. The carriage lights highlighted the panic on his face.

Suddenly everything was coming into focus. *Sarah. Daniel. Government papers. A nervous driver. McKenna and Daniel linked in espionage? No! A trap! This was Caleb McKenna's scheme! This is what he was planning all along! His revenge against Jeremiah Morgan and Seth Cooper was to implicate their children in a spy ring. It was perfect. The families would be humiliated and McKenna would be a hero for exposing them! To their parents' grief and shame, Daniel and Sarah would be hanged. For her meddling, she herself would be an added bonus. And as a final insult, history would forever record the Morgan name in a list of infamous American traitors, starting with Benedict Arnold!*

She had to warn Sarah and Daniel!

Jenny moved toward the door. Too late. Men on horses thundered past the carriage, converging on the couple in the center of the grassy knoll. Sarah screamed. Daniel stepped in front of her to protect her.

In a matter of seconds four men surrounded Daniel and Sarah. Three of them remained on horseback with pistols pointed at the couple, while the fourth dismounted and demanded that Daniel identify himself. The driver of the carriage, his hand resting on the carriage door, danced excitedly. He couldn't take his eyes off of the commotion behind him.

Jenny saw an opportunity and took it. Planting her foot on the carriage door, she kicked with all her might. The blow from the door sent the driver sprawling in the dirt.

Dropping the brown package on the floor of the carriage, she bolted out the door and climbed into the driver's seat. She snapped the reins and yelled. Startled horses reacted instantly. The carriage lurched forward, nearly knocking her from her perch.

"Go, Jenny! Get away from here!" It was Sarah's voice. Out of the corner of her eye, Jenny spied two of the horsemen reining their horses hard over to pursue her.

"Hyah! Hyah!" she urged the carriage horses to go faster.

Several hundred feet in front of her, the road made a sharp right turn around a thick outcropping of trees. Her plan was to disappear around the corner, then pray she could find a place where she could turn the carriage around quickly and double back, surprising her pursuers. It wasn't much of a plan, but it was all she could think of. The carriage was not only their means of escape, it was her only weapon.

The speed of the pursuing horsemen was surprising. They were going to cut her off before she reached the turn. So much for her plan. With pistols drawn, they were close enough that even in the dark she could make out the sneering expressions on their faces.

BLAM!

Shock and surprise flashed on one rider's face. He pitched sideways and crashed to the ground.

BLAM!

The second rider's horse crumpled beneath him, sending him somersaulting head over heals. He lay still on the ground.

Where had those shots come from? Jenny had no time to ponder the answer to her question. The turn was upon her. She pulled hard on the reins. The horses responded sharply, but the carriage resisted, its rear wheels sliding sideways.

"Hyah! Hyah!" she urged them on, hoping they could pull the carriage out of the skid.

No sooner had the skidding stopped when another carriage appeared. It was coming straight at her! She and the other driver saw each at the same instant. Jenny reined hard right. The other driver, an astonished, big-shouldered man wearing all black, matched her move. The carriages missed each other by inches. Jenny's carriage rode up the side of a ridge before settling back on the road. The other carriage was not as lucky. Its two wheels slipped off the edge of the road, threatening to send it crashing against the rocks of the cove below.

Jenny's heart pounded uncontrollably. Not only because of the near accident, but because of who she saw in the other carriage. Its sole occupant was Caleb McKenna.

The sight of the white-haired banker infuriated her. *So he couldn't resist the spectacle of his victims caught in his trap! Well, I'll just have to give him something exciting to watch!* The road widened a short distance ahead of her. After two tries, she managed to face the carriage in the opposite direction.

Her jaw clenched in fury, Jenny brought the horses to a full gallop. As the second carriage came back into view, Caleb McKenna was being assisted out of the tilting carriage by his driver. She whisked past him, showering him with dust and pebbles. Glancing over her shoulder, she saw him shaking his cane at her and screaming obscenities.

Rounding the outcrop of trees, the grassy knoll came into view. The two men who had pursued her were still on the ground. Atop the knoll one more of the pursuers lay still, his face buried in the grass. The remaining horseman was hiding behind Daniel and Sarah, using them as a shield against an unseen force in the forest. He held a forearm around Sarah's neck and a pistol in her back. It looked like a stalemate. He was slowly easing the couple away from the forest toward the road.

Jenny steered the horses onto the grass. She headed straight for Daniel and Sarah and their captor. Full gallop. The carriage bounced crazily as it hit hidden ruts in the grass.

At the sight of four horses barreling down upon him, the man with the pistol panicked. He looked at the black forest, at the horses, at the road behind him, then back to the forest. Then he turned his weapon toward Jenny.

The moment the pistol was no longer in Sarah's back, Daniel swung around and bowled into his captor with all his might. The pistol discharged harmlessly in the air. As the gunman tumbled down the knoll, Daniel jumped to his feet and pulled Sarah out of the way of the onrushing horses just as the carriage split between them and the gunman.

Jenny pulled the horses to a stop. "Hurry!" She cried to Daniel and Sarah. "Get in! Get in!"

Daniel helped Sarah to her feet. With a quick check of the gunman, Daniel placed himself between the gunman and Sarah as they ran for the carriage. The gunman had stopped tumbling. He was on his hands and knees searching for his pistol in the grass. Daniel threw open the carriage door, helped Sarah in, then jumped in after her.

BLAM!

A bullet whistled past Jenny's head. She ducked instinctively. "Hyah! Hyah!" she cried. The horses were off again, bouncing wildly down the knoll. Jenny prepared herself for another shot.

BLAM! BLAM! BLAM! BLAM!

Only sound. No bullets whistled past her. She looked back. The fourth gunman spun around and collapsed on the ground. White smoke drifted from the woods. The unseen force.

As the carriage skidded onto the road, it began to pick up speed. Daniel's head poked out the carriage door.

"Go straight down the road about a half mile, then stop!" he yelled.

Jenny nodded affirmatively. Daniel let loose with two sharp whistles, paused, then added a third. A signal of some sort. *To the force in the woods?*

Further down the road, Daniel shouted, "Pull over!"

Jenny pulled back with all her might. The horses slowed to a stop, panting heavily in the night air, their breath visible and swirling around their heads. Daniel jumped out of the carriage. He whistled again in similar manner as before.

Sarah was right behind him. She ran to the front. "Jenny, you were wonderful!" she cried. "You rescued us from those men!"

"From Caleb McKenna," Jenny corrected.

"What? I don't understand."

"He was back there," Jenny replied. "He set up you and Daniel to look like spies."

"I don't believe you!" Sarah cried.

"Look at your manuscript package on the carriage floor," Jenny said. "Maybe that will convince you."

Sarah ducked back inside the carriage.

"I'm just glad you're on our side," Daniel said to Jenny with a wink. Sarah emerged holding the brown paper package. Disbelief covered her face. Even with the proof in her hands, she was looking for some way to convince herself it was a misunderstanding.

Bushes next to the road rustled as five men in sailor's garb emerged from the forest. The force in the woods. Daniel looked up at Jenny. "You didn't think I was going to come ashore alone, did you?"

"Not likely," said one of the men with a thick Southern accent. "We don't trust Yankees."

A man with a scar on his cheek spoke to Daniel. "The local constable has been alerted. They're headed this way. We'd best move out sharply."

"So quickly? How can that be?" Daniel cried.

"Not so quick if they had advance notice," the man with the scar replied.

Daniel nodded in understanding. To Jenny: "Are you all right? Do you want me to drive?"

"No time," she said. "Jump in. Just tell me where you want to go."

"Stay on this road for a mile. There will be a path leading to a cove just beyond two large elm trees."

With four sailors packed in with Daniel and Sarah and the man with the scar riding on top with Jenny, they started out again. The additional weight, together with fatigued horses, caused them to move more slowly. They had traveled a good mile when the sailor beside Jenny pointed to two elm trees. Jenny slowed the team and led them over the edge of the road down to a cove. A sixth sailor stood guard next to a shallop. The dark silhouette of a sloop could be seen offshore.

"What now?" Jenny asked Daniel as she climbed down from the driver's seat.

"You and Sarah come with us," he replied.

"Come with you? Where?" Jenny asked.

"To the ship."

"And then where?"

Daniel shrugged. "To Richmond."

"Richmond? Are you crazy?"

"It's the only place you and Sarah will be safe!" Daniel replied. "You can stay with my mother in Manchester."

Jenny shook her head. "Out of the question."

Daniel glanced toward the road. "We don't have time to discuss it, Jenny," he said. "You said McKenna was back there, right?"

Jenny nodded.

"Who do you think the local officials are going to believe? You holding these secret documents from the war department, or him?"

"You looked at the papers?" Jenny asked.

Sarah emerged with the package.

"Sarah," Jenny said, "Daniel wants us to go with him to Richmond."

"I know," Sarah said. "Jenny, you do what you want, but I'm going with Daniel."

They could hear the soft thunder of approaching horses.

"What are you going to do, Jenny?" Daniel asked.

"Looks like I'm going to Richmond."

Jenny and Sarah stood against the railing of the Confederate sloop. They used the railing to steady themselves. Blankets were draped over their shoulders to ward off the cutting sea wind. All around them sailors bustled with activity, stealing occasional glances at the girls on deck in their formal dresses.

No sooner had they boarded the Confederate sloop when Union warships charged out of the bay after them. The Confederate captain executed a couple of crafty course changes to slow the heavier ships down, then headed into the wind and outran them. Such was the life aboard blockade-running ships, only in other instances their cargo was more profitable.

After a safe distance had been established, the captain demanded an explanation from Daniel. When he learned of McKenna's thwarted scheme, the captain flew into a rage at the personal nature of their New York escapade. He swore an oath of retaliation against the Virginian congressman, McKenna's Southern contact, who had sent them this far north. It was an oath he intended to carry out once they reached Richmond. That was, if they reached Richmond. They still had to pass through a federal blockade without getting blown up. The captain's only consolation was that with the young ladies was a package of classified government papers that might prove beneficial to the Confederacy.

The lights of the city had long since disappeared beneath the dark horizon. The eastern sky had a touch of light pink to it, the promise of another day.

"Did you bring it?" Jenny asked.

Sarah lifted the edge of her blanket to reveal the brown package. Her "manuscript."

Jenny took it and let it slip over the railing. The package hit the water, surfaced, then bobbed alongside the length of the boat.

"It didn't sink!" Sarah said.

"It will," Jenny replied.

They watched it until it was out of sight.

"What do you think the captain will do to us when he discovers we tossed it overboard?"

"I don't know. But we can't let him have those papers."

Sarah stared at the eastern sky. The sun popped up suddenly and the sky was light, almost as though God had removed a huge star-spangled lid covering the earth. "Jenny?" Sarah said softly.

"Mmm?"

"I feel so ashamed and foolish. You were right about Caleb McKenna all along, and I wouldn't listen. I was so self-absorbed that I couldn't see the truth. It nearly cost us everything."

Jenny didn't disagree with her.

"And now look at us. We're on an enemy ship, heading for enemy waters." Sarah began to weep. "We may never see our parents again. You may never see J.D. again. It's all my fault. I wouldn't blame you for hating me the rest of your life."

Jenny looked out over the water at the huge orange orb rising from beneath the horizon. "I was mighty angry with you at times," she said softly. "But I don't hate you. As for the South, what choice did we have? Besides, how bad can it be with Daniel there?"

Sarah managed a weak smile.

With the orange light reflecting in her tired eyes, Jenny said, "I have something to tell you. Something that I learned in New York." She paused. "It will change the entire complexion of your family."

"That sounds so ominous."

Jenny casually glanced all around them, checking for eavesdropping ears whether they were intentional or not. Sarah's brow furrowed at Jenny's caution.

"It's that serious?" she asked.

Jenny replied by saying, "Remember the night we argued and I got out of the carriage?"

A shamed looked crossed Sarah's features. "I remember."

"On the way home I was accosted by a man and his mother."

"O Jenny! Why didn't you tell me? They didn't hurt you, did they?"

Shaking her head, Jenny continued. "The woman was a former employee of Caleb McKenna. Years ago he tried to have her killed."

"Oh my!" Sarah exclaimed.

"For more than twenty years she has hid from him by taking on a different identity. When she heard you were visiting McKenna regularly on Sundays, she became alarmed — alarmed enough to venture out of hiding to warn you that you were in danger."

"Why didn't you . . . " Sarah left her question unfinished. She already knew the answer.

"If it hadn't been for her, I would have returned to Ohio," Jenny said. "But she convinced me your danger was real and I decided to stay. She gave me a document to deliver to your father."

"My father?"

Jenny nodded with a look of chagrin. "I made a copy of it. Unfortunately, it's back at the Society."

"What about the original?"

"Since your father didn't return to Point Providence, I had no idea how to get it to him. So I sent the original to J.D."

"What did the document contain?"

Jenny recounted the woman's written testimony to Sarah. It left the younger girl as shaken as Jenny had been when she first read it. When a Confederate yeoman informed the girls that their quarters were ready for them, Sarah was so weak in the knees she had to be helped to the cabin.

Forgotten was the fact that they had almost been caught as spies. Forgotten was the fact that Sarah's novel was lost forever. Forgotten was the fact that they were on a Confederate ship approaching a Union blockade. Sarah's only thought was for the safety of her family.

Chapter 20

HER eyes were closed. Marshall stared at the young woman lying on the bed, confounded that she had so successfully masqueraded as a Confederate private. Now that he knew her gender, it seemed so obvious. The wavering candle cast yellow highlights on the flowing brown hair that spilled across the pillow. Shadows danced across lightly freckled cheeks and nose, and lips that could belong only to a woman.

She moaned.

Reaching into his boot beside the bed, he pulled a water-soaked rag out of it. Ringing the excess water from the rag, he dabbed her forehead and cheeks. For nearly a day she had been feverish. Marshall kept her cool with the moist rag. To do so he had retrieved some water from a nearby stream using the only receptacle at hand, his boot.

Her forage cap lay nearby, atop the Confederate coat and vest. Marshall had removed them, along with her shoes and socks, to cool her down. He'd also unbuttoned the top two buttons of her Confederate issue brown shirt and sponged her neck.

She responded to his cool touch. Her head turned from side to side. Eyes fluttered open, then wrinkled in confusion as she stared at the dirt walls and ceiling. Confusion turned to fear. She turned toward the source of light and saw Marshall.

"Relax, Reb," he said. "You're safe."

"Where am I?" She lifted her head to look around. It cost her. She winced in pain.

"We're in a cave, remember? We came here to escape the shelling."

Her head sank back onto the pillow. She closed her eyes in remembrance. "A shell exploded near me," she said. "That's the last thing I remember."

"It knocked you out. That was yesterday."

Looking at Marshall, she asked, "You brought me here?" Marshall nodded.

Eyes closed again. "My head hurts," she said. She raised a hand to her forehead. Her eyes shot open in alarm. "My cap!" she cried, feeling her hair.

"It's over there with your coat and vest."

She sat up, her hands flying to her neck. She discovered the unbuttoned buttons and saw her naked feet. "Oh! Oh, how dare you!" she screamed, hastily buttoning the shirt all the way to her neck. "You cad! You low, vulgar cad!"

"What are you babbling about?" Marshall cried.

"Don't pretend innocence! You violated me while I was unconscious!"

"I did no such thing! I nursed you through your fever, nothing more. The only thing that has been violated is your disguise. How am I going to explain to the boys back at camp that I was captured by a Confederate woman? My reputation is ruined."

"Your reputation! Why, of all the crass remarks!" Swinging her legs over the side of the bed, she tried to get up.

"Where do you think you're going?" Marshall asked.

"I'm getting out of this hole in the ground before you force yourself on me again."

"You're not going anywhere, Reb."

With his hands on her shoulders, he kept her from getting

up. She tried pushing him away, slapping at his arms, punching his chest. He laughed, which only infuriated her and brought on heavier blows. Grabbing her by the wrists, he forced her back onto the bed and pinned her there. His face lingered over fiery blue eyes.

"I suppose you're going to ravage me now," she said.

"Why do you keep saying that?" Marshall cried. "I'm not going to ravage you. But I am going to see that you stay down until you're ready to get up. I don't want your death on my hands."

"Do you expect me to believe that? You've already killed so many Southerners, what's the death of one more to you?"

The words struck him hard. He had fostered friendly feelings for her back at the farm when he thought she was a boy; and now that he knew she was a woman, those feelings had deepened to admiration and something more. *What had he done that she would think he would be indifferent to her death?*

He released her wrists. She began to struggle again, then stopped abruptly, holding her head. "See?" Marshall said, "you're only hurting yourself. Now lay still and get some sleep."

She gazed up at him with distrusting eyes. "I'll not sleep as long as you're in this cave. I don't trust you."

"Well, you *should* trust me. But if it's all the same to you, I'm going outside for some peace and quiet." He plopped down on the chair and pulled one boot on. He reached for the other. Sploosh! It was filled with water. And when he forced his foot into the boot the water squirted upward, soaking his trousers.

This started the girl on the bed laughing. She grabbed her head. But in spite of the pain her laughter produced, she didn't stop laughing.

Marshall wiggled his soggy toes and made a disgusted grunt. Snatching his rifle, he said, "I'll be right outside, so don't do anything dumb." He climbed out the hole. It was twilight and peaceful, a welcome atmosphere to the one inside the cave. He leaned against the cliff and stroked his beard as he watched the stars come out.

After an hour he checked on the girl. She was asleep. Slipping out again, he made his way under the cover of darkness back to the farm. He collected a variety of stored foodstuffs from the cellar and hauled them back to the cave, sure that when she woke up she would be hungry.

The sound of someone stirring awakened him. Through groggy eyes, he saw the girl moving toward the cave exit, her hair tucked up under the Confederate forage cap. With coat and vest bundled under one arm, she carried Marshall's rifle in the other and was negotiating how to exit the cave with her hands full.

Marshall had been asleep in the chair. He'd reclined it on its back two legs against the side of the cave. "You must be feeling better," he said.

His voice startled the girl. She dropped the bundle of clothes and aimed the rifle at him. "Don't try to stop me," she said.

"Or what? You'll shoot me? The gun isn't loaded."

"How do you know I didn't load it while you were asleep?"

"Because I hid the bullets and caps, knowing that you just might wake up before me and shoot me while I was asleep."

She looked offended. "Shoot you in your sleep? How dare you accuse me of such a dastardly act! I had plenty of chances to shoot you before and didn't."

"That's true," Marshall said. "But how do I know you didn't take advantage of me while I was asleep?"

Her mouth fell open in shock. She threw the rifle at him. Marshall raised his arms to protect himself from the flying weapon; the sudden movement caused the chair's back legs to slide out from under him. He crashed to the ground.

She laughed so hard at him, she had to steady herself against the side of the cave wall. The sight of her laughing started him laughing.

Picking himself up, he said, "At least have some breakfast before you go. I went out last night and got it especially for you. You're hungry, aren't you, Reb?"

Wiping away tears of laughter, she said, "Am I your prisoner or am I free to go?"

"For now you're my prisoner. You can go after breakfast."

While he got the provisions from his haversack, she edged her way to the bed and sat down. He handed her a jar of canned peaches. "These are my mother's peaches!" she exclaimed.

"I got them from your cellar."

"You're feeding me stolen peaches from my own farm?"

"I would have grown my own, but that would have taken longer!" he replied. She stared at the jar in her hands, then at her mother's curly handwriting on the lid, which was how she had identified them. "My mother canned these last year," she said softly. "She was going to save them for when my father came home. He loves canned peaches." Tears came to her eyes. She sniffed them back and opened the jar. "Where are the utensils?"

"I don't have any."

"You don't have any?"

"This is war. Use your fingers."

Marshall removed the lid from his jar, reached inside, and pulled out a dripping peach half. Raising it high, he prepared to drop it into his mouth like a mother bird would drop a worm into a chick's mouth.

"What are you doing?" she said.

Marshall paused. The interruption caused him to drip peach

juice on his chin and shirt. He hurried the peach half back over the mouth of the jar. "What now?" he cried.

"This may be war," she said, "but that doesn't mean we have to act like heathen! We haven't prayed yet! War is a poor excuse to forget the goodness of God."

Marshall released his peach. It plopped back with the others in the jar. "All right," he said, "do you want to pray or should I?"

Her response was to set her jar aside, fold her hands, and close her eyes.

"Gracious and mighty God," she prayed, "thank You for this food which You have so bountifully provided for us. And thank You for the one who canned it. Little did she know at the time that her act of stewardship would be a blessing to her daughter in time of great need. I am also grateful that You protected us from the shelling . . . " she paused, confused by the amount of time that had passed since the night of the shelling, " . . . the other night. You know when it happened and we're grateful You kept us safe. Please Lord, stop the killing, and bring the men at war home before too many more families are scarred by death." She paused again. This time longer.

Marshall opened his eyes to see the reason for the delay. She was staring at him. With eyes wide open she completed her prayer.

"And thank you that this Northerner resisted temptation and acted like a gentleman while I was unconscious. Amen."

The prayer finished, she dipped her fingers into the peach jar and ravenously devoured two peach halves in quick succession.

"Who said I was tempted?" Marshall asked.

"What?"

"You said in your prayer I was tempted to do something ungentlemanly. I want to know what makes you think I was tempted to do anything of the kind."

"You're a Yankee, aren't you?" she shot back.

"I'm a Morgan," he replied. "Marshall Morgan."

"That's nice," she replied, pulling out a peach half with indifference.

"So what's your name?" he asked.

"You can call me Reb," she replied.

"No . . . that was suitable when I thought you were a boy. After all we've been through, I'd like to know the name of the person who captured me and held me prisoner in her barn."

She looked at him—amused and suspicious, all at the same time.

He arched his eyebrows, awaiting an answer.

"Julia Hutchinson, daughter of General Lyman Hutchinson of the Mississippi cavalry."

"Julia." Marshall said her name as if he were testing it for taste. "Julia . . I think I'll still call you Reb."

Refusing to be baited, she feigned indifference. Licking her fingers, she set the jar aside and said, "Are you always this obnoxious, or are you putting on a special act just for me?" Before he could answer, she hopped off the bed and checked her hair, making sure it was tucked sufficiently under her cap. "Thanks for the stolen peaches. I'll be leaving now. I enjoyed capturing you. We'll have to do it again sometime."

Marshall grabbed her arm. "I don't think you should go back to the house," he said.

She looked at his grip, then straight at him. Her eyes were a lit fuse, indicating an explosion could go off any second. She said, "Are you asking me, or telling me?"

"I'm asking you. For your own good."

"Then release me. I'm going home."

"All right, if you want it that way, I'm not asking you, I'm telling you!"

A sly grin formed on her face. "I knew you were no gentleman," she said through clenched teeth. "You planned on holding me prisoner in this cave to be your personal concubine all along, haven't you?"

Marshall's eyes rolled upward in exasperation. He shouted: "How can I get it through your head? I have no intention of deflowering you!" More softly: "It's not like that at all, Reb! . . . Julia. I've seen the house. There isn't much to go back to."

"It's my home," she replied. "It's all I have."

"What are you going to do? Rebuild it all by yourself?"

"If I have to . . . yes."

The way he shook his head, she could tell that he didn't think she could do it.

"When I was just a girl," she said, "my father and mother built that house from the ground up. When the chimney was in place and before the walls were completed, two swallows took up residence in our chimney. Day after day the construction activity shook bits of straw and twigs from their nest. We watched those swallows as each day, they flew down, picked up the pieces, and rebuilt their nest. Never once did they become discouraged, or give up. No matter how many times their nest was knocked apart, they rebuilt it. My father was so impressed with them that once the house was completed, he refused to light a fire in that chimney until he was sure they had flown away for the winter. As I was growing up, whenever I got discouraged and wanted to give up, my father would remind me of those chimney swallows. So you see, Mr. Morgan, I don't care how many times Yankee shells knock my house down. I'm going to rebuild it. Now will you release me?"

Marshall was captivated by this woman. Never had he known a woman to be this strong, this passionate, this beautiful.

"I didn't want to have to tell you this," he said. "But following the shelling, a battle took place around your house. Cavalry from both sides must have passed up and down this ravine a hundred times. And when I went to your farm last night, well, there are bodies everywhere. And, to tell you the truth, I don't know if your house is in Confederate or Union hands."

Without hesitation, she said, "There's only one way to know for sure."

Marshall laughed. "You are a stubborn woman!"

Julia smiled sweetly at him. "So far, it's gotten me most everything I want."

Marshall released her. She turned toward the cave exit.

"Wait," he said. "I'm going with you."

She started to say something, then held her tongue.

They approached the Hutchinson farm side-by-side, a Union soldier and a woman disguised as a Confederate private. Marshall found himself stealing glances her direction. He found it hard to believe she had fooled him for so long. Now that he knew she was a woman, signs of her gender were unmistakable—long eyelashes, petite ears, delicate fingers.

"It's not polite to stare, Mr. Morgan," Julia said.

"Sorry, Reb. Didn't mean anything by it."

Marshall scanned the countryside for some sign of occupation. Before leaving the cave, they had developed their strategy. Should they learn the area was in Union hands, Marshall would hold the gun on Julia; should they be in Confederate territory, Julia would get the gun.

"Over there!" Julia pointed to a distant row of trees. Actually, there were two parallel rows of trees with a road between them. A small band of soldiers on horseback passed between them. The stars and bars of the Confederate battle flag and a

Mississippi regimental flag flew down the road with them.

"Looks like you get the rifle," Marshall said. He handed it to Julia and stepped in front of her. She aimed it at his back.

"This is more like it," she said. "Now back to the barn. There are a pair of shackles waiting for you."

She said it seriously. Marshall couldn't tell if she was joking or not. With Marshall's hands held high, they crossed the cornfield toward the Hutchinson house. Bodies from both armies littered the field and the grounds surrounding the house. The house itself was pockmarked with rifle shot as well as suffering damage from artillery shells. The barn had a gaping hole in its side. The stench of decaying flesh filled the air. All was silent. There were no voices, no sounds of animals, no birds.

"March me around the house once before you lower the rifle," Marshall whispered.

"Who said I was going to lower the rifle?" Julia responded. Her voice quivered.

Past the barn, around the back of the house, they saw no one. The battle had passed through like a storm, leaving its morbid debris. When they reached the front of the house again, Julia slumped down on the porch step and wept. Marshall sat beside her, but offered no words of comfort. He could think of nothing to say that might help. Twice he started to put his arm around her shoulders. Both times he thought better of it.

"Will you go with me inside?" Julia asked.

Marshall nodded. He stood first and helped her up. She handed him the rifle and he preceded her into the house.

He recognized the parlor from his quick excursion through it the night of the shelling. In the light of day, it looked even more elegant even though everything was covered with dust and debris. For the most part, the room was intact. Some of the windows were broken out. There were no cracks in the chimney, the one once occupied by swallows, Marshall assumed.

The pictures that had once adorned the hallway walls were all on the floor. Marshall helped Julia pick them up and place them where they belonged. He remembered fleeting glimpses of some of them. The man and woman.

"Your parents?" Marshall asked.

Julia stared lovingly at the picture and nodded. They were a proud couple. Her father had a round head, bald on top, and a full mustache. Her mother looked almost royal with a delicate lace neckline and her hair pulled back fashionably. She had petite ears which Julia had inherited. Both of them had wrinkles in the corners of their eyes, the kind earned from generous amounts of smiling and laughing. They looked nothing like the evil, Negro-hating plantation owners Marshall had envisioned all Southerners to be.

Julia took the picture from his hands and placed it on the wall. The next picture he turned over was that of a bright, happy girl of on the verge of womanhood.

"This is you!" he exclaimed.

"You're surprised there's a picture of me in my own house?"

"The night of the shelling, when we came through here, I saw this picture and thought it was your cousin, or possibly your sweetheart. Of course, then I thought you were a boy."

Julia giggled. It was a wonderful sound, especially in the midst of so much destruction and death.

They completed their inspection of the house. More than half the rooms were unsafe or unusable. Julia's room was the only upstairs room that could be occupied. Most of the downstairs was safe with the notable exception being the dining room, where only two walls still stood.

Leading Marshall to the front porch, Julia said, "Thank you, Mr. Morgan. I'm sure you're anxious to get out of Confederate country and back to your brigade. You know, for a Yankee, you're not a bad man."

"High praise," Marshall grinned. "Will you be all right by yourself?"

"I seemed to manage before you showed up. I'll be fine. I'm a sparrow."

Marshall laughed. "Yes, you are." He took a step down. "I wish I could have known your parents," he said. "From what I saw in the hallway picture, I think I would have liked them."

"I think my father would have liked you," Julia replied, "that is, if he didn't shoot you first."

Marshall took another step down. "How is your head feeling?"

"I still have a slight headache," she replied. "But I'll be fine. Are you going back to the cave?"

"No. Like you said, I'll probably wander back to camp."

"Sorry, I can't loan you a horse," she said. "The army confiscated them long ago. I doubt I'll ever see them again."

"Thanks for the thought," Marshall replied. He took the last step. Looking around, he asked, "What are you going to do first?"

"Got to bury these bodies," she replied.

"Won't a detail come by to do that?"

"Possibly, but who knows when? I couldn't stand the stench for another day. Besides, I believe everyone deserves the dignity of a decent burial."

Marshall nodded. He took a step away from the house. "Maybe after all this fighting is over, I'll ride down here to see you. I'll bet by then you'll have this house completely rebuilt and looking like new."

"Forgive me if I don't stand on the porch waiting for you every night. But if you come, I'll treat you with Southern hospitality."

"Um . . . thanks for not placing me in shackles again . . . when you held the rifle on me a little while ago . . ."

Julia crossed her arms. She smiled coyly. "What a ridiculous thing to say! I couldn't do that to you after all we've been through together."

"No, I guess not. But thanks anyway." Marshall couldn't think of anything else to say, but he didn't want to leave just yet. After an embarrassing silence, he lifted his arm in a half wave. "I'll be going now. Good-bye." He turned to leave.

"Good-bye," Julia called after him.

Turning around, Marshall waved again. "God be with you," he said.

"He always is," she replied.

Marshall crossed the field and entered the forest, but couldn't go any farther. Turning back, he leaned against the tree and looked across the cornfield at the Hutchinson house. From a distance he could see the figure of a Confederate private pulling dead men by their legs beyond a huge oak tree on the western side of the house. It would take her several days to bury all the dead men on her property. Marshall wanted to go back and help her. *What would be the harm in doing that?*

I could get shot! That's what's wrong with it, he answered himself. *Think, Morgan! What if a Confederate detail comes by and finds you? Is helping a woman worth getting captured by the enemy?* He bent the top portion of his ear as he struggled with his desire to return to the house. *Then there's my vow. I've already broken it once, when I touched the gray-beard sniper.* More ear bending. *Two excellent reasons to head straight back to camp and forget about this whole incident.*

So the decision was made. Marshall snatched up his rifle and walked back to the Hutchinson farm.

"Just what do you think you're doing?"

Julia stood with hands on her hips as Marshall dragged a dead Confederate corporal and placed him at the end of the line which she'd begun.

"I'm helping you," Marshall said matter-of-factly.

"What's the matter with that brain of yours? Do you want to join these men? Because that's exactly what will happen if you get caught here."

Dropping the corporal's legs, he stood facing Julia. "I'll trust God to protect me."

"God doesn't protect fools," Julia retorted.

Marshall shrugged. "If you don't want me here, just say so and I'll leave."

"I don't want you here."

Going to get another body, Marshall said, "You don't mean it."

Julia followed after him. She tried to wrestle the legs of a Union sergeant out of Marshall's grasp. The best she could manage was one leg. They pulled the dead man together to the end of the row.

"I'm not going to get rid of you, am I?" Julia said.

"Not today."

"Well at least take off that uniform! Dressed like that, you're a target for the entire Confederate army! Here, follow me." She strutted toward the house. Inside, she handed him some of her father's clothes. "See if these fit," she said. The clothes were a bit small, but they fit close enough.

They were an odd couple working around the farm that day. One wore a Confederate uniform that was too big for her; the other wore civilian clothes that were too small and nearly split every time he bent over.

They dug a large trench for the bodies. As each soldier was lowered into the grave, Julia prayed a prayer over him— Confederate or Union, it made no difference. She not only prayed for the man's eternal future, she prayed for his surviving family as well. She asked God to give his parents, his spouse, brothers, sisters, a measure of comfort in their time of grief. She prayed that their loss might turn them against war forever, that their loved one's death might contribute to peace among the states.

Marshall watched, but didn't participate in Julia's ceremony. He couldn't bring himself to pray for the dead Confederate soldiers, and he thought it would anger Julia if he prayed only for the Union soldiers. So he prayed for none of them.

"Why do you pray for the Yankees?" he asked her. "They're your enemies."

Julia looked at him sadly. "Haven't you ever read in the Bible the passage that says, 'Love your enemies'?"

"I've read it," Marshall said.

"You must have a different version of the Bible then," Julia concluded.

"Why do you say that?"

"Because my Bible doesn't say, 'Love your enemies—this applies to everyone except Marshall Morgan.'"

It was a hard day's work, and still they didn't complete the task. As night fell, Marshall collapsed on the sofa in the parlor and Julia retreated to her room upstairs. Marshall tried to push the memories of the dead men from his mind. He couldn't. Like a ghastly parade they lined up and passed before him, one after another after another.

Up until now he'd managed to keep death at a distance. That's why he became a sniper. That's why he took the oath not to touch the dead. The oath was nothing more than an oath of convenience, smacking of spirituality only because it appeared in the Bible. Its real purpose was to give him an excuse to think of the enemy as nothing more than a target, never a person, and certainly not a husband or brother or father. And he could do this only if he never had to be close enough to them to look at their dead faces.

But on this day there were no enemies on the Hutchinson farm; there were no Yanks, no Rebels. There were only men who would never return home, leaving wives who were now widows, children who were now orphans. In the trench lay not only the men, but their unfulfilled dreams as well—buildings they would never build, music they would never compose, cures they would never find, children that would never be born. That night on the Hutchinson sofa in the parlor, Marshall Morgan mourned the world's loss.

The next morning when Julia emerged from the house, she found Marshall already at work dragging the last of the bodies to the trench beside the house. His face was clean-shaven.

"What happened to your beard?" she asked.

"Shaved it off."

"I can see that! Why?"

"No longer have a reason to wear it."

"I think I like you better this way," she said. "The beard made you look like you were hiding behind something. This way you're more open, honest."

"I'll take that as a compliment."

"As it was intended."

The last of the soldiers was buried by early afternoon. Julia had gone into the house to prepare some cool drinks. Marshall had just stepped onto the porch from the side of the house when he saw them. A Confederate detail coming up the road. He quickly ducked into the house.

"Julia! A Confederate detail is coming!"

Julia appeared quickly from the kitchen. She had taken off the forage cap, and her brown hair swirled around her neck as she moved.

"There's about six or seven of them," Marshall said.

Julia's eyes darted back and forth as she considered their alternatives. "Come with me," she said. She led Marshall upstairs into her bedroom. "Stand over there," she said, motioning him to one side.

"Shouldn't I get in the closet or something?" Marshall asked.

"What good would that do? If they're going to search the house, they won't skip the closets." She tore off the soldier jacket and vest and began to unbutton the brown shirt. "A gentleman would turn his back while a lady changed clothes!" she said.

Marshall turned his face to the wall. Behind him he heard the rustle of clothes. "What are you doing?" he asked.

"Trying something different," she replied. "You're sure they're Confederates?"

"Positive."

"Check the window. See if they're here yet."

Marshall moved toward the window, careful to stay out of sight and to keep his back to Julia. "They're pulling up to the house now."

"I'm ready for them," Julia said.

Marshall turned around. Julia stood before him in a pastel-yellow summer gown. She was stunning.

"What are you gawking at?" Julia whispered. "Haven't you ever seen a woman before?"

"I've never seen you as a woman before," he exclaimed in a whisper.

A male voice with a heavy drawl called from the front porch. "Is anyone in there? If anyone is in there, come out now."

Julie whispered to Marshall, "Just pray I'm not the last woman you ever see. Stay here."

She disappeared out the door. Marshall could hear her descend the stairs, calling out to the man at the door.

"Shelby? Is that you, Shelby? Good Lord, how long has it been? Really? That long? Well just look at you in that uniform. Why, if you don't look the perfect gentleman."

Marshall stood near the front window. By pressing up

against the wall and looking out the front at a severe angle, he could see a Confederate captain. Julia emerged from the front door and stood in front of him; the only thing Marshall could see of her was the bottom edge of her dress.

The captain explained to Julia that his detail had the unenviable task of burying the war dead in the area. He looked around, amazed that there were none. Julia told him she had already performed the necessary task. When he expressed surprise that a lady would do such a thing, she replied that in war everyone is called upon to perform unpleasant tasks.

The captain remained skeptical that Julia could have buried all the men without help. "Really, Shelby, do you think I'm hiding someone from you?"

"Ma'am, if you have no objections," he said, "I would like to search the house."

"Search the house? Why, Shelby Carter, I'm surprised at you! How long have we known each other? Since before either of us could walk! Do you think for one moment there would be someone in my house and I don't know about it? If I weren't such a Christian lady, I would feel insulted. Here I go and do your dirty work for you and you want to treat me like I'm a Yankee sympathizer. No sir. I'll not stand here and be insulted and then allow your men to track mud and dirt all through my house."

"Dirt in the house?" the captain countered. "It's nearly a shambles!"

"Is this what this war has brought us to?" Julia cried. "Why, Shelby Carter, you're no better than the Yankees who shelled my house. Whether you destroy it a little or a lot, you still destroy it. I'm shocked. I never thought I'd see this day when Southern manners were a relic of the past."

"Julia, please understand," the captain pleaded. "I have my orders. My lieutenant will ask me if the house and land are secure."

"All right, Shelby." Julia feigned indifference. "Do what you must! How can I possibly resist you? There is only one of me, and a woman at that; there are seven of you men and you all have guns."

The captain motioned to two of his men. They dismounted.

Julia addressed them as they ascended the steps, taking a boyish private by the arm. "Go inside to the hallway, then up the stairs. There's no need to search through all my personal things. You'll find a Union soldier standing in plain sight in my bedroom." To the captain, "You might as well know, Shelby. I captured him myself, intending to keep him as a slave to help me run the farm. But what I hadn't counted on was that he swept me right off my feet with his Yankee charms. And now I don't know what to do with him. So go ahead and take him away, it will make my life a whole lot simpler."

The captain shook his head in disbelief. "Forsythe, Swinton. Get back here. Mount up." To Julia: "Don't you take all, Miss Julia. If I weren't already married, I'd come back to court you myself."

"Well, Shelby Carter, you playful rogue," she said coyly. More seriously, she added: "I'm glad to see that at least one Southern gentleman still holds a woman's honor in high regard."

"Good day to you, Julia," the captain said. He mounted his horse and galloped away, his men right behind.

Julia Hutchinson descended the porch steps and watched the Confederate detail until they were out of sight. From the bedroom window, Marshall watched her. If he hadn't seen the transformation firsthand, he wouldn't have believed it. From awkward Confederate private to witty Southern belle in less than a minute. Seeing her standing there at the foot of the steps in her pale yellow dress took his breath away.

A solitary candle separated them. Their dinner consisted of

boiled potatoes, black-eyed peas, and a jar of canned pears. The lighting arrangement and menu were both restricted due to war-time shortages. But there was no shortage of laughter and good feelings.

Because the dining table had become a casualty of the earlier shelling, they sat at a small chess table in the parlor. Once the pieces were cleared there was barely enough room for two plates and the candle. Julia, having returned to army uniform for the remainder of the day's chores, surprised Marshall by coming to dinner in a dress. It was red with white trimming, adorned with lace and tiny bows. A matching red ribbon highlighted her hair. Marshall barely noticed the dinner. He was content to feast on the vision of feminine beauty sitting across from him.

"Tell me about your family," Julia said.

"My family. Well, let's see. Where do I begin? My father is a minister, and my mother makes the best berry pies in ten counties."

Julia laughed. "Why is it that men always associate their mothers with food?"

Marshall continued. "I have two brothers and a sister. One older brother, J.D. He's a natural leader and was considering going into the ministry before the war started. He's a captain in the Army of the Potomac. Then there's Sarah; she's a writer. The separation between North and South has been particularly hard on her and Father. You see, my father's best friend is a Virginian, and Sarah is in love with his son."

"Scandalous! Imagine being in love with a Southerner." Julia said. "How shameful!"

"It's not without its problems," Marshall said.

"Oh? And how would you know?" Julia asked.

Marshall smiled. "Getting back to my family . . . there's my youngest brother, Willy. He was born with a clubfoot, so it's difficult for him to get around sometimes. But he's really talented artistically. He draws well enough to be published in some of those major New York magazines when he wants to. He's not too far from here. I left him back at camp. He hired on as a photograph artist's assistant."

"Are you a close family?" Julia asked.

"I guess so," Marshall said. "We boys have always been close. My father and I don't always see eye-to-eye."

"The way you talk about your family, it sounds like you're close." Julia stared into the darkness. "Being an only child, I have no idea what it's like to be close to a brother or sister. I had only my mother and father. . . ." The thought of her deceased parents created tears in her eyes, then pushed them down her cheeks.

Marshall reached across the table and took her hand.

"Sometimes," she said, "I think I'm going to die from all the grief and distress this war has caused me."

A squeeze of her hand brought a smile in spite of the tears. Marshall said, "Would this be an appropriate time for me to exude some of my Yankee charm?"

Julia laughed. "What are you talking about?"

"This afternoon you told that Confederate captain that you had captured a Union soldier who had swept you off your feet with his Yankee charms."

"You were listening to that?" Julia squealed.

Marshall nodded.

"Well, don't believe what you heard. I was lying like a fool to save your neck," she said.

With a glint in his eye, Marshall said, "You also told him you were going to keep me. Are you?"

Julia blushed. The color in her cheeks, mixed with the golden light of the candle, made her look radiant. She lowered her eyes. "I only wish I could," she said.

Pushing back his chair, Marshall stood. Still holding her hand, he reached out for the other.

"What are you doing?" she asked.

"Stand up," he said.

"Why?"

"Please. For me."

Slowly, she pushed back her chair and stood. Marshall moved closer to her.

"No," she whispered softly, lowering her head.

He gently cradled her head in his hands. Her cheeks were moist and hot. He raised her head until their eyes met. She didn't resist. If there was a heaven on earth, Marshall had found it. He could spend eternity gazing into this woman's eyes. With his thumb he brushed her lower lip. Her eyes closed from the sensation.

Leaning forward, he touched his lips to hers; at first, softly like the brush of his thumb, then he pressed harder. She responded with a soft moan.

"This is wrong . . . this is wrong," she whispered.

"I know . . . I know."

They pulled each other close.

Chapter 21

BECAUSE it was a special, though sad, occasion, Julia wore a dress. For the second time in a week she stood on the porch while Marshall backed down the steps drawing out his good-bye for as long as he could. He wore his Union uniform.

"I'll come back . . . soon," he said.

"Don't make a promise you can't keep," she replied.

"I'll keep this one. If I have to join the Confederate army just to be close to you, I will."

Julia blushed. "Now you're just being silly."

"Well . . . I guess this is good-bye."

"Are you going to tell your brother about me?" she asked.

"Willy? By the time I'm finished describing you to him, it will be all I can do to keep him from coming here to court you himself."

Never before had Marshall felt like this. All his life had been guided by purpose and driven by anger. Now, for the first time in his life, his thoughts and actions were animated by love. It was an all-consuming feeling that made his previous feelings seem barbaric in comparison.

"Well," he said, "I guess this is good-bye."

"You're repeating yourself," Julia snickered.

He backed halfway **across** the cornfield, before he turned in the direction he was heading. Then he made a half-dozen more glances over his shoulder. Not until he was well inside the forest did he lose sight of her.

It took him all day and most of the next to reach the outskirts of the Union army camp. He was limping heavily, a reminder he'd been wounded. Standing picket duty that day was a fresh-faced New Yorker. Marshall recognized the boy's origin from his heavy accent. He learned it was the boy's first night on picket duty, that he'd just arrived in camp that same day. Marshall could have guessed that about the boy, for he almost shot Marshall out of sheer nervous fear.

First, the boy forgot the words with which he was supposed to challenge those who approached the camp. He shouted something like, "Stand and halt, or shoot . . . me." The boy was more intent on readying his weapon to fire than he was in speaking. This too he handled poorly. While attempting to cock his weapon, he lost control of it completely and it fell to the ground. Marshall stood and watched in amazement as the boy looked at the weapon on the ground, then at him, then raised his hands to Marshall in surrender.

Marshall shook his head in amazement and walked past him into camp.

"Morgan! Is that you? Almost didn't recognize you without the beard. Where you been?" A burly, red-headed sergeant called to him. Marshall didn't recognize him. "We was lookin' for you a couple of days ago. Couldn't find you. Couldn't find anybody who'd heard from you. Figured you was dead."

Marshall decided a little explanation was in order. "Had my horse shot out from under me by a Rebel sniper. Took me a while to make my way back here. You said you were looking for me. What for?"

The sergeant rubbed a bristled chin. "Had to notify somebody," he said.

"Notify? About what?"

"Your brother."

"What about my brother?"

The sergeant winced as though it pained him to relate the news. "He was captured by the Rebs."

Willy had heard that a reporter for the *New York Tribune* was looking for someone to supply him with battlefield photographs. When Willy relayed the tip to Zeke, he got the standard negative reply: "Too much time, too little profit."

Business had been booming for Zeke. With a fresh influx of recruits, he had a whole new crop of customers who had money for the first time in their lives and nowhere to spend it. Willy grew tired of being known throughout the camp as the boy who worked for the man who sold French pictures.

He decided he needed to break out on his own. The way he figured it, he needed to draw several pictures—six, maybe seven—and sell them. The money would get him started and the quality of his work would get him more work. But Willy never found enough time to complete even one picture; there were always horses to feed, food to cook, and fires to build. Besides, the more he thought about having to produce pictures on a regular basis according to someone else's deadlines left him cold. So Willy found it easier to complain about Zeke and do nothing to change his situation.

But when Willy discovered the handsome sum the *Tribune* reporter was offering, he was confident he'd stumbled upon something worthwhile. Whereas it took him the better part of two days to complete a pen-and-ink sketch, photographs could be made in a matter of hours. This time he had prepared a rebuttal to Zeke's standard reply.

"I know how to take pictures," Willy said. "How about if I go and take the pictures? You can stay here and sell. By splitting up, we can make double the income."

Willy chose a money theme for his argument, knowing that

Zeke would never be convinced by any other appeal.

"What do you know about photographs? Nothing! That's what you know," Zeke blustered.

"I've watched you make them!" Willy replied. "I know how to set up the camera, sensitize the plate, and time the exposure. Give me a chance, Zeke. Let me do it once. If it doesn't work out, I'll never bring it up again."

Zeke dropped down by the fire, a bottle of whisky in his hand. He guzzled the liquid, screwed up his face as he swallowed it, and said. "And who will make me my dinner? No. Out of the question. Don't talk to me about it anymore."

That was it. Willy's idea was scuttled because there would be no one to fix Zeke's dinner. But Willy was determined not to give up so easily this time; not so much because he believed in the plan, but because he'd already promised the reporter the pictures.

So while Zeke slumbered drunkenly beside the fire, Willy hitched the horses to the photographic arts wagon and set out in search of battlefield scenes. He figured Zeke would forgive him once he saw the quality of his picture compositions, and once he handed the photographer the *Tribune* money.

Dawn was about an hour away when Willy came upon an Indiana regiment that had seen some action the previous day. As he waited for the morning sun that would stretch shadows across the scarred battlefield and create the dramatic effect of a long, drawn-out encounter, he dreamed again of what it would be like to be in the midst of a major skirmish. Willy knew he could never photograph an actual battle scene because the exposure required to record the image was simply too long. The images would be distorted to nothing more than a blur. Still, he wished he could at least witness a full-fledged battle. Not a minor skirmish, but the kind of battle that changed the complexion of a war, the kind that caused people's eyes to light up when you told them you were there, the kind named after its geographical setting and spoken with awe; a battle like Bull Run, or Antietam, or most recently, Fredericksburg.

Just before daybreak Willy sensitized the photographic plates. With the sun peaking over the eastern ridges, he interviewed a couple of Union soldiers. He learned that the day before had seen several skirmishes, as up and down the valley Confederate forces tried to work their way toward Grant's army surrounding Vicksburg. The heaviest fighting took place in a peach orchard at Howard's farm near a stone bridge, not more than half a mile distant. Willy hopped aboard the wagon and set off down the road.

With the Union force behind him, he crossed the bridge and found the orchard. Like most other battlefield scenes, this one was a mixture of life and death. It was a pastoral scene of row after row of peach trees on gently sloping ground. A peaceful buzz of insects filled the air. There was a small splitrail fence which separated the orchard from the soft babble of a tiny brook. Beyond the brook was a rising embankment of scattered woods. The Howard house sat atop the hill overlooking the peach orchard. Generations of Howards must have looked out those windows at this early-morning scene. Only today something new was added to the view. Bodies of uniform-clad men lay scattered beneath the trees like fallen leaves in autumn.

Willy began to imagine what the battle must have been like as the brave men of two armies clashed under these trees. Then he reprimanded himself. He was there to take pictures before the light changed. If he didn't get right to it, he'd lose the light.

He had difficulty unloading the bulky camera without assistance, but with a few extra grunts he managed to drag it out and set it up. He chose his scene—a Union lieutenant slumped against the base of a tree, with a dead sergeant lying on his lap. *Friends who died together on the same day? It would make a good picture.* The background caught the debris of war — a dead horse, more dead soldiers, abandoned haversacks and rifles. And, of course, everything dramatically highlighted by the strong morning light with its strikingly sharp shadows. He propped a rifle against the tree trunk next to the lieutenant for composition. Aiming the camera, he composed the picture. The artist inside him approved. This picture would be worth a lot of money.

BOOM!

An artillery shell screamed overhead. It exploded in the woods.

BOOM! BOOM!

More shells. Coming from the direction of the Howard house. More explosions in the woods across the brook. A trumpet sounded a charge and Union soldiers came pouring past the Howard house, down the slope, into the peach orchard. They charged straight at Willy!

Willy fell to the ground, next to the dead lieutenant and his sergeant friend. The human wave swept over him like he wasn't there. No sooner had they passed him when they met resistance from the woods. A volley of shot slammed into the wave before they could reach the splitrail fence.

All around Willy men fell, screaming, writhing. Some who were hit tore frantically at their clothes to see how badly they'd been wounded. Then he heard another wave coming. In their haste to reach the enemy, men trampled on the dead and wounded. Artillery shells screamed overhead. Soldiers shouted and cried and cursed and moaned. With another volley from across the creek some continued to advance, others retreated. They ran headlong into each other. One soldier stumbled over Zeke Custis' camera. Both he and the camera went flying.

At first, Willy was overwhelmed by all the action around

him. After a time his senses rallied. He realized that there were no military recruiting doctors in the peach orchard. No one to tell him he was unfit to fight. No one stopping him from joining the battle and killing a dozen or so Rebels. This was his chance. He might not get another.

Willy relieved the dead sergeant of his ammunition pack. Stretching over the dead man, he grabbed the rifle he had propped against the tree for composition. For added measure, he took the dead man's hat and placed it on his head. At last, he was a Union soldier. He checked the weapon and loaded it.

The Union line was advancing toward the splitrail fence tree by tree. Willy grabbed his crutch, pulled himself up, and advanced with them. An incredible amount of smoke filled the orchard, making it difficult to see. The morning sunlight was broken into slanting lines as it filtered through the trees. Soldiers appeared and disappeared as they stepped into and out of the light.

A bullet whistled past Willy's ear. An inch or two closer and he would have taken it in the face. The man next to Willy wasn't so lucky. Hit in the cheek, he fell to the ground, his cheek ripped away showing stained teeth, his brown-bearded chin wet with red. Another bullet barely missed Willy and exploded in the tree trunk beside him—the back side of the tree. The Union side! Willy almost took a bullet from his own side!

Already he had barely escaped death twice and he hadn't even fired a shot! He steadied himself with his crutch and raised the rifle, looking through the smoke for a target. From behind him, someone ran by too closely. His foot caught Willy's crutch, knocking it out from under him. Willy fell. His weapon discharged into the tree, shattering a limb and pummeling him with leaves and splinters. Another charging soldier tripped over him, kicking him in the ribs. The man cursed as he flew to the ground with a thud.

Just then it started to rain bullets. It was a horizontal sheet that cut through everything four feet above the ground. Entire lines of Union soldiers folded over and died. One bullet hit the barrel of Willy's upraised rifle, jerking it out of his hand. Another wave of lead washed over him, and another line of soldiers fell.

This wasn't anything like Willy imagined war would be. This was chaos. Men ran blindly in every direction. Dead fell on top of dead and who was to say which side killed them? He pulled himself to the base of a tree, staying low to escape the bedlam. *Where was the glory in this? Where were the dramatic maneuvers? Where was the bravery?* There were no heroes here. Those who would return to camp tonight would have no right to boast of anything other than they had stepped into a storm of bullets and were lucky enough not to get killed.

Then he heard the most hideous sound he'd ever heard in his life. It rattled his nerves and caused his spine to tingle. From beyond the fence the hillside came alive with a high-pitched whooping cry. The Rebels were coming. A flood of them emerged through the smoke. Crossing the creek. Vaulting the fence. Sweeping through the peach orchard. Pushing the Union force back up the hill to the Howard house.

Willy pulled his crutch from under a glassy-eyed private and scrambled to his feet. All around him Union soldiers were in retreat, passing him by. With every ounce of energy in his body, Willy struggled to get up the hill. There were just too many obstacles. Bodies. Weapons. Tree branches. All of them in his way. Tripping him up. Slowing him down.

The first wave of Rebels swarmed past him up the hill. On both sides of him were Rebels. Anyone looking down on them would have thought he was running with them rather than from them.

He stepped over a body. His good foot became entangled.

It felt like something grabbed it. He pulled. It was caught good. He yanked. Still stuck. He yanked again, this time so hard he lost his balance and fell. Laying his crutch aside, he reached down to free himself. It was Zeke Custis' camera. His foot was tangled in the legs of the tripod. By pushing first, then lifting, he managed to free his foot. He reached for his crutch to get up.

Something shoved him to the ground. Willy found himself staring into the muzzle of a Confederate rifle. He wondered if some photographer would be by later to record the image of his dead body.

"It couldn't have been my brother who was captured," Marshall told the bristle-faced sergeant. "Willy isn't in the army. He has a clubfoot."

"That's him!" the sergeant cried. "Worked for that Zeke fella, the one what sells them French pictures."

Marshall knew nothing about the French pictures, but he recognized Zeke's name. "Tell me what you know," he said.

The sergeant rubbed his chin to stimulate his memory. "One of my boys spied him hobbling off with the prisoners, the ones caught at Howard's orchard. Then later, Zeke came stormin' into camp claimin' your brother stole his wagon. We found the wagon and Zeke's camera in the orchard, all shot up."

As unlikely as it sounded to Marshall that Willy would be captured as a prisoner of war, he couldn't deny that all the pieces fit. "When did this take place?" he asked.

"Four days ago."

"Where would the Rebs take the prisoners?"

A wide grin on the sergeant's face displayed tobacco-stained teeth. "You gonna go rescue him or something?"

Marshall ignored the sarcasm. With a cutting tone in his voice, he said, "When I write my parents about Willy, they'll want to know where he is."

The sergeant's grin faded quickly. "The Rebs will most likely load him on a freight train and ship him to Andersonville."

"Andersonville?"

"Prison camp in Georgia."

"Sergeant, do me a favor. You never saw me. I haven't returned yet."

"You haven't? Oh, I get it. . . . " He squinted one eye tight. "I don't know . . . if someone should ask me . . . I wouldn't want no trouble."

"If someone asks you, tell them the truth. Just don't volunteer any information. I need some time. Willy was my responsibility, with his clubfoot and all . . . "

"But if someone asks me . . . "

"You tell them. Tell them everything. Thanks, Sergeant."

Within thirty minutes Marshall had a horse and was on his way to Howard's orchard. From beside the house he stared down at the remaining litter among the trees. All the bodies were gone. Zeke's carriage was still there. Overturned. Riddled with bullets. A horse lay next to the carriage, dead. Marshall could only guess at the turn of events that would put Willy and not Zeke in the carriage and on the scene of a battle. But it wasn't hard for him to imagine that Willy's thirst for battle glory had something to do with it.

Marshall sat against the deserted Howard house. It too showed the evidence of battle with its shattered windows and bullet-spattered siding. There was no one else around as he took a piece of paper and a pencil from his haversack.

He knew what he had to do, but for some reason he couldn't bring himself to put pencil to paper. It had been so long. So much needed to be said. Spoken. Not written. But he had no choice. He wrote: *Dear Father and Mother. . . .*

It was a short letter. He told them as much as he knew about Willy's capture. He accepted full blame for it and informed them he was heading to Georgia to rescue his brother.

Marshall couldn't leave without saying good-bye to Julia. As he rode toward the house, she greeted him with a rifle, wearing the uniform of a Confederate private and looking like a boy. When she recognized him, the rifle fell to the ground and she flew into his arms.

She fixed him dinner, which they shared on the chess table in the parlor. Afterward, they snuggled in each other's arms on the sofa.

"If I had a choice, I'd stay here with you, to protect you," Marshall said. "But I have no choice. I have to go after Willy. Please understand."

Julia placed a finger on his lips. "I wouldn't respect a man who chose his own selfish interests over his brother's well-being."

"But the Union army is marching on Vicksburg," he said, "and you're all alone."

"I'm not alone," she replied. "God is my protector, and you are my love. What more do I need?"

The night was spent without sleep. The minutes were too precious to waste with slumber.

In the morning Marshall rode east. Leaving his beloved in God's care, he set his mind on his mission to rescue his brother. As he traveled through enemy territory, he hid from troop transports, avoided cities and other human contact, slept in trees, and ate off the land. After a week of riding and hiding, his beard showed promise of a glorious return. With it came his old habits and old, familiar feelings. He was on a righteous mission and he was angry enough to kill anyone who tried to stop him.

Chapter 22

THE lamp of God had gone out in England. In one sentence, that was Jeremiah's assessment of the spiritual condition of his ancestral land. From Southampton, to Winchester, to Colchester, to Bedford, to Cambridge, to Norwich he preached hot sermons in cold cathedrals to paltry gatherings of worshipers who shuffled in and out of church like it was a mausoleum. It was hard for Jeremiah to blame the people; they took their cue from the ministers.

Most of the ministers Jeremiah met were professional men who were more concerned with church politics and maintaining their living then they were about spiritual things or the condition of their country. However, they were fascinated with Jeremiah. Through him they could hear firsthand accounts regarding the oddities of the United States President, Abraham Lincoln.

"Have you stood next to him? Is he really over six feet tall?"

"Did he tell any funny stories when you were with him?"

"Is his wife really insane?"

"We've heard he still chops his own wood, does he?"

"Is it true he draws his salary in gold while insisting that the soldiers be paid in greenbacks?"

To this last question—a rumor circulated widely by anti-Lincoln forces associated with the radical Republicans—

Jeremiah defended his President. It was on the return trip to Washington from Fredericksburg that Lincoln's personal secretary, John Nicolay, fervently railed against the accusation. Not only was the rumor false, but according to Nicolay, Lincoln hadn't drawn his salary for eleven months. By not drawing it, his salary accumulated interest for the United States which, Nicolay quoted Lincoln, "needs it more than I do."

It was in Bedford that Jeremiah heard one Englishman's opinion of the American civil war. "I'm surprised it took you so long to have one," the minister of Bedford sniffed. "You colonists run to violence. Look at your revolt for independence when diplomatic avenues were still available. Is it so surprising you now turn to violence to solve your internal differences? History will prove me correct. Violence will be your undoing."

The patriot in Jeremiah wanted to bash this smug, intellectual Englishman in the nose; however the diplomat in him limited his response to words. "We're a passionate people," he said. "I'll grant you that. But then we have English blood in us. My prayer for my people now that this great conflict has begun is that from this struggle we will emerge a stronger nation. After all, wasn't your Parliament born out of civil war?"

Hopping from town to town, Jeremiah chased Seth Cooper all over England. In every city, Jeremiah heard people rave about Seth's preaching. They likened him to George Whitefield, the great English evangelist of the previous century. But though Seth Cooper drew large crowds to hear a Confederate plea for British intervention, Jeremiah discovered that the reports of his effectiveness were overrated. It was the Apostle Paul in Athens all over again—much debate, but no action. Jeremiah found no great uprising of popular opinion that would force Parliament to alter its cautious approach to pleas for Southern intervention.

Jeremiah sent a letter to that effect to President Lincoln and requested he be given permission to return home. While he waited for a response, there was one thing he felt he had to do before leaving England.

He entered the village of Edenford on foot from the north, by way of Tiverton, because that was the route and mode of transportation his ancestor, Drew Morgan, had taken. Crossing over the three-tiered stone bridge that spanned the River Exe, Jeremiah felt like he was stepping back in time. Like hundreds of other small, country villages in England, Edenford had resisted change. With minor exceptions, it looked the same as it did when Drew Morgan entered it nearly two and a half centuries earlier.

At the crossroads, Jeremiah departed Bridge Street for Market Street which looped upward into the village itself. On the village green stood the stone church of which the saintly Christopher Matthews had been curate. It was here Drew Morgan was tried for trespassing and defended by Matthews, the very man he had been sent to destroy. Making his way toward the village well and High Street, he caught the attention of the townspeople. In a town this size, no stranger went unnoticed. It was true for Drew Morgan in the seventeenth century and it was true for Jeremiah Morgan in the nineteenth century.

A black-bearded man heavy with sweat swung around from the well, his bucket full. He almost ran into Jeremiah. Water sloshed in the bucket, wetting the man's shirt. "What is this? Have we suddenly become a tourist town? This isn't London, in case you couldn't tell. Travel yonder several days and maybe you'll stumble upon it." He shook his head disgustedly and carried his bucket up a side street.

Jeremiah felt self-conscious. Being the resident of a small

town himself, he felt he should have realized the unsettling influence a stranger can have on the town's daily routine. Still, there were some places he wanted to see in Edenford before he departed.

High Street ran parallel to Market Street, the town's main thoroughfare. A cobblestone lane, it was lined with a series of small residences wedged against each other. All the residences looked identical. Resting on a granite-stone foundation, the lower portion of each residence had a wooden door and two shuttered windows. Wooden beams jutted out overhead, supporting the upper floor and providing a covering for the doorways. The exterior of the upper floor consisted of four small windows set side-by-side and surrounded by white paneling. The lane was so narrow that persons in opposite upper rooms could easily reach out over the street and touch hands.

As Jeremiah walked the lane, he felt an uncomfortable closeness due to the confines of High Street. How different it was from the open fields that separated the houses in Ohio. He stopped at the second to the last door on the left side of the lane. He didn't knock, he just looked. This was the former home of Christopher Matthews and his two daughters, Nell and Jenny. It was here that Drew met and fell in love with Nell. Together, they began the Morgan line of which he, Jeremiah, was a descendant. It was in this house that Drew decoded messages from the infamous Bishop Laud, using the very Bible Jeremiah now possessed. Jeremiah wished he could have brought the Morgan family Bible with him. It would have added something to the trip, to hold the Bible bearing Drew's name in his own handwriting while standing here in front of the Matthews' house.

"What are you doing there?" A shrill voice echoed from above. A sharp-nosed woman leaned out an upstairs window two houses up the street. "Get away from there before I call the constable!"

"I mean no harm." Jeremiah flashed his warmest smile. "One of my ancestors used to live here," he explained. "I was just looking."

"Be off with you! How do I know you're not a highwayman, or worse yet, a tax collector?"

Jeremiah raised his hands in surrender. "I can assure you, madam, I'm neither. Nevertheless, I'll be on my way."

He retreated the way he came, tipping his hat to the suspicious-eyed woman as he passed. "Be quick about it!' she ordered. "Don't dawdle!"

Returning to Market Street, Jeremiah passed between the trees that separated the road from the village green. It was a working day, so the green was unpopulated. He didn't feel he was a threat to anyone here. He ambled along, savoring the old country feeling of the village. At the bowling green, he turned and surveyed the buildings of Edenford as they rose up the side of the hill. Colorful blue and yellow and green and red serges dried on the hillside. The town still produced the wool for which it was famous. He wondered if anyone in the town still made bone lace. Two hundred years earlier they lost their two most talented lace makers when the Matthews girls fled to America.

Squinting his eyes, he located a pile of stones high up the hill. He guessed they were the remains of the old castle that lay in ruins even two hundred years ago. He breathed deeply, wishing J.D. could be here with him. The village would mean the most to him since he would be the one who would carry on the Morgan spiritual heritage that had its roots here in Edenford.

Jeremiah crossed the green, crossed Bridge Street, and stepped over a low stone wall. On the other side of the wall, the ground descended in a grassy slope to the banks of the River Exe. To his right was an old stone mill. And . . . Jeremiah couldn't believe what he saw. He looked again. Now

he understood the tourist comment made by the black-bearded man at the well. Sitting on the grass watching the River
Exe flow by the village of Edenford was Seth Cooper.

Jeremiah approached him. "Come here often?"

"Jeremiah!"

For an instant there was nothing but pleasure in Seth Cooper's face. But only for an instant. Their differences and angry
parting words came rushing back to the forefront of Seth's
mind; Jeremiah could see it in his friend's eyes. Seth now
assumed a more guarded posture.

His long-time friend had aged, but then so had Jeremiah.
Gray streaks were prominent in Seth Cooper's full beard.
And while his hair was receding, leaving a wave-like patch in
the middle of his forehead, his beard was still as thick as a
brush. The years may have added some wrinkles to Seth Cooper, but they hadn't diminished the power that his strong
eyes and firm jaw commanded.

"I'd heard you were in England," he said, returning his
attention to the river.

"Mind if I sit?" Jeremiah asked.

Seth shrugged indifferently. "You follow me here?" he
asked.

"Coincidence. I didn't know you were here. But I knew I
couldn't leave England without coming here. This may be my
only chance to see Edenford. Looks like we had the same
idea."

"You make it sound as if you're leaving England."

"I've requested it. I'm accomplishing nothing here," Jeremiah said.

"Me neither."

Jeremiah settled onto the grass next to Seth. "I don't know
about you, but I didn't exactly get a hero's welcome in the
town. At the well, a man blustered something about tourists.
I didn't know what he was talking about until I saw you."

"A big man? Black hair and beard?"

"That's the one."

"The village cobbler. He works in the same house as my ancestor, David Cooper. Probably makes shoes exactly the same way too. He was not pleased when I poked my head in and asked to look around."

Jeremiah chuckled. He could relate to the reception. "They're just cautious," he said. "I guess you can't blame them. One lady thought I was a tax collector."

Seth examined Jeremiah's face. "You look like a tax collector," he said.

"Oh, thanks! I appreciate that remark."

In truth Jeremiah did appreciate the remark. Not because he wanted to look like a tax collector, but because it was this same kind of good-natured ribbing that had been a hallmark of their relationship. It was just like old times again. For the moment at least.

"Did you go to see the dyeing vats yet?" Jeremiah asked.

"Went there first. You?"

"Not yet."

It was at Edenford's blue dyeing vat that the bond between the Morgans and the Coopers was forged. When little Thomas Cooper was accidentally knocked into the vat, it was Drew Morgan who risked his own life by reaching into the vat and pulling him out. He saved the Cooper boy's life. Although he was disfigured for the rest of his life, Thomas and Drew became close friends after both families fled to Boston colony. It was Thomas' line through which Seth Cooper traced his ancestry. If it hadn't been for Drew Morgan's heroic effort, Seth and Daniel Cooper would never have existed.

"I'm glad I came to England," Jeremiah said. "I was having my doubts earlier, but now I'm glad I came. If I accomplished nothing else, it was worth the trip just to be here. This little village puts things in perspective for me."

"How so?"

Jeremiah reached down and plucked a blade of grass. He studied it, then twirled it between his thumb and forefinger as he sought words that would accurately convey his feelings. "For most of my life I have felt unworthy to have my name in the Morgan family Bible. I didn't feel I had done anything of merit, at least not anything like the other names above mine in the family Bible, especially the first one—Drew Morgan. How does one compete with a legend? I was convinced I would live and die in obscurity in the tiny hamlet of Point Providence. My recurring prayer was that God would allow me the opportunity to do something of significance."

"God answered your prayer," Seth said. "I heard about the spiritual revival among the Union troops. And you have been a consultant to Abraham Lincoln himself."

An amused grin stretched across Jeremiah's face. "You know all that?"

"I was given a report informing me you were coming to England and why."

"An accurate report," Jeremiah said. "And that's my point! God has answered my prayer. By His grace I did those things. And now, sitting here, it doesn't matter. You know what matters most to me right now? My family and you."

Seth looked at him hard, examining his face for traces of insincerity.

Jeremiah nodded. "I have come to realize that there are forces in this world far more powerful than any of us. My family has been ripped from my house and scattered across the nation. There was nothing I could do to stop it. That same force pulled our families apart, placing my closest friend on the opposing side of a bitter and bloody war. And again there was nothing I could do about it. Why, I'd have greater success stopping a hurricane with my bare hands than I would trying to stop the winds of hate and war that have crippled our nation. For the longest time it bothered me that there were forces I could not control. After all, I was a Morgan! My name is written in the front of the Morgan family Bible!"

Seth grinned. "I understand what you're saying. Sometimes I've felt that having my name in the Cooper family Bible is more of a curse than a blessing."

Jeremiah lay back on the grass with his hands folded behind his head. "As I traveled here to Edenford, I realized it was all a striving after the wind. Why worry over things I cannot control or change? Will America become two separate countries? I don't know. And there's little I—or any other Morgan—can do about it one way or the other. But there are some things I *can* do, and already have done, that can change the course of America. Not today, maybe not tomorrow, but the change will come."

"How are you going to change the course of a nation?"

Jeremiah grinned. "I have raised four children to fear God and live according to His ways. Don't you see? This is the best thing I can do to effect godly change! Now, instead of one Morgan doing something for the good of the nation, we have six—including Susanna, of course. Then, when my children have children, we'll have sixteen or so godly people effecting godly change in whatever city they live. Seth, I've taken comfort in the fact that my greatest legacy to America is to train my children in the ways of the Lord. I can die content knowing I have done that."

Seth picked a blade of grass of his own and said, "Lo, children are an heritage of the Lord: and the fruit of the womb is His reward."

Jeremiah bolted upright. "Exactly! Where is that found?"

"Psalm 127:3."

"I like that," Jeremiah said, making a mental note of the reference.

"Speaking of children," Seth said, "what have you heard

from yours?"

Shaking his head, Jeremiah said, "Seth, old friend, you always knew how to cut to the heart of a matter. While I'm spouting theory, you want to know exactly where these Christian children of mine are exerting their godly heritage."

Seth smiled warmly. Jeremiah sobered.

"I sailed for England shortly after the Battle of Fredericksburg. When I left, J.D. was missing. Since my arrival I've learned he was wounded. That's all. I don't know the extent of his injury. As for Marshall and Willy, they ran headlong into Caleb McKenna's adopted son, Ben, and went west somewhere. We haven't heard a word from them. And Sarah . . . " Jeremiah sighed heavily, " . . . I mistakenly agreed to let her and Jenny Parsons go to New York. Sarah was offered a writing position with the Christian Tract Society." His face grew long, his eyes moist. "I received a letter from Susanna a few days ago. She's beside herself. It seems the girls are missing. The Society has no idea where they are. Again, somehow McKenna was involved. The girls were picked up in his carriage, but the driver claims they insisted on getting out at the hotel district against his wishes." Jeremiah wiped his eyes. "They haven't been seen since."

"They're in Manchester," Seth said.

"What?"

"They're in Manchester with Emma. Apparently they had quite a scare, but they're safe."

Jeremiah couldn't help himself. He leaned over and hugged his friend. "How did you ever accomplish that?"

"Thanks for the credit, but I didn't have anything to do with it!" Seth replied. "From what Emma said in her letter, McKenna hatched a plot by promising to help Sarah get a book published. He substituted secret government papers for the manuscript and arranged for her to be found with them during a clandestine meeting with Daniel."

"Daniel? How did he get involved?"

"Somehow, McKenna has ties with Confederate blockade runners. He used his influence to arrange for Daniel to be in New York. According to Emma, Jenny was the hero. She was the one who first saw through the plot and created their chance for escape. She foiled his attempt to exact revenge on us."

"I always liked that girl," Jeremiah said. He was both angry and relieved at hearing the news of Sarah and Jenny. "McKenna's adopted son is no better," he said. "I've never seen a young man his age so bitter."

"That brings us to an important question," Seth said. "How do you feel about your daughter living with the enemy?"

"What enemy? She's with Emma."

The remainder of the afternoon Jeremiah Morgan and Seth Cooper strolled around Edenford as inconspicuously as the residents would let them. They found their way up the hillside to the crumbled site of the ancient stone castle. All that was left were a few scattered stones. Except for several places where stones were still held together by mortar, it was difficult to tell it had ever been anything but natural formations.

"This is where Drew Morgan and Nell Matthews first kissed," Jeremiah said.

Seth sat on a stone and folded his arms. "How do you know so many details about your ancestor?" he asked.

"In his later years, Drew recorded his experiences in a diary. I believe Alfred Morgan still has it in Boston, if he's still alive. He's one of the wealthy Morgans. I got to read it once during a summer visit to Boston. I had to sit in Uncle Alfred's parlor and read it with him watching me. He didn't trust anybody when it came to Drew Morgan's diary. Anyway, I remember much of it and even copied portions of it."

"You realize, don't you," Seth said, "that your legendary ancestor stole Nell Matthews away from a Cooper."

Jeremiah laughed. "It just goes to show that both the Morgans and the Coopers recognize a quality woman when they see one."

The two men overlooked the village that held so much history for them. The River Exe flowed lazily by the stone mill just as it had done for the past two centuries. The colorful serges stretched out and drying in long strips made the hillside look like a patchwork quilt. The residents of Edenford moved purposefully through the streets going about their daily business.

"Jeremiah . . . " Seth stammered, " . . . it was wrong of me to leave Point Providence the way I did. I felt bad about it the moment I climbed into the carriage, but my pride kept me from doing the right thing by giving you the benefit of the doubt."

"Seth, you know I'd never do anything to hurt our friendship."

The bearded preacher nodded in contrition. "I know that. And I knew it then too. I was just too pigheaded to admit it to myself. Believe me, I paid penance for my actions, though. Emma and Daniel both chastised me mercilessly all the way home. Anyway, I want to extend my sincere apologies and ask you to forgive me. I don't want to lose you as a friend."

With a downward gaze, Jeremiah replied, "I'm glad to hear you say that. Ironic, isn't it, that we have to travel all the way to England to put our differences behind us? I knew that if we could just get together and talk things out, we would become friends again. We have too much history to let one crisis destroy what we both hold dear."

Seth jumped to his feet with a look on his face as though he'd just had a revelation from God. "Why not?" he said.

"Why not what?"

"Jeremiah, you're a genius!"

"That may be; now tell me what I said that was so smart."

Striding back and forth, Seth repeated a few of Jeremiah's phrases. "You said, 'If we could just get together and talk, we would become friends again.' And, 'We have too much history to let a crisis destroy what we hold dear.' "

"All right, that's what I said. What does it mean?"

"It means, Jeremiah Morgan, that you and I alone may hold the key to resolving our national dispute!"

"If that's so, I *am* smart! Now tell me how we're going to do it."

"You have President Lincoln's ear, don't you?"

Jeremiah was reluctant to claim any influence over the President. He said, "Whenever I've spoken with him, he seems to value what I say. How much he agrees with is hard for me to say."

"Well, I daresay he gives your opinion more value than you give yourself credit for. Now I, on the other hand, have President Davis' ear. What if we were to suggest that the two men get together and talk? Just the two of them and the two of us, in a neutral place—maybe even here in England. I've heard that Lincoln is a spiritual man."

"He is."

"So is Davis. Do you see where I'm going? If we can get them together . . . if we could get them to pray together, maybe we could become friends again. After all, as a nation we have too much good history to let a crisis destroy the things we hold dear. What do you think?"

Jeremiah liked the idea. *If it worked for him and Seth, why couldn't it work for the two Presidents? And what harm was there in trying?*

"The more I think about it," Seth said excitedly, "the more convinced I am that if we can get these two men on their knees before the God whom they both worship, through their common faith they will find grounds for resolving this conflict!"

On the hillside overlooking Edenford, the two old friends got down on their knees and committed their plan to God and asked Him to heal their nation.

Back in London, the two men made initial arrangements through diplomatic channels. Without disclosing their proposal, they arranged for Seth to accompany Jeremiah to Washington where they would meet with Abraham Lincoln. Then the two men would go to Richmond where they would meet with Jefferson Davis. As they prepared to board the ship that would take them back to America, their hopes were high.

A telegram caught up with Jeremiah just as they were boarding. It was from Susanna.

"Oh no," he said after reading it.

"What is it?" Seth asked.

"We've received a letter from Marshall. Willy's been captured by Confederate soldiers. He was taken to Andersonville Prison."

"Dear God, watch over Willy and keep him safe," Seth prayed aloud. Then to Jeremiah he said, "When we get to Richmond, I'll do everything in my power to get him released."

"Thank you, dear friend," Jeremiah said. "Andersonville. I've heard it has a high mortality rate. Is that true?"

"It's true," Seth Cooper said softly.

Chapter 23

NOT all the soldiers who died storming Marye's Heights at Fredericksburg died from ammunition wounds. Many of the wounded were burned alive in a grass fire started by an artillery shell. Those who survived the fire lay on the battlefield overnight while the temperature dipped below freezing, which was made to feel even colder by a stiff wind. Exposed to the elements was a carpet of bodies and wounded. Among them was J.D. Morgan.

Slipping in and out of consciousness, J.D. preferred the unconscious state. He didn't mind the blackness. He didn't fear death. What he feared was waking up again to the pain. He was pinned under a stack of dead men, his head spinning and his stomach nauseous, choking on the grass fire's black smoke, shivering in the frigid wind, his leg hurting beyond his ability to endure it, pushing him over the precipice of consciousness; waking up again and finding that nothing had changed, that he was still coughing, still freezing, still nauseous, and that his jaw hurt from clenching his teeth all night long. J.D. felt that if there was a place worse than hell, he was in it.

He lay facedown stretched over a dead soldier; his head bent sideways at an awkward angle, his cheek pressed against weeds and dirt. Breathing was difficult. He had to push up with all his might to give his lungs a little room to take a deep breath.

All around him J.D. heard men crying. Some cried for water, others for God to take them home, still others cried with unintelligible groans. A couple of times during the night he awoke to the delirious cry of a man calling the name of his girl back home. With chest-rattling sobs the wounded soldier called her name again and again: "Amanda . . . Amanda . . . Amanda . . . . look what they've done to me, Amanda . . . Amanda . . . please don't be mad at me, Amanda, please . . . Amanda. . . . " Then all was quiet. And as much as hearing Amanda's name distressed him, not hearing it pained him even more. It meant that Amanda would never see her man again. Tears rolled down J.D.'s temples and wet the ground. He prayed for Amanda and her dead soldier. Then the blackness came over him again.

Sounds were fuzzy. Sentences came in fragments.

"Look at this — swollen twice its size . . . "

" . . . has no head. Do you see a . . . "

" . . . charred ones go over there . . . "

" . . . did we do to get this duty?"

"I got a live one over here!"

J.D. squinted at the light. He felt a weight lifted off his back.

"This one's breathing! Bad leg wound! Can someone take him?"

" . . . at this one! Five, six, seven bullet wounds in his chest!"

"Hey! I need some help here! We've got a live one!"

J.D. felt someone grabbing his arm. Then he felt and heard no more.

Wooden rafters came into focus, supported by brick walls. The images dulled. J.D. blinked them back into focus. He turned his head. He was on the floor, his head elevated. Something soft. Gray. A folded blanket or piece of clothing.

A man lay moaning on the floor next to him, and another man next to him, and so on in a line. At the far end of the brick building was a double door. Soldiers were carrying a wounded man in on a litter.

The place reeked of sweaty men and filth and urine. And the noises hurt his ears. Men shrieking for help. Sobbing in pain. Yelling at one another and being yelled at. In the midst of the pandemonium, a perky corporal strolled by.

"Hey! Captain Lucky's awake!"

A corporal with freckles and bushy black eyebrows appeared from nowhere. A bundle of blankets was wedged under his arm. The corporal's smile showed white, even teeth, the whitest teeth J.D. had ever seen.

"Hope you don't mind us calling you Captain Lucky. The Doc started it. He was working on you and he kept saying over and over again, 'This man's lucky to be alive, this man's lucky to be alive.' When he finished working on you, he patted your head and said, 'May you have a long and happy life, Captain Lucky.' So you can see why we call you that What's your real name, Captain?"

J.D. stuck his tongue forward to wet his lips. Dry flesh rubbed against chapped skin. His mouth was void of moisture. "Mor . . ." He succeeded only in pulling up a breathy, scratchy sound from his throat. He tried again, "Mor . . ."

"You wait right here, Captain Lucky. I'll get you a cup of water. That ought to help."

J.D. watched the corporal hurry down a path between the wounded soldiers. In the interval he tried wetting his lips again. There was not enough moisture on his tongue even to make it sticky.

"Here you go!" The corporal returned minus the blankets, carrying a tin cup. He kneeled beside J.D. and lifted J.D.'s head. A pain shot up J.D.'s neck and exploded in his head like a firecracker. He winced to fight back the hurt. Lukewarm metal touched his lips followed by a splash of liquid. It was just a sip, but what a sip! It washed over J.D.'s tongue, splashed against his cheeks and teeth, then slid smoothly down the length of his throat. The second sip tasted even better.

"Not too much at once," the corporal said. He pulled the cup away and set it on the floor. J.D. followed the cup with his eyes.

"There. Is that better? Now can you say your name?"

"Morgan," J.D. said. It was still scratchy sounding, but understandable. "J.D. Morgan."

"Nice to meet you, Captain Morgan. My name is Ambrose Greeley. Yes, just like the general and the newspaper publisher. Everyone thinks of them immediately. But someday, everyone will hear my name and think of me instead of them. Because someday I'll be a famous painter."

"Oils?" J.D. asked.

"Yeah!" Corporal Greeley's eyes lit up at the correct guess. "Are you an artist too?"

"My brother is. Mostly pen and ink."

"Well, you remember my name, Captain—Ambrose Greeley. Because someday I'll be famous, just like Rembrandt and da Vinci and Rubens."

J.D. managed a half-smile. "I'll remember, Corporal." The overly-pleased look on Greeley's face indicated that the aspiring artist didn't usually get such a positive reaction to his announcement of impending fame. "Can you tell me something, Corporal?"

"What do you need to know?"

"How bad off am I?"

Greeley blushed. "You must think I'm a strutting rooster the way I'm going on about myself with you lying here in a field hospital. Tell me, how are you feeling?"

"Can't say that I feel much of anything right now. I seem

to be numb all over."

Bushy eyebrows fell forward, perplexed. "Can't be the medicine, because we don't have any that would do that. I know because most everyone is calling for something to help ease their pain and we're plum out."

"When will I be able to get up?"

Greeley looked to the far end of the building. "You really should be talking to the doctor," he said. "You wait right here. I'll go get him."

The corporal was up and gone before J.D. could say anything. Like a man with a mission, Greeley made his way through the other patients to get to the doctor. J.D. watched while the corporal tapped the doctor on the shoulder. The doctor was bent over a man whose midsection was nothing more than a bloody mess. The doctor looked over his shoulder at J.D., then back at Greeley without ever once stopping what he was doing on that soldier's belly. The doctor shook his head. Greeley said something which really set the doctor off. The doctor spoke in a low tone to the corporal, but by the way the doctor's head bobbed it was clear that whatever he said, he said in anger.

J.D. turned his attention to the oasis in a tin cup next to him. He tried to reach for it, but his arm got no farther than an inch off the floor. He regretted the attempt. Not only did he fail to reach the cup, the movement seemed to wake up his body's senses, particularly the ones that scream pain. Like a smoldering fire fanned to life, the pain started with his leg wound, then spread though his trunk to his head and arms. His eyes rolled upward in his head.

"Captain? You all right?" Greeley was standing over him.

"Pain."

"Doc said you should be hurting. Something awful is what he said. Sorry, Captain, but we don't have anything to give you. Would you like some more water?"

Gritting his teeth, J.D. nodded.

Again the corporal lifted J.D.'s head. Sips of water doused the burning in his throat momentarily, but it was of small comfort.

"The doctor isn't coming, is he?" J.D. asked.

"No, sir. He told me to tell you myself."

"Tell me what?"

The corporal glanced down toward J.D.'s feet, then back again quickly. "You've only got one leg. The doctor had to cut the right leg off."

"That isn't a very funny joke, Corporal. I can feel both legs, and the one is just about killing me with pain."

Greeley mustered up the most sincere face he could. "I'm telling you the truth, Captain. The pain may still be there, but your leg's not."

J.D. tried to sit up. He couldn't. Greeley hurried to his side and helped him. J.D. counted only one leg. A bloody bandage marked the end of his right side just below the hip. He stared, as if by staring he could make it suddenly appear. A rising tide of nausea prompted him to give up the attempt.

"Put me down," he said.

Greeley gently lowered him. "You all right, Captain?"

J.D. looked up at the rafters. It was a simple question the corporal asked. But he didn't know the answer to it right now.

"There's more," Greeley said, apologetically. When J.D. did not respond, Greeley continued anyway. "I don't know if you're a father or not," he paused for a response but got none, "but the doctor says you'll never be a father, that is, if you aren't one already."

The words were spoken, but J.D. wasn't ready to receive them. He reasoned that the words weren't true unless he acknowledged them. So he said nothing. He did nothing.

"Well, that's all," Greeley said. "Sorry to be the one to tell you. If you need anything, I mean anything at all, Captain, you call for me. I mean it!"

J.D.'s eyes were fixed on the rafters when Greeley left him. They stayed that way for over an hour before they glossed over. Tears ran down both sides of his face. He'd held off the words as long as he could. But they wouldn't go away, leaving him no other choice but to acknowledge them. By acknowledging them, they became true.

He wept. "Jenny . . . Jenny. . . . "

In his lighter moods J.D. thought, *I can't wait to get home so that Willy can give me crutch lessons.* In his darker moods he envisioned Jenny abandoning him for a man with two legs who could give her children. Thoughts of his father's reaction also haunted him. All of his life J.D. had been trained as the one who would continue the Morgan family—physically as well as spiritually. *How could he pass along the Morgan heritage if there were no children to pass it on to?*

As soon as he was able, he was sitting up. Not long afterward he was given a crutch. There were no instructions of any kind given him. No assistant to help him steady himself, or pick him up when he fell. There were just too many sick and wounded with not enough corporals like Greeley to go around.

Deciding that the faster he learned to walk with the crutch, the sooner he would get out of the hospital, J.D. set himself to the task of navigating with only one leg. Once he got the balancing part down, he had to adjust to the pain under his arm. But it wasn't long before he was able to make it all the way around the outside of the building which served as the Union field hospital. He looked forward to the twice-daily outside strolls. It got him away from the noise and pungent stench of the hospital.

It was a bright day with high, overcast clouds. Not yet spring, but warm enough that he wanted to stay outside as long as he could. Although he was able to circle the hospital in under a half hour, he deliberately slowed his pace. It wasn't a pretty enough day to make his depression disappear, but it was nice enough to make his emotions easier to live with.

On the back side of the hospital building a tent had been erected. It was here the doctor performed the surgeries. Mercifully, J.D. could not remember occupying the sole table in the tent. But it was there his leg was removed.

The tent held a strange fascination for him. He was attracted to it in an unsettled way. He reasoned he should be repulsed by it; instead he was drawn to it. And he didn't know why.

Leaning against the brick hospital building, he stared at the tent. To one side, soldiers were lined up on the ground, some conscious, some not. They were waiting their turn on the table. They sat in the midst of discarded haversacks and weapons that they no longer needed. Inside the tent, the doctor stood over a screaming soldier. He gave the man a stick to bite on. There was no time for talk or explanations or consultation. The doctor reached for the bone saw. He steadied the soldier's left leg. With the first stroke of the blade the soldier fainted. It was better that way.

In a matter of fifteen minutes, three patients were worked on in the tent. One leg, two arms. A pile of human limbs was stacked by the entrance. The doctor followed the litter of his third patient into the field hospital, leaving the tent unoccupied for the moment.

At the far end of the building a captain appeared. His eyes were fixed on the tent. For the longest time he didn't move, he just stared at the tent. Greeley came around the corner and tried to get the captain to return to the hospital. The captain wouldn't hear of it. When Greeley grabbed the man's remaining arm to turn him around, the man roared and sent the corporal skidding across the ground. Greeley dusted himself off and disappeared back around the corner.

J.D. watched as the captain with one arm approached the surgical tent. He just stood there and continued to stare.

Then a thought came to J.D. More than a thought. A revelation. Suddenly he knew what was disturbing the one-armed captain, and him too. He knew why they were drawn to the tent. And although it was too late for him, it was not too late to help the one-armed captain. J.D. realized it now. They weren't drawn to the tent. They were drawn to the pile of limbs in front of the tent.

Pushing off from the building, J.D. approached the captain and stood next to him. He waited. No words were spoken. The captain saw J.D.'s crutch, looked down at the missing leg, and then looked into J.D.'s eyes. They understood each other.

Motioning with his head, J.D. walked to the pile of limbs. The captain followed him. J.D. nodded to the captain, encouraging him to do what he must do. The captain got down on his knees and sorted through the pile of discarded legs and arms until he found what he was looking for—his own arm. Pulling it from the heap, he cradled it in his good arm. Then J.D. led the man to a field behind the tent. J.D. picked up a bayonet from the discarded weapons pile along the way.

In a quiet place under a tree, J.D. used the bayonet to dig a grave for the captain's arm. He plunged and scooped while the captain looked on in silence. When he'd made a hole roughly two feet deep, he looked up for the captain's approval. The man dropped to his knees and gently lowered the severed limb into the grave. With his good hand he helped J.D. cover the spot. The burial complete, they remained at the grave for a few minutes, then the captain stood and walked away. J.D. never saw him again.

As J.D. returned to the hospital, he felt better than he had since the day of the battle. Not so much physically, but emotionally. In his mind, he buried his leg with the captain's arm. It was no longer a part of him. And he knew he would be able to go on living without it.

Two days later he was transferred to a hospital in Washington.

"There he is! Hey, Captain Morgan! Remember us?"

Two grinning privates—one tall and skinny, the other small but manly—strode down the center aisle that separated the hospital beds. Although there was continuous noise day and night in this hospital too, there weren't the shrieks of men in agony, nor was there the stench. Large windows kept the room bright during the day. The hardwood floors were polished. And the hospital had beds, a significant improvement over the floor at Fredericksburg.

The boisterous privates had interrupted some serious thoughts prompted by recent events and correspondence. Upon his arrival in Washington, J.D. had received a visit from a Mr. Nicolay, President Lincoln's personal secretary. The bearded secretary handed J.D. a handwritten note from the President expressing the chief executive's wishes that he recover speedily. Lincoln also encouraged him to take comfort in the fact that his sacrifice was for the greater good of the nation. Furthermore, Nicolay informed J.D. that his father had been sent to England by the President to preach the cause of the Union among the British people.

As astounding as all this was to J.D., it was his personal correspondence that had the more profound effect on him. Particularly the letter from Jenny in New York. To say the contents of the letter were disturbing would be like saying that the battle at Fredericksburg was a minor Union setback.

Jenny's letter upset him so much, it was all he could do to

keep from marching out of the hospital, finding a buggy, and setting out immediately for New York. First, there was the fact that Jenny had been accosted at night on the streets of the city. Then there was the news that prompted her letter, including the document given to her by the woman who had accosted her. The document was a testimony regarding the past, but it had power to shatter the present.

He lay in bed and stewed. *What should he do? Should he send word to his father in England or wait for him to return? Should he write his mother? Should he do nothing? Something? If so, what?* J.D. prayed for an answer, but none was forthcoming. So he changed his prayer to the effect that should the need for action become evident, he would have the wisdom to know what to do and the courage to do it. He was praying this prayer when the two privates strolled down the hospital ward's center aisle yelling greetings to him.

"Hey, Captain! You're lookin' mighty good!" Rice exclaimed.

The two privates approached the bed, taking deliberate pains not to look directly at J.D.'s bandaged appendage. Both boys were recent recruits from Columbus, having been assigned to J.D.'s company a few weeks before the Battle of Fredericksburg. It was J.D. who acquainted them with the rituals of camp life with the Jehovah's Avengers.

Rice was the taller of the two boys. Lanky, hollow-cheeked, and clean-shaven, some of the men of the company had kidded him that all he had to do during a battle was to turn sideways. The Rebels wouldn't be able to see him, let alone hit him. Maybe there was more truth than fiction in the joke. The boy survived the storming of Marye's Heights. The other soldier, Dana, was small in stature, but had the build of a mature man. Although both men were the same age, nineteen, Rice looked like a big child and Dana like a thirty-year-old.

"When are you coming back?" Dana asked, ignoring the fact that J.D. had only one leg.

"Yeah, we really need you," Rice added. "The company just isn't the same without you, Captain."

"You're not going to let a little scrape like that keep you outta the war, are you?" Dana asked.

J.D. knew the men were trying to cheer him up by making light of his situation. He granted them the insensitivity of youth. They hadn't experienced enough life to realize the depth of his loss. He shifted the course of the conversation rather than join in their nonsense talk.

"How are the two of you getting along?" he said.

"We're doing as fine as can be expected," Dana replied. "'Course we haven't done much but live in the mud lately."

"And the camp's real spooky," Rice said, "walking through it knowin' that half the fellows we just met aren't there anymore."

"It's like walkin' through a graveyard," Dana added.

"We talk about them all the time. Like Wheelright—he always made me laugh." Rice held a hand to his midriff. His outstretched hand spanned the width of his body.

"And Lieutenant Logan! I sure do miss his singing. And Mr. Hawkins, I miss him probably the most."

"Yeah, Mr. Hawkins. He was the nicest man I ever met, next to you that is, Captain Morgan," said Rice.

"Our little company has almost disappeared, hasn't it?" J.D. said. There was a break in the flow of conversation. Then J.D. asked, "What about Colonel McKenna? How is he treating you now that I'm gone?"

Rice and Dana exchanged glances. Dana nodded to Rice, designating him to be the one to report on Colonel McKenna.

"It's been real strange, Captain Morgan. Something must have happened to him at Fredericksburg, 'cause he ain't been the same since. Real quiet all the time. He walks around camp and doesn't yell at anybody. Even when somebody messes up, he'll jus' tell them to fix it and he goes on his way."

"That doesn't sound like the Colonel McKenna I know," J.D. said.

"My point exactly!" Rice cried. "He spends most of his time alone in his tent. 'Course he comes out for staff meetings and the like, but with us in winter quarters and all, we've got a lot more time on our hands. He stays in his tent all alone. Captain Morgan, did he take a whack on the side of the head or something?"

"Colonel McKenna was in an observer's position during the battle," J.D. replied, "at the top of a church steeple."

"Maybe he fell down the belfry steps or something," Rice offered.

"Just don't make sense, that's all we're saying," said Dana. "In fact, Rice here walked by his tent one day and he heard the colonel singing."

"Singing?"

"That's right!" Rice recalled. "It was real low-like, not rowdy or loud, just real low and soft like he was singing to himself."

"Did you recognize the song?" J.D. asked.

"Not directly," Rice replied, "but it sounded like a hymn of some sort."

"A hymn?"

"I couldn't be sure," Rice said, "but that's what it sounded like."

J.D. grunted in contemplation. "Are you sure we're talking about the same Colonel McKenna?"

The two privates laughed at the obvious joke. "We kinda like him this way, don't we, Rice?" Dana nudged his partner who nodded his head enthusiastically.

"Shh!" Dana said suddenly. In a whisper. "Look who's at the door."

"Well, speak of the devil himself," Rice said in a low voice.

Standing at the double doors leading into the hospital ward was Colonel Benjamin McKenna. He was in full uniform, looking ready for inspection. He gazed up and down the rows of beds looking for someone. Spotting J.D., he marched toward the bed, his boots clicking on the hardwood floors. His eyes were clear, his jaw set firm.

Colonel Ben McKenna stood at attention at the end of J.D. Morgan's hospital bed. He said, "Captain Morgan, may I have a word with you?"

Chapter 24

THE Ben McKenna who stood at the foot of J.D.'s hospital bed was not the same man who had badgered him on
the training field in Ohio. Gone was the cockiness in his
posture. Gone was the naked ambition in his eyes. Gone was
the superior smirk that had, to the man, so infuriated the
Jehovah's Avengers. The man at the foot of the bed stood
with head bowed, his hat held in front of him with two
hands. He had the demeanor a man who had been whipped in
a fight.

Rice and Dana sprang to their feet and saluted him.

"Morgan, I want to speak to you," he said. Then, acknowledging Rice and Dana, he added, "But I can come back later."

"We was just leaving, sir," Rice offered, stiff-backed and
wide-eyed.

"Just leaving, yessir. We've outlasted our welcome, sir. We
were just getting up to leave, sir, . . . like Rice . . . uh, Private
Rice said, sir," Dana stammered.

The two privates saluted again, edging their way past the
superior officer as if he were a cobra about to strike.

With the two privates gone, McKenna motioned toward
J.D.'s bandaged stump with his hat. "How is your recovery
progressing?" he inquired.

"I have my good days and bad, sir," J.D. said. He started
to explain that the emotional wounds were healing more

slowly then the physical ones, but he cut short his response, interpreting the colonel's interest in his wound as mere polite inquiry.

McKenna cleared his throat. "If anyone can suffer a loss like yours and find a way to turn it around, you can," he said. A half-smile accompanied the comment. "If it were me, I don't know if I'd be able to survive it."

A compliment. Did Colonel McKenna just pay him a compliment? "You may be giving me more credit than I deserve, sir," J.D. replied hesitantly.

"No, I don't think so. I know you. If fact, for the first time, I think I understand you. You have an uncommon inner strength, like your father. For the longest time it baffled me. I was taught that a man's inner strength was self-generated through ambition and pride and sheer willpower. Yet you and your father know nothing of these things. And lately I've realized these things can burn a man up inside. At least, that's what they were doing to me."

This isn't right, J.D. thought. *Why is McKenna doing this?* Then he remembered Jenny's letter and this new McKenna began to make sense. In her letter, Jenny had described how Caleb McKenna was showering Sarah with compliments and praise, earning her gratitude—but to what purpose? Jenny was convinced that whatever his purpose, it was no good. *Was Ben McKenna doing the same thing? Like father, like son?*

"I came to apologize," McKenna said. "I'm . . . " he glanced uncertainly at the bandaged stump, "I'm responsible for the loss of your leg."

J.D. looked at his stump, then at the colonel. "I don't understand," he said. "How are you responsible? This is the result of a Confederate bullet."

McKenna lowered his gaze. He fidgeted with the brim of his hat. It was so unlike him to fidget, let alone lower his gaze. There wasn't a man in the Jehovah's Avengers company who had not felt the chill of Colonel McKenna's icy stare boring into him.

"Do you recall the story of King David and Uriah?" McKenna asked.

J.D. nodded. "To cover his adulterous relationship with Uriah's wife, Bathsheba, King David sent orders to have Uriah placed in the front of the battle, then to have the other soldiers pull back, leaving Uriah vulnerable. When the orders were carried out, Uriah was killed."

McKenna looked impressed. "You know your Bible," he said. "I had to look it up."

"For what purpose?"

Taking a deep breath, McKenna said, "My father instructed me to do something similar to you. I purposely placed the Jehovah's Avengers in the front lines knowing that they would suffer the greatest casualties. It was not a tactical decision, but a personal one. I did it so that you would be killed."

"Why would you do such a thing?" J.D. cried. "Why would you and your father want to kill me?"

McKenna looked into J.D.'s eyes and couldn't hold the gaze. Staring at his hat he replied, "Are you aware that your father married my adopted father's only daughter? And that she died in childbirth? And that Caleb McKenna adopted me to compensate for his loss?"

Cautiously, J.D. said, "Yes."

"My father blames your father for his daughter's death. Have you ever met Caleb McKenna?" the colonel asked.

"No, sir. I have not."

"If you knew him you would understand that he is a powerful force. He is not a man to forgive wrongs he perceives have been done to him, nor does he forget them. And he will do everything within his power—which is considerable—to destroy the people who have wronged him."

"My father," J.D. said. "Is he in danger?"

"Though my father has never told me this directly," McKenna replied, "the way I figure it, he wants to inflict upon your father the same pain he felt when his daughter died. He will not rest until Jeremiah Morgan mourns the death of one or more of his children."

"Sarah and Jenny!" J.D. cried breathlessly.

" . . . have eluded him," McKenna said.

"They're safe? Where are they right now?" J.D.'s hands pressed against the bed. He was lifting himself out.

"I don't know," McKenna replied. "And neither does my father."

J.D. plopped back onto the bed.

"I received a cable informing me that if I saw them I was to inform the Secret Service that they were transporting valuable government documents to a Southern agent."

"What!"

McKenna shrugged. "All I know," he said apologetically, "is that they are currently out of his reach. That in itself is good."

J.D. sank back onto the bed in an attempt to digest this information. The more he thought, the more intense became his emotions. He remembered the kind-hearted cabinetmaker who had survived the Mexican War only now to be killed because of one man's personal thirst for revenge. "You deliberately sent good men to the slaughter just to get to me?" he said with clenched fists. His voice shook. "Vern . . . "

McKenna cut him off, completing his thought, " . . . Hawkins. Yes, I know their names! Every one of them! Chase, Wheelright . . . " McKenna cried angrily. "I watched every one of them die! I watched through my telescope as artillery shells blew them apart! I watched as wave after wave of them melted on the ground like snowflakes. Don't you think I haven't been tortured by their memories? Every night I close my eyes and see them! Every night!" His voice quivered uncontrollably. "Every night . . . every night!"

McKenna looked away, fighting to rein in his emotions. The low din of hospital routine and other conversations spilled into their area.

After several moments, J.D. said, "Why are you telling me this?"

"To ask your forgiveness," McKenna said. Matter-of-factly, he added, "I don't expect you to grant it. But I felt I had to ask." He turned to leave.

"Wait! Colonel . . ."

McKenna continued walking.

"Ben . . ."

At the sound of his name, McKenna stopped, but didn't turn around.

"Ben . . . please come back," J.D. said. "There's more to it, isn't there? You didn't come here just to ease your guilt. Tell me! I want to know why you came!"

When Ben McKenna turned around, his cheeks were tracked with tears. He started to say something, but couldn't. He swallowed, looked up at the ceiling and tried again.

"I want to be like you," he said, "and your father." He bit his lower lip in an unsuccessful attempt to hold back a flood of grief.

"Like me?"

McKenna nodded. "I'm tired of hating, of hurting people, of using people, of being afraid of everyone . . . afraid that they'll bury me before I can bury them. When I saw you and your father at the revival services . . . the love you have for each other . . . I always thought that kind of thing was a weakness . . . but then I saw the way it changed men's lives . . . how it brought them together . . . gave them peace . . . and how they looked up to you." He brushed back tears. "Do you have any idea how much those men loved you? They weren't charging into enemy guns because they believed in a cause! They were following *you!* They would have followed you anywhere!"

He broke down. Sobs punctuated his sentences. "Do you know . . . what I was thinking when I was up in that church steeple? I was thinking that if they knew I was trying to kill you, they would charge up that hill anyway . . . and that they would most assuredly surround you . . . protect you . . . jump in front of a bullet if it would save you! Do you realize how much I hated you at that moment? Truly hated you? I hated you because you made me realize how miserable I was — how worthless my life was!"

He produced a handkerchief and dried his face. "That night I was sure you had died. Do you see the irony of that? The miserable creature was still alive and you were dead! I was going to kill myself . . . but I didn't have the nerve to do even that! Then the thought came to me, that maybe I could replace you . . . do the kind of things you did . . . be the kind of person you were. At first I thought I was only fooling myself, but then I remembered what your father said during the revival services. That it was God who changes us, recreates us into His image. So, instead of killing my body, I killed the old Ben McKenna and asked God to make a new one." He wiped his face again.

J.D. said nothing. It was almost too much for him to accept. But the proof was standing in front of him.

"Do you realize how fortunate you are?" McKenna asked. "I'm not talking about the fact that you're alive. I'm talking about your family. At the enlistment camp I hated you and Marshall and Willy because you cared for one another. You stuck up for each another. And then there's your father. Do you realize that I would give anything to have a father like yours? Let alone to have a faith like yours?"

J.D. was stunned. He was reeling from the revelatory blows. Ben McKenna's unexpected confession was only part of it. This was the answer to his earlier prayer! And not only had God given him the wisdom to recognize it—just as he had prayed—God had given him the words he needed to verify it! Two words. Like Gideon's fleece. J.D. laid them out between him and Colonel Ben McKenna to see what would happen.

J.D. said, "You can."

"Can what? Have a faith like yours?" McKenna smiled. It was a warm, confident smile with no hint of boasting in it. "Someday, perhaps. I have a lot to learn and a lot of bad attitudes to overcome. But I've begun the journey, and that's the important thing. Jesus Christ is my Lord now. I've been reading the Bible so that I might know Him and His ways better."

Just like Rice and Dana reported. "You've also been singing hymns in your tent," J.D. added with a grin.

An astonished look appeared on McKenna's face.

"One hears rumors," J.D. explained.

"As for having a father like yours . . . " McKenna said.

J.D. said the two words again, "You can."

Ben McKenna looked puzzled. Then a patronizing smile formed on his lips. "I know what you're going to say, 'Nothing is impossible with God.' But believe me, you don't know my father."

"I know him better than you think," J.D. said.

"I thought you said you'd never met my father," McKenna said.

"I said I'd never met Caleb McKenna."

McKenna's expression mutated from a look of puzzlement to one of hopeful surprise. "You know my birth father?" he asked.

"Yes, I do," J.D. answered. "I've known him all my life. He's my father too."

Ben McKenna stared at J.D., his mouth open, his head shaking slowly from side to side. He heard the words, they just didn't make sense.

J.D. explained. "You are the son of Jeremiah Morgan and Elizabeth McKenna Morgan. Their baby did not die as Caleb McKenna would have us believe. He is standing before me at this very moment."

Ben's head shook harder.

"I have in my possession a letter from New York," J.D. said. "In it is the handwritten testimony of the midwife. It's true. You are my half-brother."

Ben McKenna Morgan had to steady himself against the metal bed frame to keep from collapsing.

"Are you all right?" J.D. asked, swinging his leg over the side to get up.

Ben motioned him back into bed. "I'll just sit down for a moment," he said. He worked his way around the edge of the bed and sat on the corner. For a long time he just stared at the floor. J.D. was content to let him have the time he needed.

"Can I see the midwife's letter?" Ben asked.

J.D. reached to his stack of correspondence on the floor. As he did a suspicious thought burrowed into his mind. *The midwife's letter. It was the original. If this was an act—a McKenna trick—he could be handing over the only tangible proof of the woman's testimony! It was just the kind of scheme Caleb McKenna was capable of devising! On the other hand, what better way was there for J.D. to know for sure if Ben McKenna was really changed?* J.D. held the letter in his hand, debating what to do.

He handed the midwife's written statement to McKenna.

Ben read it carefully. When he finished, he didn't offer it back. He began to chuckle.

"What's so funny?" J.D. held his breath, never taking his eyes off the letter.

"This!" Ben held up the letter and shook it. "This is just like him! This is vintage Caleb McKenna!" He handed the letter back to J.D. "Do you know what I used to call him? The puppet master. Because he's a master at pulling strings to make people do whatever he wants them to do!" He threw his head back in disbelief. "What kind of warped mind would steal a child from his own son-in-law? Incredible!"

J.D. tucked the letter away. "I thought you'd be furious," he said.

Ben laughed as he spoke. His was laughter laced with bitters. "Of course I am! I'm livid! To think that old man robbed me of nearly thirty years of my life! I'm furious!" Then, in a sober, soft voice he added, "But more than anything else, I'm relieved. Because thanks be unto God, I am set free!"

It was true. J.D. could see it written on his face. This was not something McKenna was capable of enacting. This was no trick. The only reasonable explanation was that God had worked a miracle and changed Ben McKenna.

"I am Jeremiah Morgan's son!" Ben bellowed. The entire ward stopped what they were doing and stared at him. Then, one by one, they returned to what they were doing before the outburst. "Does Jeremiah . . . does my father know?" Ben asked.

"No, he doesn't. He's in England, so Jenny forwarded the letter to me."

Tears filled Ben's eyes. He shook his head sadly. "I almost killed my own brother . . . I almost killed my own brother!" he wept.

J.D. reached over and touched him on the shoulder. "God was watching over us," he said. "Ye thought evil against me; but God meant it unto good."

"Is that in the Bible?"

J.D. nodded. "Genesis. A great story about brothers. We can read it together."

"What about Marshall and Willy? Do you think they'll ever

accept me?"

With a nod, J.D. said, "It will be a shock to them just like it has been to all of us, but they'll come around. They're good men. And Sarah . . . now Sarah will have four brothers instead of three. But I'm sure she can handle it."

McKenna threw his head back. "I have a sister!" he cried.

The curious looks from the other men on the ward set the brothers to laughing.

John Nicolay, the President's secretary, escorted Jeremiah Morgan and Seth Cooper to the White House by carriage. Jeremiah had been instructed to give the secretary a synopsis of the report he would be making in person to the President. Jeremiah would have preferred speaking to Lincoln first, before his advisors had time to line up against the plan. But he felt he was in no position to dictate the terms of his meeting with the President. *Wasn't it enough that the President was allowing him to bring a Southerner into the White House?*

When Nicolay heard their plan to bring the two Presidents together, he was more than skeptical. *Idealistic* and *a chasing after the wind* were the words he used to criticize the plan. "The radical Republicans would lynch Lincoln if he invited ol' Jeff Davis to the White House; they'd banish him forever if he stepped one foot in the South!" Nor could the secretary be persuaded that there was a neutral country suitable for such a meeting.

Jeremiah and Seth refused to be disheartened until they talked to Lincoln himself. Seth replied to Nicolay's pessimism by saying he imagined Moses most likely received similar reaction when he informed the Israelites in what manner they would be crossing the Red Sea. "Furthermore," he stated, "if God—who parted the waters for the Israelites—wants Presidents Lincoln and Davis together, He will find a way of bringing it to pass. Even if He has to part the waters of the

Potomac to do it."

Nicolay was not amused.

It was during this carriage ride into the heart of Washington that Nicolay informed Jeremiah his son was recovering at the military hospital there. With two days separating them from their meeting with Lincoln, Jeremiah and Seth decided to see J.D. right away. Two marines accompanied Jeremiah and his Southern guest for security reasons. They rode behind Jeremiah's carriage at a discreet distance.

"Does J.D. know you're in Washington?" Seth asked.

Jeremiah was almost giddy in his response: "I thought I'd surprise him. And having you with me, it will be a double surprise!"

Upon arriving at the hospital, the two men scanned the ward from the double doorway. Seth spotted him first.

"Looks like he already has company," Seth said.

Jeremiah reacted in disbelief at what he saw. "That's McKenna's boy!" he exclaimed.

Ben McKenna was sitting on the edge of J.D.'s bed. The two men were laughing and carrying on.

"Are you sure that's McKenna's boy?" Seth asked. "I thought he hated J.D."

"I'm at a loss!" a bewildered Jeremiah exclaimed. "A total loss! But I can tell you one thing, I don't like it. This would be just like Caleb McKenna . . . " he didn't finish his sentence, but strode purposefully down the center aisle of the hospital ward. The escort marines took up a position at the double doors.

The two preachers were halfway to the bed when J.D. spotted them. His eyes lit up excitedly. "Father! And Mr. Cooper?" he cried. "What a surprise!" To his father: "I thought you were still in England!" To Cooper: "Don't mistake my surprise as an affront, Mr. Cooper, but is the war over and nobody told me?"

Ben leaped up and stepped to the end of the bed, allowing Jeremiah and Seth Cooper to greet J.D. Both ministers nodded to him, their faces portraits of suspicion.

Jeremiah bent down and hugged his son. "I'm glad to see you in such good spirits, J.D. Believe me, if I'd known you were injured, I never would have left Fredericksburg."

"I know, Father," J.D. replied. "It all worked out for the best. I mean that."

Seth Cooper shook J.D.'s hand vigorously. "None of this Mr. Cooper nonsense," he said. "You're a man. Call me Seth."

With an anguished expression, Jeremiah examined J.D.'s bandage. In a serious tone, he said, "How are you doing, son?"

J.D. looked at a sheepish Ben McKenna standing at the end of the bed. He threw his head back and laughed. "Never better! This is the best day of my life!"

With raised eyebrows Seth said to Jeremiah, "I think the boy's delirious."

Jeremiah was indeed perplexed. He took a long look at Ben. The young man wore a mischievous smile. Then at J.D. He looked like a grinning fool.

J.D. said, "Father, you had better get a couple of chairs. We have something to tell you and it's best if you're sitting down."

Jeremiah's lips pressed together, a combination of suspicion and fear. He looked at Ben a second time. Seth too was growing a worried look on his face.

"It's good news!" J.D. cried at their expressions. "Better than that, it's great news!"

Seth found two chairs. "Are you sure you want me in on this? I'll leave."

"It is a family matter," J.D. replied, "but if I know my father, he'll want you in on this."

The two preachers exchanged glances. Jeremiah nodded at his friend. They lowered themselves into the chairs, but neither man sat comfortably.

"There's really no easy way to tell you," J.D. began. "Probably the best way is for you to read this." He retrieved the midwife's confession and handed it to his father.

Jeremiah read the letter with his best friend reading over his shoulder. Their heads moved back and forth down the page. The further down they read, the more their mouths hung open. When he finished, Jeremiah's hands dropped to his lap. He looked in dismay at the man standing at the end of the bed.

"Father," J.D. said, "I'd like to introduce you to your oldest son, Ben Morgan."

When Caleb McKenna stormed into the hospital ward, it looked to him like the Morgans and Seth Cooper were arrayed against his son. Moments before his arrival, the whole story had come out—Jenny's late-night encounter with the midwife; Caleb McKenna's scriptural instructions to Ben to kill J.D.; the deaths of the greater male portion of Point Providence on the hills of Fredericksburg; the impact of the revival on Ben, eventually resulting in his spiritual conversion; and J.D.'s two-word fleece and ultimate revelation that Jeremiah Morgan was indeed Ben's father.

White curls of hair swung side-to-side as Caleb McKenna leaned heavily upon his cane with every other stride.

"Two Morgans and a Cooper versus one McKenna. Hardly seems fair," he growled. To Ben: "I was told I would find you here. Didn't I raise you better than this? Didn't I teach you not to pick on the poor and lowly, but to concentrate your energies on strategic adversaries?"

Jeremiah and Seth stood as their old enemy neared. J.D. looked around for his crutches. His father motioned him to remain in bed, a silent order J.D. reluctantly obeyed. It was the first time he'd laid eyes on the formidable Caleb McKenna. He found the man to be caustic and bitter in speech as well as appearance. It was difficult for him to imagine the charming side of the man that had seduced his sister. *But then, didn't the Bible portray unspeakable evil as both repulsive and alluring in appearance?* Piercing eyes blazed at him behind wrinkled lids.

"So, you must be John Drew Morgan," McKenna said flatly. The old man looked at J.D.'s stump. His commentary comprised a single word: "Unfortunate," he said. It was a wooden word tossed at J.D. like a penny to a beggar. He saved his emotion for Jeremiah and Seth. "I hear the two of you are up to your old chivalrous roundtable diplomacy that goes something like this . . . " His tone changed to the singsong, mocking voice of a child. " . . . If we can just get everyone to sit down and talk with one another, this world would be a better place."

Jeremiah and Seth exchanged startled glances. Surely he couldn't know about their plan already. They had just briefed Nicolay a few hours ago!

"It's a stupid idea," McKenna said. "Even if the two Presidents were to meet, and even if they agreed between themselves that the war should end, there's nothing they could do about it. Neither of them has that kind of power. The real power of this country lies beneath the surface."

"In men like you?" Seth taunted. A boiling cauldron of emotion bubbled inside him, staining his face and neck red.

McKenna's response was a superior smirk. "When I heard the two of you were returning from England aboard the same ship I knew it had to be for something like this. Believe me, gentlemen, your plan doesn't have a prayer. But I suppose you still believe in prayer, don't you?" To Ben he said, "Come on, son. It's best that you not be seen with traitors and Southerners."

"Just one minute, McKenna!" Seth thundered. "If there are any traitors in this room, you are their chief! And I intend to see you get exactly what you deserve!" Jeremiah took his friend by the arm. "This isn't the place for this," he whispered.

All around them patients and hospital staff were watching. Many of the patients wore pleased expressions. The drama being played out before them was an exciting interlude to a boring afternoon. The two marines at the door also followed the action intently, but for different reasons.

McKenna replied coolly, "I remind you that you are on enemy soil. Don't say anything that could cause a diplomatic incident."

"I wouldn't say anything that isn't completely true," Seth replied, "nor would I say anything I couldn't prove! First, you support the effort to blockade Southern ports; then you run your own blockade with contraband goods for profit!"

A bony finger raised in warning. "Lies!" McKenna shouted. "I could have you imprisoned for such accusations."

"Like I said," Seth replied, "I'm not saying anything I can't prove. You are indeed a parasite, old man. You feed off both sides of this war for personal gain. And the tragedy is that in times of disunity, unscrupulous leeches like you thrive. But once friends from both sides reconcile, the truth comes out. And bugs like you scurry for some dark place to hide."

McKenna looked to Ben. "These men are not worthy of our time," he said. "Let's leave."

"Just a minute!"

Seth grabbed McKenna by the arm. The two marines came running. Seeing them coming, Seth released the old man and they stopped. "A word of warning," Seth said to McKenna, "you stay away from my boy!"

McKenna turned his back on Seth. "We're leaving, Ben!"

"Son! Don't go!" Jeremiah cried.

The old man whirled around, his face ashen white.

Jeremiah to Ben: "We have a lot to talk about. Please stay . . . for a while at least. I'd like to tell you about your mother."

McKenna came storming back. "What kind of lies have you been feeding my boy?" he screamed. To Ben: "Don't believe anything they've told you. These men are dangerous. Look at them. Consorting in this sacred ward with the enemy against whom so many gallant men have fought. Let's get out of here before they soil your good reputation."

Ben didn't move. "Is Jeremiah Morgan my father?" he asked.

McKenna to Jeremiah: "Is that what you've been telling him?" To Ben: "Jeremiah Morgan is not your father. I took you in after your father and mother died."

"But they have a letter from a midwife which documents my birth and abduction."

"Impossible! She . . . " McKenna cried.

Jeremiah spoke up. "She escaped your attempt to silence her. In truth, her testimony records details that could only be known by a person who was present at Ben's birth."

McKenna pointed an accusing finger at Jeremiah: "He must have forged the testimony!"

Ben to McKenna: "Then tell me. What were my real father and mother's names? Can you produce documents that verify I am *not* Jeremiah Morgan's son?"

McKenna: "It's been so long ago . . . " he stammered. "I can't recall their names at the moment. . . . "

Ben: "Surely there were some kind of documents."

McKenna· "I'm sure there were . . . someplace. Come back to New York with me. We'll talk to my lawyer and see if we can find them."

"Ben. . . . " It was J.D. speaking. "Search your heart. You

know we're brothers. We both know it."

The man standing at the end of the bed looked exhausted, depleted, worn out, like a field that had been trampled upon by two opposing armies. He lowered his head and bulled his way past Caleb McKenna and out the double doors.

"Ben!" McKenna called after him. "Where are you going? Ben, listen to me! Don't you run away from me!"

The old man whirled around to face Jeremiah.

"You've turned my son against me!" he bellowed. With a raised cane he charged at Jeremiah. Seth stepped between them and blocked the blow intended for Jeremiah. A moment later the two marines were on the elderly man, restraining him from using his cane, and ushering him from the room. McKenna's obscenities could be heard long after he could no longer be seen.

Seth was the first one to speak. "Interesting afternoon," he said. "Did you plan all that for my entertainment?"

J.D. asked, "Do you think we'll ever see Ben again?"

Jeremiah: "All we can do now is pray for him."

Later that night there was a knock on Jeremiah Morgan's hotel room door. When he answered it, he saw a haggard colonel.

"Come in, Ben," he said.

Ben remained in the doorway. He said, "Tell me about my mother."

Chapter 25

JEREMIAH couldn't help but think God was smiling down upon them. Spring sun shone through the Oval Office windows, filling the room with the promise of a bright new day, not just for the Union but for the Confederate states as well. Seth sat next to him on the sofa, stiff and rigid in anticipation of meeting President Lincoln. Nicolay had ushered them into the room expecting the President to be behind his desk. He wasn't. The embarrassed secretary left the two men alone in the office while he conducted a one-man search for the chief executive.

"Nervous?" Jeremiah asked his friend.

"No," came a stiff reply.

"So am I."

Two pairs of eyes roamed the walls, the carpet, the desk.

"I don't think I could ever get used to being in here, even if I came in every day for a year," Jeremiah said. He looked at his friend. "When we were back in school did you ever once imagine we would be meeting with men like Abraham Lincoln and Jefferson Davis?"

Before Seth could answer, the door swung open. Lincoln entered with long strides; Nicolay trailed behind him. Jeremiah and Seth stood and greeted the President. Seth's eyes were wide with amazement at Lincoln's height.

"Dr. Seth Cooper!" the President greeted him warmly.

"I've heard some mighty impressive comments about your preaching ability. I hope someday I have the good fortune of hearing one of your sermons."

"Thank you, Mr. President." Color rose in Seth's cheeks.

"And Jeremiah . . " Lincoln held Jeremiah's hand as he spoke. "You have done a good service to your country. I want you to know your President is grateful."

Jeremiah's hand was lost in Lincoln's oversized grip. "Your kind words mean a lot to me, Mr. President."

"Please, gentlemen, sit." The President motioned them to the sofa. He sat opposite them in a chair. Because of his long legs, there was extra distance between him and his guests. "Can Mr. Nicolay get you something? Coffee? Tea?"

"No, thank you, sir," the men replied in unison.

With a nod, Lincoln said, "Then let's get to the subject at hand. I understand you have a unique proposal."

Long discussions between Jeremiah and Seth had gone into determining the best way to promote their plan. *Would it be better for each man to present the plan to his own President; or would it be better for them to present the plan to each other's President?* In the end Jeremiah insisted Seth make both recommendations. He reasoned that Lincoln was already impressed with Seth Cooper's reputation and Jefferson Davis regarded him as a trusted advisor. Besides, Seth had always been Jeremiah's superior in the art of verbal persuasion.

Lincoln listened thoughtfully to the plan. His fingers formed a steeple as he concentrated on Seth Cooper's clearly worded proposal. When Seth was finished, Lincoln chose his words carefully in response. In short, he said, he liked the simplicity of the plan. His concern was that should he publicly endorse the plan and Davis reject it, the American people might interpret Lincoln's action as a sign of capitulation or weakness. Lincoln admitted to the two ministers that there were several men in his cabinet who argued strenuously that he reject the plan outright.

Jeremiah found his hopes sagging until Lincoln concluded: "But having discovered the power of prayer in time of personal tragedy, how can I arbitrarily discount its power in time of national tragedy?" President Lincoln agreed to consider such a meeting if President Davis would give a positive, verifiable signal that he too would be willing to meet.

Although the President's response was cloaked in qualifications, Jeremiah regarded it as half a victory. The other half would come if they could get Jefferson Davis to agree.

"Mr. President," Jeremiah said, "might I request that two others be granted the necessary protection to travel with us to Richmond?"

"And who might they be?" Lincoln asked.

"The first is my son, J.D."

"The young man wounded at Fredericksburg? How is he?"

"He lost a leg, sir," Jeremiah said. "But his spirit has rallied and his mind is as clear as ever. It was my thought that since he can no longer service his country as a soldier, he might serve as my assistant in this matter."

"He is able to travel?" Lincoln asked.

"By carriage," Jeremiah replied. "He is getting stronger as each day passes."

"Very well," Lincoln said. "And the other?"

Jeremiah hesitated, searching for words. "The second person I would like to accompany me is also my son—Colonel Benjamin McKenna."

"McKenna?" Lincoln said the name as though he was trying to get something nasty off his tongue. "Isn't he the adopted son of Caleb McKenna?"

"You know them?" Jeremiah asked.

"My acquaintance with the McKennas goes down a long, unpleasant road," Lincoln said. He repositioned himself in the chair. Not finding a comfortable position, he repositioned himself again, as though the chair had suddenly sprouted thorns. "My association with Caleb McKenna in not a friendly one. He is a formidable force among the radical Republican block and has made it clear that he is opposed to my administration."

Jeremiah couldn't keep himself from grinning. "Forgive me, Mr. President, but now I see how you got into the White House. That is the most diplomatic description of Caleb McKenna I have ever heard."

A huge guffaw burst forth from the President. "I like you, Morgan!" he boomed. "Few men are able to see through the thick fog of Washington vernacular as quickly as you."

"Unfortunately," Jeremiah added, "we are speaking of the same Caleb McKenna."

"Yet you called Benjamin McKenna your son. . . . "

As briefly and dispassionately as he could manage, Jeremiah described his recent discovery that Benjamin was indeed his son by Elizabeth McKenna. He went on to describe Caleb McKenna's foiled attempt to ensnare Sarah and Daniel in New York, which resulted in Sarah and Jenny's flight to Virginia. From the beginning of the narration Lincoln shook his head in disbelief and didn't stop until the tale was completed.

"Caleb McKenna has been my ruthless adversary ever since I gained the nation's attention," Lincoln said. "I have always regarded him as a dangerous man, but in all my dealings with him, never have I heard such Machiavellian tactics."

With lowered head, Jeremiah agreed. "Since the death of Elizabeth, I have done my best to stay out of his way," he said, "but lately he has given me no choice. I cannot abandon my firstborn son. However, I also realize I am no match for McKenna. Therefore, I must depend upon the goodness of God and friends who can match him in authority."

Lincoln nodded. He understood the reference to him. "How will Ben's accompanying you to Richmond gain a victory over McKenna?" he asked.

"Caleb McKenna is using his influence to get Ben transferred to the Western army, to remove him from my influence and that of his brother."

"And what does J.D. think of having a new brother?"

Jeremiah laughed. "Before, they were enemies; now, they are the best of friends, or should I say the closest of brothers."

Lincoln turned his head and stared out the window behind his desk. Until this moment, Jeremiah hadn't considered that Lincoln might suffer personal political reprisals for granting this request. The President's sad eyes indicated the reprisal could be significant. Jeremiah wished he had never made the request.

"I make it a practice not to involve myself in army personnel matters," he said. "My generals grow uneasy whenever I tell them how to do their jobs. So I have found it prudent to be cautious in picking the times I involve myself in their business."

"Forgive me for asking, Mr. President. In all truth, I did not consider the consequences to you personally when I made the request. My only thought was for my son, Benjamin."

Lincoln studied Jeremiah for a long moment. Then he stood abruptly. Jeremiah and Seth joined him. He extended a hand to Seth. "Dr. Cooper, present your proposal to your President Davis. Should he be willing to adopt it publicly, I will match his good faith. May God go with you."

"Thank you, Mr. President," Seth said.

Lincoln took Jeremiah's hand. "We share a common bond, you and I—we both love our children deeply. I'll see that the necessary documents are prepared for J.D. to accompany you. I will do what I can to ensure the safe return of your daughter and her friend to the Union."

"Thank you, Mr. President!" Jeremiah said.

"As for Benjamin," Lincoln hesitated, "I can think of nothing that would give me greater pleasure than to be partner to a victory over Caleb McKenna. If Ben is willing, I will appoint him to accompany his father to Richmond for this peaceful endeavor."

"Thank you, Mr. President," Jeremiah said with tears in his eyes. "God bless you."

It was like old times at the Cooper household—almost. Susanna was absent, as were Marshall and Willy. Still, the spirit of reunion was strong. The Morgans and Coopers were together again.

Seth had succeeded in securing Daniel a leave of absence from military duty to assist him in his presentation to Jefferson Davis. During the carriage ride south it occurred to the elder Cooper that the presence of two families—one Northern and one Southern—was a visible argument for their proposal. *If two families—two men and their sons—could set aside their differences, why not two Presidents? Or two governments?*

As for the matter of the Confederate government's involvement with Caleb McKenna's blockade running, Seth Cooper's protest hit a brick wall of resistance. He was informed that the South was dependent upon Union men like McKenna to maintain a meager flow of incoming supplies, and that if a Union banker wanted to betray his country, they were obliged to help him do it.

When Seth argued that Daniel's near capture was McKenna's personal attempt at revenge, and that a Southern ship was endangered in a dangerous foray into Union waters that netted no supplies, officials replied that according to reports the ship had succeeded in capturing classified Union government documents, that at some point the documents disappeared, and that all the evidence regarding their disappearance pointed at the two Union women. Seth was warned that should he press the matter further, the women would most likely be convicted of espionage.

With great reluctance, Seth backed away from the matter. McKenna and his Southern partner had won this battle.

At the Cooper's Manchester mansion, Jeremiah enjoyed the cool of the covered porch with Seth and Emma. She had just joined them with glasses of cool mint tea. The view from the porch was of a sprawling, undulating grassy expanse dotted with elm trees with massive trunks, some hundreds of years old. The shade beneath three of the ancient trees was occupied.

Daniel and Sarah sat beneath one of them, both with their backs against the trunk, their eyes closed. An occasional waft of Sarah's laughter reached the parents on the porch. A few trees away were J.D. and Jenny. While Jenny sat against the tree, J.D. reclined with his head in her lap. She lovingly caressed his cheek as they conversed.

Since she was young Jenny had always impressed Jeremiah, but no more so than when they arrived at the Cooper mansion. With Seth's assistance, she had received a letter forewarning her of J.D.'s injury, so she already knew of his missing limb and his inability to father children. There was insufficient time for her to reply to J.D.'s letter before their arrival, and Jeremiah was concerned how the young woman would react to his son's injury. He need not have worried. When the carriage arrived, Jenny burst forth from the house like an artillery shell from a cannon. She was all over J.D., covering him with kisses, yet gentle enough that she did not once cause him to lose his balance. His injury made no difference to her. It was as though J.D. had been crippled all his life.

The third shady tree behind the Cooper mansion was occupied by a lone figure—Ben McKenna Morgan. Before leaving Washington, Ben filed the necessary papers to have his name changed on all his military records. He did this of his own accord. Ben explained to J.D. that not only did he want the name change to reflect his true parentage, but his transformed spiritual nature. While reading in the Old Testament he had learned that in times past men changed their names to reflect a spiritual encounter—Abram became Abraham, Jacob became Israel, and so on. In similar manner, Ben McKenna Morgan's new name reflected his encounter with God.

Standing alone under the ancient elm, Ben took in a panorama of the plantation while absentmindedly folding a piece of grass. Tossing the grass aside, he returned to the porch and sat next to his father.

"I was just telling Jeremiah," Seth spoke to Ben, "that I received word from Charleston today. Our meeting with President Davis has been postponed again. Possibly for a month or more."

"A political tactic?" Ben asked.

"Possibly," Seth replied with unconcealed disappointment in his voice. "If the proposal is never presented, Davis doesn't have to respond to it."

"Have you gotten any indication that he would dismiss it outright?" Jeremiah asked.

Seth shook his head. "I don't know. I hear rumors among the staff members. Although we've not talked to anyone officially, they know the essence of our proposal."

Jeremiah's eyebrows shot up in surprise. "Spies?"

Seth laughed at his friend's comical expression. "You always have been politically naive," he said good-naturedly to his friend, "even in denominational politics. Does it really surprise you that the South might have spies in Washington, and that Richmond might have Union operatives?"

Assuming an air of maturity, Jeremiah replied, "Of course

I know these things are going on if I stop to think about it; but I don't normally stop to think about it. It just strikes me as odd that information regarding a prayer meeting between Lincoln and Davis is worthy of a spy's effort."

"Oh?" Seth said inquisitively. "And what is the goal of such a meeting?"

"A cessation of hostilities," Jeremiah replied.

"And then what? Would we remain one country, or two?" Seth asked.

"If it were up to me, we would become one country again," Jeremiah said.

"That's my desire too," Seth replied. "But there are a lot of Southerners who would consider me a traitor for expressing such a view."

"Besides," Ben added, "there are a lot of people who don't want the war to end. Some are making money because of it; others are launching careers."

Jeremiah shook his head sadly. "I understand what both of you are saying," he said. "But isn't there a better way to build financial empires and launch careers than by sending our young men into fields to kill each other?"

To chase away the gloomy feeling that was descending upon the porch gathering, Seth called to the two couples to join them. Once everyone was gathered, he made an announcement.

"It seems as though God is going to bring something good out of our government's delay," he said. "It wasn't easy, but I managed to secure an appointment with General John Henry Winder of Andersonville Prison."

"Willy!" Sarah exclaimed.

"Now don't get your hopes up!" Seth cried. "I only have an appointment with the man to discuss the spiritual well-being of the prisoners. But while I am there I have been given liberty to discuss Willy Morgan in particular. Because Willy is technically a civilian — a fact officials are reluctant to admit since he was captured while firing upon Confederates — there might be a chance I can get him released into my care. But, mind you, Winder is under no obligation to do me this favor."

Jeremiah crossed over to his friend. Placing a hand on Seth's shoulder he said, "I could ask for no greater hope than to place Willy's future in your hands, or should I say on that golden tongue of yours?"

Everyone laughed except Seth Cooper.

"Can you take anyone with you?" Jeremiah asked.

"Not into the meeting," Seth replied.

"You're certainly not traveling alone," Daniel said. "It's not safe. I'm going with you."

"So am I," said Jeremiah.

"Me too," J.D. and Ben said simultaneously.

Seth shook his head. "That's too many," he said. "Besides, J.D., the ride may be rough. It would be better if you stayed behind."

"That's my brother in that prison," J.D. said. "I'm not going to sit here and wait for someone else to bring him home."

Jeremiah approached him. "J.D., maybe Seth is right."

J.D. backed away and defiantly faced everyone staring at him. "Not until this moment did I fully appreciate how Willy has felt all these years! Well, let me tell you something. You will have to tie me to a bed to keep me from going. And once I break lose, I'll be right behind you!"

Emma spoke to Jenny: "Please talk to him, dear. He'll stay if you ask him."

Jenny shook her head. "I won't ask him to stay," she said. "I agree with him. In fact, if I thought I could get away with it, I'd go with you too! Willy needs help. If his brothers don't help him, who will?"

"It's too many," Seth said.

Jeremiah replied, "We'll stay out of sight of the prison itself."

Daniel added, "I, for one, welcome the company. There is little law and order outside of the cities; not to mention raiding and scouting parties. The more men we have, the safer I'll feel."

Everyone looked to Seth. "All right. We all go!"

There weren't any cheers following his pronouncement, just determined head-nodding. As each man went to his room to prepare for departure, Seth pulled Jeremiah to one side. He spoke in low tones.

"There is more news than I spoke in front of the women," he said. "I didn't want to alarm them needlessly."

"Go on," Jeremiah said, grim-faced.

"Andersonville Prison is nothing more than a stockade in squalor. The officials I conferred with did their best to discourage me from making the trip." He paused in an attempt to soften the words that came next. "Jeremiah, the chances of Willy's survival are not good, especially considering his clubfoot. The way it was described to me, many of the heartiest men survive only a few weeks."

"Are you saying we shouldn't go?" Jeremiah asked.

"No. I think you know me better than that. If my son were down there, no matter how little the odds, I would go."

"I'm glad you said that," Jeremiah replied. "Those are my thoughts exactly. I'm going with you or without you."

Seth nodded. "I just wanted to forewarn you."

"How long has it been?"

Ben asked the question as he paced furiously between two trees, walking to one tree and pushing off, then to the other; back and forth, back and forth. J.D. sat on a log, his watch in hand. Daniel and Jeremiah stood with their backs to the dead campfire, facing the direction of Andersonville Prison which was too far distant to see.

"It's five minutes since the last time you asked," J.D. said.

The four of them were awaiting the return of Seth Cooper, who had gone to the prison alone to meet with General Winder. The journey into Georgia had gone without incident. While Jeremiah and J.D. shared driving duties in a small carriage, the others accompanied them on horseback. The two-family party had been stopped a number of times along the way, but between Seth's papers and Daniel's Confederate uniform and orders, no one challenged their right to travel south. While the other four stayed out of sight in the woods, Seth completed the journey to the prison to negotiate Willy's release. He had been gone over an hour.

"I never have been good at waiting," Ben said. He picked up a fallen tree branch and tapped it nervously against one tree trunk, then another.

"Here he comes!" Jeremiah cried.

"Are you sure it's him?" J.D. asked.

"That's my father," Daniel said. "He always leans to the right when he rides."

"Is Willy with him?" Ben asked.

"He's riding alone," Jeremiah replied, his tone guarded. Just because Willy was not with Seth did not mean that the meeting had gone badly.

Jeremiah's optimism evaporated the moment Seth Cooper's facial features came into focus. Seth's face and ears were beet red. He clenched his teeth, released, then clenched them again, causing his jaw muscles to bulge from the effort. There was an uncontrolled fire in his eyes that grew ever hotter; they looked like they would spit brimstone at any moment.

Seth Cooper dismounted hastily, angrily flinging the reins aside. He removed his hat and slammed it against a tree with all his might. Never, in all the years Jeremiah had known him, had he seen Seth so angry.

"Father, calm down!" Daniel cried. "Tell us what happened."

The four men who had been waiting for his return gathered around. They would have to wait several moments longer. Seth Cooper's rage overpowered his attempts to form intelligible words. With an uplifted hand he put off all well-meaning attempts to help him gain control of the monster within. Leaving them behind, he walked a short distance into the woods. With a single hand he leaned against a tree, his head lowered.

"I've never seen my father like this," Daniel said in a hushed tone. "Never."

"He has to work through it himself," Jeremiah said. "Give him time. When he's ready, he'll tell us what happened."

Ben started to say something, took one look at his father, and swallowed his words. His lips pressed tightly together, he walked away a short distance. J.D. and Jeremiah exchanged glances.

A quarter of an hour passed before Seth regained his composure and returned.

"General Winder is an arrogant, pompous, blowhard who thinks he's Napoleon and that Andersonville is France," Seth said, still fighting an internal war of control. "Do you know what he told me? He boasted that he was killing more Yankees in his camp than twenty regiments of Lee's army!"

Jeremiah winced.

"That's right!" Seth replied to his friend's reaction. "And I wouldn't doubt that he's doing it. Men are jammed together inside that stockade, but instead of expanding it, Winder is counting on natural attrition by death to keep the population under control. He told me that to my face!"

"Did you inquire about Willy?" J.D. asked.

"Willy? What's one Willy to a man like Winder?" Seth's

response was explosive. Signaling an apology with his hands, he added, "I tried. Several times. The man refused to acknowledge that the prisoners had individual identities."

Seth walked over to Jeremiah and placed a hand on his shoulder. "As unpleasant as it is for me to say this to my best friend, I don't believe Willy could have survived in that place for more than a week. Some of the men I saw inside were nothing more than skeletons too weak to even walk. Some who were healthier were scrapping over a fruit can they use as a skillet. There were no guards to break up the fight. Winder watches the prisoners kill one another for recreation."

Ben spoke up. "What if you went to Winder's superiors? Maybe you could convince them to order Winder to produce Willy. At least then we would know if he was alive."

Seth shook his head. "My fear is that even if I succeeded in seeing Willy, Winder would then kill him in retaliation."

"He would do that?" Daniel asked.

"The man I met would do that," Seth said.

Jeremiah closed his eyes, fighting back his own emotions. "You're saying we have no further recourse."

A hardened look formed in Seth Cooper's eyes. "I'm saying that if my son were in there, I would never leave this place without him."

J.D., Ben, and Daniel grinned.

"We're going in to get him?" Jeremiah asked.

"As God is my witness," Seth said, "if Willy is alive, we're not leaving Andersonville without him."

They needed a plan.

Using rocks and sticks, they constructed a miniature of the camp based on Seth's recollections.

"It's an immense pen. About thirteen acres worth." Seth drew lines in the dirt outlining the camp's perimeter. "The walls are formed with pine logs about twenty-five feet long buried vertically in the dirt. In the center, the yard is divided by a creek running east and west."

"It flows under the fence?" J.D. asked.

"Yes, but I know what you're thinking and it won't work. The creek is only about a yard wide and ten inches deep at best."

J.D. nodded.

"Inside the fence perimeter is railing made of stakes about twenty feet from the stockade." He drew another line inside the first one. "It's called the Dead Line. Any prisoner crossing the Dead Line is shot. No warning. No questions. Winder told me that sometimes prisoners commit suicide by crossing the Dead Line. Other times prisoners are murdered by being tossed across the Dead Line by other prisoners. The first man to be killed crossing the Dead Line was retrieving an old piece of cloth that had blown across it. Winder thought that was funny."

"Where are the guards posted?" Ben asked.

Seth drew boxes to indicate the positions of the guard posts. "The entrance is a double gate." He drew a larger box to indicate the entrance. "Only one gate is opened at a time A person entering the prison is let into the box, searched, then let into the camp. The same procedure is used upon leaving."

Once the miniature replica of the camp was completed, Jeremiah turned to Ben. "You graduated from West Point," he said. "What strategy would you use to get Willy out of there?"

All eyes turned to the newest member of the Morgan clan.

"Our objective is clear," he said. "The plan should be a simple one. Get inside and find Willy; then get out. Here's what I suggest. . . . "

Everyone leaned over the crude representation of Andersonville Prison as Ben proposed his plan.

Chapter 26

WILLY protected himself from the midday sun under the lean-to that had become his home. He watched as a white maggot crawled out of the warm sand a couple of feet away from him. For a few minutes Willy and the maggot lay side-by-side in peaceful coexistence. Then, the livelier of the two of them sprouted wings. After several aborted attempts, the maggot managed a clumsy flight, dropping down upon Willy's arm and stinging him like a gadfly. Willy brushed the maggot away absentmindedly.

"Morgan! Morgan!" A hollow-cheeked figure with dull black hair ran toward the lean-to. "He's dead. Gerrish is dead!"

Willy stared vacantly at the messenger and now his sole remaining friend. Teddy Gerrish, Isaac Cutler, and Willy arrived at Andersonville the same day. Together the two soldiers had scrounged to make a shelter by bribing the guards with brass buttons from their uniforms. In return they managed to secure wood and a piece of woolen cloth. Through the last stages of cold weather, the three of them shared a single overcoat under which they huddled to keep warm.

Gerrish was the son of a Rhode Island butcher, a boy of eighteen with freckles and a lopsided smile. Cutler, the oldest of the three at nearly thirty, was a Philadelphia journalist who grew tired of reporting history and joined the army to help make it. As it turned out, he made little history, if any at all. He was captured outside Corinth, Mississippi in a minor skirmish with the Rebels, his first encounter with the enemy.

The older Cutler looked after Gerrish and Willy like they were his own boys. One day, when Willy was idly scratching in the dirt, the newspaperman recognized his artistic talent. The ink in the journalist's blood stirred to life as he realized the value of Willy's talent. Here was a boy who could visually record the atrocities of Andersonville so that someday the Union would know the horrors and squalor of the prison camp. Cutler proposed a deal. He would look after Willy, whose prospects for survival were not good, considering men of far healthier standing lasted only a few weeks; plus, he would secure Willy some kind of artistic media; in return, Willy would record life in Andersonville Prison for all the world to see.

At first, Willy accepted the terms simply to survive. But soon the scenes he recorded began to have an effect on him. The more pictures he sketched, the angrier he became. More than ever before, he wanted people to view his sketches. He wanted his portrayals of life in a Confederate prison to turn their stomachs, just so they might know a glimpse of life at its lowest level. And even then, he knew his sketches were inadequate. For they might capture a moment of horror, but they could never convey the foul stench of a sewer. They couldn't adequately communicate the hollowness of life without hope. Pictures alone could never communicate to civilized people the meaningless existence of this filthy, lice-infested jungle of dying humanity.

Willy's desire to live died a little more each day. He had lost all feeling. Even as Cutler raced up to him with the news that Gerrish was dead, Willy felt nothing for the boy who shared their tent. His only feeling was for his pictures. He had reconciled himself to death, but his pictures must survive.

At all costs, his pictures must survive.

Reaching for a large scrap of paper that he had been saving for an important work, he said flatly, "Tell me how it happened."

Cutler reminded him that Gerrish had taken their fruit cup to get water from the stream. This was Gerrish's daily task, one which he took seriously. It was his part of keeping the three lean-to occupants alive. Because the stream was polluted with filth once it entered the camp, every day Gerrish would walk the width of the camp to the west side where the stream first emerged under the wooden fence. A majority of prisoners took their water in the same spot and on this day the crowd was heavier than usual. Gerrish worked his way toward the stream, getting as far upstream as he could. While reaching for the water, his arm touched the railing of the Dead Line. A shot startled the prisoners. It hit Gerrish in the back of the head. He fell dead into the stream, polluting the water with his blood.

Some of the prisoners took up a chant, "Thirty-day pass! Thirty-day pass!" It was a common assumption that every guard who killed a prisoner earned himself a thirty-day leave of absence. The other prisoners cursed Gerrish, kicking his lifeless body for polluting their only water supply.

With his stub of a pencil, Willy sketched the scene as he saw it in his mind. A boy's face frozen in surprise the moment he felt the bullet. A guard high above, his rifle spitting smoke. Hundreds of hands with an assortment of cups reaching into the river. An instant in time. The instant before a splash in the river, the boy's face so close to it his shocked reflection could be clearly seen. The instant before one Union soldier's spiritual escape from the Confederate's version of hades.

When he was finished with the sketch, Willy showed it to Cutler. The journalist held the picture in his hands a long time. "You captured Gerrish's face well," he said, his voice choking. "Anybody who knew him would recognize him." Shaky hands offered the picture back to Willy. Cutler stood and walked away from the lean-to that housed only two occupants. As he walked, he sniffed and wiped away tears.

Willy took the picture and placed it with the others in the back of the lean-to. He flipped through his collection: prisoners handing guards brass buttons in exchange for a few pieces of wood; a bloody fist fight between an Indiana bugler and a Chicago street tough; a band of New York toughs roaming the camp looking for things to steal; a prisoner cradling his emaciated friend as the death rattle sounded in the friend's chest.

Without the slightest emotion, Willy arranged the sketches and hid them under a rock in the back of the lean-to.

The next day a gang of twenty New York toughs swept through the lower portion of the camp, carrying off boots, tins that were used as skillets, and Willy's pencil. Prized possessions all. It was a regular occurrence. The New Yorkers would raid, then dare anyone to cross the stream to reclaim the stolen items. No one ever did. Until now.

The death of Gerrish and the loss of Willy's pencil worked like stone against flint in Cutler's soul. First a spark, then a fire. With journalistic passion he spread the flame of his anger among the other prisoners. A gang of forty men quickly formed, tired of the New Yorkers' disdain for their property. Led by Cutler, they marched toward the stream to take back from the New Yorkers what was rightfully theirs.

His back against the trunk, his leg stretched out along the branch, his rifle resting across the leg, the sharpshooter rested easily high in the branches of the tree. Squinting into the distance he could see all of Andersonville Prison. Two riders approached the front gate. The shooter squirmed to one side to get his pocket watch. Two twenty-eight in the afternoon. The riders' presence didn't conform to any schedule he'd been able to discern. Nor had he seen them before. One was tall and fat; the other couldn't be more than a clean-shaven boy, guessing by his size.

The man in the tree yawned silently, stretched, and ran his hand through white-streaked hair. Marshall scratched his beard. It had been a week since his last bath; itching skin and an unpleasant odor reminded him. It had been that long since he'd been observing the prison, looking for a way to get to Willy. He was baffled. The enclosure was a putrefying, stinking lake of humanity. When the wind shifted, the stench from the distant camp overpowered his own odor. The seething ripples of life within the wooden walls reminded him of the Dead Sea. There was a fresh inlet, but no outlet; except for death, of course. *How was he going to locate Willy amongst all those tents?*

A twig snapped below him. Marshall's senses jumped to the ready; his breathing slowed until he was hardly breathing at all. Quick eyes jumped back and forth. It was a deadly game he'd played too often. *Whoever spots the other first wins; the loser dies.*

A figure appeared from directly beneath him. A civilian. Alone. At least for the moment. The man walked to the edge of the forest. With his back to Marshall, he placed his hands on his hips and stared at the prison. Marshall didn't see a weapon, but that didn't mean the man didn't have a pistol or a blade tucked in his waistband. A man would be foolish to travel far without a weapon. Slowly, silently, Marshall raised his rifle to a ready position. For a long time the man studied the prison. Marshall waited. Patience.

The man was a statue. Marshall kept an anxious eye in all directions. It would be foolish to think the man was alone. Just as Marshall was scanning around the tree as he did periodically, the man turned toward him. Marshall didn't catch the man's movement until he was completely turned around. Fortunately, Marshall was up high and the man was looking on the ground for something. A place to sit.

Just then a lightning bolt of recognition struck Marshall. It hit him so hard, he nearly toppled from the tree. *Colonel McKenna! What is he doing here?*

Marshall's jaw set in anger. With the eyes of a predator, he watched as Ben McKenna settled onto the ground, his back once again to Marshall. His chest heaving, Marshall stared so hard at McKenna's back he was surprised the man couldn't feel it.

God was delivering the man into his hands, Marshall was convinced of this. He remembered the way McKenna did everything he could to humiliate J.D. He remembered the way McKenna looked upon Willy as less than human. He remembered the sneering remarks the colonel had made about their family, their town. *Puffers, that was what he called us.*

Marshall tucked the rifle against his shoulder and aimed through the telescope sight. He was so close to his target, he didn't need it. There was no way he could miss from this short distance. With the sight resting on McKenna's neck, Marshall could clearly distinguish one hair from another. He quieted his breathing and pressured the trigger.

No.

Marshall eased up on the trigger. If he shot McKenna in the back, the man would never know who it was who killed him. Marshall wanted him to know.

As silent as a cat, Marshall climbed down the tree, keeping the trunk between himself and McKenna at all times, should an unexpected sound cause him to look behind him. Marshall reached the ground without being detected. Quietly, he emerged from the tree and moved to within ten yards of

McKenna.

In a quiet voice Marshall spoke: "A rifle is pointed at your head; move and you're dead."

McKenna started, then froze.

"Stand to your feet, but don't turn around. Keep your hands to the side."

McKenna did as he was told.

"Now. Turn around slowly. You reach for anything and it's the last thing you'll ever do."

A slow rotation brought the two men face-to-face. Ben's eyes lit up. He smiled. "Marshall!" he cried.

The friendly greeting startled Marshall; it was completely unexpected. He expected surprise, but also fear. There was no fear! The man looked glad to see him!

"What are you doing down here? You're a traitor, aren't you? I should have expected that from you."

"I'm not a traitor!" McKenna protested, still smiling. "We've come to get Willy."

The mention of Willy's name set off an explosion of anger inside Marshall. With two quick steps he slammed the butt of his rifle across Ben's cheek, sending him flying backward.

"Get up!" Marshall shouted. His emotions teetered on the edge of control and emotional chaos.

His hand rubbing his cheek, Ben picked himself up. "I don't want to fight you," he said. "I'm here to help. J.D. is here too, and . . ."

Marshall moved to strike again. Ben jumped backward. "You are a Satan!" Marshall cried. "Do you expect to confuse me with your lies? Until what? One of your companions sneaks up behind me?"

"It's not what you think!" Ben said.

"I'll tell you what I think," Marshall cried. "I think I'm going to fight you. And then, I'm going to kill you."

"I won't fight you," Ben said, lowering his hands.

"I'll kill you outright!" Marshall screamed.

"Then you'll just have to kill me," Ben said.

"With pleasure!" Marshall raised the rifle and aimed it at McKenna's chest. Ben didn't move. His hands at his side, he calmly looked Marshall in the eyes.

Marshall lowered the rifle.

"I knew you couldn't do it," Ben said.

Marshall threw down the rifle. "Well, there's one thing I can do . . . I can give you the thrashing of your life."

"I told you already. I won't fight you."

"What's wrong with you?" Marshall screamed. "Why won't you fight?"

A voice came from behind Marshall. "Because he's your brother, that's why."

Marshall swung around. "J.D.?"

With the aid of his crutch, J.D. walked toward him. Behind him came Jeremiah and Seth and Daniel.

"It's good to see you, son," Jeremiah said. "Though I'd hardly recognize you with all that hair."

Marshall was convinced it was all witchcraft until his father put his arms around him and embraced him. Then it was just like he was a little boy again in Ohio, so many years ago. Still in his father's embrace, Marshall could see the grinning faces of J.D. and Seth and Daniel.

With one arm draped around Marshall's shoulder, Jeremiah turned him back toward Ben. "It's a long story, son," he said. "But the short version is this: Ben is your older brother."

Chapter 27

THE key to the rescue plan revolved around a gruesome fact of life in Andersonville: the daily death of Union soldiers. According to Ben's observed estimate, between fifteen and twenty men died each day. He derived this figure from the body cart that emerged from the gates every Monday and Thursday at noon carrying a pile of bodies the short distance between the camp and the mass grave a half-mile distant. What made this grisly transport attractive to him was the fact that the soldiers didn't do the burying. A cart came from town, entered the prison, loaded the bodies, then dumped them in a wide trench that served as a mass grave. It was always the same cart that performed the task, but not always the same two men driving it.

The plan was that Daniel, wearing his Confederate uniform, would deliver a "captured" Ben to the guards at the prison gate. Once inside the prison Ben would have three days to locate Willy. On Thursday at noon, the cart would appear as usual, but this time with two new workers—Jeremiah and Seth.

Because Seth had already been seen by the guards, precautions were taken to disguise his identity. He would wear an old pair of overalls and a wide brimmed hat. And at great personal sacrifice, he would shave off his bristly beard which he had worn ever since his early days in college. From Ben's observance of the guard rotation, the chances were slight that any one of the same guards would be on duty that day. Still, these precautions were worth the effort.

Once they were inside the compound, Jeremiah and Seth would perform the task of loading the bodies onto the cart. If all went well, two of the bodies would still be alive—Willy's and Ben's. They would then be smuggled out of the camp with the stack of dead bodies.

A safe distance away, Daniel would be waiting with a horse for his father at a designated rendezvous. J.D. would be waiting a little further up the road with a carriage for the Morgan getaway.

It was Jeremiah who insisted on the two rendezvous points. He was reluctant to include Seth and Daniel in the plan at all. If their participation in the escape became known, they would most surely be put to death as traitors. But Seth insisted on helping. He argued that no one deserved to live in the kind of conditions he'd seen inside the stockade, war or no war. As a concession to his friend, Seth agreed to part company with them as soon as the wagon was out of the guards' sight. On horseback, he and Daniel would then distance themselves quickly from the much slower wagon.

After the Morgans transferred from the wagon to the carriage, the plan was for them to travel north to the Flint River, follow it upstream into the mountains, then cross the mountains into eastern Tennessee. It would be a difficult journey, but the rough terrain would give them greater cover than by traveling along the open fields and roads. The carriage J.D. was driving would take them as far as the river; after that they would travel on foot.

This part troubled J.D. He understood how Willy had felt all his life. J.D. knew their lack of mobility would slow down the rest of the men, and possibly endanger them all.

The plan did not include early discovery and alarms while

the wagon was inside the camp. Once outside, the only plan was to try to outrun their pursuers, who could muster a considerable force. First, there were guards in the towers. The only good news in this regard was that Ben had not observed any rifles with telescopic sights attached to them. Then there was the guard camp a half-mile away. Should an alarm sound, men on horseback would come flooding from that direction. Finally, there were the hounds. It was one thing to outrun and outsmart human pursuers, quite another thing to lose persistent hounds.

The plan was settled until Marshall appeared; he unsettled it. Ben, for one, welcomed Marshall's sharpshooting skills as a bonus. He could cover the wagon from a distance as it passed in and out of the camp. Marshall, however, insisted on being the one to go inside the compound to rescue Willy.

"I'm responsible for him!" Marshall shouted. "He's my brother!"

"He's my brother too!" Ben retorted.

"What makes you think you can get Willy to trust you?" Marshall retorted. "He remembers you like I do. And it's not a fond memory."

"It's already been worked out. I'll carry a note from Father. Besides, you're needed on the outside as a sharpshooter."

"Take my rifle," Marshall said, "You can be the sharpshooter. I'm going in."

"I'm a lousy shot!" Ben cried.

It was a stalemate. Both brothers insisted they were the best choice to go inside the camp. It was left to Jeremiah to decide between them.

While Jeremiah pondered his decision alone, J.D. came and sat beside him.

"There's something you should know about Ben," he said.

Jeremiah gave J.D. his full attention.

"First, let me say that if I were to encounter Ben today and

I hadn't seen him for years, I wouldn't believe he's the same man; that's how much he's changed."

"You don't think Willy will come out with Ben?"

"A note from you should be sufficient to convince Willy, that's not my point." J.D. looked at the ground. "Father, I don't want to speak ill of Ben," he said slowly, "it's just that . . . "

"What are you trying to tell me, J.D.?"

J.D. looked his father in the eyes and said, "Ben was less than heroic on the battlefield. At Bull Run we couldn't pry him from a tree during the charge. On the other hand, he may have changed in that regard too! I just don't know. . . . Anyway, I thought you should know that when you make your decision."

The next morning Jeremiah announced that Marshall would be the one to go into the camp to find Willy.

Ben didn't argue with his father's decision. The night before the plan was to be carried out, he asked Marshall to instruct him in the use of the telescopic sight. For the remainder of the evening, Ben picked distant targets and practiced his aim, doing everything Marshall had taught him.

Later that night, after everyone had gone to sleep, Ben slipped out of camp and made his way toward the stockade. He wore no shoes and his clothing was ragged and torn. He left behind a note posted to a tree with a knife. It read:

Sorry, Marshall, this is something I must do. I have to prove to all of you, and to myself, that there is Morgan blood in my veins. As for the remainder of the plan, it is unchanged. Better this way. I never was good with a rifle.

Under his arm Ben carried several shirts. These he ripped into long strips, tying them end-to-end to make a cloth rope.

When the rope was finished, he tied a sturdy stick about a foot long to one end of it. Then, he lay down on the bare ground and rolled around, covering his head and face, neck and arms with dirt.

It was a moonless night as he made his way to the stockade. The size of the wall and the stench from the other side hit him like a one-two punch. He began to wonder if he was doing the right thing. Maybe Marshall was the better choice for this mission. At the foot of the fence he paused. There was still enough time for him to return to camp. He hadn't been spotted. He could sneak back and remove the note from the tree before anyone woke. *After all, Jeremiah had chosen Marshall for the assignment, hadn't he?* He must have had good reasons for doing so.

Ben surveyed the fence. He thought of Willy on the other side. Something stirred inside him. It was a new feeling for him, unlike anything he'd ever experienced. It was a feeling of family. A sense of belonging, of being a part. Of having the privilege to put someone else's needs above his own. He took a deep breath and proceeded.

Taking the cloth rope in hand, Ben tossed the bulk of it over the fence, holding onto the stick portion until the momentum of the rope pulled it from his hands. The rope wedged between two pilings, with the stick serving as an anchor. Had he been on the other side of the fence, everything would have been in place for him to scale the fence. Ben fell to the ground, clutched an imaginary ankle sprain, and screamed in pain.

Guards appeared instantly. They surrounded him. One of the guards looked up and saw the stick wedged high between the pilings. Yanking Ben to his feet, they shoved him toward the front gate. Ben favored his perfectly healthy right ankle. All the way into the compound they cursed him, jabbed him, and berated his Yankee stupidity for being unable to make good his escape.

◆ ◆ ◆

Ben was dumped unceremoniously into the New Yorker section of the compound. Unlike his pretended ankle injury, this time the pain was real. His right eye and cheek were black and swollen. His back bore fresh red stripes. These were the penalties for his attempted escape the night before.

Pushing himself up from the ground, he surveyed his surroundings. The early morning light broke over the stockade. There were stirrings of life among the ragged rows of tents. He had studied the camp for hours from a distance. It hadn't prepared him adequately for this. He gagged on the smells and the filth. Beneath the flimsy shelters all around him he heard men coughing up phlegm or retching. The emaciated bodies that emerged from the tents had forsaken any attempt at personal hygiene. Diseases of every sort were open to public viewing, particularly scurvy and diarrhea. A man brushed by him without stopping to excuse the intrusion. His lip was cancerous. The disease had eaten the whole side of his face.

Three days. He had three days to sort through this maze of filth and find Willy.

"New Yorkers! Defend yourselves! To the stream! To the stream!"

A red-headed Irishman raced up and down the rows of tents like Paul Revere calling minutemen to action. From his place on a mound of dirt, Ben gazed dejectedly in the direction of the stream. It was Wednesday. He had searched two days without success. No one claimed to have ever heard of a Willy or a Morgan.

Ben had the rest of the day to find him. Otherwise, tonight he would sit among the dead and wait to be carried out— alone. This whole ordeal would have been a waste of time. A gnawing feeling in his belly told him Willy had already visited the pile in a legitimate role.

During Ben's search he had met unexpected resistance. He learned quickly that the entire camp was hostile to New Yorkers; and if the comments thrown at his back when he passed by held any truth in them, it was a reputation well-earned. The commotion at the stream was just one of many reputation-making incidents for the camp New Yorkers.

Nearly fifty prisoners stood at the edge of the stream challenging the New Yorkers to come out. Their leader, a hollow-cheeked man with black hair, stood in the middle of the stream. With an upraised fist he shamed the New Yorkers for raiding the lower camp. He demanded the return of three items in particular: a pair of boots, a skillet, and an artist's pencil.

"These what you lookin' for, Cutler?" A brawny New York tough taunted the man in the stream. Wading into the stream to meet him, the tough stopped to lift one foot from the water to show he was wearing the boots in question. With his left hand he held up a small skillet; with his right, the stub of a pencil. "Come and get 'em if you want 'em!"

The black-haired Cutler stood his ground. "Return the items to me and we'll leave," he said. "Otherwise, suffer the consequences."

The tough grabbed his heart. He turned to the gathering New Yorkers behind him. "I'm scared!" he cried. "Please don't hurt me, Mr. Journalist!"

The crowd of New Yorkers laughed at the tough's antics.

Cutler turned to address the men behind him. "Do you want to know how tough this man really is?" he asked. "I'll tell you! See that pencil? He stole it from a cripple who uses it to draw pictures!"

Cutler's side of the stream burst out laughing.

The journalist waited for the laughter to subside a bit, then he added, "And the cripple nearly won the fight!"

The lower side of the stream erupted even more with laughter.

Ben jumped to his feet. *Willy! A cripple who draws pictures!*

He had to get to the man named Cutler, to see if he knew Willy. Ben began working his way toward the stream.

It didn't take the New York tough long to realize that in a battle of wits he was woefully ill-equipped. Abandoning words, he raced toward Cutler with fists flying. The scene that followed was like two dams bursting at the exact same instant, releasing two floods of screaming men that converged in the middle of the stream. It was a battle without rifles. With amused expressions, the guards watched from their towers.

Ben stopped. The clash of bodies unnerved him. *What was he going to do? Wade into the middle of it and expect to have a conversation with Cutler? No, it was best if he wait. Yes, that was the best course of action. Stay out of it and wait. If he charged into the middle of the fight, there was no telling what might happen to him. A person could get killed in there. Or worse yet, he could get injured and miss the appointed rendez-vous, in which case he would be stuck in Andersonville forever.*

Ben's heart pounded wildly as he watched the battle. Hitching up his pants, he waded into the fray. *I have to find Willy.*

He pulled and elbowed and shoved and ducked his way toward the stream looking for Cutler or the New York tough, thinking that if he found one, he would surely find the other. But there were too many bodies and hands and legs. It was hard to distinguish one from the other.

Then, like a curtain parting, he saw a gaunt, black-haired man. The man was on his knees in the stream of filth, holding himself up with one hand as men fought over him.

"Cutler!" Ben screamed. There was too much noise. Ben could hardly hear his own voice.

The curtain of bodies closed. Ben pushed his way toward the man he thought was Cutler. Pulling two men apart, he found himself standing over the black-haired man.

"Cutler!" he screamed. The man looked up. It was the journalist! Ben offered him a hand. Cutler shrank away from him. Ben pushed away men who tumbled in all around them.

"Do you know Willy? Willy Morgan?"

A light of recognition shined in Cutler's eyes.

"Willy!" Ben screamed again. "You know him, don't . . . "

Something rock-hard smashed into the back of Ben's head. There was a flash of white, then everything softened to a blur. He felt his knees growing weak. Either the sun was crashing or he was fainting, because everything grew dark. He fell on top of Cutler, sending them both momentarily underwater.

With his head half in the polluted stream and half out, the last thing he remembered was seeing the stub of a pencil float in front of his eyes. He reached out and grabbed it.

Ben awoke beside the stream. Someone had pulled him out. He was not alone. Scattered all around him were men in similar condition, or worse. He reached behind him and felt the back of his head. It was sticky wet. As he touched it, the skin at the base of his scull stung, sending waves of pain deeper into his head. Moaning, Ben struggled to sit up. To do so, he had to open his left hand which was clutching something. Willy's pencil stub.

As twilight covered the camp, Ben balanced himself on unsteady legs. He had just a few hours left. He had to find Willy. Splashing across the stream, he made his way to the lower camp.

As before, no one wanted to have anything to do with a New Yorker, especially now. Several men threatened to escort him back across the stream if he didn't leave immediately. Then, Ben had an idea. He held out Willy's pencil.

"I came to give this back to the crippled man," he said. Their response was a suspicious gaze.

"When was the last time a New Yorker came down here to give something back to someone?" he argued.

Suspicion turned to puzzlement, then to curiosity. Finally curiosity got the better of one British prisoner. "I can show you where the cripple lives," he said. "If you let me watch when you give him his pencil back."

Escorted by the Brit, Ben found Willy alone beneath the lean-to. Willy's eyes were closed, his breathing shallow.

"Willy?" he said.

Willy's eyes fluttered open. It took several moments for them to focus. When they did, Willy said in a raspy voice, "McKenna?" A wry smile crossed his face as his eyes closed again. "So you finally got what you deserved, eh, Colonel?"

Ben extended an open hand. Laying across his palm was the pencil stub.

"Look what he brought you, mate!" Ben's British guide cried excitedly.

Willy had to raise up to see what Ben was offering him. His eyes filled with questions. With a trembling hand he carefully plucked the pencil stub from Ben's hand as he would a price-less diamond.

Chapter 28

WOULD I return the pencil to you if I wasn't telling the truth?" Ben shouted at Willy. He was exasperated. Nothing he said seemed to have any effect.

The two of them sat in the lean-to. Willy had worked his way as far back into the lean-to as possible as Ben fervently pleaded his case. He told Willy nothing of their common bloodlines, choosing instead to focus his line of argument regarding this one unexplainable act of kindness—the return of the pencil stub. Their common heritage would not only be unbelievable, but inconsequential given the life-and-death setting. But the pencil . . . that was something Willy could understand.

The pencil was such a prized possession in camp that Willy would have understood if Cutler, a friend, had retrieved the pencil, then decided to keep it for himself. Such was life in prison. But this . . . an *enemy* returning his pencil to him . . . this wasn't done . . . it just wasn't done!

Speaking in whispers, Ben said, "Tomorrow at noon, your father and Seth Cooper will drive a wagon into the camp. They're posing as undertakers. They'll haul us away with the dead bodies."

Unbelieving eyes blinked back at him.

"J.D. and Marshall are here too. They'll assist us once we get out."

"Why didn't Marshall come in to get me?" Willy asked.

"We need a sharpshooter to cover us while the wagon passes in and out of the gate."

"What about J.D., why didn't he come in to get me?"

Ben looked away. He said, "J.D. was wounded in battle. He isn't able to do it."

"Wounded bad?"

Ben nodded.

Willy inched further back into the lean-to. Reaching behind him he fingered the rock that hid his pictures. "I don't believe you," he said.

Ben leaned toward him earnestly. "I brought you back the pencil, didn't I?"

Willy refused to leave until Cutler returned. As darkness fell, Ben began to fidget. Time was running out. He didn't want to wait too long. Once the camp was settled for the night, any singular movement would attract too many eyes.

"We have to go now," Ben said.

Willy fidgeted, but made no attempt to get up.

"What if Cutler doesn't come back?" Ben cried.

Willy made no attempt to answer.

Ben stood and surveyed the camp. Signs of life were scattered here and there, but for the most part it was still. "We can't wait any longer," he said. He decided on another tact: "Your father is going to want to know why you didn't come with me. What should I tell him?"

Staring at the ground Willy made no sign of having heard the question.

"Good-bye, Willy," Ben said. He turned to walk away.

"Wait."

Ben turned back to see Willy lifting a rock in the far reaches of the lean-to. Underneath the rock were more than a dozen pieces of paper of various sizes. Willy handed them to

Ben. "Take these with you," he said. "They have to get out. They have to."

Ben leafed through the papers. He saw a moving compendium of sketches vividly portraying life and death in Andersonville.

"They must get out," Willy repeated.

Ben handed the pictures back to Willy. "No," he said. "I won't take them with me."

Willy stared helplessly at the pictures.

"If you want those pictures to get out, you'll have to take them yourself. I won't do it for you."

He waited for a response. There was none. Silent eyes stared at the returned pictures.

"If we leave right now, these pictures will be out of camp by tomorrow afternoon. You can do it, Willy! Are you with me?"

It was barely a nod, but it was the first affirmative Willy had given, so Ben acted on it. He helped Willy tuck the sketches inside his clothing. Then he told Willy to play dead. Sticking a shoulder into Willy's abdomen, Ben hoisted him up. He was surprised at how little Willy weighed. Solemnly he carried Willy across camp, surprised at how little attention he received, until he remembered that the sight of a dead man was a common one in Andersonville.

Ben hesitated as the pile of dead prisoners came into view. This close, the view was revolting. A mess of tangled limbs. Heads bent at awkward angles. Eyes wide open but unseeing. Then there was the smell of decay. The stench burrowed through his belly like a worm. Ben didn't know if he was going to be able to go through with this part of the plan.

Two guards were positioned in front of the pile, their backs to it. Better not to look at it. Above them, another guard leaned against the railing of his guard tower.

With Willy still folded over his shoulder, Ben stooped and

picked up a good-sized rock. "Here we go, Willy," he whispered.

"Another one?" the taller of the two guards said as Ben approached.

"Do I give him to you?" Ben asked.

The guard made a sour face and cursed. He scoffed, "I wouldn't touch a live Yank, much less a dead one. Drop him on the heap yourself."

Without a word Ben split the guards. They gave him plenty of room to pass. He walked to the far side of the pile of human carcasses. He glanced up, hoping the guards weren't watching him. They weren't.

With their backs still to the pile, one of the said, "That must be twenty today!"

The other guard laughed. "My, my, my, how them Yankee boys do love to kill one another."

Ben lowered Willy onto the pile. Willy was playing his part well. His arm fell limp to one side. As Ben released him, he checked the guard in the tower. Something in the distance held the guard's attention.

Raising up, Ben pitched the rock in his hand a good distance. With a thud it hit the stockade pilings across the Dead Line. The heads of all three guards snapped that direction. The guard in the tower aimed his rifle at the sound, shouting, "He's mine! He's mine!" The two guards on the ground readied their firearms and ran a few steps in the direction of the sound.

Ben took advantage of the distraction. He dove onto the pile of the dead, worming his way under an outstretched arm. Closing his eyes, he fought back a rising tide of nausea. He tried not to think of where he was. His heart beat so loudly, he thought for sure the guards would hear it. He lay still and waited.

Several moments passed before he heard the guards speaking again.

"Hey, where'd that Yank go?" he heard one of them ask.

No immediate answer was heard. *Were they looking at the pile? Had they spotted him?*

Coarse laughter. "He must have skedaddled something fierce!"

The other guard clucked his tongue. "Ain't surprising. You know how scared Yanks are about dead things."

For the remainder of the night Ben listened to the two guards pass the time by talking about their favorite foods. He fought back wave after wave of sickness. With his head buried against the torso of a dead Union soldier he prayed that the night would pass quickly.

With the light and warmth of the sun came the flies and the swarms of lice. Ben had to guard against voluntary and involuntary movement every minute. He wanted so badly to climb off this pile of death and brush away the things crawling on his arms and legs and face, to flee from the pile of stench before the arms of the dead reached up and claimed him as one of their own.

The baking sun made the smells and insects even more unbearable. To take his mind off of them Ben relived the day of surprising revelation in the Washington hospital. *You are the son of Jeremiah Morgan and Elizabeth McKenna. . . .* That was the day he was reborn. He had a family. Repeatedly he told himself that this was all worth it just to be part of a family who loved each other like the Morgans.

"What do we do if they're not there?" Seth asked.

The two old friends shared the only seat on the heavy, lumbering wagon. Jeremiah held the reins loosely in his hands. Two black mules pulled them dutifully toward the entrance to the prison. A mile behind them Daniel and Marshall finished securing the wagon's original drivers to the trunk of a sturdy tree.

"They'll be there," Jeremiah replied. "Ben has a stubborn streak in him. Witness his insistence that he go in after Willy."

"A stubborn streak . . . " Seth echoed, " . . . is that a Morgan family trait?"

Jeremiah laughed. "The boy must have picked it up from his mother." He looked, then looked again at his friend sitting next to him. "Promise me one thing when this is all over?"

"Anything."

"Promise me you'll grow your beard back. You look ridiculous without one."

The wagon drew near the gate. Seth leaned over and whispered. "Let me do the talking. I don't sound like a Yankee."

At the gate a Confederate corporal approached them.

"We've come to bury the dead," Seth told him.

The corporal motioned to two other soldiers who swung open the gates. Jeremiah urged the mules into a boxlike enclosure. The gates closed behind them. Jeremiah found himself surrounded on all sides by tall timber and Confederate soldiers.

Seth repeated his statement to a sergeant.

"Where's Pollard?" the sergeant growled.

"Couldn't come today," Seth said.

"I ain't seen the two of you before."

"Probably because we haven't done this before."

With squinting eyes the sergeant stared at them. He looked like he'd just tasted something disagreeable.

"Look, Sergeant, if you want Pollard, that's fine with us. We don't want to do this anyway. You can bury them dead Yanks yourself for all I care. Just open those gates behind us and we'll back these mules right out of here."

The sergeant sniffed. Turning to the gatekeepers, he ordered them to open the interior gates. Jeremiah urged the mules forward. The sprawling tent city appeared in front of them.

Seth whispered softly, "Well, we're in."

"That's not the part I'm worried about," Jeremiah replied.

As the wagon approached the pile of deceased Union soldiers, Jeremiah's heart sank within him. It was all he could do to keep from racing to the pile and tossing aside the carcasses of the dead until he found his two sons. Sensing his impulse, Seth reached over and gripped Jeremiah's arm.

"Let's get them loaded and get out of here," Seth said calmly.

While Jeremiah turned the wagon around, backing it toward the pile, Seth jumped down and donned a pair of gloves. Two guards watched him. With hands on hips, he studied the pile. Using the pretense of surveying the job ahead of him, he searched visually for Ben and Willy. He didn't see them. To the guards he said, "Care to give us a hand, gentlemen?"

One guard wrinkled his nose and turned his back. The other said, "They don't pay me enough to do that."

Jeremiah joined his partner. One by one they lifted the corpses onto the wagon.

He saw Willy. Motioning Seth over to him, Jeremiah bent low to pick up his son. "Lay still, Willy. We'll get you out of here."

There was no response. Jeremiah didn't expect one. They loaded Willy onto the wagon just like all the others.

Seth cleared his throat. He'd found Ben.

Jeremiah bent a little lower than he normally did. "Ben. It's your father."

Goosebumps appeared on Ben's arm. Jeremiah bit his lower lip hard to keep from crying out.

High atop a tree Marshall followed the progress of the wagon as it made its way across the prison yard. In mournful silence he watched his father and Seth Cooper load the bodies onto the wagon. As he watched, he worked the knuckles of his fingers. He wanted them to be limber should he need to aim and fire his rifle quickly.

A half-mile from the camp, under the shade of a tree a short distance from the road, Daniel held the reins of two horses. He watched for any sign of an approaching wagon. Further down the same road J.D. checked his watch. A quarter to one. Forty-five minutes had passed since the two men had entered the camp. He prayed for their success.

"That's the last of them!" Seth cried, indirectly informing the guards that they were finished.

Jeremiah climbed aboard the wagon. He couldn't resist looking at his boys one last time. They were both loaded close to the driver's seat. Unlike most of the others around them, their eyes were closed. Still, they looked dead. Jeremiah fought back tears. *Hold on, boys, just a little longer,* he thought.

Minutes later they were stopped inside the box-shaped portal again. Guards on the ground and guards in two towers examined them—all of them keeping a distance from the death wagon. One guard got down on his hands and knees and looked under the wagon.

The outer gates swung open. Jeremiah could see freedom. He controlled an urge to whip the donkeys into action; instead, he spoke gently to them. The wagon lurched and they passed through the gates.

Just then Jeremiah heard a moaning sound behind him. Seth heard it too. So did the sergeant. Jeremiah pretended not to hear.

"Hold up!" the sergeant cried.

Seth turned around in his seat. As he did, without moving his lips he whispered, "Keep going!" To the sergeant, he formed a quizzical look on his face and tapped his chest as if to say, "Are you talking to us?'

The wagon continued to make steady progress away from the gate.

"Yes, you!" cried the sergeant.

Just then Willy stirred. His eyes opened. He blinked them into focus. Seeing the dead man laying next to him, he sat up abruptly, recognizing his friend. "Cutler! Please, God, no! Not Cutler!"

"Let's get out of here!" Seth cried to Jeremiah.

Jeremiah slapped the mules into action.

At the sound of the commotion Ben's eyes flew open. He raised up.

Behind them the sergeant was beside himself. Pointing excitedly at the wagon, he ordered the guards in the towers to shoot.

"Stay down!" Seth shouted to Ben. Willy was oblivious to what was going on around him, he was weeping so profusely over his friend Cutler. Seth pushed Willy down. Guards were positioning themselves to fire.

BLAM!

One of the guards toppled over the railing, somersaulting to the ground.

Marshall!

The other guard got off a shot. It hit the pile of bodies with a sickening thud.

"Are you hit?" Seth screamed.

"No," Ben answered.

Willy shook his head.

BLAM!

Another tower guard took a bullet from Marshall. It spun him around. He crumpled onto the floor of the guard tower.

At the foot of the guard tower soldiers scurried everywhere to mount a pursuit. *What was it Ben said they could expect?*

Cavalry. Hounds.

"Faster!" Seth cried.

"These are mules, not thoroughbreds!" Jeremiah shouted.

Marshall climbed down from his post. The wagon was out of the guards' range. His mind raced as he ran to join J.D. They were going to be caught. A carriage was no match for men on horseback. There had to be some other way.

He thought of Julia. He would never see her again. It was all his fault. He never should have left Willy on his own. All of them—his father, J.D., Willy, and now Ben—all of them were going to end up in Andersonville Prison. That is, if they weren't shot first. And it was all his fault. He ran. As fast as his legs could carry him, he ran.

In the distance a train whistle sounded.

Marshall ran faster.

"I heard shots!" Daniel cried.

Seth jumped from the wagon. "Go! Go!" he screamed.

"Good-bye, old friend," Jeremiah said. "Now get out of here!"

"Go!" Seth screamed, slapping the mules.

As the wagon picked up speed once again, Jeremiah heard the voice of his best friend behind him. "And God go with you!"

"I heard shots!" J.D. cried as Marshall approached.

"Two were mine," Marshall said. He jumped into the carriage. "Let's go!" he said.

"What? Where's the wagon?"

"Let's go!" Marshall screamed. "The entire prison guard is headed this direction!" He tried to wrestle the reins from J.D.'s hands. J.D. fought back.

"We can't just leave them!" he cried.

"Let's go!" Marshall screamed again. "I'll explain on the way!"

"Which direction?"

"Straight ahead, toward the train tracks."

The carriage jumped forward. "What are we doing?" J.D. asked.

Marshall rubbed his beard. He stared at J.D.'s stump. "I'm not sure yet."

"Do you see them?" Jeremiah called over his shoulder.

Ben was sitting up, looking behind them. "Not yet!"

Jeremiah whipped the poor mules. He knew they couldn't go any faster, still he whipped them out of frustration. They weren't going to make it. He thought of Susanna. *She would be all alone. Permanently. Seth would take care of her.*

He whipped the mules again. He thought of the quiet days, the boring days in Point Providence when he used to wish for an exciting life, a life to match the other names in the Morgan family Bible. *Be careful what you wish for. Well, it was exciting all right. After his death Susanna could write in the Bible that he was the first Morgan to destroy his entire family. Some legacy.*

"Where are J.D. and Marshall?" Ben called from the back. "They should be right here!"

Ben was right. They were approaching the rendezvous point. Neither the boys nor the carriage were anywhere in sight. Jeremiah pulled back on the reins.

"No! No!" Ben screamed. "Keep going!"

With the carriage stopped beside the tracks, J.D. shredded the lower portion of his trousers with a knife, the part that draped past his stump.

"Give me the knife," Marshall said. He pricked a couple of his fingers, squeezing blood from them. He rubbed the blood on the exposed stump.

"What are you doing?"

Marshall continued to squeeze and rub. "We have to make it look real," he said.

J.D. nodded. He pricked a couple of his fingers, smearing the stump red. "I'm not sure this is a good idea," Marshall said.

"It was *your* idea!"

"I know! But it's too risky."

"We have no other choice," J.D. said.

"Are you sure?"

"We have no other choice," J.D. repeated.

Marshall slapped his brother good-naturedly on the shoulder. "I've always admired you," he said. "Don't disappoint me now by getting yourself killed." Marshall jumped from the carriage and ran through a thicket of bushes farther up the tracks.

J.D. picked up the carriage reins with a steady hand. He checked the train's progress up ahead. It was slowing. Marshall said he'd spotted a station when he first arrived. What he was about to do would be hard enough, impossible if the train was going full-speed. J.D. waited for the right moment. Not too soon, he couldn't give the engineer time enough to stop the train; but not too late either, or he'd get himself killed.

Now.

J.D. eased the carriage onto the tracks and pulled the horses to a stop. A frantic engineer leaned out the window of the locomotive, at the same time yanking on the whistle cord over and over again. The train screamed at J.D. to get off the track. Brakes shrieked in fright. But it was too late. The train could never stop in time.

J.D. waited. *Not yet. Not yet.*

At the last possible second, he yelled at the horses. The carriage lurched forward. With his good leg, J.D. pushed off, jumping as far as he could. The locomotive clipped the back wheels of the carriage as it passed him. J.D. slammed onto the sloping ground and rolled over and over and over.

Still screaming, the train ground to a halt.

The engineer and brakeman bounded from the locomotive, running toward J.D. When they saw his bloodied stump they gasped and rushed to his aid.

"If you'll kindly step away from my brother," Marshall said.

The engineer and brakeman whirled around to see Marshall Morgan pointing a rifle at them.

While Marshall held the engineer hostage, he ordered the brakeman to assist J.D. aboard the locomotive. Curious passengers poked their heads out. Marshall ordered them back inside. Just before he boarded himself, Marshall oversaw the separation of the locomotive and tender from the rest of the train. Then, hopping aboard, he handed the rifle to J.D. "Cover us," he said. Turning his attention to the controls, he said with a boyish grin, "I've always wanted to do this."

"They're coming!" Ben shouted.

A cloud of dust covered the trail behind them. The storm producing the cloud was Confederate cavalry. Jeremiah shook his head. They couldn't outrun cavalry in the carriage, let alone this wagon.

He steered the wagon around a bend, looking for Marshall and J.D., looking for some kind of alternative. A marshy forest was on their left. To their right was a field and railroad tracks with a locomotive and tender creeping along further back.

The train's whistle blew three short blasts.

Jeremiah looked over his shoulder. The cavalry was gaining. Ben and Willy and the corpses were bouncing crazily.

Three more train whistle blasts.

If it were a long train, Jeremiah thought, he might be able

to beat the cavalry across the tracks, cutting them off with the train. A locomotive did him no good. Three more train whistle blasts.

"It's J.D.!" Ben cried from behind him.

Jeremiah looked over his shoulder, then up the road.

"On the train!" Ben was on his knees, pointing at the locomotive.

Jeremiah looked toward the tracks. J.D. was hanging halfway out the engineer's window, waving furiously. Signaling them up ahead.

"Cross the field to the tracks!" Ben yelled. "Get ahead of the train!"

Jeremiah nodded. He steered the mules off the road. The initial bump sent several bodies flying from the wagon. Willy slipped toward the edge. Ben grabbed him and pulled him back.

They reached the tracks ahead of the train.

J.D. was hanging out the window, yelling. "We can't stop! They'll catch us." He motioned forward. "Run! Run! We'll pull you on board."

Jeremiah jumped down from the wagon. The cavalry was closing. He went back for Willy.

"Run!" Ben yelled. "I've got him. Run!"

Jeremiah urged his aging bones into a run just as the train was catching up to them. J.D. and Marshall had exchanged places. Marshall leaned out the locomotive on the second step. With one hand he held on, the other hand was extended to his father.

"Grab my hand!" he shouted, the train catching up with his father.

Just as the train was about to pass him, Jeremiah reached up. With all his effort he increased his speed. A thought flashed into his mind. *If those old mules could do it, so can this old mule.* He grabbed Marshall's hand. Marshall pulled him on board.

Right behind him, Ben carried Willy in his arms like a baby, running with all his might.

"Slow it down a little!" Marshall cried to J.D.

"Can't do it!" J.D. cried. "We'll lose too much momentum." Marshall to Ben: "You can do it!" He stretched out his hand for Willy.

BLAM! Ping!

A pistol shot ricocheted off the side of the train. "Hurry!" Marshall cried.

Ben's face was scarlet and pouring sweat. His breathing came in violent puffs. Just a little faster. Willy's arms bounced up and down with Ben's strides.

Marshall stretched out as far as he could. "A little more!" he yelled.

Ben was beginning to slow.

Jeremiah joined Marshall and he held onto his son allowing Marshall to stretch even further.

Ben increased his effort. The gap closed.

BLAM! Ping!

Marshall instinctively drew back because of the shot. Then he reached out again. He touched Willy's fingers, then lost them. Touched them again.

Ben lunged. Marshall caught Willy and pulled him swiftly aboard. Ben's effort threw him off-balance. He tumbled to the ground.

"Ben!" Marshall cried. He started to jump off the locomotive. His father grabbed him.

"I've got to help him!" Marshall cried.

Jeremiah shook his head. "Look!"

Ben was on his feet again, running, closing the distance between him and the locomotive.

BLAM!

A geyser of dirt erupted near Ben's feet. He kept running.

Marshall grabbed his rifle. BLAM! He picked off the lead

soldier. The man's fall obstructed the two horses immediately behind him, slowing them down.

Ben was close to the landing. He reached up.

Marshall swung down, grabbing his hand.

Ben stumbled, causing Marshall to lose his balance, pulling him down. Jeremiah grabbed Marshall's shirt to hold him in. Marshall regained his footing and hauled his oldest brother aboard.

"Let's go!" Jeremiah yelled.

J.D. shoved the throttle forward.

A hail of bullets hit the side of the locomotive.

Ahead of them the station loomed into sight. J.D. pulled the whistle cord repeatedly, warning people away as the locomotive picked up speed.

The train burst past the station. Buildings and baggage beside the track cut off most of the cavalry from following. The train picked up more speed and the distance between them and the riders increased until there was no Confederate cavalry in sight.

Jeremiah's four sons huddled around him with cheers and tears and congratulations.

Shortly afterward, they stopped the train long enough to cut telegraph wires. Marshall was reminded of Harper's Ferry. The fact that the lines were down would not be nearly as alarming as the fact that a train had been stolen. This would buy them some time.

They stopped the train shy of Fort Valley and abandoned it. From here on out, they would travel by foot until they reached Union territory. With Marshall assisting Willy and Ben assisting J.D., the Morgans made their way up the Flint River and into eastern Tennessee. Jeremiah and his boys were headed home.

EPILOGUE

The nation barely had time to breathe a collective sigh of relief following the end of hostilities at Appomattox Courthouse, Virginia on April 9, 1865, when the serpent of tragedy rose up and inflicted them with another grievous wound. Five days later, on April 14th, President Abraham Lincoln was shot in the back of the head while attending a performance of *Our American Cousin* at Ford's Theater in Washington. He was carried across the street to a boarding house where he died.

The assassin, John Wilkes Booth, was tracked down by government troops to Richard Garrett's farm near Bowling Green, Virginia and shot to death. Rumors and charges of conspiracy jumped and spread like spot fires on a dry hillside. Radical Republicans, some in Lincoln's cabinet, came under suspicion, including Lincoln's Secretary of War, Edwin M. Stanton.

During a highly publicized conspiracy trial, nine people were identified as conspirators in Lincoln's assassination. Five of them were sentenced to life in prison, including New York banker Caleb McKenna. McKenna was caught with secret government documents at his New York mansion. Several high-ranking government officials in Washington, including Secretary of War Stanton, named him specifically in their testimony. Four others were sentenced to hang within twenty-four hours of the verdict. They were: Lewis Payne, an unemployed ne'er-do-well; George Atzerodt, a carriage maker; David E. Herold, a drugstore clerk; and Mary E. Surratt, a boarding-house owner.

These five conspirators were hanged on July 7, 1865.

During the war crime trials of the Andersonville Prison officials, Willy Morgan's graphic portrayals of camp atrocities figured prominently in the guilty verdicts of the officials in charge.

If there was anyone in Point Providence who hadn't heard about the upcoming October garden wedding at the Morgan house, he had either just arrived in town or he had been unconscious for three months.

On the day of the wedding, the two ministers, Jeremiah Morgan and Seth Cooper, stood side-by-side under a floral arch. Their pretense of dignity was frequently disrupted by humorous asides which they whispered in each other's ears.

Emerging from the house, the bride and groom slowly made their way down the grass aisle which separated the wedding guests into two equal sides.

"Sarah looks magnificent," Seth whispered.

"Daniel looks like he's ready to bust," Jeremiah whispered back.

"Can you blame him?" Seth replied.

"It's been a long time coming, that's for sure." Both men wiped back tears as their offspring stood before them. Sarah's eyes sparkled with joy; Daniel's eyes were fastened to his bride.

There was a pause in the ceremony. Jeremiah looked past the couple at the house as the second bride and groom appeared. With one arm draped over a crutch and another linked to his bride, J.D. and Jenny followed the same green path to the ministers.

Sarah and Daniel made room for the second couple. Jeremiah felt like he was going to burst with pride.

Lifting his eyes to the house a third time, he watched as Marshall and Julia appeared. The boys and their father hadn't been home more than a week from their Andersonville escape when Marshall rode south to the woman he loved. For the remainder of the war he helped her rebuild her family's home.

With Willy sitting on one side of Susanna Morgan and Ben sitting on the other, the ceremony began. It moved smoothly from couple to couple as each one exchanged wedding vows separately. Then, the couples kissed simultaneously to seal their vows for all eternity and to mark the beginning of the celebration. Jeremiah could contain himself no longer. Tears flowed freely.

"May I have your attention?"

Jeremiah called out as loudly as he could over the babel of the wedding party.

"Please be seated everyone! There is more! This momentous day is not over yet!"

Seth and Emma and Susanna helped him shepherd the guests to the chairs. When everyone was seated and quiet, Jeremiah and Seth once again stood before them.

"As everyone here knows," Seth began, "it is the tradition of our two families to present our families' Bibles to the next generation. This tradition was begun over two hundred years ago. It was the hope of both our families' forefathers that in doing this, there would always be a generation of Coopers and Morgans in America who continue to believe and espouse the spiritual truth as set forth in these Bibles." He looked to Jeremiah to continue.

"Seth and I were reminded of our spiritual heritage during our recent sojourn to England. Unplanned by us, we met in Edenford. The memories of our forefathers are as rich as the clotted cream they still make in that part of England. Seth and I were reminded of the suffering and hardships our ancestors endured, and how through it all, they never lost their faith. Their hardships only served to make them more determined to believe, to trust, to love. This is the heritage our families share. Then . . . " he looked at Seth, " . . . and now."

It was Seth's turn again.

"Daniel Cooper, will you please come forward."

Daniel joined his father before the assembled guests. Seth spoke directly to Daniel: "As you know, this Bible first belonged to a man who had a disfiguring accident as a result of a fall into the dyeing vats of Edenford. Though he suffered physically the remainder of his life, he grew stronger spiritually day by day. This Bible and his faith comprise the legacy he passed down to his son, and thereafter from son to son. And now it is my privilege to pass it to you."

Seth opened the Cooper family Bible.

"Daniel, I have written your name beneath mine. And just as my father challenged me to keep the faith and hand it down to his son, so I now challenge you." Looking at Sarah, he said, "And I want it known to everyone here that I couldn't be happier with the woman you have chosen to be your wife and the mother of future Coopers." He winked at Sarah.

Clearing his throat, he added: "And beside your name, is this Scripture passage—Psalm 127:3: *Lo, children are an heritage of the Lord: and the fruit of the womb is His reward.* My son, with this Bible, you carry the hopes and dreams of generations of men and women who have proudly owned the Cooper name."

Seth embraced his son. The assembled friends clapped enthusiastically.

It was Jeremiah's turn.

"J.D. Morgan, will you please come forward."

Jeremiah waited for J.D. to join him before continuing. Holding the Morgan family Bible in his hands, he said, "The Morgans trace their spiritual lineage back to Drew Morgan." He opened the front cover of the Bible. "Five names separate Drew's name from mine. Included among them is my grandfather. His listing is different from all the others because there is a second name on the same line, Esau, his twin brother.

From what I understand, these twin brothers competed for everything, even the honor to possess this Bible. But never have I heard of a Morgan declining the honor of possessing this Bible. Until now."

Whispers rippled across the gathering of guests.

"Marshall, Willy, and Ben, will you come up here?"

When all four of his sons were standing with him, Jeremiah said proudly, "These are my boys!"

The gathering applauded. Jeremiah fought back tears.

"Any one of these boys—young men, actually—" he inserted sheepishly, "are worthy to be selected as the bearer of the Morgan family Bible. Three of them came to me separately with the same recommendation. And, with the full agreement of my wife, I have decided to follow their recommendation and present this Bible to Benjamin Morgan."

Ben's three brothers all pounded him on the back with congratulations and made fun of him for the surprised look on his face. They ushered him to Jeremiah's side.

Ben's father opened the Bible and read aloud the names of the men who were listed:

Drew Morgan, 1630, Zechariah 4:6

Christopher Morgan, 1654, Matthew 28:19

Philip Morgan, 1729, Philippians 2:3-4

Jared Morgan, 1741, John 15:13

Jacob Morgan, Esau's brother, 1786, 1 John 2:10

Seth Morgan, 1804, 2 Timothy 2:15

Jeremiah Morgan, 1833, Hebrews 4:1

"And to this list, I have added the following name:

Benjamin McKenna Morgan, 1865, Romans 8:28

"Ben's inscription is the first three-name inscription recorded in the Bible, and there's a good reason for this. First, to honor his mother, Elizabeth McKenna, who gave her life that he might be born. And second, so that future generations will see the three names and ask why. Then, they will be told the story of Ben Morgan and they will know the power and grace of God as described in Romans 8:28, *And we know that all things work together for good to them that love God, to them who are the called according to His purpose.*"

Jeremiah handed the Bible to Ben and hugged him fiercely.

"If I might say one thing more," Jeremiah began.

"Get these preachers started," Seth exclaimed, "and you can't shut them up!"

Everyone laughed, including Jeremiah.

"It's just that I can't help but feel that God has had His hand on us throughout this terrible Civil War. There is not a person among us who does not know of a family who sacrificed one or more sons on the battlefield. And though we have not been without our losses, not only has my family survived the ordeal, but we've increased! I found a son I never knew! I have a new son-in-law who is like a fifth son to me! And I have two lovely new daughters-in-law—Julia and Jenny. Of all men, I am most blessed!"

Later that afternoon, Jeremiah Morgan gathered his immediate family around him. And as his ancestors did for five generations before him, he related the saga of the Morgan family faith.

"The story begins at Windsor Castle," he said, "the day Drew Morgan met Bishop Laud. For it was on that day his life began its downward direction. . . . "

AFTERWORD

The Civil War is without doubt the most scrutinized era in our nation's history. This is both a boon and a dilemma for historical researchers. On the one hand, unlike other eras of history, facts are relatively easy to find; on the other hand, there are so many facts to find that it is easy to get buried under an information avalanche.

One of the greatest difficulties was for me to choose which parts of this great civil conflict I wanted to incorporate into this novel. Some authors solve this dilemma by writing entire series set in this time period. For this series I was limited to one volume and the choices I was forced to make were hard ones. To accomplish this, the Morgan family in this book is larger than in the previous books. This was done to include as much of the rich history as possible.

The Morgan family is fictitious. So are the families Cooper and McKenna. Point Providence and its residents situated along the Ohio River are also fictitious, though Adams County is not. The Jehovah's Avengers company is fictitious. I chose to create a town and company so that I could select the Civil War battles that best suited my story, without being restricted by the history of an actual company and regiment.

Jeremiah Morgan represents our desire to control our world. Early on, he faces the unpleasant reality that there are forces in our world over which we have no control. Against his will, his family is ripped apart and scattered across the states. However, he also discovers that when these forces are met with steadfast faith, unexpected blessings sometimes emerge from seeming tragedy.

J.D. is a noble character in that he is his father's favorite but, unlike Joseph in the Old Testament, he does not alienate his brothers and sister by constantly reminding them of his favored status. He does not covet the role for which his father has groomed him.

Marshall is the hyper-righteous zealot who makes life easier for himself by interpreting everything as black or white. Through his experience with Julia Hutchison, he learns compassionate Christianity when he falls in love with the enemy.

Sarah is a bright-eyed optimist who allows her optimism and passion for getting published to overcome her good sense and the advice of close friends. She learns that life is best viewed through the twin lenses of optimism *and* reality. Her writing is a precursor to the Horatio Alger rags-to-riches stories that became popular in the latter part of the century.

Willy is the tragic figure in the story. He discounts the talent he has and longs for the things that can't be. Consequently, he leads a miserable life. Not until late in the story does he appreciate his God-given gift.

As for the historical characters and incidents, they are many:

John Brown, the accounts of Bleeding Kansas, Harper's Ferry, and Brown's attempt to establish a free Negro state in the mountains are all historical. So is Preston Brooks' beating of Charles Sumner in the U.S. Senate chambers. This was a violent time when passions and blood flowed freely.

Cyrus Hines' account of the murder of Elijah Lovejoy in chapter 5 is a true account. And the preacher quoted by Mother Kinney is historical. Hundreds of men—white and black—traveled great distances to hear John Jasper preach.

Mother Kinney's account of his sermon orations are based on actual funeral records.

Of course, Harriet Beecher Stowe was a well-known personality during the days of the Civil War. When Abraham Lincoln greeted her at the White House, he took her by the hand and said, "So this is the little lady that started this great war." Lincoln and historians agree that her book, *Uncle Tom's Cabin*, a work of fiction, crystallized the conscience of America against the evils of slavery. The account of her writing her famous novel is based on a historical incident recorded by her friend and confidant, Annie Fields. In addition, I used the Negro dialect as recorded in her work as a guide for the early chapters in my novel.

The battle accounts recorded by name are historically accurate—First Bull Run, Antietam, Fredericksburg, and the shelling of Vicksburg with the area residents hiding in caves. Generals Ambrose Burnside and Joseph Hooker each took turns leading the Army of the Potomac. Neither of them was successful.

The Battle of Fredericksburg is the most detailed battle in this book. The battle is a reminder that good men, when pressured to perform, often make unwise decisions with tragic results. The quotes attributed to Confederate General Robert E. Lee are a matter of record. I also discovered references to a revival prior to the Battle of Fredericksburg; however, the revival and preaching portrayed in this book are a product of my pen.

The story of J.D. helping another captain find and bury his severed arm is based on the historical accounts of Mary Ann Bickerdyke, a woman who volunteered her services to keep the conditions of the field hospitals sanitary. Hundreds of soldiers called her Mom.

Unfortunately, the portrayal of Andersonville Prison and its infamous Dead Line is based on historical record. Of the

32,000 Union prisoners-of-war at Andersonville, 13,000 of them perished. Following the war, Captain Henry Wirtz, one of the prison's commanders, was found guilty of war crimes. He was hanged on November 10, 1865. In the historic Andersonville, the bodies of the dead were carried outside by prisoners to the grave. In return, they were given a few minutes to grab pieces of wood from the forest for fuel. I placed the pile of dead bodies inside the perimeter of the camp for story purposes.

While researching this novel, I gained a profound respect for President Abraham Lincoln. All of his notoriety and fame came after his death. During his presidency he was vilified and hated, a favorite target on both sides of the war. Besides the pressures of his office in the midst of our country's greatest unrest, he suffered numerous personal crises and tragedies. Yet he treated others with a respect they did not give him. In addition, he had a joke for every occasion. And, as history records, in spite of his detractors, it was his dogged persistence that preserved the unity of our nation.

The death of his son Willie, the pardoning of the doll, and comments regarding General George McClellen's reluctance to attack are true. The conspiracy trial and hanging deaths of four of the nine conspirators in his assassination are historical, the exception being the imprisonment of Caleb McKenna who is a fictitious character. Naturally, Lincoln's conversations with the fictitious Jeremiah Morgan never really occurred.

If the Civil War is our most scrutinized era in history, Abraham Lincoln is the most well-known and best-loved President. It is a reputation well-deserved.

Jack Cavanaugh
San Diego, 1995

The Morgan Family

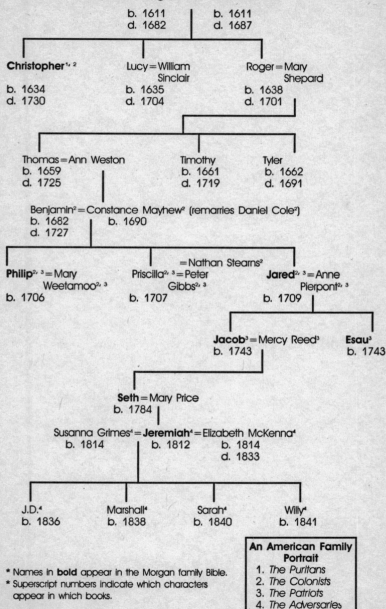

Drew Morgan[1] = Nell Matthews[1]

b. 1611   b. 1611
d. 1682   d. 1687

Christopher[1, 2]   Lucy = William   Roger = Mary
                                    Sinclair   Shepard
b. 1634   b. 1635   b. 1638
d. 1730   d. 1704   d. 1701

Thomas = Ann Weston   Timothy   Tyler
b. 1659   b. 1661   b. 1662
d. 1725   d. 1719   d. 1691

Benjamin[2] = Constance Mayhew[2] (remarries Daniel Cole[2])
b. 1682   b. 1690
d. 1727

                            = Nathan Stearns[2]
Philip[2, 3] = Mary   Priscilla[2, 3] = Peter   **Jared**[2, 3] = Anne
          Weetamoo[2, 3]   Gibbs[2, 3]   Pierpont[2, 3]
b. 1706   b. 1707   b. 1709

                    Jacob[3] = Mercy Reed[3]   **Esau**[3]
                    b. 1743   b. 1743

          Seth = Mary Price
          b. 1784

Susanna Grimes[4] = **Jeremiah**[4] = Elizabeth McKenna[4]
b. 1814   b. 1812   b. 1814
                                    d. 1833

J.D.[4]   Marshall[4]   Sarah[4]   Willy[4]
b. 1836   b. 1838   b. 1840   b. 1841

* Names in **bold** appear in the Morgan family Bible.
* Superscript numbers indicate which characters
  appear in which books.

> **An American Family Portrait**
> 1. *The Puritans*
> 2. *The Colonists*
> 3. *The Patriots*
> 4. *The Adversaries*

Don't miss a single book from the American Family Portrait Series!

Jack Cavanaugh's epic of faith, love, and sacrifice follows the Morgans through the years, chronicling the triumphs and tragedies of one of America's first families of faith.

Look for *The Puritans*, *The Colonists*, *The Patriots*, and *The Adversaries* in your local Christian bookstore.

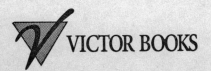

VICTOR BOOKS

Enter a medieval world of ancient secrets, an evil conspiracy, and a mysterious castle called Magnus.

The year is 1312. The place, the remote North York Moors of England. Join young Thomas as he pursues his destiny—the conquest of an 800-year-old castle that harbors secrets dating back to the days of King Arthur and Merlin.

You'll find *Magnus* at your local Christian bookstore.

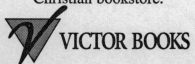

It's 1942. World War II is raging. And Marcel Boussant must make a decision.

The young Frenchman must decide whether or not to help Isabelle Karmazin, a beautiful Jew trapped in Nazi-occupied France. Torn between a safe existence for he and his family and a stranger's plight, Marcel must act quickly.

Look for *A Legion of Honor* in your local Christian bookstore.

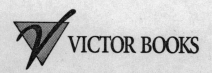

VICTOR BOOKS